JESSICA A. MCMINN

THE BLOOD CURSE

GARDENS OF WAR & WASTELAND

— BOOK II —

THE BLOOD CURSE

GARDENS OF WAR & WASTELAND
BOOK II
JESSICA A. MCMINN

ALSO BY
JESSICA A. MCMINN

Novellas

The Collector's Lost Things

Call of the Huntress

Gardens of War & Wasteland

The Ruptured Sky

The Blood Curse

For friends, new & old.

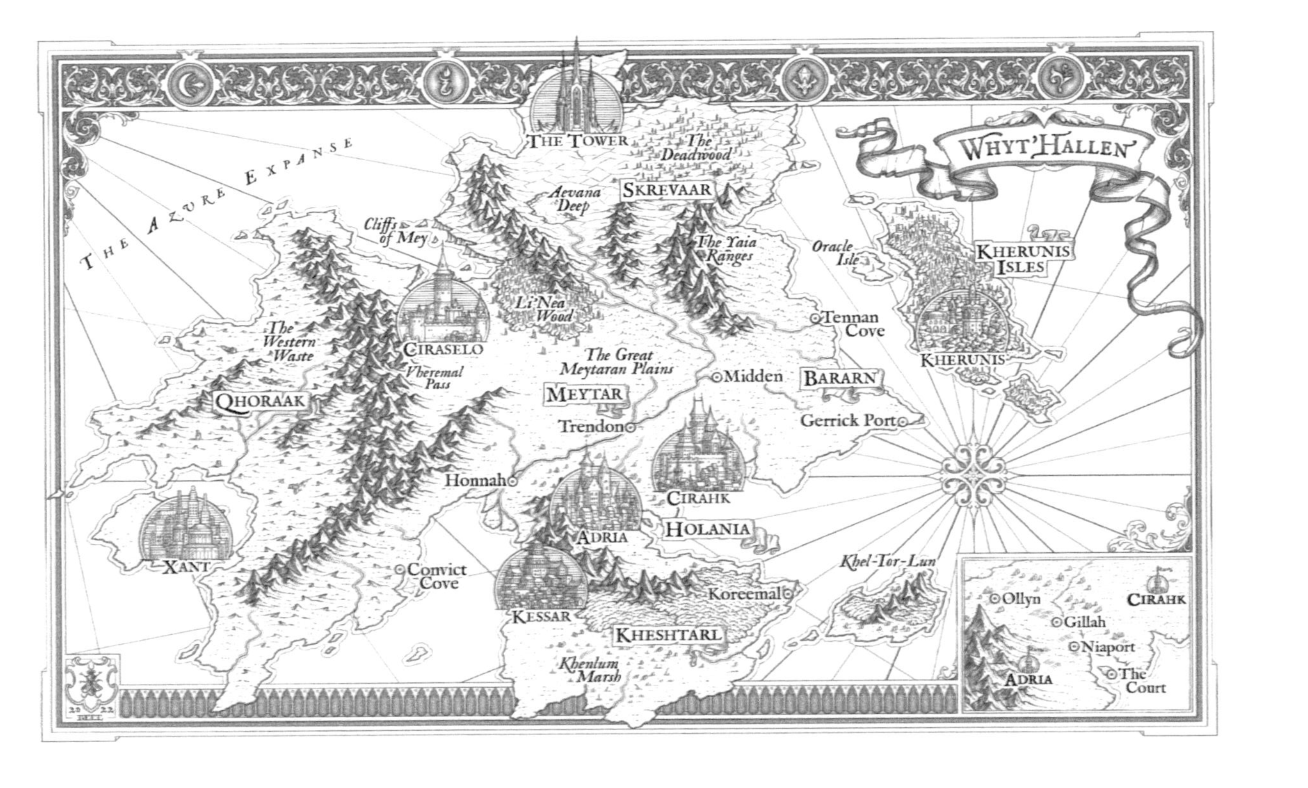
WHYT'HALLEN
THE TOWER
The Deadwood
Aevana Deep
SKREVAAR
The Yaia Ranges
Cliffs of Mey
Li'Nea Wood
Oracle Isle
Tennan Cove
KHERUNIS ISLES
KHERUNIS
CIRASELO
The Western Waste
The Great Meytaran Plains
Midden
BARARN
QHORA'AK
Vheremal Pass
MEYTAR
Trendon
Gerrick Port
Honnah
CIRAHK
HOLANIA
ADRIA
Khel-Tor-Lun
XANT
Convict Cove
Koreemal
KESSAR
KHESHTARL
Khenlum Marsh
THE AZURE EXPANSE
Ollyn
CIRAHK
Gillah
Niaport
ADRIA
The Court

Trigger Warnings

Gardens of War & Wasteland is a dark fantasy series that contains the following content and trigger warnings:

Strong language
Violence (blood, murder, torture)
Gore
Alcoholism
Sex scenes (explicit)
Sexual Assault (past event; discussed on page)
Child abuse (off page; past event)
Birth trauma/child loss (off page; past event)

If you are impacted by any of the above events, this may not be the book for you.
Please proceed at your own discretion.

The Story So Far ...

Amikharlia — runaway princess and huntress born with the ability to perceive and wield *khe'torla*, the magic used by the immortal Meah-Hyren to break the sky and flood the world with demonspawn.

Amika is the first of four prophesied Chosen destined to break the seal on the Goddess Miatha's soul and return her to her seat of power.

But doing so will tear the world asunder once more, poisoning the land and ushering new evil into the realm.

Despite her reservations, Amika's hand is forced and now the Prophecy is set in motion, it cannot be stopped.

Rei-Hai Shaw — childhood friend to the Holani siblings and member of the Tower brethren of assassins.

Rei abandons his creed when he learns Amika's the target of his masters' latest mission, effectively sealing his own death.

But he was condemned to die long before betraying the Tower: as a Siephymn, the product of human and demon, his life is short and destined to end at the tip of a hunter's blade.

All Rei wants is to see Kio one more time before he devolves into demonspawn—even if it means returning to Qhoraak.

Kiokharen — Amika's older brother who has spent years trying to control the fall out of Amika's disappearance while grappling with the loss of his wife and unborn son.

Crippled by doubt and drowning in drink, Kio makes one poor decision after another—eventually landing in the dungeons of Cirahk for attempting to kill their prince.

Any hope of being reunited with his childhood love, Rei-Hai Shaw, is quickly dashed when Kio learns he is to be shipped to Qhoraak as a slave.

Kriah — the Meah-Hyren halfblood created specifically to fulfill a role in the Prophecy.

After breaking the Skrevaar seal and watching his grandfather die, Kriah is disillusioned by the path he's been forced to walk.

But as a new threat arrives on the shores of Whyt'hallen, Kriah now accepts the end really can justify the means ...

PROLOGUE

The floor was cold beneath his feet. The boy shivered, pulling the thin blanket around his narrow shoulders, though it did little to stave off the chill of the stone.

He hadn't moved in three days. This room was all he'd seen of his new home. A pile of straw for sleeping. A pail for relieving himself. A sad blanket for warmth. He'd never known cold like this. Or loneliness. Here in the dark, he would even welcome the companionship of his father's fists.

A shadow stopped outside his room. The boy swallowed. It wasn't time for rations. No one had been to visit him since he'd arrived. A strange blend of hope and fear swirled in his chest. The knob turned with a greasy squeak.

A girl's head poked around the opening door, a flickering lantern clenched in her small fist. She was youthful and fair-haired and she gave him a smile that was not warm, but not exactly inviting either.

'You're a Siephymn,' she said.

'I'm Rei-Hai,' the boy corrected her.

'Elles. But that's not what I meant.' She padded into the room. The door groaned shut behind her. She couldn't have been much older than he, but was certainly larger. Rei had always been small, and at thirteen years of age he was often mistaken for a child far younger.

'You're part of my batch.'

'Your what?'

'Batch. It means we'll train together. We're still waiting for others to arrive, though.'

Rei hadn't asked too many questions the night they'd taken him away. When a white-haired woman came through a puddle in his wall, he'd thought he was dreaming. The woman had not been threatening or even unkind, but when she gave the command to leave, Rei simply nodded and followed. He understood power when he saw it.

'I'm from the Ice Coast,' Elles said, stabbing a thumb into her chest. 'Northern Bararn. Mam said it was the Tower or the pleasure house. I chose here. What about you? Where're you from?'

'Adria.'

The girl frowned. 'But you're a Siephymn.'

'What's a Siephymn?'

'Don't really know. A curse from the south? At least that's what the man said, and he looks just like you.'

So he *looks different, too,* Rei thought, picturing the blood-red sheen of his own hair, which his father always insisted he shave to the scalp; the way his pupils grew narrower with each passing year; the luminescent golden sheen he saw in his eyes whenever he caught his reflection in a certain light ...

The blackness of his blood.

'My mother was from Kheshtarl,' he said softly.

'Guess that explains it, then.'

It really didn't. Rei looked down at his hands, his fingernails bloodied from scratching against the floor to try to calm the dread that had been building inside since his arrival. The scabs were as dark and dry as charcoal.

'The Siephymn man's downstairs. Wanna see him?'

Rei hesitated, looking around the cold and empty room.

'Are we allowed to leave?' he asked, voice small.

The girl shrugged. 'Not like the doors are locked or anything. You coming or not?'

Rei nodded this time and clambered to his feet, legs stiff and numb from sitting. Thin blanket still draped across his shoulders, he padded after Elles, stunned by the light spilling in from beyond the open door. He squinted and raised an arm to shield his eyes. He'd been in the dark so long, even the dim illumination from the wall sconces stung.

'Have you only been here three days, too?' Rei asked, head turning left and right in cautious wonder as he trailed the stone corridor after Elles. There were no windows. No paintings or wall scrolls. Just yards of grey rock dotted with flickering torches, spiralling down what Rei assumed to be some sort of spire.

'Maybe four,' Elles admitted with a casual shrug. 'Could be five. But definitely not more than seven. Was still the Hirathi Moon when I left home. But look.' She pointed to the first window they'd seen since leaving Rei's chamber. 'The Myrahn Moon's waning now.'

The crescent was partially hidden by a swathe of cloud, both pale and grey against the night sky. Rei shivered at the icy breeze blowing through the paneless opening.

Snow, he realised. *Nothing but snow. As far as the eye can see.*

He turned back to Elles, almost accusingly. 'Where are we?' he demanded.

The girl shrugged. 'I don't know. Somewhere north, I guess. You should ask the Siephymn man. He might know.'

Elles hurried on, her bare feet quiet on the stone, dust motes dancing in her wake. Wherever they were, this tower was old and disused; the scent of mildew itched the inside of Rei's nose.

They'd travelled here by magic. Through whatever tunnel of water had opened to his room and come out the other side in that cold stone box. The woman had left again straight after, not saying a single word. He had no idea how far from Adria they'd travelled, or if anything existed out there beyond the snow. He wished now that he'd asked more questions.

He wished that he'd said goodbye.

'Hmm,' Elles said as she came to a stop. The floor had finally evened out onto a solid landing, and a heavy wood-and-iron door lay ajar at the end of the room, a stronger—*warmer*—light crackling from within.

'The Siephymn man's usually here.' She placed her hands on her hips as she thought. 'Never would let me go any further. Guess now's our chance. Come on.'

Elles hurried through the open door, her excitement and carelessness making her oblivious to the dark spattering of blood across the floor.

But Rei saw it.

'Elles—' he called, but the girl was already skidding to a shocked halt inside the adjoining room. A strangled sound escaped her lips, part gasp and part scream. Rei raced after her.

A red-headed man hunched on all fours spewed torrents of viscous black blood onto the stone. His back arched grotesquely like a drawn bow, vertebrae and ribs protruding at odd angles beneath the shroud of his robes.

'Deities dead ...' Elles breathed, hand reaching out for Rei in shock.

But Rei didn't take it. He couldn't move. Couldn't tear his eyes from the sight before him. From the man—the *creature*—screaming and writhing and clawing at his own face with fingers like talons. There was blood, so much blood, and screaming and pain, and all Rei could think was *This is me—Elles said this was me.*

He turned to run, but a door at the other end of the room burst open. The white-haired woman appeared, with a shining blue crossbow in her hand.

And put a bolt in the man's brain.

1

KIOKHAREN

Each cresting wave brought fresh bile to Kio's throat, burning and choking his airways like the cheapest liquor he'd ever had the misfortune of drinking. He'd forgotten what it was to be still; the rocking beneath his feet was so constant it reminded him of a night on the wine without the pleasure of its taste on his lips.

This was his life now.

No more council meetings or state dinners or decadent banquets dragging into the early hours of the morn. No—Reminas had stolen those, along with his name. His dignity. His home.

Prince Kiokharen Erhin Josten Holani was dead.

'This one sounds desperate fer some sex,' jeered the mess captain—a hulking lump of a Kheshtarli by the name of Bryn-Daal—from the bunk above. 'Calls out for a lover in his sleep. Likes us southerners, by the sounds of things. Better watch meself, eh, lads?'

Kio rolled over in his cot to face the wall.

Fourteen days at sea. Fourteen days locked in a box with the most insufferable creatures he had ever known: rapists, thieves and murderers all bundled onto a convict trawler bound for Qhoraak, sentenced by those with enough coin to see their enemies gone. Kio didn't belong here. He wasn't a criminal. He'd been trying to bring one to justice. And yet he was the one confined to a mess day and night with the likes of Bryn-Daal, a petty thief called Ylan, and Davyn the Wife Killer, in what he could only describe as a new kind of torture.

'You reckon he'll try 'n' 'ave a go?' Davyn sniggered. 'Don't got the sack, I reckon.'

'Slow in the head, I'd say,' grunted Ylan. 'Not said a single word. Nothing except, "Uhh, Rei-Hai. *Uuuuugh*." Maybe we ought to remind him what he's missing.'

Callous laughter erupted among the mess. Kio huddled down deeper into his cot. He hadn't dared to speak—not since he'd been dragged half-conscious from the dungeons of Cirahk only to watch a man's head blown off on the docks. The horrors he'd endured at Reminas's hands felt a lifetime ago, eclipsed by the misery of the ever-swaying ship, filled to the gunnel with shit and rot and disease.

But it was the phantom persistently haunting his dreams that kept the real agony raw and inflamed in his mind. A recurring vision he'd first seen in the dungeons, of Rei-Hai appearing before him, desperate and distraught. A tormenting, vivid hallucination—one where he could still taste Rei's kiss on his lips. Feel the touch of his skin, smell the sweetness of his hair. It almost felt like a memory. A distant, blurred memory, but a memory all the same.

Only it wasn't. Rei-Hai Shaw was a spy, their relations just another job—a truth Reminas had so cruelly shared, boring a hole through Kio's chest so deep he had no hope of ever plugging it closed.

Kio squeezed his eyes shut and hugged himself a little tighter. Ylan and the others continued to grunt and groan, no doubt accompanying their noises with a string of equally obscene gestures. But their cackles were cut short by a baton rattling the barred door to their mess.

'Quiet down in there, you lot!' the guard shouted. 'You know the rules—no noise after lockdown. Shut yer faces or I'll rouse the Boatkeep.'

The Boatkeep. The threat of her fury hung over them like storm clouds. She ran the ship with a spear in her hand and a sword on her hip. Her tongue was her sharpest weapon, one she wielded sparingly but with precision—or so Kio had heard. He had not yet had the displeasure of crossing her path, but if he kept his head down and did as he was told, then perhaps he never would.

Bryn-Daal grunted and rearranged himself in the bunk above. His great hulking body dipped the mattress, bringing his stinking girth inches from Kio's face. He hadn't had a decent sleep since boarding the ship. Between the snoring and the rocking and the fucking *stench* of these painfully small confines, the former prince had given up hope of ever feeling comfort again.

The mess captains were roused before dawn to prepare the slop that would be breakfast. Bryn-Daal descended from the bunk with a tremendous thud. He cursed and snorted, scratched and farted, lumbering around in the dark for his boots. When he finally trudged out, complaining about the hour, the cabin smelt a bit sweeter.

And so began another morning. While they waited for their turn to wash, the inmates were given their daily rations: water, a couple of hard, stale biscuits, and citrus. Today it was a scruborange, lifting Kio's spirits ever so slightly. Breakfast was a bowl of sticky, tasteless oatmeal; dinner salt beef and hard cheese; and supper, more salt beef, a sprinkle of dried peas, a slice of bread and a thimble of fortified wine. Kio would have traded his entire weekly allowance of beef for a full flagon of wine, but that would mean engaging with these beastly men more than necessary.

'Dally, yer on scullery. Up yer get.'

It took Kio a moment to respond. Dally Grant was his name now. A farmer's boy sold to the convict ship for treasonous crimes against the crown. Named for the dog Reminas kept as a child—a sickly runt of a thing Reminas used to beat so often it would piss itself whenever he passed. Kio burned at the continued insult every time the name was called.

Of all the shit duties aboard the ship, scullery came with one small perk: a chance to go above deck. Kio had not yet been assigned to the task and almost salivated at the thought of fresh air hitting his lungs after so many weeks behind bars. He swallowed his eagerness and waited for the other men to finish their meals so he could collect their plates to take above. But his impatience was palpable. Ylan dropped utensils on the floor to absorb more time; Davyn chewed slower. Snarling, Kio gritted his teeth and snatched the spoon out of the Wife Killer's crooked mouth. They hooted and guffawed as he stamped after the guard, unable to smother his bubbling rage.

Even before he laid foot on the ladder, Kio's heart began to quicken. It had been an age since he'd last seen the sun and he could already feel its warm glow against his skin. He squinted, pre-empting the sting in his sensitive eyes ... but what he found above deck was an undersaturated world, the sun a sad, dull orb in a battered and bruised sky.

Kio rubbed his eyes. Had weeks of darkness ruined his vision? No—the muted veil persisted. A sickly red hue spread from the north-west, staining the horizon like blood.

And there, above the swell of coastline in the distance, a great crimson scar tore across the sky, jagged and raw.

He'd heard the others speak of the wound in the clouds, but he hadn't seen it with his own eyes, hadn't been able to imagine it. Seeing it for the first time made his palms sweat. Unsettled nerves skittered beneath his skin. A horrible knot tightened in his chest.

That was when he saw her—the Boatkeep. Perched upon the fo'c'sle, telescope in hand, she pored over sea charts, leather tricone precariously balanced atop her head. Kio swallowed dryly.

The woman from the docks.

The night he'd come aboard, when numbers had been branded into his flank, he'd seen a woman—*this* woman—kill a man in cold blood with a stick that belched fire. A firearm, he'd since heard it called. A weapon so devastating it blew a body away like a leaf in the wind. No wonder the prisoners spoke about her in fear.

She was tall for a woman, almost of a height with Kio himself, with taut and toned arms the colour of the midnight sky. At ease in breeches and jerkin, she commanded a presence as sure and powerful as any military general he had known. There were gold rings on her fingers, and ornaments of bronze, brass and bone in her sun-bronzed locs, all twisted together into a larger braid hanging down to her waist.

'Right, get washing,' the guard barked, shoving Kio in the back. His boots collided with a trough filled with dishes brought from the other messes. 'Utensils go back in that box when done.'

The washing water was a putrid grey, thick with half-eaten food, a film of grease, and deflated foam Kio hoped was soap and not an accumulation of scum. He battled the instinct to gag as he submerged the plates he carried in the trough, trying instead to focus on the fresh air filling his lungs. Unless in charge of cooking or cleaning, the prisoners remained below, confined to their messes of four. It was his first time even seeing the ship itself, his eyes having been too swollen and bleary to take it in the night he came aboard.

It was a barque—a hundred feet long with three masts and an iron hull. A far smaller ship than the galleons of the mighty Bararnite armada, but grander than any vessel Holania owned. Being a landlocked kingdom, Holania's only boats were single-manned fishing crafts on the Faethou River. Kio might have appreciated the craftsmanship had he not been locked in a cage below deck, filled with contempt for how he got here, and—

A smack rattled the back of his head.

'Didn't bring ye up 'ere to daydream!' the ashen-eyed crew member growled. 'Move it along or ye'll be emptying the shitters fer a week.'

The threat did not make him hurry. He'd already spent most of his time aboard emptying the bucket for his mess; it almost didn't bother him now. At least he *had* a bucket to shit in. He'd not been left to stew in his own filth like he had in Cirahk. He still didn't feel clean.

Kio continued to dally, and must have rinsed the same cup eight times before moving on to another. The sun felt so good on his shoulders, even if it was muted by the shroud of the Tear. The fine salt spray tingled on his skin. The breeze made him suddenly aware of the length of his hair, the thickness of his beard. He was so used to being clean-shaven that it made him itch and his face feel heavy.

'Look at that,' a bronze-skinned young man remarked to a fellow officer across the deck. 'Don't oft see elkaven this far from the coast.'

Kio dropped the cup and glanced skyward, hope filling his throat. *Piren-Ha!*

The officer scoffed. 'Prob'ly them witch-fuckin' jungle dwellers sending demonspawn to spy on us. Don't trust nobody this side of Khel. Think every ship that comes in their way gonna steal their damn fish. Paranoid bastards.'

'Shhh,' the young man hissed, glancing towards the Boatkeep, who was still engrossed in her charts. 'Boatkeep don't like us talkin' like that about them folk. Remember what happened to old Dyxx?'

Kio's heart plummeted back where it belonged. Rei-Hai had a bird just like that—a messenger they used to communicate when they were apart, which was always. Piren-Ha used to linger on his windowsill, waiting for Kio to pen his response before returning to Rei's side. He never saw her otherwise. Probably wouldn't see her again.

Dinner came and went. As did supper. Dusk fell and the prisoners were once again locked in their mess for the night. Kio rolled straight into his cot; Bryn-Daal and the others gathered about the rickety wooden table between the bunks. The lantern had but a drizzle of oil left in its base and the orange glow rendered the convicts' faces skeletal and haunting.

'Alright, which one o' yer witch-fuckers wants a game of Um-Narl?' Bryn-Daal produced a pair of misshapen wooden dice from his meaty fist.

Ylan whistled. 'Now where the fuck'd ye get dice from, Bryn?'

'I smuggled them in me arse 'fore I came aboard!' the Kheshtarli guffawed, and the whole table shook. 'Yer daft pricks! Got 'em from one of the crew. At least one of them poor witch-fuckers got some balls about 'im.'

Davyn scowled. 'Aye. Takin' orders from that Boatkeep bitch. What business a woman got being cap'n o' a ship?'

'What business a woman got bein' anywhere but a brothel?' Ylan added, and they all cackled.

Kio released an involuntary scoff. All eyes snapped in his direction.

'Ah, look who found his tongue!' Davyn chuckled. 'What's the matter? Mam sent to a pleasure house, was she? Sister, maybe? That why you won't stick yer prick in a woman? Worried you'll be pokin' family?' His laugh gained volume with each lashing jeer, the others soon joining him.

'Maybe his prick's no good,' said Bryn-Daal.

'Or too small,' Ylan chuckled.

'Would you like to see for yourself?' Kio growled, sitting up on his elbows. 'No? Then shut your fucking mouth or I'll shove it down your throat.'

There was a hoarseness to his voice Kio did not expect. Blood pumped hot in his ears, eyes burning as he denied them the will to blink lest it betray the weakness he felt.

'Alright then, Princess, settle down,' Bryn-Daal scoffed, holding up his palms in mock placation. 'Yer want yer dick sucked, all yer gots to do is ask. Why don't we up the stakes in our little game here. Loser pops the winner in his gob. Feelin' up to it, boy?'

Kio grunted and rolled over, the fire gone from his veins. When had he become such a coward? A fearful boy subdued by the pathetic taunts of insignificant lowlives?

You're not a prince anymore, Kio. You're Dally. Dally the dog. Less than nobody.

When the light from the lantern finally died and the others packed themselves off to bed, silence overtook the mess as the guards made their rounds to check the locks. But even in the still of the quiet night, Kio could not sleep. His mind returned to the dungeons, as it invariably did. Rei-Hai stood before him, obscuring the hollow stare of his dead mother's face. He was there in the darkness—pale and real and beautiful—stroking Kio's face and kissing his lips, fingertips a cooling salve upon his many bruises.

Kio pounded his fist against his forehead, desperate to rid himself of the images. He couldn't trust them. Phantom pangs of hunger and thirst had whittled away his mind, rendering it unreliable. Dreams felt like memories; memories like nightmares where everything was blurry but vividly tangible all at once. Then there was the elkaven flying overhead—was it her? He should have whistled. Piren-Ha would have responded, would have recognised him.

Even if he no longer recognised himself.

Once Kio had met Bryn-Daal's torments with a vulgar threat of his own, the big Kheshtarli attempted to initiate a somewhat strange form of friendship. Rather than the intimidation he had planned, Kio's foul outburst instilled a kind of awkward respect among the group, an acknowledgement that Kio was perhaps just as fucking horrid as the rest of them. The taunts soon turned to questions, and despite himself, Kio found he answered more often than not. They may have been some of the worst people he had ever met, but at least they were people—living, breathing people.

'What the fuck you doin' that for?' Davyn asked with a scoff as Kio poured the contents of a waterskin into his empty bowl to drink. Bryn-Daal and Ylan also paused in their breakfast to watch with curious eyes as his fingers stiffened and trembled.

This was a truth that he would not—*could* not—share. It was hard enough to even look at the wrinkled leather of the waterskin, let alone drink from it. It was too much like the greying face of his mother's severed head. Just holding it made his flesh crawl, his stomach clench and churn.

He brought the wooden bowl to his lips and drank, the tepid water tasting faintly nutty from the porridge. But he didn't care. He was just thankful the bowls were made from wood and not clay, which was so, so similar to bone, and conjured flashbacks of drinking from Ty's fractured skull.

'Don't know where it's been, so I'm not putting it in my mouth,' Kio tried to say casually. He popped a sliver of scruborange onto his tongue, attempting to swallow without gagging while the memories were fresh in his mind.

Bryn-Daal snorted, picking at what was left of a dry biscuit. 'What'd a rich bastard like you do to get put on a prison ship with this dumb lot?'

'And what makes you think I'm rich?'

'Yer talk all fancy,' said Ylan.

'That makes me educated, not rich.'

'Aye, and only the rich are educated. So what'd yer do?' the Kheshtarli pressed.

Kio tossed the flakes of citrus skin into a pile on the table. 'Tried to kill the prince.'

That earned him a hearty laugh. Crumbs burst from Bryn-Daal's mouth as he chortled. 'More like yer tried to fuck his whore.'

'Maybe I did that too.'

'Aye, maybe ye did.' Bryn-Daal slipped his now empty plate across the table towards Kio. 'Alright then, yer dangerous witch-fucker. Go clean up me plates like a useful wench.'

It was the only good part of his day—heading above deck for scullery duty. He rolled Ylan's neglected fruit onto the table and collected up the final plate before pattering up the stairs into freedom. The day outside was overcast, but the vermilion rays bouncing off the swollen clouds only made the scene more ominous. Kio tried not to look at the sky, focussing instead on the crew scattered around the deck. But the guards all seemed tense, as if things were somehow worse than before.

The Boatkeep stood upon the fo'c'sle, eye pressed to her telescope as she peered at a cluster of islands rising before them on the horizon. The ship was headed straight for them—or rather, for a narrow channel between the isles and the mainland. Kio frowned. Koreemal was the westernmost point of the Khesh Cape, and no map he'd ever seen depicted islands off its coast.

'Why are we headed for that channel?' Kio heard himself ask. The sea before them was shallow and speared with sharp rock below the surface. Drift too far either direction and the hull would be torn to shreds. He was no seaman, but even he could see the obvious danger.

The guard eyed him suspiciously, likely because most of the crew thought him mute. 'All ships take the channel,' he said.

'Why?' he questioned. 'Risk a shipwreck to save a few days at sea? What utter madness!'

'Because those who go round the Dread Isle don't oft return.'

As Kio made to argue, a sharp cry pierced the air: an elkaven circling overhead.

The same foolish hope overcame Kio once again. He broke away from the guards, bringing his fingers to his lips as he raced for the gunnel. His shrill whistle reverberated off the rocks of the narrow crossing.

The bird's trajectory did not falter.

Kio's heart retreated from his mouth and sank back down where it belonged, sullen and defeated. The crew were staring at him, shocked and silent. Ice crept up his spine.

The Boatkeep spun on her perch, huge braid whipping like a tail as her green-brown eyes found Kio. She stalked towards him, a predator on the hunt, lips drawn back in a vicious snarl. 'What the *fuck* is he doing?' she whisper-shouted. 'Get him below deck—*now!*'

Several more elkavens burst from the island's peaks like a puff of dispersing leaves. Panic rippled through the crew. The birds gathered overhead, descending closer and closer ... until Kio saw they weren't birds at all.

Each the size of a stallion, the beasts were huge black blights in the crimson-tinged sky: four-limbed and draconic with scaled serpentine bodies and leather wings. Their claws were scythes, their jaws filled with multi-rowed teeth the length of daggers.

With a harpy-screech, they dove for the ship.

2

AMIKHARLIA

The rain hadn't stopped for days. Amika adjusted the cowl on her cloak as she and Rei trudged into the township of Honnah, Holania's westernmost district, known for its pear orchards and little else. The runaway princess had not been here in years.

'The Tower has a safe house here,' Rei said, voice lower than the exhausted slouch of his shoulders. 'We should avoid the tavern. And the inn.'

'Perfect,' Amika said, the word heavy with sarcasm. Her boots left squelching imprints in the sodden path as they snaked through the town square.

The miserable weather did not deter the townsfolk from their daily lives. Farmers displayed their produce on trestle tables around the square, more engaged in conversation with one another than hawking their goods. But there was a wariness in their eyes, and it wasn't from the arrival of strangers.

The Tear in the sky.

It had darkened on the day of Amika's wedding to Reminas—the day Kriah must have succeeded in breaking the seal in Kherunis. The angry fissure had widened and lengthened, stretching across the Great Meytaran Plain from Ciraselo to Adria like a festering wound.

Mud hardened to cobblestones as they moved away from the markets and into the residential area. The houses, no longer the feeble thatched-roof dwellings of the commonfolk, grew into two-storey structures that culminated in a large manor at the end of a cul-de-sac, overlooking the town. It had a grey shingled roof and an ornate steel fence surrounding well-manicured gardens. A memorial had been erected out the front: a statue of a blank-featured woman with a babe in her arms. Wreaths of white flowering dogwood were laid at the effigy's feet as well as little bunches of colourful pansies. Amika swallowed; Rei bristled beside her.

This was the Berne residence.

Moyna's home.

Amika first met Moyna Berne when the heir of the Honnah estate was fifteen years old, after she was determined to be the best match for the increasingly fussy Crown Prince Kiokharen. When the betrothal was finalised, Moyna moved to the Holanian capital of Adria, where she boarded with a distant cousin in the upper echelons of the city. She was a good match for Kio, Amika agreed; Moyna was steadfast and pragmatic where her brother was impulsive and tempestuous. She'd been excited to see them wed, but the ailing health of Moyna's father saw the nuptials delayed until after Amika had fled to Ciraselo. Moyna and Kio would have ruled well together.

But then there was Rei-Hai Shaw.

Amika edged towards the monument. It had been here for months, a year perhaps; moss had begun to grow across the surface of the stone.

'I always thought he really loved her,' she said softly.

'He did,' Rei agreed. He stood several paces away, huddled into the shroud of his woollen cloak, his golden eyes surveying nervously.

'And you?'

Rei rubbed his elbow, gaze diverted. 'A different kind of love. Let's keep moving.'

Amika exhaled slowly. Her brother had known two great loves and she was yet to find a single one. Love was a complex emotion, one she only seemed to half understand. But she saw its power, saw how it enslaved Rei-Hai every bit as much as the Tower had. His love for Kio kept him on his feet when all he wanted to do was collapse. Amika saw the pain he struggled with growing stronger each day. And yet he kept moving.

The rain was setting in now; the misty sprinkle turned to a heavy downpour, with icy winds whipping down from the mountains that lay before them. The western road through the delta flats led on to the Crags in the distance, the ranges that divided Qhoraak and Meytar. Snow dusted their jagged peaks—something Amika had not seen in all the years she could remember. Winter would be bitter this year.

'Rei, stop,' she said, eyes coming to rest on the town's noticeboard. The wooden placard was pinned with a great many flyers: parchments outlining the dates of town events; advertisements for the local barber; posters for the lost, wanted and found. Many were old and fraying, but right in the middle was a freshly pinned notice, complete with a crude charcoal etching of a monster.

Amika ripped the parchment free. 'Someone's posted a mark.'

'Who cares?' Rei grunted. 'Let's go.'

'*I* care,' she hissed. 'Kio would care. These are our people, Rei-Hai. Something's tormenting them.'

Amika inspected the listing as Rei came squelching back through the mud. The creature described was like nothing Amika had ever encountered on the plains, or even in the depth of the Li'Nea Wood.

'Looks like a wannari,' Rei muttered, glancing over Amika's shoulder. 'They're supposed to be extinct.'

She raised an eyebrow at his unexpected knowledge as he took the parchment from her.

'There was a bestiary in the Tower archives that I spent a great deal of time reading,' he clarified. 'Call it morbid curiosity, if you will, but ever since I found out what I was, I was determined to learn what I could *become*. Never did get that answer.'

'So if this demonspawn is extinct, then what is it doing here? In *Honnah*, no less.'

Rei shrugged, his right shoulder stiff from the wound he still carried from the Tower. He pushed the flyer back into her hands. 'Come on. It was last spotted where we're heading. May as well check it out.'

Night fell as they arrived at the westernmost arm of the Faethou River delta, where the demonspawn sighting had been reported. The wintry downpour had subsided to an irritating sprinkle that left Amika sodden and shivering. Rei had managed to kindle a little campfire upon a rocky outcropping among the marshes, but the meagre flames provided them with little warmth or light.

Amika shifted through her supplies for her bedroll and dry blankets. 'I'll take the first watch,' she said, plumping the bundle of fabric under her backside to soften the stone seat.

Rei gave no protest; he was already hunkering down to rest. Dark circles bagged under his eyes and his pale complexion was more pallid than usual—if that were even possible. At least the colour had returned to his hair; now that the black dye had washed out, it shone like a brilliant crimson flame, visible even in the dark. But still, he was not the same.

She wasn't the same.

Amika cleared her throat. 'Rei-Hai.'

Rei's eyes snapped open, exposing golden irises.

'Have you ... ever been with a woman?'

A smile lit his tired features. 'Are you propositioning me, Princess? At this hour?'

'What? No!' Amika blanched. 'Of course not! Look—have you?'

'Once or twice. Didn't much enjoy it.'

'You didn't?'

'I like men, Amika.'

'With my brother, then? You enjoy that?'

Rei sat up, face hard. 'Why are you asking me this? Are you *bored?* Surely you can find a farmer to entertain you, or some beast to go slay. Anything is preferable to this conversation.'

'I just ...'

I just feel wrong.

Amika prodded at the dull coals with a nearby stick, well aware of Rei's steady gaze on her. She wasn't so much avoiding his questions as struggling to put her racing thoughts into words.

'I don't understand the love you share with my brother. I *can't* understand it. It's like a language I can't seem to learn. That night with Reminas in my bed, I felt nothing but anger, hate, disgust ...'

'Understandable.'

'But even with Tallas. Beautiful, kind Tallas. There was no desire, no passion. I gave no more thought to our wedding night than I give the style of my hair. Oh, I don't know.' She threw the stick into the fire. 'How did *you* know? How did you know you loved my brother?'

Rei considered his answer in silence. 'When I look at him, I stop breathing.' A distant smile grew. 'Kind of like how Kriah looks at you ...'

Kriah.

Amika's pulse tripped at the thought of him. It had been two months since they parted ways on the Meytaran Plain, when she left their mission for Kherunis to liberate her people. She would have gone with Kriah, had Kio's life not been at stake. Had Rei not been so recklessly desperate to save him from Qhoraak. She cared for Kriah. She missed him. But ...

'Why is this bothering you?' Rei asked after a while.

'I don't know,' Amika confessed. 'Maybe there's something wrong with me.'

'Because you didn't want to fuck Reminas?'

'Because I don't want to *fuck* anybody.'

The redhead shrugged, irritatingly nonchalant. 'Some people seek pleasure from men. Others from women. Some from both and others from neither. There's nothing wrong with you, Princess. Now get some sle—'

Amika opened her mouth to question Rei's sudden pause, but he raised a finger to his lips before she could speak. Golden eyes scanning the darkness, he reached towards his boot.

'Something is watching us,' he whispered, a dagger in his hand.

'The Tower?'

'I said some*thing.*'

Amika drew her sword. She knew Rei's affinity with demonspawn and was grateful for the forewarning. Years of experience had taught her how quickly these monsters could sneak up on their prey.

'Where is it?'

Rei dipped his head towards the riverbank. 'I can't get a clear sense of it,' he said, edging closer to Amika to form a defensive stance. 'It's concealed somehow.'

Amika was blind in the blackness. Even Rei, with his impeccable vision, was struggling to focus his gaze on any one spot. They couldn't fight an enemy they couldn't see.

She glanced over her shoulder at their pathetic little fire. Its *khe'torla* resonance was faint but rhythmic, and she was confident in her ability to stoke it to a vicious flame, but the blaze was still too far behind them to see what lay ahead.

'Move back,' Amika instructed, also taking a step away from Rei. 'I'm going to give us some light.'

She'd transported flame to her hands before, without even meaning to, when she'd burned Reminas alive in her bed. If she concentrated, perhaps she could control it. Amika outstretched her palm towards the coals, closing her eyes to focus on the thrumming pulse in her veins. When the beats synchronised, she clenched her hand.

Her fingers peeled open, and fire danced above her skin.

Rei gasped. Amika, too, could not hide her shock at her success. The glowing flames licked and curled around her flesh, but never burned it; the warm glow was an ally. She drew strength from its presence—and from her own power.

'Direct it that way,' Rei suggested, pointing at the water's edge. Amika nodded and unleashed the flame in a spiralling torrent, illuminating a path across the marshy plains. Light bounced off tufts of spiky grass, off glistening rocks. Ripples on the river's surface quickened.

A great maw burst from the water, snapping at Amika's fireball. She and Rei ducked to shelter from the falling spray. Amika tugged on her *khe'torla*, and the fire came spiralling back to hover over them like a chandelier.

The creature slithered towards them on short, stocky legs, belly almost dragging on the ground.

'What ... is that?' Amika breathed. Her grip tightened on her sword.

'Nothing that should still be alive.'

The wannari had a long snout, slender and rounded like blacksmith pincers, filled with row upon row of sawblade teeth. The muck and river weed revealed patches of obsidian hide, thickly scaled like a reptile. This demonspawn was old: ancient battle wounds pocked its flesh in silvery craters, and its golden eyes held little sheen.

'I can't get a hold on it,' Rei said, grimacing from some unseen strain. 'It doesn't recognise my presence. I'll run decoy—I'm sure you can handle taking it down.'

He flashed a brief grin before darting off into the darkness, flinging an ineffectual shower of poison-tipped needles towards the beast; they clattered off its scaled hide into the mud.

'Thanks,' Amika muttered. She assessed her options. Unlike the ukarats she poached on the Meytaran plains, this demonspawn was armoured. Unless she could stick her sword in its soft underbelly, weapons would be of no use.

She'd have to use magic.

'I'm going to try something,' Amika said. 'Think you can keep it busy?'

'What do you think I've been doing?' a voice shot out of the darkness, followed by a throwing knife. It pierced the wannari's left eye and sent it howling.

Snarling and snapping, it lunged blindly in the direction from which the blade had come, great jaws open in search of meaty purchase. Rei rolled out of its path and into the light of Amika's fire lantern. Sweat beaded on his forehead and his breath came quick and heavy, far more forceful than Amika expected from such little exertion.

'Don't get too close,' the princess warned as she reached her *khe'torla* down into the soil. The earth's thrumming pulse was low and deep; distant and difficult to grasp. Amika had harnessed its power once before, when she'd unleashed an earthquake that rattled the old capital. This time she would have to be more precise.

Rei's needles clattered off the demonspawn's flank like pebbles on a wall. Black blood streamed from the wound to its eye, which did little more than aggravate it. Rei kept his distance but made the odd daring dash to collect his deflected weapons.

Once he was clear, Amika waited for the magical beats to synchronise before sending a surge through the ground. She could see the disturbance moving through the earth, like an animal tunnelling too close to the surface. It approached the wannari with speed Amika hadn't expected. She clenched her fist. A sharp spear of stone burst from the ground near the beast's jaw.

It missed.

Rei tumbled out of the way. He didn't get back up. In her panic, Amika sent another burst of *khe'torla*, larger and less controlled than the last. The ground rumbled beneath her feet; the demonspawn snarled and whipped its great head around, anticipating an attack but unsure from where.

Six, seven, *eight* stone spears erupted below it, piercing its soft underbelly and raising it several feet in the air.

Amika dropped to her knees. The beast quivered with residual life; one of the spears impaled its head through the throat.

She rose shakily to her feet and strode over to inspect her kill. Its jaw was open, leaking thick dark blood onto the earth. Once she would have eagerly scoured the corpse for a trophy. Now, she looked at it with guilt.

Rei groaned as he walked stiffly towards her, hand pressed to his hip. A graze cut his forehead above his eyebrow, sending a trail of black blood down his face. Amika looked back at the wannari's broken form, remorse swelling anew at the reminder of the connection between her friend and the demonspawn.

'Could this have been one of them?' she asked. 'A Siephymn?'

'Not any time recently,' he said, jaw clenched. He reached up to pull his dagger from the beast's eye. It released with a *pop* and shower of blood and clear jelly. 'This thing is centuries old. I don't know how it's been alive all this time. It must have been in some kind of hibernation.'

A cold shiver raced down Amika's spine as an uncomfortable thought stole into her mind. 'What if ...' she began, swallowing. 'What if the Great King never banished the demonspawn from Holania? What if they just went into hiding? What if breaking the seals has awakened more than just the Tear?'

Rei wiped his dagger on his cloak and returned the blade to his boot. 'Then we have far bigger problems than we realised.'

3

KRIAH

'You should ask Lomi for a job,' Amika said, propping herself up on an elbow, bedsheets twisted around her naked form. 'She's always complaining that she can't find helpers who know an onion from a radish.'

'I don't know much about Qhoraakese food,' Kriah confessed, rolling onto his side to face her. 'But I do know what a radish is.'

'*And* how to cook it.' She leant in for a quick kiss. 'Speaking of cooking, are you going to leave your mother to fix breakfast on her own again?'

He waited for a moment, Amika's fingers fiddling with his curls, before answering. 'I'd really rather stay here.'

Her smile broadened and his heart sang. 'No regrets, then?' she asked.

None, he thought. He regretted nothing. Not his decision to abandon Greist'hal's quest, denying his destiny as Chosen and choosing instead a life in Ciraselo with his mother and Amika. And he certainly didn't regret his decision to stay in bed.

'Never.' Kriah took her lips passionately, wrapping his arms around her battle-hardened body. Amika melted into him and time slipped away into a perfect dance of tangled—

Rough hands pawed at his shoulders. Kriah hit the ground with a wooden thud, water spilling from his lungs. A fist thumped at his back to help expel the ocean.

'I told yer to hold his bloody arms!' a gruff voice barked. 'Yer damn near nearly drowned the poor lad!'

'I wasn't expectin' him to start thrashin' around like that!' An equally rough reply. 'Thought he was dead, to be honest.'

Kriah groaned as he was rolled onto his back. He blinked in the sun, struggling against the horrific glare. Dark silhouettes hovered over him like phantoms. He opened his mouth to address the faceless figures, but his tongue was fat, his lips cracked.

'Deities dead, look at the poor lad. Dry and shrivelled as an ol' prune. Get 'im into the shade.'

Hands gripped him under his arms and dragged him across the deck. Out of the sun's harsh bite, Kriah could still feel its searing kiss, his entire body taut and stretched and raw. He tried to speak again, but no words came out; instead, a waterskin was thrust between his lips, sending cold liquid splashing down his throat. He choked on the deluge.

And then he passed out.

He didn't dream this time. Having lost consciousness, Kriah had been unable to conjure a dreamscape, and instead opened his eyes feeling disorientated, with no concept of time. How long had he been out?

Stretching his legs, he rolled onto his side and sat slowly upright. He was in a cabin of sorts. A kitchen—no, a mess. The sailor's mess on *Amikharlia's Tears*.

Kriah hoisted himself to his feet, using an uncorked barrel of wine as a crutch, then taking a seat on top of it. His head spun a little at the movement, but at least his senses had returned—even if his memory had not. He tried to piece together what had happened since he'd fled Grey and Azet'haal's battle on Kherunis, but the relentless sun had left him delirious. Fragments flashed before him: the endless ocean. Sails on the horizon.

The sea parting.

How did I get back to the Tears? *Did I really see—*

'Yer awake!' a gentle voice said from the doorway. Kriah looked up to see the one-eyed boatswain, Nell, holding a tray of food, a coarse blanket over his arms. He set the tray down on the table in front of Kriah, then draped the blanket around him. 'You were shivering, so I thought you'd need this. It's a terrible case of sun fever yer got there. Had to use a whole tin of salve.'

Kriah looked down at his red-brown arms, now slick and shiny with an earthy-smelling ointment. His face was tacky to the touch, as was the back of his neck, and suddenly his whole body felt sticky—and sore. He ached from head to toe, and there was a persistent throbbing at his temples. Never had he felt so ill.

Another familiar face joined Nell in the doorway. Rhenar, first mate of *Amikharlia's Tears*, strode into the room, arms folded over his round belly as he inspected Kriah. 'Ah, so yer awake now. Gave us all a mighty scare out there on the deck, lad. Thought we'd hooked ourselves a corpse.'

'I—I'm fine,' Kriah managed, his voice dry and hoarse. 'I think.'

He'd never been sick a day in his life. His Meah-Hyren blood protected him from common ailments, so aside from the fatigue of hard labour, he had no idea how it felt to be anything other than well—or how long it'd take to recover.

'Not ev'ry day yer see a nomad boy floatin' off the Silver Coast on 'is own, that's fer sure,' Rhenar said. 'Raises a question or two.'

'I'm sure he'll answer them in time, Rhenar,' Nell said, picking up the meal tray and setting it on Kriah's lap. 'Goddess only knows what he's been through.'

Kriah considered the bowl before him: a watery broth, filled with still-hard salt beef and partially rehydrated peas. His stomach howled and he brought it to his lips, gulping it down with enthusiasm as though it were a flavourful creation he'd made on his own hearth.

'Yer got a name, boy?' the first mate grunted.

'It's Kry—'

He paused. No one remembered him here. Not Rhenar, or Nell, who'd been his bunkmate; not the crew or Captain Yless, who'd welcomed Kriah and his grandfather aboard when they set out from Gerrick Port. Their memories had all been lost. Addled by Greist'hal's *khe'torla* before he and Kriah abandoned ship for Kherunis.

'My name is Kriah,' he said eventually. 'My family are travellers from the plains. While wintering in Midden, we caught wind of a rumour out of Tennan Cove that promised riches too good to ignore.'

He scrambled to piece together a story from bits of information he'd acquired in his travels. Kriah had known nothing of the world before leaving the Li'Nea Wood, and the chance of misremembering what he'd heard and making a fool of himself was high. But Rhenar and Nell watched him earnestly, waiting for him to continue; his lies were going down well.

'My clan had lost much of their flock to ukarats—'

'What's an *ukarat*?' Nell asked, head cocking slightly to the side.

'Uh …' Kriah took a long drink of his hot soup. Were there no demon-spawn this far east? 'It's, uh … the nomads' word for "wolf".'

He glanced across the rim of his bowl at Rhenar and Nell; they were both nodding in acceptance. Kriah exhaled a careful breath and continued.

'My father heard a rumour of giant snow crabs up the Ice Coast, on the ocean shelf off Kherunis. Sent me out to find them.'

Rhenar and Nell exchanged a glance. The first mate unfolded his arms and pushed himself off the bench where he'd been leaning. 'Looks like we caught the same wave,' he said, taking a seat on another makeshift chair opposite Kriah. His beard had thickened in the short time Kriah had been away, or perhaps his cheeks had just grown more hollow.

'Though it seems we fared a little better than you, lad,' Rhenar continued. His hand curled around an empty cup left on the table, but his searching eyes found no ale to fill it. 'Might not've found any bloody crabs, but at least the crew's intact. Mostly.'

Nell lowered his head. Kriah sensed more to this story. *Amikharlia's Tears* had been wracked by more than rough seas. Thunder rumbled outside with its ever-present temper. Incessant storms had raged ever since Kriah fled Kherunis after breaking the Skrevaar seal, leaving Greist'hal behind.

His grandfather was dead. There was no point in hoping otherwise. It was a fact as clear as the ocean was wet. He and Azet'haal had been trapped inside a shield crafted from Greist'hal's own life force, keeping the effects of the battle bottled inside. When it failed, the resulting flood of *khe'torla* was enough to disrupt the very world around them. No wonder the storms were so violent.

'Well, not much we can do about it now,' the first mate muttered, raising the cup to his lips, forgetting it was empty. He sighed and looked into its dry bottom. 'Yer must need some rest. Now yer belly's full and body's dry, looks like yer can barely keep yer head up. Find a cot for him, Nell.'

The sandy-haired boatswain nodded at Rhenar's suggestion and gestured towards the door. Kriah set down the soup bowl and stood to follow. Rhenar was right: every inch of his body longed for sleep now that it was no longer distracted by more pressing needs. As half Meah-Hyren, he did not require sleep as often as the mortal Second Born, but he could not even remember the last time he'd closed his eyes to truly rest.

'There's a spare bunk in my cabin,' Nell said as he closed the door to the officers' mess behind them. He glanced briefly at a room across the narrow corridor. A soft, pained wail resonated within.

The captain's quarters, Kriah recalled.

Nell coughed gently and directed them up onto the deck. Kriah squinted as he emerged and was greeted by large, heavy raindrops splashing on his face. The rest of the crew watched on as he passed, their faces sullen and full of pity for the shipwrecked sailor they no longer recognised as one of their own.

'It's away from the other lodgings,' the boatswain continued, 'but you'll rest better away from the noise of the crew's mess.'

He descended back into the ship's bowels below the fo'c'sle, where the scent from the galley rose up to meet them. Kriah's stomach growled the moment his nostrils caught a whiff of the rations boiling for the evening's meal, despite him having just consumed two bowls of the reheated stew.

'I'm sure Cliff will scrounge up something extra for yer,' Nell said, noting Kriah's gaze on the galley door. 'He'll complain, but he'll do it.'

Kriah smiled faintly as he recalled the curly-haired cook he'd swindled out of a win in his first game of Um-Narl.

As Nell opened the door to his narrow lodgings, Kriah was filled by the comforting warmth of familiarity. The crate the young boatswain used to keep his ledgers was strewn with additional documents and sea charts. Candles, melted down to stumps, spread across the makeshift table in dry, waxy puddles.

'What happened to your father?' Kriah ventured, recalling the moaning from the captain's chamber.

Nell turned back towards him, head cocked curiously. 'How'd yer know Cap'n Yless is my da?'

'Uh,' Kriah floundered, 'just a guess. You reacted strangely when Rhenar mentioned the toll this voyage has taken.'

The boatswain rubbed his forehead where the bandages concealing his blind left eye wrapped around his temple. He suddenly seemed every bit as exhausted as Kriah; Rhenar, too, had worn the troubles of a weary man. Whatever ill had befallen the captain had left its mark on his son and first mate, too.

'Aye, he's my da,' Nell conceded with a heavy sigh. 'Though not too many folks know it. Yer got a sharper eye than most, uh ... Sorry. Yer name slipped my mind again.'

Kriah's heart fell a little. 'Kriah. My name is Kriah.'

Nell gave a smile as slight as his nod—his mind appeared to be far away now, most likely with his father.

Kriah sat down on the cot that had once been his. 'What happened?' he prompted, then remembered he was a stranger. 'I'm sorry, I shouldn't—'

'No, it's fine.' Nell too eased himself onto a swaying hammock. 'Nice, actually. Rhenar 'n' I've tried to keep the cap'n's condition from the crew. We don't even know what happened to him, really. One mornin' we woke up not really rememberin' much of anything, 'cept that we'd been at sea for weeks with not much to show for it.'

Kriah's belly clenched. That had been Greist'hal's doing. He was the one who'd planted the seeds of rumour that sent the *Tears* off course to bring them closer to Kherunis.

'Cap'n kept mutterin' somethin' about snow crabs 'n' how we can't turn the ship around now. He was ravin' mad! One minute he was shoutin' orders, and the next he was whimperin' 'n' moanin' 'bout bein' swindled by a witch. Rhenar 'n' I locked him in his cabin for his own good. He'll be right, though,' Nell said with sudden certainty. 'Just gotta get him home to Mam.' His good eye drifted towards the stack of ledgers on the makeshift table. 'Gonna be a grim ol' winter, though.'

Kriah's fists curled as guilt screamed in his ears. He had no words of comfort to offer Nell. 'I'm sorry,' was all he muttered, but the placation felt hollow.

Nell just shrugged, somewhat defeated. 'Nothin' yer've done, Kriah. I'd wager yer losses are greater.'

Neither of them had any more to say after that. Kriah kicked off his boots, swung his legs up into the suspended cot, and waited for sleep to find him.

The crew treated Kriah differently in the days that followed. He was not so much a stranger as an outsider, no longer ordered to pitch in and pull his weight. Jyn, the wiry seaman who'd once shared the dice table with him, nudged Kriah aside when he tried to help, shouting for him to get back to his cabin and let the real sailors work. It stung more than Kriah expected. While he'd never been a *real* sailor, for a time he'd been one of them. He'd felt like he belonged.

Kriah was on the fo'c'sle with Rhenar when the Whyt'hallen coastline finally rose from the horizon. The first mate's lips drew thin and taut as he lowered his brass telescope.

'Call for Nell, will yer, lad?' Rhenar asked.

Eyes straining, Kriah tried to follow Rhenar's gaze, but the clouds—no, smoke—hung too low and thick in the distance.

'Now, lad,' Rhenar barked, sending Kriah scuttling down the deck in search of the boatswain.

He found Nell on the quarterdeck, arms folded and face stern as he oversaw the repairs to the mainmast's rigging during a brief respite from the rain. The boatswain's posture softened as he spied Kriah's approach.

'Rhenar's called for you up top,' Kriah said, chasing his breath.

Nell nodded and turned to his sailors. 'Finish up 'ere, then move on to the mizzenmast.'

He followed Kriah back to where Rhenar was perched on the bow, unhurried so as not to cause alarm—a junior seaman racing across deck to deliver a message was one thing; a ranking officer another. Wordlessly, Nell took the telescope from Rhenar's grasp and pressed it to his good eye. After a moment, he lowered it again and looked gravely across at the first mate.

'That smoke's comin' off the beach, not the town,' he said.

'Aye,' Rhenar agreed softly.

Kriah's brow furrowed as he struggled to discern the importance of the observation. 'The beach?' he asked. 'What would be burning on the beach?'

The mate swallowed, jaw clenched. 'Bodies.'

4

KIOKHAREN

'Hit the deck!' the Boatkeep yelled, and someone tackled Kio to the floor. His cheek smashed against the slick wood, shame welling up inside him as he covered his head with his arms. A great screech whirred overhead. Kio felt the vibrations of the soldiers now scooping up weapons and racing to the gunnel to defend against the attack. Panic choked the air. Commands flew in tongues he didn't understand. Screams and drums, horns and firearms sounded all around—a cacophony of confusion that assaulted his senses and seemed to drive the winged beasts mad.

'All prisoners below deck—*now!*' the Boatkeep shouted, firearms cracking as smoke filled the air.

An unseen hand hauled Kio back to his feet by the collar of his tunic. 'You 'eard her, down you g—aagh!'

The man's head disappeared into the great maw of a winged beast before it dragged his flailing body overboard. The weapon he had brandished—a short, iron-tipped spear—fell where he stood.

It wasn't a sword, but it would do. Kio plucked it from the deck just as another creature came careening out of the clouds towards him. With an upward thrust, he pierced its belly. Blood and black viscera slopped onto the deck in a slimy puddle. Kio gagged at the putrid smell, thick with shit and rotting fish. He kicked the skewered monster aside, tore the spear free and raced for a group of sailors currently under siege along the stern.

A smaller creature flitted about the group like an irritating fly in the summer. It plucked firearms from their hands with its agile claws while onlookers aimed misplaced shots at the leathery membrane of its wings. The distraction allowed larger beasts to descend with ease, snapping and tearing at the confused guards around the mizzenmast.

Are they ... intelligent?

Kio's thought died when the wail of a young man caught his ears.

A winged beast hoisted the Qhoraakese guard into the air, talons hooked through the meat of his shoulders. Kio skidded to a halt. Readjusting his grip on the spear, he sent it catapulting towards the creature, where it embedded in a sinewy flank. The beast howled. Pounding its wings, it released its grip on the guard as it fled.

Kio was too far away to catch the boy with any grace. He threw his body across the deck, trying to cushion the young guard's fall by catching him on his chest. The impact forced air from his lungs with a groan and the prince lay stunned on his back, staring up at the red sky. The horde of beasts hovering above had started to thin as the ship cleared the channel and passed out of their territory. The guards continued to shoot at their retreating assailants, cheering as the creatures dropped from the air into the ocean below.

But the joy was short-lived. As the shooting died away, the screams of pain became all the more prevalent—none so desperate as those from the boy strewn across Kio's chest. The prince wiggled out from beneath the wailing young sailor and scrambled to his knees to assess the damage. The boy's arms were hunched over his chest, trying to stem the blood that flowed from several punctures. The wound on the left was most severe, the white of his clavicle visible among the gore.

'I need a chirurgeon!' Kio called, glancing frantically around the deck. 'Someone help him! A healer, please!'

No one came to his aid.

'Healer!' he called again, a touch of desperation in his voice. Didn't anyone speak his language? Or, as a prisoner, was he simply invisible?

The boy gurgled a bloody cough. 'No! Come on, hang in there.' Kio pressed his hands to the bubbling wound, blood spilling faster than he could plug it. 'Come on, come on—'

Kio found himself plucked away from the boy and restrained by two men. He struggled against their grip, adrenaline still strong in his veins.

'Enough!' a commanding female voice boomed. 'He is gone.'

Heavy footsteps clacked across the deck; Kio dared not face the approaching sailor, knowing full well who he'd turn to find.

The Boatkeep.

She stood over him now, tall and imposing, her tricorn hat askew and a smoking firearm over her shoulder. She wiped a trail of blood from her cheek.

'This one's a prisoner?' Her Meytaran was clipped but fluent, and the man who responded spoke with a native lilt.

'Aye.' He lifted Kio's tunic to inspect the brand on his side. '57892.'

'Where is he from?'

'I'd have to check the manifest, Boatkeep,' the guard explained. 'But … I believe he boarded with the main shipment in Cirahk.'

Her hazel eyes narrowed. 'Have him and his papers brought to my cabin,' she said, then straightened and turned away. 'And review the full manifest for any prisoners who may be experienced with healing arts.

Bring them to the sick bay to assist with the injured. Strip the fallen and throw the corpses overboard. We'll hold a vigil at sundown.'

They dragged Kio to his feet and prodded him back across the deck. But instead of being shoved down with the messes, he was marched towards the captain's quarters at the aft end of the ship. There was no point in struggling, he knew that. His body had grown weak since his time in Cirahk; still, that did not stop him fighting against the restraints as they pushed through the doors.

The captain's quarters comprised a spacious cabin, lavishly decorated—even by Kio's standards. A double bed, heavy with embroidered quilts and throw pillows, consumed the far wall, framed by ornate wooden panelling. The centre of the room was filled by a large table with a single high-backed chair; the multi-purpose space held a half-finished tray of breakfast rations, a pewter goblet, and an array of papers and sea charts. Even with the mess, the quarters made the ship seem more like a royal frigate than a convict trawler.

Perhaps this ship once lived a grander life, just like me, Kio thought bitterly as he was forced into a sitting position on a large oak barrel, opposite what must be the Boatkeep's chair. The wood smelt heavily of rum and his mouth salivated. He could use a drink now more than ever.

'Wait here,' one of the guards barked as he fastened Kio's wrists together.

'We're in the middle of the ocean,' Kio observed coolly. 'Where could I possibly go?'

He received no answer aside from the standard clip around the head. He was alone now, the door swinging in the guards' wake.

With a huff of frustration, he gave a futile tug on his restraints. Anxiety wheedled its way back through his body. Adrenaline left him, leaving a sick, heavy feeling at the base of his gut. His head swirled from his first encounter with the Boatkeep, the memory quickly joined by the distant *splash* of a headless corpse hitting the water.

If she was going to kill him, surely she would have done so already. Made an example of him in front of the crew, just as she'd done back on the docks in Cirahk. But what exactly had that man done wrong?

What have I done wrong?

The door creaked open, and Kio's skin prickled. The footsteps were unhurried as they crossed the cabin, the Boatkeep finally coming into view. She set her firearm down on the messy table, loosening the buttons of her stained blouse with the other hand. She tossed the leather jerkin aside altogether and took a seat on the edge of the table, legs straight and ankles crossed. Her hard stare fell on Kio. He met her gaze.

'You can fight,' she observed, folding her arms. 'Not an undisciplined brawler like all the other cockstains on board, but a true, trained swordsman.' Her lips thinned to a fine line as she mused. 'What were you? A knight? A lordling's personal guard?'

'A prince,' Kio said.

The woman laughed. 'A prince, aye. Of course.'

'I am Kiokharen Erhin Josten Holani, Crown Prince to the throne of Adria.' There was little point in lying. She would either believe him or she would not; no amount of charading on his behalf was likely to change her mind. 'I was sent here as a captive of Reminas Bara after I attempted to murder him for his attack on my people. This is his idea of justice.'

Her expression shifted to one of vague amusement. 'Ah, so you're *him*. I heard the crew gossip about a prisoner sold by the Bararnite throne. Well, well, well. Tried to kill the prince, did you?' She snorted. 'I've had dogs with brighter ideas.'

The insult stung. He bristled and clenched his jaw as he considered what allegiance this Qhoraakese woman held to Bararn. Had this revelation signed his death? She was in Reminas's employ, after all.

The Boatkeep straightened, her fingers toying with a knife retrieved from the table. 'Fool or not,' she said, admiring the blade, 'you can fight. And you protected my men.'

'Not all of them,' Kio muttered. He still felt the young man's blood on his hands, dry and sticky.

She nodded. 'That boy was beyond saving. But we all benefited from your bravery and prowess. My men could learn from you.'

She threw the knife towards Kio, smiling when he did not flinch. It impaled the rum barrel between his legs. She swiped a goblet from the table and sauntered closer. As she crouched between his knees, the cavalier grin on her lips grew wide with delight.

'I don't care what bought your berth on this ship,' she said, twisting the knife in the barrel. Amber liquid spilt from the cracks in the wood. 'I care what it is you can do for me.'

'And what exactly is that?' Kio swallowed, acutely aware of the proximity of their bodies, of their faces. Of the rich, smoky bouquet of rum wafting upwards.

The Boatkeep thrust her goblet under the spilling liquid. 'I need fighters. Actual trained soldiers. Not just violent ruffians who can mindlessly swing a sword and take orders when they feel like it. I need discipline. I need respect.' She knocked the rum back in a hearty swig, then wiped her mouth with her forearm. 'How'd you like to get out of those chains?'

It was Kio's turn to place a bet. The cup was still face down, dice hidden within, and all three men before him had wagered their nightly rum ration on high-even. Kio was new to Um-Narl, and he used this inexperience as an excuse to deliberate. There was no skill to this stupid game—it was just luck, something Kio wasn't very familiar with these days. But he really wanted those *fucking* drinks.

'Even ... Low.' He thrust his thimbleful of rum across the low table, bracing for Bryn-Daal to reveal his fate.

'Deities fucking dead, two 'n' two,' the burly Kheshtarli groaned. 'Low evens.'

Kio nearly fell off the stool, mouth growing thick with saliva as Davyn and Bryn-Daal reluctantly slid their rations across to him. Ylan hesitated, a sneer forming under his flat nose.

'Can I suck your prick or something instead?' he mumbled, but Kio was already knocking back the first of his takings. He grimaced as the dark liquid roared down his throat; he'd never been fond of rum, but it was the first time in a long while he'd had more than a drop just enough to wet his tongue.

'Not a fucking chance,' Kio said, slamming the little pewter cup on back on the table and reaching for the next. 'Pay what you owe, Ylan.' Drink. Exhale. 'Besides, you're not my type.'

Ylan's scowl deepened and he slapped the cup sideways. Kio scrambled to right it, saving most of the precious alcohol from spilling onto the table. He drank it just as fast.

Sweet, burning bliss.

'Holy mother Miatha, you fucking lucky bastard,' Davyn moaned, licking parched lips as he ran his hands down his distraught face.

Kio choked on the last of his drink. 'Lucky?' He coughed. 'How *lucky* can I be? Imprisoned here with you lot? Some definition of *luck*.'

'Alright, alright. You're not the first daft fucker in here to think himself hard done by.' Bryn-Daal flapped his hand, dismissive. He picked up his plate to continue eating his salt beef and dried peas, both of which were immensely unappealing without the rum to wash them down. ''Cept you can't be too down on luck when the Boatkeep herself has taken a shine to yer.'

Kio froze, wishing he hadn't been so quick to drink down his rum. The hair on the back of his neck stood at attention, though he tried to act calm.

'That's right, we heard,' Bryn-Daal continued. 'All anyone could talk about this morning was how some crazy bastard up on scullery held his own against a demonspawn ambush. Took down three before the guards took *him* down.'

Kio picked up a previously shunned strip of salt beef from his own plate and popped it in his mouth. The meat was dry and fibrous on his tongue, but it served its purpose in the absence of drink.

'Demonspawn?' he asked, eyebrows raised. 'There haven't been any demonspawn in Whyt'hallen for centuries.'

The mess captain bellowed a great laugh in response. 'Deities dead, you Middle Kingdom fuckers are ignorant pricks. No demonspawn in Whyt'hallen? None in Holania, perhaps. Southern Bararn, most of Meytar. But in Kheshtarl ... Well, let's just say folks don't do much travelling after dark.'

'Crew says Qhoraak's even worse,' Ylan said. 'Where those white-haired witches tore the damn sky that let the fucking beasts through in the first place. Heard they keep demonspawn as pets.'

Davyn hawked up a wad of phlegm and spat it on the floor beside the stack of empty plates Kio had been building at his feet. 'And that's the place we're fucking heading.'

A sombre silence fell over them, as if the gravity of their sentence was only just registering. Terror flared in Kio anew. To think his greatest fear when getting on this boat had been a life of slave labour toiling away in a mine. Now all he saw were fangs and claws and blood; all he heard were screams.

Iron creaked behind him as the guard struggled with the lock. All four of them turned towards the door as Bryn-Daal squirrelled his dice away to wherever he kept them hidden. No one entered the messes after supper; the plates weren't cleared until morning scullery, and night call was just a brief banging on the bars.

Kio recognised the man as one of the guards who'd escorted him to the Boatkeep's quarters a few days before—a solid, bald man with a nose that had been broken one too many times and several pink scars carved into his rich russet skin.

'57892. Dally. Dally Grant,' he said, looking directly at Kio.

'Yes?' His heart was hammering, but the extra rum he'd won at least kept the tremble out of his hands.

'The Boatkeep summons you,' the guard barked.

Though he'd been invited to share in her supper, and even been offered a chance at freedom, the Boatkeep kept Kio on edge, senses alight and ready for battle. He did not trust her, as she clearly did not trust him, having posted two guards by the door of her cabin while they dined.

The Boatkeep ate and drank without reserve, and even offered Kio food from her own plate. But he couldn't bring himself to accept, despite still being hungry after his own meagre meal.

'Was that your first time seeing Siephymn?' she asked, washing her mouthful of food down with a chaser of rum.

Kio stared at her blankly.

'Siephymn. Demonspawn. The beasts you slayed.'

Siephymn ... Why did that sound familiar? The word was foreign, but he'd heard it before. He soon placed the memory: Rei-Hai Shaw—one of his cagey conversations about the Tower. Kio'd always assumed it was something to do with the brethren, a title or insult his childhood friend had earnt ...

'Kheshtarl has been known to ship their Siephymn off to Khel-Tor-Lum—the so-called Dread Isle—when they devolve, so they don't attack their farms or villages.' The Boatkeep speared a wedge of boiled potato and popped it into her mouth, worryingly nonchalant. 'The only thing worse than watching a loved one turn is having to *end* them once they do.'

Kio's heart was thundering now. Sweat broke out on his brow as fractured pieces of memory fell together in his mind. The black blood, the golden eyes. Skin so pale it lacked colour at all.

Demonic little bastard.

Geraad Shaw had cursed his apparent son endlessly. Beaten and neglected, Rei was ultimately sold to the Tower. Kio always thought it the result of a grieving husband, bereft of his wife and drowning in drink.

'S-Siephymn...' His gaze settled on a second goblet left on the table; the Boatkeep dipped her head towards it. Kio knocked it back without hesitation. The rum snaked hotly down his throat. 'What are they? Demonspawn?' he asked, lips tingling from the liquor.

The Boatkeep tore a sliver of salt beef from the pile on her plate and added it to her mouth. She chewed thoughtfully, considering her answer. 'Not exactly. They're beings, like us. Born to a mortal mother but fathered by a *khaaja*—the Kheshtarli word for alpha,' she elaborated in response to the confusion that must have passed over his face. 'We know them as the First. The first beasts to pass through the Tear. They take our form, impregnate our women.' She shrugged casually. 'And that leaves us with Siephymn.'

Kio's throat was dry again; he coughed to find his voice. 'Can it be ... undone?'

'They're not cursed, Little Prince.'

He bristled at the new moniker.

'A Siephymn cannot amend their parentage any more than you and I. Besides, why would they want to? It is an honoured existence. One of power and pride.' Under her breath, she added, 'At least, it used to be.'

The Boatkeep brooded, and Kio fell into the same heavy silence. He listened to the crew chatting out on the deck, their voices subdued. They had mourned their fallen comrades and the Boatkeep herself had led the brief vigil. She was not the tyrant she had been portrayed as when he first boarded—the prisoners may fear her, but the crew did not.

But she still shot a man in cold blood.

Kio stood and paced the room. The woman's hazel eyes followed him with caution, but she made no attempt to stop him. His mind buzzed with questions he couldn't find the words to breathe into life. Instead he reached for another drink.

'You offered me a chance at freedom,' he said, deciding to steer the conversation back to the reason he was here, if only to stop thinking about demonspawn and Siephymn and Rei-Hai fucking Shaw. He downed the fresh cup of rum, no longer grimacing at the burn but delighting in it. His muscles finally grew heavy and relaxed.

'I told you: I need fighters,' she said calmly, balancing her knife and fork on the edge of her plate. 'You're not the first convict I've liberated on one of these journeys and I doubt you'll be the last. Some of my best men and women have been exiles from the Middle Kingdoms. I hope you'll be one of them. If not,' she added with a shrug, 'you can go back to your mess and travel on to whatever prison camp you've been assigned.'

Kio swirled the rum around his goblet, watching a fleck of residue from the barrel float on the surface of the liquid. 'Who are you?' he asked.

'Emanais Ulande,' the Boatkeep said flippantly, as if her name had never been a secret.

'Yes, but who *are* you? What do you need all these fighters for?'

Emanais leant back on her chair, elbow propped on the table as she considered Kio from across the cabin.

'To wage war.'

5

REI-HAI

Rei wasn't sleeping well. That wasn't anything new, but there was now an ache deep in his bones that went well beyond fatigue, made worse by the battering and bruising he'd sustained from the encounter with the wannari. He grimaced as he rolled onto his side. The wound Jahaanya Yai had left him had still not fully healed and, although it no longer bled, the skin was red and angry around the scar.

'Shit,' he groaned, clutching his shoulder as he sat up on his paper-thin bedroll.

'You should rest more,' Amika suggested from her perch on a rocky outcrop overlooking the camp. Her sword lay across her lap, unsheathed and ready. 'It's not exactly light out.'

It was well before dawn. A faint orange glow had started to break on the horizon, but visibility beyond their campsite was poor. There were no stars out, and the moon was obscured behind a swathe of cloud, stained crimson by the Tear. Rei had lost track of the days that had passed since they'd left Adria, of the days Kio would have been at sea. He would reach Qhoraak before them—of this Rei was certain—and while he was confident in his plan of getting *into* the seclusive kingdom, he had no idea where to start looking once they arrived.

'It's alright,' he muttered. 'I'm up now.'

'You look terrible.'

'Good morning to you too, Princess,' he snorted.

She was right, though. His head pounded and his body felt so heavy he was unsure he could even stand, let alone travel another day on foot. He'd never felt fatigue like this before. Despite the inflammation of his wound, he was sure it was not infected—his body battled no fever, nor was it wracked with bouts of nausea.

But he was certainly ill.

Rei had felt the Tear's influence ever since Amika first aggravated the celestial wound back in Ciraselo. It hung over him like a miasma and had grown stronger since he'd left Adria, likely due to the first seal falling at Kriah's hands. Cursed blood pumped hotly through his veins, bubbled over shifting bones and stretching muscles. With the help of Ka'ella's decoctions, he'd managed to keep the transformation at bay, but with only one phial left ...

'We could rest today,' Amika said, hopping down from the rock. She stretched upon landing, her limbs long and lean. 'I know you're desperate to find my brother, but what help will you be if you can barely stand?'

'Amika,' he coughed, his voice hoarser than he expected. 'I just ...' He swallowed the words before he could speak them.

I just need to see him again.

Amika nodded, apparently satisfied with the reason he never gave. She bent to heave up his pack to shoulder alongside her own. 'We'd best get going, then.'

The terrain became steep and increasingly rocky the further west they moved from the delta flats. Hampered by the steady incline and his own poor condition, Rei grew frustrated at their slow progress. With the regular breaks Amika insisted upon, they couldn't have managed more than ten miles before the sun began to set and they made camp for the night.

Rei guzzled his waterskin, ignoring the spillage that snaked down his chin. He stretched out his heavy legs, the ache bone-deep, and grimaced away the words of gratitude for the early rest that threatened to burst from his lips. He would not let Amika see how weak he was; he would not let *himself* see it either.

'There's a stream not far from here,' Amika said, pointing down the grassy hillside away from their rocky perch and the setting sun. 'I'll fill a pot for dinner. We still have some salt meat we can soften in a st—'

'We should hunt while there's still game around,' Rei insisted. 'Save our rations for when we hit the caves into Qhoraak.'

He salivated at the prospect of it. Thick, red meat, hot from a fresh kill. The thought jumped unbidden into his mind and was hard to push aside. He swallowed dryly.

'We don't have a bow,' Amika said, her expression troubled. 'I mean, I could try with my magic, but—'

Rei touched the satchel strapped to his thigh. 'I have plenty of needles. Should be able to get a hare or two without much exertion.'

Provided I can keep myself steady enough to aim ...

The princess nodded, clearly too tired to argue. 'Toss me your waterskin. I'll fill it up and brew some tea for when you're back.'

Rei's stomach churned at the thought of tea, but he nodded his agreement before struggling to his feet and hobbling away.

Kio was stroking his hair. Slow, tender movements unperturbed by the sweaty slickness of his skin. The fever had still not broken, the toxins still holding their grip on his muscles, on his mind. Pain radiated through every nerve.

'This is foolish, Rei-Hai—I'm calling a healer,' the prince said, and made to stand. Rei snatched his hand back.

'N-no.' He squeezed Kio's hand so hard he felt the knuckles crack. 'It'll pass.'

It has to pass.

'Let me at least send for mandrake tea. So you can—'

'That will only cause questions,' Rei hissed between clenched teeth. 'Leave it. Please.'

Kio sighed, defeated. 'Why won't you let me help you?' He reached out with his other hand to brush damp hair back from Rei's face, leaning close so Rei could finally see him through his blurred vision. 'There has to be something I can do. I hate seeing you suffer.'

Rei knew it was wrong to have come here, to make Kio watch him go through this. He should have made for the safe house in Trendon the moment he broke free of Qhoraak. There, he could have sweated the remaining poison from his body alone and without concern. But the moment he'd seen Adria's spires rising black against the setting sun, he'd known where he needed to be.

'Just stay with me,' he begged weakly.

With a nod, Kio clambered over the bed and wrapped himself around Rei's curled and shivering body, holding him close. Rei allowed himself to relax.

'Mother wants to plan a summer wedding,' Kio began after a moment's silence. 'I can't keep hiding behind Amika's disappearance as reason to delay, she says. Like that's the only reason,' he added more softly.

Rei had been content with just the prince's quiet presence, but he was suddenly grateful for the distraction, the deep, gentle hum of Kio's voice every bit as warming as his embrace. His body grew heavy as sleep finally crept closer.

'Do you think she's still alive? It's been two years, and—nothing. I'd have thought she'd have come home by now. But I suppose it took you longer to find your way back to me.'

'I didn't run away, Kio,' Rei mumbled groggily.

'And suppose Amika didn't either?' Kio's fingers traced idly down Rei's arm as he spoke. 'What ill fate has befallen her?'

'If she were at the Tower, I'd know it.'

Silence fell again. Rei drifted somewhere between sleep and wakefulness, soothed by the comfort of Kio's touch. His body had lingered so long in pain now that exhaustion conjured its own analgesia. He would have slept, had a knock not come to the door.

Kio froze, a child caught sneaking food from the kitchens. After a hesitant pause, Rei felt him roll from the bed and pad towards the door on bare feet.

'What is it?' His harsh whisper was almost a bark.

'I could see light coming from your chamber. Why are you awake? Can you not sleep again?'

The woman's voice was familiar, but it took Rei a moment to place it. *Moyna.*

The door clicked open. 'Something like that,' Kio said, his voice softer now. 'The maids took my wine.'

'That will bring you no peace, my love. *Tea* will help you sleep. Something herbal and soothing. I'll get it for you myself.'

Rei pressed his face into the pillow, stifling a groan as another wave of pain surged over him.

'Mandrake,' Kio said suddenly. 'From the chirurgeon's stores. Tell Master Antor it's for me and he'll give it to you.'

'I will not get you that.'

'Valerian root, then. Please, Moyna. I need to sleep.'

The delay in her response spoke of her hesitation. Finally, she said, 'I'll see what I can do.'

Kio closed the door and returned wordlessly to the bed; Rei felt the mattress dip as the prince took a seat beside him. A soothing hand rubbed his thigh as he peeled his face from the pillow. Kio's eyes were soft. Warm.

'I hate you,' Rei groaned.

'No you don't.' Kio smiled and placed a kiss on his forehead.

Rei awoke, face in the dirt, dry grass scratching at his cheek.

He sat up with a start. The world spun. He vomited. He wiped his mouth and his hand came away bloody. *Red* blood.

Panic rose in his throat with more bile. The blood coated his arms from fingertip to elbow, dark and crusty. The skin of his chin and neck was stiff and sticky where it had already begun to dry.

It's not mine. He knew that, but patted his body down for wounds all the same. Giving himself the all-clear, he glanced around for any sign of whatever—*whoever*—he'd killed.

A deer lay in the grass beside him, broken and bloodied and disembowelled. Its slender neck fell at a sharp angle and the soft skin of its belly was torn and shredded, flies gathering about the shiny entrails that spilt from the gaping gash. Rei shuddered, and the tremor shook his entire body. He threw up once more, this time tasting the raw flesh on his tongue. He felt ill, but oddly ... satiated.

He'd turned. He must have. And ripped apart the nearest creature he could find. But now he was back and felt more himself than he had in weeks.

Rei rose to his feet, but found them to be heavy and unresponsive. He stumbled a few steps before regaining his balance, groaning at the stiffness in his joints. Sighing, he glanced down at the ruined corpse of the deer. He couldn't bring this back to Amika—not without an interrogation.

The moon struggled to find its place in the night sky as Rei went in search of the stream to follow back to camp. He didn't remember wandering so far—but he didn't remember the deer, either. Rolling up his sleeves, he submerged his bloodied hands in the water, hissing at the cold bite of its touch. He began to scrub, softly at first but then with desperate vigour, as if trying to leach wine from a beloved shirt.

His right hand failed to lighten. He rubbed and rubbed, but the dark smear remained like a black glove, fading just above his wrist.

This wasn't blood.

Rei ran his fingers over the back of his hand. It was tough and leathery, the nails thick and sharp.

'Fuck.'

Splashing water on his face, he cleaned himself up, ignoring the gnawing pit in his belly.

He was running out of time.

The fire had burned down to charcoal and Amika was curled up asleep by the time Rei returned to camp. There was a pot of cold tea by his bedroll, which he sheepishly crawled onto without making a sound. He glanced at the glowing fire and found two small hares skewered on spits above coals, one little more than a carcass picked bare.

'I was hungry,' Amika said through the darkness. 'Good thing I didn't wait.'

'I got lost.'

'No you didn't.' The princess sat up and lifted the scrawny hare from the spit, passing it to him across the dim fire. 'Why won't you let me help you?'

Rei snorted, recalling Kio's similar words from his dream—his memory. He took the skewered animal from her and looked at the dry, overcooked flesh. Images of the bloody deer flashed through his mind. His tongue tingled, but he was no longer hungry. Not for *this*, anyway.

'I'm beyond help, Amika,' he mumbled.

'Only if you give up.'

Rei took a bite of the hare. His throat closed and he gagged, but he forced it down anyway. He tossed the rest of it back into the fire. Sparks scattered like startled mice.

'I'm changing, Amika. I can't stop it. *You* can't stop it.' He held up his hand in the dim light, unsure whether she could see the dark stain. 'No one can.'

Amika nodded solemnly, silent as she thought. She didn't look at him, and he couldn't blame her. He was hideous.

'What about the cure Ka'ella made?' she asked.

'It's not a cure—'

'If a single dose can stop a change, then surely a lot could—'

'There isn't any more, Amika!' He hadn't meant to shout. 'I have one phial left. And since you and Reminas ...' He shook his head. 'It doesn't matter.'

After rummaging in his bag, he tossed the last glass ampoule her way. Despite his lack of care, she caught it effortlessly.

'Why are you giving this to me?' the princess demanded, her face hard.

'I need you to be ready to use it,' he swallowed, scratching the back of his neck. 'In case I can't.'

'And then what?'

'And then you'll have to kill me.'

They didn't speak to each other well into the next day. Amika rose moodily at daybreak and packed her things in silence. The pace she set was brisk, but after turning yesterday, Rei was feeling temporarily refreshed and able to keep up.

Clouds, heavy with snow, gathered overhead. They had been building for days now, growing darker by the hour. Rei cursed under his breath when he felt the first flake on his cheek. If the falls turned heavy and blocked the entrance to the caves, they'd have no choice but to take the road over the sea cliffs—a path that was perilous in the best of weather.

'How much further to this secret passage of yours?' Amika asked, noting his distraction with the sky.

'A day. Maybe more.' Rei reshouldered his pack and strode past her. 'Or less, if we pick up the pace.'

'You're the one who stopped,' she grumbled.

Rei exhaled heavily. He hadn't been foolish enough to think Amika would accept last night's request without question, but he hadn't been prepared for an outright refusal. They'd quarrelled heavily after his *casual* plea for her to end his life before he lost himself completely. He was a *selfish coward* for *dumping such a great burden* on her without any consideration for her feelings.

'And what of my feelings?' Rei had shot back bitterly. 'You think I want to become a monster?'

'Who says you will?'

Rei had scoffed. He expected this stubborn ignorance of Kio, not of Amika. Perhaps that was why he'd never told the prince.

'Rei,' Amika called now, pulling him back from dwelling on the argument. He stopped and turned back, finding her hand on her sword hilt. With a flick of her chin, she gestured towards a rocky outcrop rising to the south. She drew her blade.

'Look out!'

Rei tumbled aside as an explosion erupted at his feet—firesand. He reached for the dagger in his boot and brandished it defensively before his chest, just in time to block the shadow swooping in. Rei kicked the assailant back, their hood falling to reveal a flash of golden hair tumbling free of a long braid.

'So they finally gave you a band,' Rei scoffed. 'Or are the masters just getting desperate?'

The woman grabbed a fistful of her left sleeve and tore the fabric free. 'More like *four* bands,' she snarled, nodding down at her inked forearm.

'You're still a hack, Elles,' Rei shot back. 'A frontal assault when you're outnumbered? Do better.'

'So be it.'

Elles flicked her wrist, sending a small blue spark careening towards him. He sprang back at the last minute as a crater opened up where he'd stood.

Magic? No—

Amika and Rei scattered as Elles flung another assault in their direction. Another, soon after; Amika deflected it with her sword, sending fractured slivers of the defused Skrevaari magic stone fizzling to the ground. Rei returned the volley with a spray of needles. Elles jumped aside, two needles piercing holes through her cloak.

'What are you doing with Tears of Yaia, Elles?' Rei demanded, raising his dagger.

'Levelling the playing field.' She reached into the pouch at her hip, sending a barrage of stones towards him in quick succession, explosions blossoming every which way. Rei scrambled to escape the flurry of broken earth. It should have been easy to evade, but the wound in his shoulder throbbed; he'd fallen on it hard to escape the first attack. A stray stone chip clipped his thigh and he slipped on the dusting of snow that had begun to fall.

'Rei!' Amika shouted, rushing to cover him.

'I'm alright,' he grunted. He pulled his hand away from his leg to find blood.

Elles laughed. 'Jahaanya said you'd been winged. Time to come home, little birdie.' Her hand went for the bag of stones.

Light burst from Amika's outstretched palm, blasting the satchel from Elles's belt. A fierce wind howled and snow flurried in earnest.

'You want to fight with magic?' she hissed. 'Then let's fight with magic!'

The air began to swirl. Rei's hair whipped, snow stinging his eyes as the flakes danced, engulfing them in a concentrated blizzard. He gasped as something stung his cheek, his hand instinctively rising to check. A pinprick of blood dotted his fingertips.

Elles gasped, too, as a wound opened on her forearm. On her shoulder. On her forehead. She fumbled aimlessly, flapping her arms as if caught in a swarm of bees.

The snow.

Rei glanced towards Amika. Her eyes were closed, her brow furrowed, sweat beading on her forehead as she concentrated, hands outstretched towards the frigid maelstrom. She was pouring *khe'torla* into the snow, tempering the flakes into millions of tiny daggers. Every now and then, one nicked her own flesh, sending a spray of red mist into the whorl.

She was growing powerful.

Even since the demonspawn ambush in the Li'Nea Wood, Rei's skin crawled whenever Amika unleashed her magic. The earthquake, the wannari, the shocking aftermath of her encounter with Reminas ... When she wielded *khe'torla* in battle, the results were devastating.

And she was only just getting started.

'Amika,' he said, climbing back to his feet. Another snowflake bit into his arm. 'Amika!'

She couldn't hear him over the howling wind.

'Amikharlia—*stop!*' Rei barged her with his shoulder, knocking her off balance.

The spell faltered and the clouds dispersed. Amika blinked slowly and shook her head as if emerging from a trance.

'Wha—' Elles gasped and skittered backward on her hands and heels, blood streaming from a thousand wounds. Her emerald eyes were wide with a fear the Tower should have beaten out of her long ago. 'Wh-what are you?'

Rei pulled his dagger and stalked towards Elles. She frantically pawed through her clothes, grabbing a fistful of *something* that she hurled behind her. The ground rippled like a pond—a portal.

Elles scrambled to her feet and made a dash for the watery window. Rei gave chase, but she was too fast. He threw his dagger, watched the blood spray as it embedded in her shoulder. With a scream, she fell and tumbled into the pool.

'Fuck!' Rei shrieked, falling to his knees, fist pounding the earth. The portal flickered and collapsed. 'The Tower will know where we are now!'

'Then why did you stop me?' Amika asked, stomping towards him.

'Did you even know what you were doing?'

'Of course I did!'

'Oh really?' Rei gestured to the cuts on his face, on his arms. 'Nothing like a bit of collateral, hmm?'

Amika looked humbled. 'I'm sorry. The snow was harder to control than I thought.'

'Or you got carried away. Wouldn't be the first time.'

He felt the princess bristle and waited for a rebuke; instead she silently folded her arms and stared.

'You've gotten powerful, Amika,' Rei said bluntly. 'Very quickly.'

She shrugged. 'I've been practising.'

'Maybe. But do you remember what Grey told us in Ciraselo? How when a Meah-Hyren takes life, they absorb the victim's *khe'torla*?'

'I'm not Meah-Hyren.'

'No. But you manipulate magic like one.' Rei sighed. He was not one to be lost for words, but he suddenly felt the need to tread carefully, to express his observations with tact. 'What if ... What if you took something from Reminas when you killed him? After all, all mortals have *khe'torla*.'

Amika's grip on her arms shifted from defence to comfort. She seemed to shrink. Not with shame, but with ... fear.

'You didn't want me to kill her in case it sent me mad.'

'I didn't want you to kill her because *I* wanted to do it.' Rei clapped a hand on her shoulder, gave it a squeeze. 'Fucked that one up, didn't I?'

Amika did not return his attempt at cheer. She walked off, sulking.

'Let's not do any more than we need to, okay?' he called after her, trying to ignore the blackness stretching further up his arm.

6

KRIAH

The smoke grew thick as *Amikharlia's Tears* approached Gerrick Port. The docks were sparsely manned, but those lingering around the wharf had their faces covered and their hands full of whatever dry wood they could carry. Pyres dotted the sandy coastline like flies on rotting meat, and the smouldering mounds puffed white plumes into the air.

The crew was silent. Everyone had gathered on deck to observe the approach with anxious resignation—a far cry from the jubilance Kriah expected after a long stint at sea. How many of these sailors no longer had loved ones to welcome them home?

'Was the town attacked?' Kriah asked, joining Nell and Rhenar at the gunnel. The first mate paused his attempts at signalling a dockhand to answer.

'Aye, it could've been,' he said grimly. 'But it wouldn't make a lick o' sense.'

'The dead would've been buried,' Nell added quietly. 'We only burn when—' He glanced at Rhenar for confirmation or support, but the older man said nothing, just shook his head and turned back towards the docks.

Kriah had read of the plague that brought the Mey to the shores of Whyt'hallen. The Sickness, they called it, fearing it so much they never could give it a name. There had been no record of it in these lands, but the way the citizens of Ciraselo had responded when the Tear appeared in the sky over their city suggested its return was always at the forefront of their minds. Kriah was certain the breaking of the seals was not responsible for unleashing any kind of pathogen, but the timing was certainly suspicious. Guilt bubbled up from his gut once more. Could he have somehow done this?

The Tear was visible from the coast now, no longer just a thick bruise of storm clouds on the western horizon as it had been when he'd left for Kherunis. It was a red, raised scar, crackling across the sky like a single bolt of lightning frozen in time. He'd watched the faces of the crew grow grim as the wound in the sky came more into sight. No one voiced their concern, but their fear was as tangible as the salt spray on his cheeks.

'Pull us in, lad!' Rhenar shouted at a dockhand as he hauled great coils of mooring ropes overboard. 'Nice 'n' steady, now. She's a big girl, the *Tears*, but she's had a rough ol' time at sea.'

Under a steady coat of rain, the crew unpacked the ship, hauling their minimal barrels of catch onto the docks with shoulders hunched in shame. Nell took Kriah by the arm and pulled him away from the other sailors.

'I 'ave a job for yer,' the boatswain said, voice low. 'I need help gettin' the cap'n to shore. Don't want the crew seein' 'im like this.'

Kriah nodded and followed the young man down into the bowels of the ship. Rhenar kept the crew focussed on their tasks, giving Nell a knowing nod as they headed below. With all hands busy unloading the bounty, the rooms at the stern were silent and abandoned. Nell entered the great cabin after a brief knock, and pried the door open to an empty chamber.

Kriah sucked in a sharp breath at the disorder and disarray, the acrid stench. Flies buzzed around uneaten food on the long table; parchment, torn, crumpled and stained, lay strewn about the spacious room. It smelt of rot, of vomit, of human waste—the neglected cage of an animal and not the dwelling of a captain.

Nell eased his way around upended chests and drawers towards the adjoining room, where the captain was detained. Kriah lingered a pace behind, but was tall enough to see over the boatswain's shoulders and into the bunk.

Captain Yless was huddled in the corner, arms wrapped around his knees, rocking back and forth. He muttered what sounded like non-sensical gibberish, but Kriah caught the odd word between his groans: 'White... haired... witches...'

There were scratches on his face from where he'd clawed at his skin and his previously restrained hair fell about his shoulders in sweat-slicked coils of rope.

'Time to go ashore, Cap'n,' Nell began formally. 'Stores are unloaded and the *Tears* is secure. Nothin' left but to get yer home to yer family.'

Nell inched closer and reached a hand towards the captain's elbow to help him stand; Yless whimpered and retreated further into the corner like a scared dog. Kriah swallowed, looked away. Back in Ciraselo he had learnt that careless manipulation of another's body could splinter bones like dry kindling. Now it was time to see what happened when *khe'torla* was applied to the mortal consciousness. This man's mind had shattered—and Greist'hal had been the one to do it.

Kriah turned back to Captain Yless's pitiful form to find Nell silently pleading for assistance. He racked his brain. 'Do you have any herbs to sedate him?' he offered after a moment's deliberation.

Nell shook his head. 'Nothin' I can get him to take. We tried lullin' him with whiskey, but even that was a struggle.'

'Was there a healer on board? A chirurgeon or apothecary?' No names or faces came to mind from his previous time aboard, but surely there was *someone* skilled enough to take care of the crew's ailments when at sea.

'Aye, a chirurgeon. His quarters are right below this one.'

Captain Yless started keening in distress, grinding the heels of his palms into his eyes. Nell rushed to his father's side to try to calm him and Kriah took this chance to leave. He located a ladder to the lower level tucked away in the far corner of the great cabin and descended two rungs at a time, his adrenaline fuelled by guilt over the damage Grey had done. Kriah was loath to bend the captain's mind anymore, but Nell was desperate to get him off the ship without revealing his condition.

The damage is already done, he told himself. It was poor consolation. But first he needed a charade—a distraction that wouldn't expose his magic. A fake sedative for the captain to inhale if they couldn't get him to drink. Any decent healer would have a stash of valerian, he recalled his mother saying, so there must surely be some among the ship's wares.

The chirurgeon kept a chaotic cache, a far cry from the organised clutter of Ka'ella's apotheca. Kriah examined the bundles of herbs and flowers strung up to dry. Valerian had a small pink flower, he remembered, and a sweet scent. There were several bunches fitting the description. Kriah grabbed two and gave each a good sniff. There was little difference between them. Shrugging helplessly, he chucked them into a grinding bowl he found on the table and gathered up some lengths of cloth to use as masks. Inhaling the fumes of burning valerian would have no effect, but Nell didn't need to know that—he just needed to believe it would be helpful.

All the lanterns had been extinguished since the ship had docked and Kriah could find no alternate source of fuel. He closed his eyes and reached deep, hoping for but a memory of flame hidden in the candle's wick. The slightest spark caught the edge of his senses, the mutterings of a slow requiem. Kriah caught the beat and shifted it to the bowl in his hands. The dry fronds crackled and fizzed smoke into the air. After wrapping a length of bandage around his nose and mouth, Kriah clambered back up the ladder.

Captain Yless was holed up in the corner, arms shielding his head. Nell continued to inch closer to his father, spouting increasingly persistent requests for him to stand.

'This should help,' Kriah announced, moving into the room. 'Cover your face so you won't be affected, too.'

Nell did not hesitate or question the directions. After securing his own makeshift mask, he took a step back to allow Kriah to work. He mingled *khe'torla* with the smoke tendrils, slipping it into the captain's body with an unheard, undulating melody. Once inside, it made him heavy, and dragged him down to sleep.

Yless's eyelids drooped and the arms over his head grew slack and fell by his sides. Slumped against the wall, he looked more a drunkard in an alley than the sturdy sea captain Kriah knew him to be.

'Alright,' Kriah said, setting the smoking bowl aside. 'Help me carry him out.'

Slowly, they carried the captain from the ship as though he were a roll of expensive carpet—one on each end. Kriah breathed evenly in and out through his mouth against the stench of the big man, exhaling with great relief when they set him down on the dock.

The mood here was as grey as the sky. Families reunited in tearful embraces, but there was no joy in the exchanges. Everywhere crestfallen sailors moved to join their loved ones, but not a single person seemed untouched by whatever tragedy had occurred while they were away.

'Nell, where's your mother?' Kriah asked, scanning the crowd for a woman who resembled the pale-haired boatswain.

'I don't see her,' Nell said gravely, his single-eyed gaze also perusing the sea of faces. 'I don't understand. She's always here to—Vynalla!' He pushed through the gathering villagers towards a scrawny blonde girl standing on one of the crates that had been unloaded from the ship.

'Benell!' She hopped down into Nell's waiting arms and he spun her about in a tight embrace.

'Vynalla, what're yer doin' here? Where's Mam?'

'Where's Da?' she countered. 'And who's this? Don't remember seein' 'im before.' She turned towards Kriah, who lingered behind them, unsure of what he should say or do, or even where he should go now they had made land.

'I, uh, I'm Kriah,' he said awkwardly with a small wave of his hand.

'We found him at sea, Nalla,' Nell explained, hand still on his sister's shoulder. 'He helped me with Da. Here, c'mon.'

Nell led them back to the dock where they had left Captain Yless unconscious among the cargo.

'Deities dead!' Vynalla breathed, hoisting up her skirts and running the moment she saw her father's slumped form. She collapsed at his side and reached for his vitals as though she were a healer. 'What's happened to him? Is he—'

'He's just sleepin',' her brother said.

Was he? Kriah wasn't so sure. Wasn't sure if the captain would ever wake. The extra nudge of *khe'torla* needed to get the man to rest may have been too much for his already addled mind. Once again, guilt clenched his belly in its claws.

'Good thing I brought ol' Bess,' Vynalla sniffed.

Using the distraction of family reunions to slink back through the crowds unnoticed, Vynalla led Nell and Kriah to the stables outside the local tavern where everyone had hitched their beasts. Among the horses and pack mules was a gnarled grey donkey hitched to a small two-wheeled wagon.

'I thought yer'd need some help carryin' yer sea chests,' the young woman said, a twinge of sadness in her voice. Indeed, it was not their belongings they needed to lug back home, but the captain himself.

Once he was loaded into the muddy tray, Nell pressed a few coins into the innkeep's hands to store the packs they'd now have to return for. They set up off a sloped, rocky path that wound up to the Ylesses' home on the headland. Rain began to fall more earnestly now, no longer an irritating sprinkle but a persistent pounding atop their shoulders. It was an arduous hike; Kriah's legs were clumsy after weeks at sea and the ground seemed to wobble and shake under his feet.

'What's happenin' here, Nalla?' Nell pressed now they were away from the bustle of the docks. 'The pyres on the beach? And where's Mam?'

Vynalla closed her eyes and let out a long breath. 'Abed with fever fer three days now,' she said, stroking Bess's bristly mane. 'I can barely keep fluids in her. She has it, Nell.'

'Has what?'

'The Sickness.'

Captain Yless was moaning in his sleep when they arrived at the house. Kriah moistened a strip of cloth with his waterskin and pressed it to the man's forehead. Relief trickled in through the hard walls of his doubt—the captain may not have been coherent, but his consciousness was not entirely lost.

Vynalla unhitched Bess from the wagon and fixed her reins to a stake by the house. She splashed water into a trough and gave the old girl a good scratch about the ears. Nell fell into step alongside her, going about the chores and retrieving a biscuit of hay for the donkey. Kriah stood by, forgotten and redundant, until it came time to move the captain indoors.

'Wait,' Vynalla said, stopping them on the front step. She brushed dirt from her apron before removing it from her waist. Tearing it in half, she handed a strip to both Kriah and Nell and fixed her own scarf about her nose and mouth. Nell nodded and followed suit; Kriah did the same, however unlikely it was that he'd become infected with whatever malaise had seized their mother.

The Ylesses' home was far less grand than what Kriah expected of a sea captain. It was a single-room dwelling, sparsely furnished, with no lavish decorations or symbols of status. The steep pitched roof allowed for storage within the ceiling cavity, and most of the family's belongings seemed to be stored up in the rafters and off the damp, compacted earth floor. A cast iron pot hung above a central hearth fire, where a sleeping woman lay bundled under a mound of furs on a wooden pallet cushioned with straw. They placed Captain Yless beside her.

'I haven't finished preparin' supper,' Vynalla confessed sheepishly. 'Between handlin' all the chores, lookin' after Mam, meetin' you and Da at the docks ... All I've managed to do is boil water. Mam would've had a right welcome feast waitin' fer ya.'

'I'll cook,' Kriah offered with enthusiasm he hadn't known he had. 'I mean ... it's the least I can do. Nell saved my life.'

Vynalla shared her first smile since meeting them at the docks. Her eyes crinkled into little green crescents and he imagined her lips parting over slightly crooked teeth beneath the scarf in a cute, girlish grin. His face grew hot at the image he'd conjured.

'Mam'd simply die if I—' She stopped abruptly, hearing her own words. 'I mean—yer our guest. Can't have yer cookin' yer own meals. Wouldn't be proper.'

'Then allow me to help. Please. I insist.'

Vynalla turned to her brother for permission; he gave a dismissive shrug and kicked off his boots before taking a seat on the pallet beside his mother. He wrung water from a towel and placed it on her forehead.

'After supper I'll head back to the docks,' the boatswain said wearily. 'I'm sure Rhenar had our catch secured, but there're ledgers to balance. Crew'll be right stroppy if their wages aren't in order 'fore we ship out for Cirahk in two moons' time.'

'Yer can't be shippin' off again so soon,' Vynalla protested from the ladder. Despite her initial reservations about Kriah helping fix dinner, she had set about preparations immediately and was already passing down ingredients from their food stores in the ceiling cavity. Several potatoes balanced precariously in one arm as she hung off the ladder with her other hand. Kriah hovered nervously below, waiting to receive whatever she passed down—or her, should she fall.

'Cirahk's the biggest market, Nalla. We've only unloaded a small portion of our catch for the land routes—the rest goes on to the capital by sea. It's the way Da's always done it.'

'But the Sickness ...'

Nell bit at a jagged thumbnail. 'She's not got the Sickness,' he muttered. 'No one does. That plague died back in Old Mey.'

From what Kriah knew of the Sickness, it was a blood plague that started with fever and lethargy before progressing to haemorrhages and then death. No one was believed to have recovered—at least no one who was ever documented. At the height of the pandemic, the Mey had built ships to flee their homeland, and those with even the slightest symptoms were left behind. Historians estimated that less than three percent of the population made it off Old Mey. The rest ...

'She's been three days abed,' Vynalla said, descending the ladder. 'The bleeds will start soon. That's how it's been fer the others.'

'How many others?' Nell was clearly trying to sound ignorant to hold onto hope, but Kriah knew it was denial speaking. They'd both seen the pyres on the beach.

'Must be half the town by now.'

She unburdened her arms onto a small table that was to serve as a chopping board. Kriah moved to help her cut and peel the assortment of root vegetables, listening intently as they worked.

'A rider from Tennan Cove came about a month ago,' Nalla said, hacking an eye off a potato that was probably too soft for eating. 'During the Sixth Skrevaar Moon. He warned of an illness runnin' wild in the docks. Was quarantined at the inn even before he fell sick, but it was too late by then. Others started to complain o' fever, Wyl Porter among 'em. Few days later 'n' they're all dead.'

Nell's face fell; Wyl must have been a friend. Kriah had no words of comfort. He knew how brightly that pain seared—and that nothing but time would bring solace.

'Last I heard it'd spread to Midden,' she continued solemnly. 'Won't be long before it reaches the capital.'

Kriah scraped the prepared vegetables into the pot hanging above the hearth and inspected the other ingredients Vynalla had laid out. He picked up something that looked like a charred piece of driftwood and gave it a sniff. It was pungent and fishy—some sort of dried fermented mackerel or sardine. He'd seen similar produce at the markets in Ciraselo, but never had the chance to try it. Even though he recoiled reflexively at the strong odour, his belly fluttered at the thought of tasting something new. If only he still had his father's cooking journals to document the experience. If only his worries extended as far as lost books ...

'Deities dead,' Nell cursed, running both hands through his hair. 'How is the Sickness back? Why here? Why now? It doesn't make any sense.'

'Folks say it's the sky,' Vynalla said. 'A death omen. How do we know our ancestors didn't see the same thing?'

'It's not the sky.'

Kriah didn't realise he'd spoken until both siblings turned to stare at him.

'I mean, someone would have written of it. It's coincidence, I'm sure.'

'But he said—'

It was Vynalla's turn to draw the full attention of the room. She faltered under the scrutiny of her brother's gaze as if she'd spoken out of turn.

'What aren't yer tellin' me, Nalla?' Nell pressed.

She set aside the knife and picked at her nails. 'A wanderer came by the inn on the turn of the Nirhana Moon,' she said quietly. 'He claimed to be a healer and that he could cure those inflicted by the Sickness if they were brought to 'im before the bleeds started. No one believed 'im at first. But then Urinnie Blayke's kid came down with fever and she marched right up to the stranger and demanded he prove his claims. The man took a pitcher of water from the bar, muttered words of prayer, then poured it down Urinnie's boy's throat. Fever was gone within the hour. Boy's been fine since. And he's not the only one.'

Nell frowned sceptically; Kriah listened on in silence, stirring absently at the thickening stew.

'I wouldn't be tellin' yer this if I hadn't seen it with me own eyes. This healer—Kohle Mak, he calls himself—he's a miracle maker. As powerful as the Goddess herself. He can save Mam if I—'

'And what does he want fer one of his miracles? I can't imagine it's free,' her brother scoffed.

'Three golds—'

'*Three golds!*'

'—which I already 'ave!' Vynalla paused, eyes darting nervously around the room even though they were alone. 'I sold Bess and the wagon,' she muttered, almost inaudibly. 'I have to leave her with Feldah at the inn when I take Mam in to see the healer.'

'You *what?*' Nell jumped to his feet. 'Da's had ol' Bess longer than us. How could yer sell her?'

'We're fishermen, Nell. What d' we need a wagon fer? Luggin' belongin's from the ship? Da's never home long enough to warrant unpackin'. It's just a waste of coin keepin' her fed.'

Her brother let out an exasperated sound, but Vynalla remained silent, jaw set and defiant. The air was tense and unbearable and every bit as suffocating as when Kriah's mother and Greist'hal had shared a room.

Kriah raised a ladle to his lips to taste the soup, audibly slurping. He coughed awkwardly. 'Uh, supper's ready?' he said, not sure whether the interruption would ignite the spark or defuse it.

Nell came to collect his bowl and took his meal seated beside his parents; Vynalla retreated to the far end of the room, where she ate leaning against the lowest rung of the ladder to the attic.

Kriah stood by the stew pot, feeling as alone and forgotten as he had adrift at sea.

7

KIOKHAREN

Emanais was a gleeful drunk. She had a rumbling laugh like a summer storm and a smile that burned brighter than any lantern in the room.

She was also *fucking* crazy.

Having been invited to one of her suppers alongside the highest-ranking officers of her crew, Kio watched in silent horror as she fired a shot through her own cabin door when one of the scullery boys from the galley spilt her cup; in the same breath she merrily offered a copper to whomever dared suck the mess up. Three sailors dropped their lips to the deck as she cackled and sprinkled coins over their drunken, prostrate forms. Kio never knew what to expect each time he was summoned to her cabin to dine, but it always involved a great deal of rum, and of that he could not complain.

'Tell me, Boatkeep,' Polk started merrily. A man with a belly like a keg and a thirst to match, he was Emanais's first mate and the guard responsible for ferrying Kio to and from his mess whenever the Boatkeep insisted on an audience. 'What is it you plan on doing with the Little Prince here? 'Bout time we tossed him back to the fishes, isn't it? Or you plan on making him one of the crew?'

Emanais slouched in her high-backed chair, heel resting on the seat and tricorn perched on her bent knee. She fingered the trigger of the cocked pistol over her shoulder as she stared at the burly mate.

'I think I will keep him,' she said measuredly. 'He's nice to look at, isn't he?'

'What? And we're not?' Polk grunted, feigning offence as he gestured to the other officers around the table.

'You're like a slaver's cock pimple compared to him. Now piss off, the lot of you; I'm sick of smellin' you.'

Complaints were muttered, but the loyal crew obeyed. Kio made to rise with the rest of them, but Emanais levelled her pistol at his chest.

'Not you, love. Take a seat.'

He glanced at the departing sailors as they filed past him to the door; Polk clapped a hand on his shoulder, but it gave little reassurance. Kio downed his remaining rum, blinking slowly as the potent liquor burned down his throat, and steeled himself for whatever carnage Emanais was about to summon.

The Boatkeep strode over to where he sat and propped her arse against the table. Casually, she placed her tricorn hat on his head. It smelt of sweat and tobacco.

'So,' she said. 'You given any thought to my little offer?'

'I'm not a sword for hire,' Kio said defiantly, though he may have slurred a little.

'No,' the Boatkeep agreed, flicking the brim of the tricorn. 'You're a prisoner. And once we reach Qhoraak, you'll be a slave. Maybe you'll mine the tunnels under the mountains. Perhaps you'll be a bedboy in Xant. But most likely, you'll work the Siephymn farms on the Waste.

That is the Allchief's greatest passion, after all. I don't think you'd much like that.'

Kio sobered. He looked past Emanais, at the long table covered in plates and upended goblets in place of the charts and maps that were usually sprawled everywhere. Evenings spent with Emanais and her inner sanctum were certainly a cosier alternative to Bryn-Daal and the mess below deck. But to become a sword in another's army ... It went against the very core of his being, against every lesson that had been drilled into his head.

Emanais pushed away from Kio and wandered back towards her own seat at the opposite end of the table. Candles sputtered as they approached the ends of their wicks, melted wax consuming the tapers so they looked like malformed stalagmites growing up from the wood. The crimson glow bleeding in from the narrow windows encircling the room added to the unsettling weight on Kio's chest.

'What is this war of yours?' he asked. 'You said you need soldiers. What are you fighting against?'

Emanais picked at the scraps left on the table, checking the cups for neglected rum. 'A tyrant and his regime of exploitation,' she muttered, mouth full of something. Then, opening her arms in a flourish: 'I want to kill the Allchief.'

Kio sputtered a laugh. 'And you want *my* help? I think you'll find I'm not very good at regicide.'

'Yes, that's because you're a fool. A fool with naught but foolish fool schemes in your foolish fool head. Stab the Prince of Bararn at a political engagement? Are you mad?'

Kio sprang from his chair and joined her in pilfering the leftover drink. He took a long, angry swig from someone else's cup. 'Apparently.'

Emanais wiped her mouth and sauntered back around the table towards Kio. She wrapped her long arms around his neck, stretching on her toes just slightly to bring her lips close to his ear. 'Listen. I don't care what stupid crimes you did or did not commit. I care that you can fight. I need every foot soldier I can get to dismantle the Siephymn trade, farm by *fucking* farm. If you don't want to help, I'm sure there's plenty of others aboard who will.'

Kio turned his head towards her ever so slightly. It had been a long time since he'd felt someone's breath on his skin. But it wasn't just her close proximity that sent a shiver through his body.

'When you say *farm* ...' Kio hesitated. 'Do you mean...?'

'A breeding program, yes.' Emanais's tone was flat. Detached. 'Siephymn farms breed Siephymn.'

'*Why?*' The question blurted incredulously from Kio's lips as memories of the demonspawn assault flooded back into his mind. 'Why create more—' *Monsters*, he wanted to say, but the word died on his tongue. Rei-Hai Shaw was not a monster. He was not—

'Because they're powerful, Little Prince. And, to a tyrant, power is worth more than gold.'

Kio nodded, her motives suddenly making sense. 'You want to weaken his power by dismantling the farms,' he surmised.

'No,' Emanais said softly. She closed her eyes and took a long, deliberate breath before speaking again. 'I want to save my sister.'

Kio took his time returning to the mess. He'd been allowed to leave unescorted, and so he dallied, savouring the freedom with long, slow gulps of fresh air drawn down deep into his lungs. It was a clear night, still and calm, and even the crimson wound in the sky didn't seem as menacing.

As he commenced the descent into the ship's bowels, Kio caught the murmur of a familiar sound. He paused, his eyeline all that remained above deck as he scanned for the source of the disruption.

There, in the shadow of the main mast's rigging, a couple met in secret. Lip-locked and frenzied, the amorous pair unlatched buckles and removed clothing as though they had no fear of being caught. Kio felt his pulse quicken, his skin grow hot, as one of the figures dropped to their knees, teasing a moan of ecstasy from their partner.

Kio ducked below deck, drawing deep gulps of air to calm himself, to rid the sights and sounds from his mind. He didn't like the way panic rose alongside his arousal. How quickly the cold fingertips of fear dashed all warmth from his pleasure. He slipped a hand inside his shirt to feel his thundering heart and closed his eyes as he breathed. No, he didn't like this at all.

As he approached his mess, he could hear Bryn-Daal's snore rumbling deep within. The stocky Kheshtarli was so loud they could probably hear him on the mainland—something for which Kio was grateful as he pulled the heavy bolt from the door and snuck his way inside. Someone would be back to tighten it later, no doubt, but his mess-mates didn't need to know he'd been afforded the liberty to wander freely around the ship at night.

He slipped into the bunk below the snoring Kheshtarli and gave the bulging weight a prompt kick; it did nothing but elicit a sudden snort and a pause before the same droning rhythm resumed. Kio groaned. His head pounded from all the rum and he wanted nothing more than to sleep off the hangover before it set in.

But that wasn't likely to happen. He wasn't drunk enough to silence Bryn-Daal's snoring or the thoughts swirling through his brain, and so he lay awake, mulling over the Boatkeep's offer. If he accepted, he would be raised from the ranks of prisoner, given a berth among the crew, better rations, more privileges … but he'd have to fight someone else's war. Win someone else a crown. Rei-Hai had been forced to live a life in service of another and he'd hated every minute of it. Kio had hated it for him. But Rei hadn't had a choice—it had been servitude or death.

Were the options placed before Kio really any different?

'Hope the Boatkeep chooses to offload that witch-fucker at the Cove,' Davyn grunted from his bunk across the room. 'Won't get a wink o' sleep till then. That fat fuck would wake me dead Mam.'

Kio rolled over to see the Wife Killer lying awake, his scowl deep and angry in the crimson-tinged pre-dawn light seeping in through the porthole. 'I've never known anyone to snore like him,' Kio muttered.

'Then you've not known many men.'

I've known plenty. 'How long until we reach the Cove?'

'I saw the Khenlum Marsh off starboard last time I was up on deck,' Davyn said. 'Reckon we got four or five nights left listening to this bloody racket.'

The easternmost port of Qhoraak, Convict Cove, would be the first place the ship docked since Kio had come aboard in Cirahk. He'd forgotten what it was like to have solid ground beneath his feet, to not always feel like he was drunk when he was irritatingly sober. The thought of dry land made him forget how little he actually knew of the western kingdom. Was it as cursed and poisoned by the devastation of the war as the Middle Kingdoms feared?

Kio was about to ponder aloud about the Qhoraakese settlement when the mess door was flung open. Bryn-Daal woke with a short, sharp snore, rocking around so violently in shock Kio was sure he'd fall through the cot and crush him.

Ylan stomped through the doorway with little regard for having disturbed the other members of his mess. Kio sat up on his elbows, glancing up at the bunk over Davyn's; he'd not realised it was empty.

'Where have you been?' Kio asked, a touch more demanding than he intended. The unexpected authority in his voice caused Ylan to chuckle.

'Miss me, sweetheart?' he jeered, kicking off his boots. 'Turns out you're not the only one who's caught the Boatkeep's eye.'

'I thought you were a petty thief. What could she possibly want with—'

'I'm good with a blade, boy. And plenty of other things that are long and hard, let me tell you.' He gave a brief, crude guffaw, but fell silent when his merriment was not mirrored. Ylan gave a bitter sneer before continuing to boast. 'The bitch wants to make me crew, and I intend to do it. We'll be leaving you lot at Convict Cove, and I for one can't wait to be done with you sorry pricks.'

So she really did find more soldiers, Kio realised, flopping back on his cot. A weird sensation curled in his chest, one not fuelled by liquor. Was this ... jealousy? He may have been disinterested in the Boatkeep's advances, but he was not oblivious to her flirtations. Had she really turned to *Ylan* of all people when he'd evaded her charms? What exactly was she after—a stiff prick or a good sword arm?

You can't give her either.

Nausea swept over him, threatened to heave the meagre contents of his stomach up onto his blanket. Keeping himself in check, Kio sucked down long, slow breaths.

I'll be off the boat in five days if I say yes, he thought. Five days and he could be on land and out of shackles. The Cove wasn't too far from the Holanian border. All he need do was pass the Sea Cliffs and he'd be on his way to Honnah. If Emanais put a sword in his hand, perhaps he could—

No. The time for scheming was over. He had to play it safe if he was to survive—had to roll over and submit. Ylan had done so without hesitation, and now he was set to get off this damn ship.

Kio clenched his fists and willed the sun to rise faster. At dawn he would find the Boatkeep—and hope that it wasn't too late.

As soon as he was done with scullery, Kio went in search of Polk. He found the first mate up on the fo'c'sle, telescope pressed to his eye as he surveyed the land to the north.

''Bout a day out from Kessar,' he was saying to a deckhand when Kio approached. He turned away from his conversation to eye Kio up and down. 'What are you doing out of your mess, Little Prince?'

'I want to speak with Emanais,' he commanded.

Polk and the deckhand chuckled. 'Certainly, Your Highness. Now fuck right off.'

'She made me an offer and I intend to take it,' Kio said. 'Tell her that, will you?'

He was returned to his mess below deck to wait out the afternoon in the same dank drudgery as countless days before. But as expected, he was summoned to the Boatkeep's quarters after sundown once most of the prisoners had been locked in for the night.

A guard posted outside her cabin waved Kio inside without any announcement to alert the captain to her guest's arrival. Beyond the door, Emanais bent over the table, inspecting several curls of parchment. Her locs, which she usually wore bound in a single, thick braid, fell freely in ropes over her shoulders. A white linen shirt hung loosely off her chest, cut for a much larger man, with her belts and leather jerkin discarded on a chair. Her pistol sat on the table, out of reach.

An elkaven, black and silky as the night, squawked from its perch by the window.

'Piren-Ha?' Kio gasped, shocked and confused and dubious over the hope rising in his chest.

Emanais looked up, finally acknowledging his arrival. 'Svern,' she corrected.

The bird cawed and flapped its wings in recognition of its name. Kio's mood plummeted. Rei had been a fever dream; he was not coming after him.

'You summoned me?' he grunted, turning away from the elkaven.

'I hear you wish to join us,' Emanais said simply. 'Good. Because I have work for you.'

The prince raised a sceptical eyebrow.

'Or rather, I am in need of your opinion.' She gestured towards the scrolls sprawled across the table. The largest depicted a map—a schematic of a military base of some kind. The other was a letter, written in a script he could not read.

'You're castle-born and educated,' Emanais said. 'What, in your training, would you say is this camp's weakness? From where would you launch an attack?'

Kio looked at the map. It was a basic charcoal etching likely completed in haste. Crosses marked several intervals around the perimeter, which he assumed were entry points or guard posts. Based on the crudeness of the illustration, it was not likely drawn to scale and gave no indication of surrounding terrain or natural cover.

Kio shrugged. 'I wouldn't know. I'm just a foolish fool with foolish ideas, remember?'

Emanais smiled in curious observation. 'I didn't take you for someone so easily bruised.'

'I'm not.' He was, but she didn't need to know that. 'Even if you hadn't insulted me so emphatically, I'm not confident in offering any strategic advice on this.'

'No, me neither,' Emanais sighed. She straightened and reached for the goblet and open bottle sitting on the table before her. 'I was hoping a fresh set of eyes might help, but it's useless.' She poured rum into the goblet, wordlessly passed it to Kio, then drank directly from the bottle. 'I may as well be looking at chicken scratchings.'

Kio glanced down into the cup, unsure of what to say. He never quite knew how to react to Emanais. Every time he spoke to her she was a different person, a rehearsed act tailored to the audience. Which mask was her true face? Was he seeing it now?

Moyna, too, had been a difficult person to know, but for reasons different to the Boatkeep. Moyna's mask had been stone, an impenetrable case hiding her true thoughts and feelings—the same as every other highborn person Kio had known. But she had been quick to remove it in favourable company, revealing the warm, caring companion she was. Kio's heart ached anew.

Emanais was still taking broody swigs from the rum bottle when Kio asked, 'Why do you have an elkaven?' The bird's presence had bothered him the whole time he'd been in the room. It set his skin crawling with the same unease as Piren-Ha. This one—Svern—was much larger. Solid and meaty where Piren-Ha was sleek.

'He belongs to my sister,' Emanais said. 'We use him to communicate when we're apart. She sent these maps to me. No doubt through some significant effort. I wish they could be put to good use, but ... this is hopeless.'

'Do all ... Siephymn ... use demonspawn as couriers?' Kio asked carefully. He'd been wrong about Emanais's motives for destroying the farms; he'd hate to get this wrong, too. Emanais had not strictly *said* her sister was Siephymn but it all seemed to make sense now.

The bird cocked its head to the side. Emanais stretched across the table to scratch beneath his beak. 'No ...' she said slowly, as if confused by the question. She turned back towards Kio. 'Who is your Siephymn? A brother? A sister? A lover, perhaps.'

Kio chewed on his lower lip, wishing his cup was not already empty. The question was painfully difficult to answer. What *was* Rei-Hai Shaw? A dream? A jest? A mission?

'How did you know?' Kio asked instead, setting the cup aside. Without being prompted, Emanais refilled it.

'The day when I told you about the demonspawn that attacked us,' she said, continuing to pour until the rum spilt a little over the rim, 'you looked horrified. And not just because of what you'd killed. It was fear that you're going to lose someone you love. I've worn that face myself.'

Bringing the rum to his lips, Kio went in search of a seat. He was tired. Tired of this ship. Tired of losing people he cared about.

Tired of being alone.

'H-how long does it take?' He tried to swallow the grief down with the liquor, but it stuck in his throat like a burr.

'To devolve? About twenty years. Some make it to twenty-five. Most don't.'

Kio closed his eyes and exhaled slowly. Rei would be twenty-three this coming Myrahn Moon.

A soothing hand rubbed his back. He found Emanais sitting beside him, her brow furrowed in shared sorrow.

'I've had my whole life to come to terms with Yeni's fate,' she said. 'You grieve all you need to. But then I need you to turn it inward, sharpen it into hate, and help me destroy every last witch-fucking Siephymn farm on this witch-fucking Waste so no one has to suffer as she has.'

His eyes had grown hot, but he blinked back tears, nodding in agreement. He needed to do something—*anything*—to stop feeling so useless, so foolish.

Destruction sounded good.

8

AMIKHARLIA

The tunnel through the mountains was dark and damp. Amika struggled to keep her footing on the occasional sharp descent, her well-worn boots slipping on slick limestone with every unexpected drop. Rei fared little better, despite insisting he could see just fine in such dim light.

'I spend most of my time travelling by night, Princess,' he said when they paused to catch their breath. 'We don't need a torch.'

'Yes, but you usually have the moon and stars to guide you,' Amika replied, wrapping a length torn from her cloak around an old branch she'd been using as a walking stick. 'We only get a break in the rock overhead once every mile.' She paused as she thought about that more closely. 'It's strange. Almost like they've been carved on purpose. Natural waymarkers.'

'They were,' Rei shrugged. 'There's a whole network of tunnels under here. Mined by the convicts Meytar used to dump on the west. It's how they move goods to the Middle Kingdoms without paying sea tax to the ports. Your Qhoraakese friends in Ciraselo never told you?'

Amika blanched. 'No. Nylah always ships her wares out of Cirahk.'

'Well, she's an idiot.'

Rei stood and shook circulation back into his right hand. The skin was still black and leathery, the nails sharp and hooked like claws. He did his best to keep it hidden, but Amika hadn't forgotten how he had changed—or what he had asked her to do.

'We'd be fools to traipse through here blind,' she insisted. 'We need a torch.'

'Good luck finding flint.'

I don't need flint.

Amika was becoming confident in her ability to manipulate fire. First the Li'Nea Wood, then Reminas, and most recently with the wannari. But each time there had been a source to draw from—a candle or even a dying campfire. Could she summon it out of nothing?

Amika closed her eyes and listened to the cave around her. Water dripped from stalactites, and aside from the sound of her own breathing, that was all she could hear. She focussed on the water. It was a sweet melody. A twinkling etude, as difficult as air to seize. The ants marched beneath her skin, but it was no longer an itch she couldn't scratch. Amika grabbed the *khe'torla* and wrenched it towards the crudely fashioned torch.

Be fire, she willed, but nothing happened.

Kriah had never said it was possible to turn water into flame—but he'd not said it *couldn't* be done, either.

Be fire.

Sparks flicked across the cloth.

BE FIRE.

Flames erupted and filled the cavern with a warm glow. Amika gasped and then smiled triumphantly, glancing up at Rei to share her glee.

Her friend's face was stony.

'What?' She got back to her feet, ready to press on.

'I didn't say anything,' Rei said as he followed after her.

No, but you were thinking it.

Without further discussion, they continued, moving quicker now guided by torchlight. The passageway was a curious mix of natural caverns and manmade tunnels weaving through the rock. Stalagmites stretched from the slick ground, reaching up to trip them, and the odd claw mark or catch of dead fur on jagged edges alerted them to the fact that they were not alone.

'Are there many demonspawn in Qhoraak?' Amika asked, bringing the torch close to a large slash carved in the wall.

'Thousands,' Rei said. 'Why do you think the Meytarans blocked all known land paths to the west?'

Amika traced her fingers across the rocky gash. Whatever made this had been huge. Bigger than an ukarat—possibly larger than the wannari.

Have we awoken something ancient?

'Amika,' Rei said, tone grave.

Her hand went for her sword. But there was no demonspawn waiting to assail them. Instead, Rei crouched before a withered corpse lying crumpled in a pool of dry, dark blood.

Black blood.

He nudged the figure with his boot. The body rolled back to reveal a rusted dagger embedded in the woman's throat. Fire-red hair fell limply around her grey, leathery face.

'Deities dead,' Amika gasped, noting the angle of the blade. 'She killed herself.'

Rei squatted down and brushed the hair off the nape of her neck. A small diamond had been branded onto the skin with hot iron, leaving a silvery scar behind. Rei scratched at the back of his own neck.

'What is it?' Amika asked.

'She escaped a farm,' he said grimly. 'No wonder she wanted to die.'

Amika crouched opposite him, inspecting the body herself. She couldn't have been older than fourteen, dead less than a week—unless the cold of caves had kept her well preserved. But Amika sensed it wasn't just her age that had Rei so unsettled.

'You've been in one,' she breathed. 'You were a prisoner too.'

Rei said nothing, but the fleeting microexpression on his face told her she was right. As a former brethren, Rei had travelled extensively during his work for the Tower, but he had always been cagey about his time in Qhoraak.

'Three years ago, the Tower sent me to Qhoraak to retrieve the Hirathi Blade,' Rei began, shifting into a more comfortable seated position. 'I was captured.'

He lifted his hair, still ashen in patches from Ka'ella's temporary dye, and turned to reveal a similar pattern to the girl's burned into the back of his neck.

'Siephymn have always been prolific in Qhoraak,' he continued, dropping his long locks. 'Each clan had at least one among their ranks, and to be born Siephymn was once a great honour. Chieftains didn't fight their own battles—the Siephymn did. They were their proxies. Their champions.'

Amika recoiled.

'Demonspawn are naturally drawn to Siephymn,' Rei continued. 'With practice, we can summon and control them at will.'

'Like Piren-Ha,' Amika said, recalling the strange bird Rei had adopted as a pet.

'Like Piren-Ha,' Rei nodded, 'only these monsters weren't being summoned to ferry letters. When challenges to another chieftain's lands were raised, the Siephymn would battle their summoned demonspawn until one surrendered—or was killed. The latter was the preferred victory.'

Crowns weren't inherited in Qhoraak. Amika had learnt that from conversations overheard in Lominah Deen's tavern. The Allchief won his throne through conquest, and any monarch could be challenged by a rival at any time. No one had ever mentioned *how*, though.

'The current Allchief, Waqar Koll, has been in power for over a decade now,' Rei continued. 'And he knows the game well. The stronger the Siephymn, the stronger the demonspawn, and it's long been thought that the offspring of two Siephymn would be exponentially more powerful than its sire. So Waqar set about creating farms in hopes of breeding the perfect warriors. Not just to be his proxy, but to be his *army*.'

'Goddess,' Amika gasped. She watched Rei grow distant, detached, as he had done in Ciraselo when he'd first told Amika of his heritage. But he clearly wanted to open up, no matter how difficult, and so Amika sat silently until he felt ready to continue.

Eventually, he drew his arms about himself and went on, his voice a bitter whisper. 'They pump you full of poisons until you can't control your body, and force you to couple over and over and over again. I don't know how many nights I was there. How many—'

Amika threw her arms around him and held him close. His skin felt fever-warm in the icy chill of the caves. Tears splashed on her shoulder like water dripping from the stalactites, and for a moment she wasn't sure if they were hers or his. Rei was not one to cry, but he was not one to open up about his past, either. So she didn't ask, or pull away to check his tears; just silently held him until he decided it was time to let go.

When he finally shrugged her off, his eyes were dry, albeit a little puffy, and he wore the same cold, distant expression that'd become the norm lately.

Rei was looking at the girl's corpse when Amika said, 'We should bury her.'

'Why?'

'Because it's the decent thing to do,' she insisted, shocked at his protest.

Rei stood. 'She's dead, Amika. I really don't think she cares.'

'*I* care. Go if you want; I'll catch up.'

He scoffed and trudged off into darkness, leaving Amika to kneel beside the Siephymn's body in the flickering torchlight. She looked around the sprawling cavern, breath clouding before her face. She had no way of burying the poor girl; the ground was solid stone and she wouldn't risk blunting her blade trying to dig. With a sigh, she picked up the torch and stood.

Fire was becoming familiar to her now. Its pulse was hot and strong, and the easiest *khe'torla* to control. Amika shifted the flames of the torch to the girl's body and stood a solemn vigil as the brief and violent fire reduced her to ashes. She wasn't sure whether it was appropriate for a daughter of Qhoraak, but she whispered the old prayer to Nirhana, wishing her safe passage back to the Goddess's embrace.

It hadn't occurred to Amika until now what would happen should they succeed in raising Miatha. Reverence for the Goddess and the Deities had all but faded to obscure traditions rather than genuine worship. Amika had heard that Hirathi was still celebrated in Qhoraak, but in the other kingdoms ... Would Miatha be wrathful upon her resurrection? Would she help return the world to the way it had been? Stem the rising threat of Azet'haal and his Meah-Hyren?

Would she even want to be reborn?

After three days of darkness, Amika was finally able to breathe fresh air into her lungs. Daylight hit her eyes in a crimson assault as they stumbled out of the caves and onto the parched earth of the Western Waste. A part of her had expected a flat expanse of dry sand, but the landscape was anything but: sharp rocks broke the horizon like a stone forest, mountains whittled down to their bones from years of wind and erosion. The ground beneath them dropped away in a sudden slope, dangerously gravelled with pebbles, making the path down from the caves perilous if they rushed. Everywhere she looked was red, red, *red*. The rocks, the sand, the sky. The Tear was vivid here—a jagged, pulsating scar.

'I'll call ... Piren-Ha ... to ... scout ahead,' Rei panted.

Amika turned back to see her friend doubled over, hand pressed against the stony mouth of the cave for support as he chased his breath. He pulled forth a hidden needle and pricked his thumb, then brought the bead of blood to his mouth. He whispered the elkaven's name before collapsing to his knees in the dirt.

'Rei-Hai,' Amika gasped, rushing to his side. She helped him to sit upright and wiped the sweat from his forehead. 'Are you alright?'

'Something's coming ...' He closed his eyes and leant his head back against the rock. 'There are so many.'

'So many what?'

'Demonspawn,' he groaned, face contorted in a grimace. 'Six?'

Needles appeared in his hand. With a flick of his wrist, one went whistling past Amika's ear; a sharp squeal sounded behind her.

'Make that five.'

Amika drew her sword and spun to see the creatures scuttling towards them. They were small, wiry things, no larger than cats, with hairless rat tails whipping back and forth. Judging by their oversized eye teeth, their bite would cause the most damage, meaning they'd have to get close to attack. All she need do was keep—

'Ah—*ow!*' she cried as one of the demonspawn launched and latched onto her forearm. Its jaw was vice-strong; the more she shook, the more it bore down. Blood oozed from the punctures, trickling down her arm to drip from her fingers. There had to be a way to pry it off.

Amika tossed her sword into her other hand, raised it high and brought the pommel down on the creature's skull. After a hollow crack, the beast fell limp into the dirt, eyes bulging from its concave head.

'What the fuck are these things?' she hissed, clutching at her wounded arm.

'No idea.' Rei was on his feet now, a fan of needles readied between his fingers. One of the creatures made to pounce, then froze when confronted with Rei's outstretched hand. Amika glanced around, looking for an unexpected ally who could control *khe'torla*, before realising it was Rei, utilising his influence over the demonspawn to hold it still. Amika swung her sword at the creature as it struggled to break free, cleaving it clean in two. Inky blood splashed across the dry earth.

'They look like skampils, but they're supposed to be solitary scavengers,' Rei said, tumbling aside before unleashing another spray of needles. 'They shouldn't be in a pack like this. We'll exhaust ourselves trying to fend them off.'

Rei was right; Amika's blows missed more targets than they hit. The skampils were agile, and her sword was not the ideal weapon for dealing with such pests. Rei and his dagger were more suited to this fast, close combat, but he was hardly at his best. She couldn't rely on him to help her right now.

So she reached upward.

She reached for the Tear and the angry red thunderheads bubbling around the gaping wound like festering flesh. There was power there. Not the syphoning void of the Tear itself, but pools of *khe'torla* crackling through the clouds around it. Amika could feel it like goosepimples on her skin.

'I think I might be able to strike them all at once,' she said, glancing towards Rei. He was bleeding from a cut on his forehead, though Amika suspected he had hit it during a clumsy evasion rather than a bite.

'Whatever it is, do it quick,' Rei panted, running a needle through a skampil as it made to lunge for his face. Three little corpses now littered the ground around them, but more were skittering out of cracks and crevasses to take their place.

Demonspawn held no internal *khe'torla*, so to strike them directly Amika would need to use unstable magic and risk a reverberation that could do more damage to the already fragile world.

But what if she used an anchor?

She heaved her blade skyward. She had to trust herself. Letting intuition take over, she summoned *khe'torla* down onto the blade, groaning under the strain as it sputtered with bolts of white lightning. The crackling energy coursed through her. She felt power—more than she had ever felt before. And it felt *good*.

With a scream, she released her grasp on the lightning, swinging her blade in a great arc before her. The bolts zipped towards the demon-spawn like electric homing pigeons, drawn to little pockets void of *khe'torla*.

Amika hit the ground hard, collapsing to her knees and then her face, sword clattering from her slackened grip. Keeping her eyes open was a battle; her head throbbed and her body fought against the weight of a thousand boulders.

Eventually she succumbed to the darkness.

When she awoke, the air smelt burnt. Grimacing, she pushed herself out of the dirt and sat back on her heels, surveying the surrounds. The skampils were gone, reduced to scorch marks on the dry earth. Amika exhaled her relief. That cast had rendered her dangerously vulnerable. It had been some time since expelling *khe'torla* had left her in such a state. Then again, she'd never unleashed a power quite like that before. What would Rei—

'Rei?' Amika glanced around, pulse quickening. 'Rei!'

She found her friend face down a few yards away, faint wisps of smoke rising from his body. Amika raced to his side. How could she be so foolish? Of course the spell would have hit him! He was Siephymn. He was—

A blow collided with her chest, knocking the wind from her lungs as she landed on her back. Desperately sucking in air, she rolled aside as the smouldering assailant descended on her in a flurry of flashing claws and snapping teeth. Amika scrambled for her sword and spun to face the new threat.

Rei snarled as he crept towards her, hunched on all fours like a beast. The fine features of his face had distorted, lengthening into a wolfish muzzle complete with a maw of vicious teeth. Three bone horns protruded from his skull, and his back was bent and misshapen, bulging as though something were trying to break through the skin.

Amika took a cautious step to the side, keeping her distance from the creature that was once her friend as he began to pace threateningly. A low rumble bellowed from his throat.

He was not Rei anymore.

He was demonspawn.

Amika white-knuckled her sword. He'd asked her to kill him and she'd refused—but what choice did she have?

Think, Amika!

She scoured her brain for options. Manipulating *khe'torla* seemed to only aggravate him more. And subduing him through combat could cost his life.

There has to be another—

The potion!

The last phial of the decoction Ka'ella had crafted from Amika's blood was still nestled safely in her pack. She looked desperately around for their supplies and found them by the mouth of the cave where they had dumped them prior to the attack. But Rei stood between them. She would need some sort of distraction to get around him, one that wouldn't cause him any more pain.

Amika summoned a ball of *khe'torla* and shot it at his feet. He jumped back in fright. Thunder rumbled overhead at the unstable cast. She fired another, and a sharp wind began to rise. Amika used the carefully aimed bursts to spin them around without ever having to turn her back on her friend.

The storm was raging now. Rain fell in heavy drops, propelled by the ferocious breeze. At least the disturbance was localised, Amika thought, relieved to see her unstable casts had not caused a more devastating reverberance.

She fired one last bolt, larger this time, enough to send Rei sprawling backward in a shower of stone shards. While he was stunned, she reached for her pack, shoving her hand inside to paw blindly for the phial.

Rei shook his head and rolled back to his feet.

Come on, come on!

A needle pricked her finger and Amika withdrew her hand swiftly, phial gripped in her palm. Rei was bounding towards her. She raised her arms to shield herself, holding him back with a fierce grip on his throat. His teeth snapped, clawed hands scraping for purchase. Amika screamed—then rammed the syringed ampoule into his neck, pushing the bright vermilion liquid through his veins.

His golden eyes widened and the thrashing of his body slowed. He grew limp and heavy in her arms, eventually crashing down upon her.

Amika lay still, winded and exhausted. The brief but violent storm had abated, dumping enough rain to leave the ground slick and muddy. Threatening clouds still hung overhead. They'd need to find shelter while they recovered their strength—*if* they recovered their strength.

Swallowing her fear, Amika slipped out from under Rei. Breath held in her chest, she rolled him onto his back. He was himself again. His face had smoothed to delicate features, looking serene and youthful as he lay unmoving; Amika pressed her fingers to his throat and sighed relief when she felt a steady pulse.

Once she had dragged him back to the mouth of the cave, she set about bandaging her wounds. The skampil's jaw had done a number on her forearm, leaving a dozen little punctures deep in the flesh. The gashes from Rei's claws were worse, red and wide. The bleeding had stopped, however, and it didn't look likely that she'd need to stitch any closed.

Had she healed herself again? She recalled Grey's words from when they had first met after the ukarat attack in the forest. Both he and Kriah had thought that wound should have killed her. She had constantly surprised Kriah with the things she could do, as if she were more powerful than a Chosen should have been.

Would he be afraid of me now, too?

Amika leant her head back against the wall of the cave. She glanced down at Rei resting beside her and brushed his hair back from his face, her fingertips lingering where horns had once been.

'I understand now,' she said, tears growing hot in her eyes. 'I'll do it. I promise.'

For a brief moment, she thought she saw Rei smile.

9

KRIAH

Tensions were high between the Yless siblings. Nell spent the night pressing cold towels to his mother's forehead while Vynalla slept fitfully against the cot beside them. Kriah watched from across the hearth, thankful neither noticed that he remained awake. Just as dawn was breaking, the young boatswain started to nod off and Kriah seized the opportunity to rise in search of food. He wasn't hungry, but fixing a meal for the siblings was the least he could do.

Guilt gnawed at his insides as he climbed the ladder into the rooftop storage vaults, head foggy with worry. Would the Yless siblings lose both their parents? Kriah felt directly responsible for the ill fate that had befallen Captain Yless, but the mother …

The illness spreading in Gerrick Port could not be the same devastating affliction that had driven the Mey from their homeland centuries ago. Had the Sickness crossed the Azure Expanse with the refugees, it would have spread long before this. Could more explorers have arrived on Whyt'hallen's shores?

Kriah descended from the ceiling, arms full of an odd assortment of ingredients, a cold sweat on his neck. He saw vague images of a parting ocean—remnants of a fever dream he'd had while adrift at sea. A delirium brought on by dehydration. Why think of that now?

'Nalla will keel over if she sees yer doin' that.'

Kriah startled at the sound of Nell's voice, an egg tumbling from his hands to shatter on the floor.

'Shit,' he cursed. 'Sorry.' The apology felt redundant when the pong of rot wafted up from his feet.

Nell flashed a crooked smile. 'Looks like yer saved us from sore bellies.'

The boatswain's words were in good humour, but fatigue and grief were clearly written on his face. He had risen from his prostrate position by his mother's cot, stretching out his back as he stood. But even in the poor light emanating from the hearth between them, Kriah could make out the glistening blood on his friend's fingers—and where it seeped from his mother's ears.

'I don't suppose this healer—this Kohle Mak—can really work miracles?' Nell said softly, wiping the blood from his fingertips on the leg of his trousers.

Kriah said nothing. False hope served no purpose here.

Leaving the eggs to the side, he sorted through the other ingredients he had found: wax-dipped cheese, dry sourdough, some sort of cured sausage. He brought the meat to his nose. It was heavy and richly fragrant with chilli and spice.

'Do yer think there's any hope fer either of 'em?' Nell ventured cautiously. He blotted the blood away from his mother's ears with a cloth this time, all the while glancing across at his sleeping father. Captain Yless had never fully roused since Kriah sedated him with *khe'torla* back on the ship.

Sedated or killed? Kriah wondered bitterly for a moment, before admitting aloud, 'I don't know what ails your mother. Or what miracles this healer offers. But this sickness of the mind ... I'm sorry. I don't think your father is likely to recover.'

The words were hard to voice, sticking in his throat like tacky pine resin. He should have known further use of *khe'torla* would do more harm than good, especially given the captain's precarious state. Even if he were to open his eyes, he would not be the same man.

Nell nodded solemnly. 'Da'd hate to live like this. Life lyin' down wasn't livin' at all, he always said. Would be kinder to just ...'

Kriah was shocked to hear a Second Born speak in such a way. Their lives were so short, so precious. Did they not wish to delay death as long as they could? He let silence pass between them as he got to work on breakfast, cutting the cured sausages into slices to be cooked in the pan.

'Do you think that's what he'd want?' Kriah hazarded after a while. 'To die?'

'Aye,' Nell said with confidence. 'A few years back we had an old sailor collapse on the *Tears*. He was talkin' to me Da, then 'alf his face went slack 'n' he dropped to the deck. When he came to, he couldn't do nothin' 'cept blink.'

He had moved to his father's side now and peeled back an eyelid; the pupil showed no response.

'I remember seein' Da sit with him,' he continued, his voice breaking slightly. 'Just lookin' into his eyes as if they could speak. Course he didn't, but after a long while Da nodded 'n' cleared the cabin, askin' me to stay behind 'n' lock the door. When we were alone, he picked up a pillow ... 'n' held it down over ol' Pyrse's face.'

Kriah stopped pushing the sausages around the pan.

'He never struggled—not that he could've—but I saw his eyes when me Da approached. There was no fear. Only thanks.'

Tears had welled in Nell's eyes. He sniffed, wiped his nose with the back of his hand and glanced towards his sister, who was still sleeping soundly with a slight snore.

She must be exhausted, Kriah thought, his eyes also falling on the young woman. She didn't look comfortable, sitting on her knees as she was, her upper body draped over her mother's low cot, head resting on her forearms as a pillow. But she did not stir. Not even with Nell's talking or the breakfast sizzling over the hearth.

'I want yer to go with Nalla 'n' take Mam to the healer,' Nell said, having dried his tears and regained his composure. 'While yer gone I'll …' He dipped his head subtly towards the captain. 'It's what he'd want.'

Kriah nodded. 'Of course.'

Nell released a long sigh. 'D'yer think the Goddess'll forgive me?'

'I think the Goddess would understand.'

'Do yer think *she'll* forgive me?' Nell's one-eyed gaze went to his sister.

Kriah remained silent. That was a far harder question to answer.

Kriah helped Vynalla hitch the wagon up to old Bess for one last journey with the Yless family. Vynalla stroked the mule's bristly mane lovingly as Kriah assisted Nell in loading their mother onto the wagon.

'Yer've been good to us, Bessie,' she cooed. 'But it's time fer a new home. Feldah's got some friends for yer too. Won't be long till yer as fat as they are.'

'Don't leave her with Feldah till that coin's in yer hand, a'ight?' Nell cautioned sternly.

'I know how good business's done, brother,' Vynalla grumbled. 'Who d'yer think's been doing all the shoppin' n' sellin' while you lot're at sea?'

Nell ruffled his sister's golden hair, then pulled her in for an embrace. He squeezed tightly and seemed to hold her longer than usual; Vynalla grew uncomfortable and pushed him away.

'I'll do what I can to get the healer to see Mam,' she said. 'Won't come home till she's well. Take care o' Da fer me.'

Kriah and Nell exchanged a look before the boatswain nodded. 'Travel safe.'

Vynalla climbed up beside her mother, fixing her scarf tightly around her lower face. Kriah took Bess's reins and started off down the rocky trail towards the village proper. It was a grey, drizzling day, with a ripe wind fresh off the ocean—not unlike the first time Kriah rode into Gerrick Port. Winter was in full swing now, and extra smoke thickened the air from household hearths, joining the black plumes rising from the beach. The number of pyres seemed to have increased, despite the so-called miracle healer having come to town.

'Suppose it's only a matter o' time 'fore I get it now,' Vynalla mused soberly.

'You can't know that,' Kriah said without turning.

'Don't even know where Mam got it from. Must've been that Gregan fellow who kept comin' by tryna sell us his damn goose. Horrible thing it was. Wouldn't buy it if it laid gold.'

The young Bararnite woman was quite chatty, though Kriah couldn't be sure whether that was her usual disposition or how she chose to keep her mind distracted from all that was happening. He was used to a life of relative silence; Grey had never been fond of frivolous conversation, even when he was in one of his better moods, and so Kriah lapped up Vynalla's stories the same as he enjoyed the sharp banter between Amika and her childhood friend, Rei.

Amika.

Kriah's chest ached as he thought of her. For all his lies and manipulations, his grandfather had been right about one thing: they were fools to let her go alone. Azet'haal was aware of her existence—and of their plan to break the seals—and so if he came looking for her, he'd undoubtedly succeed. She was so careless with her gifts without Grey's guidance. Kriah cursed inwardly. He should have been with her, teaching her—*protecting* her.

'Do yer think the Goddess is mad at us?' Vynalla asked.

'What?' Kriah stumbled, dragged from his thoughts, glancing back at Vynalla for clarification.

She pointed at the blistering sky to the west. 'Well, yer said the Sickness didn't come from that. So where'd it come from, then? The Goddess Herself? No one worships Her much these days. Her, or Her children. Well, I hear they do in the west, but I think I'd still pray if I lived in such a wasteland. Maybe that's what I should do—start prayin' to Nirhana again. Or Miatha herself. I don't mind, really.'

She didn't speak much the rest of the way to the tavern. Kriah wondered if she was already deep in her prayers to the Deities; however, when he went to help her disembark, he learnt that her mother's fever had spiked.

'She's never burned like this before,' Vynalla said, looking at Kriah with wide, worried eyes.

'I don't want to haul her through the town like this,' Kriah said carefully. 'Let's book a room to keep her safe. And then go find this Kohle Mak.'

Vynalla nodded and handed him a leather drawstring pouch, heavy with coin. 'Tell Feldah we've brought old Bess, too.'

Kriah took the coin purse and left Vynalla and her mother in the wagon while he headed for the tavern. Inside, it was much the same as what he had come to expect of Meytaran public halls: a long bar ran the length of the establishment, with private tables and booths spread about the venue for patrons to eat, drink or entertain. Guests were sparse, and those he saw kept their distance and their faces covered. All eyes turned to Kriah as he entered.

He stumbled under the cold scrutiny. 'I, uh ...'

'Don't take it personal. No one likes an outsider these days, lad,' a man behind the bar said. He was slim, dark-haired and bronzed like a nomad. 'Where'd yer stumble in from?'

'I, erm, was a crew member on the *Tears*,' Kriah began. '*Amikharlia's Tears*. Um, Captain Yl—'

'Aye, I'm familiar with the *Tears*. Heard she docked the other night but not seen hide nor hair of ol' Yless yet. Been waiting for his daughter to show, too.'

This must be Feldah, Kriah surmised, and approached the bar to keep their conversation more private. 'Vynalla Yless is outside with her mother. We've come to see the heal—'

'Don't be speaking of that too loudly in here, lad,' Feldah said, glancing towards a couple of patrons still interested in Kriah's business at the tavern. 'Nalla told me of Fiolla's ... situation, and, aye, I did agree to help. I got a room out back where you can stay and await Kohle Mak's services—if he'll come to yer, that is.'

Kriah frowned. 'What do you mean?'

'Business been pickin' up for him. Can't see everyone. Can't save everyone, either. He and his cohort've set up camp down the other end of town. Quite a crowd he's drawing with his public miracles. Folks even started callin' him a god.'

Kriah's skin prickled. He tried to imagine what sort of man would seek to capitalise on people's suffering as Feldah rummaged around in his tunic and produced a semi-rusted key on a simple leather strap.

'An old storage shed round back,' the publican said. 'She's not much, but there's pallets in there for Nalla to keep Fiolla comfortable until ... Well, give her my best will yer, lad?' He pushed the key into Kriah's palm and gave him a familiar pat on the shoulder before breaking away to serve a customer who had approached the bar. Kriah lingered a moment, flesh still crawling, before heading back outside to meet Vynalla.

'How'd yer go?' she asked when she spotted him.

'Kohle Mak is performing his miracles across town,' Kriah said. He held up the key. 'Gave us a room for your mother. Said we should leave her there to rest while we plead our case to the healer. Apparently, it's getting harder to win his services.'

Vynalla snatched the key with determination. 'Then we'll have to be extra persistent.'

Kriah raised an eyebrow at her use of *we*.

'Oh, come on, Kriah, *please*,' Vynalla begged. 'Besides, Benell will kill yer if he hears yer left me on me own to traipse through town.'

Seeing little effort in further protests, Kriah helped Vynalla settle her mother into the room Feldah had offered them. The barkeep wasn't wrong when he said it wasn't much: the small, boxy room had gaps between the rotten wooden panels that constituted a door, and the beds were mounds of straw covered over with old hessian grain sacks.

'Set her down here,' Vynalla said, gesturing to the pallet along the far wall. She brushed her mother's sweaty hair back from her forehead, her expression turning soft and slightly pained. Blood trickled from Fiolla's nose now, as well as her ears.

'You should stay with her,' Kriah said, lingering awkwardly in the doorway. 'She shouldn't be alone, in case …' He trailed off, realising how insensitive it was to breathe those words into reality. But Vynalla didn't fall apart at the thought. She didn't even sob. Instead she smoothed her skirts across her thighs and took vigil at her mother's side.

'Yer right,' she conceded. 'I'll stay with Mam. Please, Kriah—make him see us.'

Kriah nodded pathetically. He wasn't sure this Kohle Mak had any answers for them, but refusing her seemed unreasonably cruel. The least he could do for her was try.

He closed the rickety door behind him and headed towards the beaches on the southern side of Gerrick Port. Kohle Mak was said to perform his miracles on the sand beyond the docks. Kriah tried to recall the streets he had taken when he'd disembarked *Amikharlia's Tears* days before. He found the path easily enough; as he neared the water, people started to congregate despite their obvious fear of the Sickness. Some wore pomanders on leather thongs about their necks; most covered their faces with scarves; a brave few brazenly went without either. As Kriah grew close to the crowd, he heard a single voice ring clearly through the intermittent cheers from the gatherers.

'… Mak offers salvation,' the man cried. 'Kohle Mak offers protection. Protection from the blight your gods invite down from the heavens!'

'We believe in Kohle Mak!' a voice rose from the crowd.

'The Deities are dead!'

Unease swirled in Kriah's gut like a tempest. The man at the centre of the crowd continued to yell, touting Mak's benevolence like a fishmonger at market. There was something off about his appearance, about the snowy white hair and the ebony of his eyes, pools of deep night sky against youthful, milky skin.

Meah-Hyren, Kriah realised, though no one else in the crowd seemed to make the connection. Was this man wearing a different face that Kriah could not discern, the same way his grandfather had done around unfamiliar company? Was Kriah the only one who saw the telltale signs of the stranger's heritage? He felt no unusual tug of *khe'torla*—but that wasn't to say magic wasn't being spun.

'Kohle Mak stands with you, when the Deities have chosen to hide,' the man shouted. 'Behold—his gifts!'

He gestured towards a small tent erected behind him on the sand as the crowd erupted like an eager audience welcoming a bard to the stage. But the man who burst through the flaps to the sound of applause was no gawdy entertainer—just a figure in a simple rough-spun linen robe, face hidden behind a solid silver mask with no opening for eyes, nose or mouth. He raised his hands and the crowd hushed to an eerie silence.

'Fear not, my children,' he said in a voice as slippery as honey. 'I shall save you all.'

Kriah's hands tightened to fists by his sides, heart pounding. He knew that voice. Would *never* forget that voice.

Azet'haal.

10

KIOKHAREN

Convict Cove came into sight just as the sun was setting over Qhoraak. However ominous the bruised and bleeding sky had become, Kio could not deny that it made sunsets spectacular. He had always thought there was no more glorious vista than the sunsets of Adria; but sundown over Qhoraak was different—crimson, orange and indigo. Black silhouettes of clouds obscured the sky like ink spilt across an artist's canvas.

'It always feels good coming home,' Emanais said, appearing on the deck beside him. Her locs were loose of her usual thick braid, and exhaustion slackened her posture.

'I lost track of how many days I've been at sea,' Kio admitted quietly. He'd counted them compulsively when he first came aboard, etching them into his brain before sleep like notches in a belt. The last one he remembered was day twenty-three.

'Fifty-four,' the Boatkeep said with certainty. 'Since we set out from Cirahk, at least. It was summer when I last set foot in Qhoraak. I'll sleep well tonight knowing my family all walk the same strip of solid ground again.'

It was strange to hear a captain speak of land with such regard; Kio had always thought seafaring folk felt uneasy when separated from their ships. Instead of prying, he asked, 'What family do you have waiting for you? You mentioned a sister, but—'

'That's all there is,' Emanais said quickly. 'A sister. And a nephew. There is no one else.'

'No husband?'

The Boatkeep snorted.

'A wife, then?'

'I am unwed, Little Prince. Such things do not concern me, for I have no clan I wish to join to another, and that is the only purpose of marriage in Qhoraak.'

'Doesn't sound all that different to Holania,' Kio mumbled. At least not for the highborn houses. Marriage was a transaction, no different to trading coin for goods or services. Moyna was to be his partner in the business that was ruling, for it was a weight too heavy to bear alone. He'd never given thought to finding another to be his queen. But if he wanted to take back his crown ...

'And what of you?' Emanais turned to look at him, their eyes connecting at almost equal height. 'Have you left a wife behind?'

'She died.' He said it so matter-of-factly that it made his grief sound distant and not the shadow that still clung to his every step, driving his thirst and poisoning his mind. 'A son along with her.'

Emanais did not speak, just stood with Kio in silence as they watched the dark shapes of Convict Cove grow closer in the dusk.

'I'm sorry,' Emanais said finally. 'This wife of yours ... Was she not your Siephymn?'

Kio closed his eyes and swallowed. 'No,' he said. 'She was not. She was a woman I loved, but not one I was in love *with*.'

Emanais's brow creased in confusion. 'To love, in love ... Is it not the same? We have no such difference here.'

He was considering how best to explain himself when Emanais's boorish first mate Polk approached, looking grim.

'Boatkeep,' he said, glancing at Kio then back to the captain.

'Speak,' Emanais urged.

'A blue flame burns in the lighthouse.'

Emanais swore. 'I'll be in my quarters,' she hissed. 'The deck is yours, Polk. Little Prince—with me.'

Kio trotted after her, mind swirling. 'What was that about?' he asked, quickening his stride to match hers. 'What does a blue flame mean?'

The Boatkeep exhaled slowly through her nose, teeth spearing into her lower lip. 'We've got a welcoming party.'

Emanais paced the length of her quarters while the *Leviathan* eased into her berth along the crowded docks of Convict Cove. From the small porthole, Kio watched the rush of deckhands below as they tossed and tied ropes to bring her in. Rows of wooden tenement houses, several stories tall, lined the foreshore, and people of all types filled the boardwalks, hawking wares before they were even unloaded from the ships.

It was the messiest market Kio had ever seen—and the most competitive. In the short time he spent watching, he witnessed three fistfights, one of which left the weaker party immobile in a pool of his own blood. Nobody helped him up; passersby only stopped to filch his body for valuables. He was probably dead, Kio realised belatedly. His pulse quickened.

Heavy boots marched along the boardwalk, parting the crowd like a curtain. A dozen Qhoraakese soldiers with rifles in one hand and spears in the other made their way down the dock to welcome the *Leviathan*. The fiery mark of Hirathi was emblazoned on their bronzed breastplates, marking them as some sort of royal guard.

Kio turned to Emanais and found her biting at her fingernails. 'What have you done?' he asked, panic suddenly rising like a tide in his throat. While it seemed ironic that a captain in charge of ferrying criminals to face justice may be something of an outlaw herself, seeing Emanais cower below deck certainly made it seem like she had something to hide.

Kio swallowed hard. *What have I gotten myself into?*

'I'm forbidden from going ashore,' Emanais said—not the denial of wrongdoing Kio had been expecting. 'I'm in exile—an enemy of the Allchief. Why do you think I've been tasked with such a hateful witch-fucking job as running convicts to the capital?' She spat a sliver of thumbnail from her lips.

Kio's eyes narrowed, and he asked again: 'What have you done?'

Emanais sighed. Kio's mind raced as he tried to pre-empt what she was about to reveal. Mass murder? Treason? Regicide—or a previous attempt thereof?

'I rescue Siephymn, Kiokharen,' Emanais said gently, as though giving a casual reminder. 'In doing so I destroy the farms that house them. And sometimes'—she gave a nonchalant little shrug—'people die.'

'You're a ... You're a *terrorist?*' Kio gasped, too busy grappling with the shock of her admission to acknowledge the warmth he felt at the use of his real name.

'I'm a *hero!*' Emanais shot back. 'Waqar Koll is the terrorist. Capturing Siephymn. Imprisoning them. Breeding them like cattle. Not a single person of Siephymn blood can sleep safely on Qhoraakese soil thanks to him. *That* is terrorism. Waqar's men dying in the destruction? I call that a casualty of war.'

Emanais swiped a bottle of rum from the table, pulled the cork with her teeth and took a lengthy swig. Liquid dripped off her chin as she drained the bottle, then tossed it aside to smash against the wall. Kio watched as her chest heaved with a rage she could barely contain. 'Siephymn have suffered so much because of him,' she continued. 'My *sister* has suffered so much. And still you call me *terrorist?* I'm not the villain here!'

'No, I agree,' Kio said. He turned to look back out the porthole and watched a grim-faced Polk usher the soldiers on board. 'Doesn't look like you're on the winning side, though.'

'Well,' she muttered, flopping into her high-backed leather chair, 'heroes don't always win.' She toed off her boots and went back to chewing her fingernails, sliding so far down in her chair that she looked small and afraid.

Outside, the people of Convict Cove had stopped their jostling to watch the raid unfold on the *Leviathan*. A portion of the guard had broken away from the main entourage to restrain a number of rowdy hecklers. Were they vocalising in support of Emanais and her crew—or against them?

'I had no idea Qhoraak was so divided,' Kio said, turning back to Emanais. She was inspecting the inside of empty bottles, looking for a drink. Kio's tongue swelled with a thirst of his own.

'When the Middle Kingdoms started sending us the very worst of their criminals, what exactly did you think would happen?' she grumbled. 'They work off their debt, and then what? Go home now that all is forgiven? No—they were stuck here. Had to make a life for themselves somehow. For most, violence was all they knew. Waqar was a monster when he came here and is a monster still.'

Kio straightened. 'Waqar was a *convict*? How did he become your king?'

'Allchief,' the Boatkeep corrected. 'The position is claimed through conquest, not bloodlines. Were it simply by inheritance, then I—oh, get me a fresh drink, damn you.' She pointed towards the wall of cabinets where rows of dark glass bottles sat behind lattice shutters. The hinges screeched as Kio opened them to retrieve a bottle still sealed in a thick lashing of red wax. He blew dust from the faded label.

'This is wine,' he observed. His mouth salivated and a tremor shook down his arm.

'Is that a problem?' Emanais stretched out her hand. 'Not fancy enough for your princely palate?'

'N-no, it's not that.'

The wine was from Honnah.

Moyna's estate.

Kio remained silent as Emanais took a knife from her belt and started stabbing at the thick wax seal. After several failed attempts, she tossed the blade aside and whacked the bottle's head on the arm of her chair, shattering the glass neck. Rich red merlot splashed down onto the decking. Kio's heart lurched at the waste.

She drank from the broken bottle—spilling wine down her chin to avoid cutting her mouth—before offering it to Kio. He took it without hesitation, pouring it down his throat like a man long parched. A flood of warmth filled him. Of comfort. Of memories. He wiped his lips with the back of his hand, tongue curling out to scavenge every last drop. He was soon thirsty for more.

Emanais eyed him curiously, lips parting to speak, but a knock came to the door before she could say anything.

'Boatkeep,' a low voice rumbled. It wasn't familiar.

'What is it?'

The door opened and in came a young man, head shaved to the scalp, with neat, thick eyebrows and a sharp, strong jaw. He was strikingly handsome, Kio noted, and the warmth spread to his groin as the man's green eyes washed over him before settling on Emanais.

'Ema,' he said, voice dropping. 'They wish to check the captain's quarters. Polk's stalled them in the messes, but they won't clear us to dock until they've done a thorough sweep.'

'*Kaeya magh,*' Emanais spat; Kio didn't need to understand Qhoraakese to know that it was nothing good. 'You've got the papers?' she asked, rushing towards the wall where her coat and tricorn hung from a peg. She handed them to the man as he nodded. 'Good. Help me with this, then.'

The Boatkeep manipulated an ornate carving that adorned the framework of the recessed shelving along the wall of the cabin. There was a hollow *click* and the shelves moved away to reveal a very narrow compartment. The shaven-headed man helped pry the stiff hidden door open just wide enough for Emanais to squeeze herself in with all manner of huffing and cursing.

'Sickness take you if you leave me in here a second longer than needed, Dhenka,' she growled. 'I swear on Hirathi that I'll—'

The man—Dhenka—shouldered the door closed, the woodwork once again sealing flush as if there were nothing there. Kio heard a faint thud as fist met wood inside the compartment.

'Now then,' Dhenka said, spinning on his heel to address Kio with a wide, charismatic grin. He swung Emanais's coat about his own shoulders and set the tricorn aloft on his head at an angle. 'We've not been introduced, but Ema's told me all about her little pet.'

Kio's eyes narrowed. 'You're awfully familiar with your—'

'Uh-uh, don't speak.' Dhenka raised a finger to Kio's lips, and the former prince saw red. 'You are to listen, nothing more. It's very important that this all goes to plan, so you do not open your mouth, even if a Spear addresses you. Do you understand?'

'I—'

The long finger mashed into Kio's lips. 'I said don't speak. Nod. Do you understand?'

Kio nodded, jaw clenching. Just who the fuck was this man?

'Good.' Dhenka dropped his hand and pressed it to Kio's chest instead, guiding him back across the room to Emanais's bed. 'Now sit here and be silent.'

With a push, he forced Kio back on the mattress, piled high with a tangle of sheets and pillows. Dhenka stood over him, smirking as his fingers tugged at the laces of Kio's shirt.

Kio snatched his wrist. 'Do not,' he growled, forgetting the earlier instruction not to speak.

A roguish smile spread across Dhenka's lips as fire coursed through Kio's veins, expedited by the increasing thump of his heart. Dhenka was attractive—seductive, even—and despite himself, Kio longed for the other man's touch.

Or any man, really.

How long had it been since he'd taken someone to his bed? He hadn't even thought about sex, let alone yearned for it. Who had his last man even been? Flynndel Mont? No—Erryck, the stable boy. Both felt an age ago.

But not as long as Rei-Hai.

Memories of the tortured fever dreams rose unwelcome in his mind. The desperate press of Rei's lips. The touch of Rei's fingers against his cheeks. Heat swarmed his body.

'I can see why Ema has so much fun with you,' Dhenka smirked, slipping his wrist from Kio's grip, which had gone slack in his distraction.

Kio went to grunt a retort, but was stopped by banging at the door. Dhenka spun on his heel and waltzed unhurriedly towards Emanais's chair, where he plonked himself down, crossing an ankle over a knee as he did so.

'Come in,' he called to the unwelcome guest, eyes still locked on Kio.

Polk entered ahead of two guards who still wore their firearms cocked over their shoulders. Kio's jaw hardened. He'd seen the devastation those weapons could inflict when Emanais had blasted a man's head off on the docks of Cirahk. If one were to be fired in the close quarters of the cabin …

'Who're you?' one of the guards, who had a shiny pink scar cutting the width of his face, demanded of Dhenka, his finger curled around the rifle's trigger.

'The acting captain,' Dhenka said casually, inspecting his nails for dirt.

'Shouldn't that be him?' The guard gestured at Polk, the first mate.

'Well, it's not.' Dhenka stood now, rummaging around in the pouches on his belt until he produced a yellowed stub of parchment. He handed it to the scarred man. 'Here. Dock papers from Kessar. You'll see the port stamp right there. Stopped a few days ago to take on a fine vintage red. Loaded up our cargo ... Offloaded our capt'n.'

The guard scrutinised the crumpled offering before handing it to his partner to do the same. Kio had no memory of docking anywhere, let alone as recently as Kessar.

'And who's he?' the other guard said, pointing his chin in Kio's direction.

'Capt'n's consort,' Dhenka said with a nonchalant shrug. 'Left him for me to enjoy.'

Kio burned for an entirely different reason now: being a prisoner was one thing, being thought a whore another. He clamped his jaw to swallow his words, breathing slow and deliberate through his nose.

The guard gave a disapproving sneer before handing the stamped stub back to Dhenka.

'You're clear to dock,' the scarred man said, nodding at his partner.

'Many thanks,' Dhenka said coolly. 'We're due to arrive in Xant around the turn of the Nirhana Moon. We'll give our regards to the Allchief then.'

The guards said nothing more as Polk followed them from the room, closing the door behind them. They remained frozen for a moment, silent and immobile; Kio trying to cool his indignation while Dhenka no doubt waited to be sure they were alone. He turned back towards Kio, smiling at a job well done.

'I am nobody's consort,' Kio growled, low and menacing. In truth, he was as shocked as he was insulted by the insinuation—everyone on board seemed privy to his preferences thanks to Bryn-Daal's loose lips.

Dhenka sauntered towards him, shrugging out of Emanais's coat. For the briefest of moments, the Qhoraakese man's eyes flicked to his lips. Kio's heart thundered, fire ripping through his veins.

'Pity,' Dhenka said, voice barely a whisper. Pale green eyes still locked with Kio's, he set the tricorn hat down on the chair and exited the room, leaving Emanais to bang on the wall for her freedom.

11

KRIAH

The crowd fell silent in Kohle Mak's presence. Even the wind grew still, the waves lapping with extra care across the shore. Kriah's skin prickled.

Mak—Azet'haal—kept himself hidden in heavy robes. His white hair was covered by a deep cowled hood, his face obscured behind an expressionless mask of silver. The features were allusions at best—a narrow slit between the crest of thin lips for a mouth; a long straight bridge of a nose. But the eyes ... The eyes were solid. No holes or slits to see from. Kriah recalled the terrible burns that marred Azet'haal's face. Burns that melted an ear and cost him an eye. But this mask was more than a vain attempt at modesty. It was an act, a lure to draw people towards the mysterious blind man who could heal.

And it was working.

The crowd was transfixed, watching Azet'haal as if under some sort of spell. Was that what he was doing? Kriah's toes curled in his boots against the growing unease. He felt the faintest of ripples, silent and subtle, but could not pinpoint exactly what was being pulled.

'People of Bararn—of Whyt'hallen!' Azet'haal said, his words disembodied behind his unmoving mask. 'A new blight has befallen you in the absence of your gods. Spread the word of my coming and I shall grant you succour.'

He dipped his cowled head towards the Meah-Hyren who'd announced him and the man disappeared briefly inside the tent. When he returned, he carried a young woman in his arms, limp and lifeless in a pale linen shift. Her skin had a sickly grey pallor and dried blood trailed from her ears, nose and the corner of her mouth.

The crowd gasped; Kriah's fists clenched.

'This girl was walking not two days past,' Azet'haal proclaimed. 'Now she barely moves at all. Selflessly working to aid the village, she too was struck down by this blood plague—this blood *curse*. I will not have her sacrifice go unrewarded!'

The Meah-Hyren lay the young woman down at Azet'haal's feet, her blonde hair pooling around her head like a cloud. Azet'haal lowered to his knees. He pulled a crystalline flask from the expansive sleeves of his robes and held it up for the onlookers to see. It was filled with a clear liquid, unremarkable until he flicked the side of the bottle with his long fingers. The liquid shone like sunlight, sparkling like a freshly polished crown. The closest audience members shielded their eyes, forced to look away from such a brilliant glow.

He plucked the glass stopper from the bottle's neck and poured the glittering liquid into the woman's mouth, clamping a hand over her nose and lips to ensure she swallowed. Then he pressed a palm to her forehead and another against her chest and began chanting a strange mantra. The words were not Meah-Hyren, or even a Yaian dialect—they were simply gibberish.

Kriah felt the slight tug of *khe'torla* permeate the crowd, but no enchantment he knew manifested in such a way. Light crackled from beneath Azet'haal's hands and the woman's body arched as if shocked by lightning. Her limbs shook with seizure. Azet'haal rolled her to her side and she vomited onto the sand, a frothy pink mix of blood and potion. Soon she began to cough. Slowly, she opened her eyes.

The people of Gerrick Port were silent for a moment. Then someone broke the lines and rushed to the girl's side—a friend or relative eager to scoop her into their arms.

'My power grows as your faith in me does!' Azet'haal proclaimed from behind his silver mask. 'Show me your devotion and I will heal your loved ones of this sickness!'

The crowd surged forward, stepping around the cured girl still spread across the sand, more focused on their own agenda than the fortune of another. The Meah-Hyren guard helped arrange them in some sort of queue leading back towards the tent. *Khe'torla* swirled through the chaos—calming or creating it, Kriah couldn't say.

He would not allow Vynalla to come here, would not allow her to fall into whatever trap Azet'haal had laid. He didn't offer these people salvation—if anything, he had caused this. Kriah just had to figure out what *this* was.

Using the crowd's preoccupation to his advantage, Kriah slipped away unnoticed. He hurried back towards the inn, passing not another soul as he raced through the streets. Bess the old mule was crunching weeds from an overgrown garden bed outside Feldah's tavern, still hitched to the wagon they'd used to cart the Ylesses' mother into town.

In his haste, Kriah barged the rotted door of the old shack open with his shoulder. Vynalla knelt beside her mother, sobbing into the scarf she wore wrapped around her face. There were stains on her apron where she'd tried to mop away the blood now streaming from Fiolla's nose and ears.

She turned to Kriah with a flash of hope in her puffy eyes. 'Did you speak with the healer?' she asked desperately.

Kriah's chest grew heavy, his stomach tight. He swallowed dryly and approached Vynalla, turning the words over on his tongue before daring to give them voice. 'Nalla,' he began awkwardly. 'Do you remember the stories of the Meah-Hyren?'

Vynalla turned over her shoulder, one golden eyebrow raised in confusion. 'The white-haired witches who broke the sky?'

'Yes. Aze—Kohle Mak is one of them. He's using magic to cure people. The same magic that ruptured the veil between realms. We can't trust him, Nalla. He's not here to save you.'

Vynalla glanced at her mother, then back to Kriah, her green eyes glistening as she fought back tears. 'But the Meah-Hyren ...' She pulled the scarf from her face as her attention shifted to Kriah entirely. 'They live on their islands to the east. They haven't stepped foot on Whyt'hallen for centuries. It can't be true.'

'I saw it with my own eyes, Nalla,' Kriah said, gripping both her shoulders tight as the faded memory of his time adrift at sea suddenly found clarity. 'I saw the ocean part. And the Meah-Hyren walked through it.'

For a moment he expected Nalla to laugh. It certainly made him sound crazy. She did not, but her face crumpled strangely as if she didn't quite understand. Or maybe she just pitied him.

'So what?' she declared stubbornly. 'So what if he's using magic? If it could save my Mam, then—'

'But it *won't*.' Kriah pulled her closer, their foreheads almost touching. 'He might restore her body, but at what cost to you? Life in his service? He is not a *god*, Nalla. He will only bring you pain.'

The air around them grew heavy. Silent and still like the gathering night. A tear finally escaped Vynalla's eye, rolling down her cheek where it dripped from her chin on Kriah's forearm. He raised a hand to wipe it from her soft skin.

'You care that much about what happens to me?' she said softly, lips trembling.

'Yes,' Kriah breathed. 'I don't want a—'

Vynalla swallowed his words with a kiss.

It took Kriah a moment to react, to realise what was happening. It had been years since he'd known the touch of a woman's body—decades, even. Only once, and so very long ago. He'd been young, a mere adolescent by Meah-Hyren standards, he supposed. She had been one of the first nomads he had traded with. He'd been stranded in their camp during a violent summer storm and she had offered refuge in her tent. It had been years after Brenneck, his very first friend, and his use of the Meytaran tongue had turned sloppy. But he hadn't needed words, not really. The woman had guided his hand to her breast and there wasn't anything else to be said. His body had reacted on its own, much as it did now.

Their kiss deepened, mouths parted by dancing tongues as Kriah raised his hand to tangle in her golden hair. She was warm and soft and everything he didn't know he needed. And most importantly, she was here. Not a dream or a memory or a distant hope, but *here*. Together they could forget everything they didn't have, everything they'd lost or would soon have stolen from their grasp.

Within moments, they tumbled towards the bed.

Kriah awoke to the cool light of early morning. He sat up with a start. It was not like him to fall asleep without intent, and he was groggy and disoriented. He rubbed at his eyes as he tried to piece together the time he had lost, recalling the warmth spreading through his body with burning shame. It had been wrong to lie with a woman so entangled by grief, and he cursed his foolishness for succumbing to such basic lust.

He reached across the bed beside him to rouse Vynalla from sleep, but his hand found nothing but cold straw. She was gone. Flinging back the thin sheet that had covered him, Kriah scrambled around in the semi-darkness for his clothes. The room was empty; Fiolla was gone too.

Still in a state of undress, Kriah burst through the rickety door and out into the icy morning. Old Bess and the cart were nowhere to be seen.

'Shit,' he cursed, a swell of panic, rage and guilt rising in his stomach. He shouldn't have fallen asleep. How had she left without making a sound?

The questions were a pointless distraction. Piecing the answers together would not change what had happened—nor help him reach Vynalla any faster.

Kriah headed straight for the beach where Kohle Mak had performed his miracles the night before. Smoke bellowed from smouldering funeral pyres where the dead were left to burn, discarded like rubbish. Kriah's gut churned as he thought of the sick game Azet'haal was playing with the Second Born. He had the power to save everyone—why did he pick and choose?

Shadows moved in front of the healing tents set up by Mak's followers. Kriah caught the flash of golden hair as someone ducked inside the tent flaps—Vynalla. He went to call her name, to demand that she stop, but another figure appeared behind her, hooded and masked.

Azet'haal.

Kriah stopped dead, his blood running cold. The masked face was turned towards him, and despite the solid metal covering his eyes, Kriah could feel Azet'haal's gaze boring into him. Somehow, Kriah knew he was smiling.

It was too late. The sorcerer's claws were hooked in Vynalla and there was no way to wrest her free—not without exposing himself and opening the people of Gerrick Port up to further disaster. He'd given Vynalla every chance, every reason, not to turn to Kohle Mak, and he had failed.

There was nothing more he could do.

Kriah was breathless as he staggered up the hilly incline to the Ylesses' cottage. The muscles in his thighs burned with every step, and despite the wintry air, sweat beaded on his forehead from exertion now that the sun had fully risen.

Nell was in the front garden, digging a hole in what was once a vegetable patch. A *deep* hole.

Kriah slowed to a halt.

Nell looked up to welcome him, tears cutting lines through the dirt and grime on his cheeks. So he had done it. He had put his father to rest.

There was nothing more I could do, Kriah reminded himself, feeling the phantom press of Vynalla's lips against his. He had berated himself for not doing more to dissuade her, for not using *khe'torla* to bend her actions to his will. But now he was reminded of the captain, and how Greist'hal had left him damaged beyond repair.

'I ... did it.' Nell swallowed. 'He's gone.' He dropped the shovel and pressed the heels of his palms into his eyes in an attempt to block the tears. It did not help.

Kriah quickened his stride and pulled his friend into an embrace, burying Nell's face in the breadth of his shoulders. He quickly fell apart, wailing like a babe. Kriah remained silent, unsure of what else he could say or do. He'd never had to console anyone before. He'd never even really consoled himself. Not after Brenneck. Not after Grei—

The reality of his grandfather's death hit him with the full force of an axe swing. Their relationship may have been complicated, but for eight decades, Greist'hal had been the only other person Kriah had known. And even then he'd been kept at a distance. His grandfather had done a lot wrong, but after seeing Azet'haal in person and catching a glimpse of the madman's ambitious plans, Kriah couldn't help but wonder if Grey's actions had truly been as bad as he'd first thought. Perhaps the end really did justify the means.

The two men stood embracing for some time, joined in their grief. When Nell finally pulled away, his eyes now dry, he looked around and asked, 'Where's Nalla?'

Kriah had known the question was coming, but he was still unprepared to answer. He stepped back from Nell, rubbing at his neck and scratching his hair.

'The healer ... Kohle Mak. He's not ...' He swallowed. 'He's not here to help you—he's here to enslave you.' There was no way to say it without sounding insane, so Kriah just blurted out all he had surmised about Azet'haal's plans and hoped for the best.

Nell stared at him as if he was, in fact, crazy. 'Is that what you told my sister?' His face was dark. 'Where is she, Kriah?'

'I told her he wasn't to be trusted. That he was dangerous. She didn't listen. No doubt she's already been turned into one of his followers.'

Nell rolled his eyes and made to storm past Kriah towards the town.

Kriah grabbed his arm. 'Listen to me,' he pleaded. But he could tell by the look in Nell's eyes that time had already passed. This was a man damaged by grief. Poisoned by fear. Simple words would not reach him now.

Once again, Kriah felt the urge to twist his mind with *khe'torla*. Surely one little nudge wouldn't hurt? Nell had already come through the memory wipe unscathed. But what if—

Nell yanked himself free and continued down the gravelly slope.

'Nell, *wait!*' Kriah lunged for his arm again, hooking his wrist. He pulled him in close and pressed a palm to the young boatswain's forehead.

A wave of shock hit him immediately.

When his mother had dragged him into a shared projection with her and Greist'hal back in Ciraselo, they had all been there, trapped in a moment as Ka'ella recounted the nature of Kriah's birth. The fate of his father.

But in his rush and inexperience, Kriah was unable to conjure the same conscious space for himself and Nell to inhabit. Instead he filled the young man's mind with a rapid flux of his own memories. Everything from their forgotten first meeting to the showdown with Azet'haal flashed in quick succession, pouring through Kriah's palm and into Nell's head like water through a funnel.

When he pulled away, they were both on the ground, propelled from each other with magnetic force. Nell was face down in the dirt. Kriah shuffled across the ground on his hands and knees to his friend's side. He pressed a tentative hand to Nell's shoulder, half expecting him to recoil in disgust. When Nell didn't respond, fear seized him in a vice-like grip.

'N-Nell,' he whispered, voice cracking as he gave the boatswain a little shake.

After a moment of agonising silence, a small groan escaped Nell's lips.

Kriah loudly breathed his relief and sat back to allow his friend space to sit up. Nell clamped a hand to the side of his head, just above his blind eye, and gave Kriah a pained look.

'Kriah ...?' he began, then glanced around their immediate surroundings, as if to check where they were. 'What was that? Was that ... Was that all real?'

Kriah's breath froze in his chest as he considered how Nell might react. Would he shun him? Drive him away for being a magic-wielding fiend? But it was a little too late to lie now. Slowly, he nodded.

'Well,' Nell said, wiping his hands on the legs of his pants. 'Then we need to tell as many people as we can.'

12

KIOKHAREN

Despite all the effort it had taken to get into Convict Cove, Emanais did not plan on staying long. She informed the crew who were disembarking that they would have three days in town to gather supplies and unwind before heading inland to join with the rest of the Boatkeep's little army.

More terrorists, Kio thought, before mentally correcting the derogatory term. It would take some time to readjust his views, he realised. Having been raised a prince, he found it hard to think of anyone working against the crown as anything other than treasonous scum—even if it wasn't his throne they rebelled against. It was just ... habit.

But Kio wasn't a prince anymore. Reminas had stripped him of that. As an exile, he didn't even have a home, let alone a crown. One day he might strive to win it back, but now he was here to follow orders. Perhaps if he played her game well, Emanais would lend him her army to reclaim Holania. That only solved half the problem, though.

Convict Cove was a busier town than Kio had expected. It was small—far smaller than Adria—but not the dingy slum he'd thought it would be. No one from the Middle Kingdoms knew anything of Qhoraak except that it was a wasteland; an expanse of scorched, barren earth good for nothing but the gems that could be mined there.

There was no distinct food or market district as there was in the neat, orderly arrangement of Adria's castle town; instead, vendors hawked their delicacies from wheeled wooden carts and narrow hole-in-the-wall eateries where the windowsill served as counter and dining table both. But it was the aromas that called the loudest. Sizzling meat fresh from the charcoal; curries rich with fragrant spices; syrup cakes, steamed pudding, fresh—

Kio paused. A crowd was gathering around a noticeboard outside what appeared to be some sort of workshop. Black smoke billowed from the chimney stack and the greasy stench of iron and oil overwhelmed the enticing scent of the food stalls.

'That looks like the brand on me skin,' a man said, pointing a grimy finger towards the length of parchment stapled to the board. The people gathered were mostly Meytarans from the Middle Kingdoms, though a couple of Kheshtarli and even a Qhoraakese rounded out the throng.

Convicts, Kio surmised. He thought of the brand seared into his own skin, a ridge of bubbled numbers down his flank—57892.

Kio approached the noticeboard, grateful his height and keen eyesight allowed him to see over the crowd. 'It's a list,' he muttered, mostly to himself, but many heads turned towards him.

'It's a what?'

'You can read?'

'What's it say about me?'

The questions rang out in quick succession, and the crowd parted as Kio stepped forward to get a better look. The left side of the sheet was a list of numbers; the right a mix of Meytaran letters and Qhoraakese script Kio could not read.

'67823,' he said, reading the first row of the list.

'That's what they called me,' a robust middle-aged man with thinning brown hair said, raising his hand to identify himself.

'It says "food". Were you a cook back home?'

'A baker, sir. Worked for a wealthy estate in Holania. The masters let me go, and soon my debts started piling up and that's when my creditors—'

Kio raised a hand to cut the man off, his chest growing tight. To think the convict trade was happening in his kingdom, under his nose—

'What's it say about me?' a man from the front interrupted. He pulled up his shirt to reveal swollen red numbers burned across his hairy chest.

'89291,' Kio read, then turned back to the board, running his finger down the list. 'It says ...' He squinted; the letters were poorly formed. 'Blacksmith?'

'That's me!' the man bellowed, dropping his shirt and pounding his puffed-up chest with pride. 'Best damn ironworker in Cirahk!'

Before anyone could respond—in awe or refute—the shutters on the window next to the noticeboard burst open, causing the crowd to jump. A bald Qhoraakese man stuck his head out, skin shiny with sweat and face obscured behind an eye mask of glass and leather. He slid the goggles up his forehead, hazel eyes darting left and right across the crowd.

'Who work iron?' he barked, his Meytaran crude.

The Cirahkian blacksmith raised his hand slowly, glancing sheepishly to his peers.

'You work forge,' the Qhoraakese said. 'Come, come. I have job. Pay coin.' He beckoned the man over with an enthusiastic flap of his hands.

The blacksmith stumbled out of the crowd, a bewildered grin on his lips as he headed towards the building.

So that's what these numbers mean. Kio had assumed they were brands indicating ownership—a scar to permanently mark them as convicts. But it was more than that. It was a code to denote skills so one might find work to earn a living or pay off their debts.

I wonder what my skills are?

Kio scanned the list, but could not find his number among the tutors and tailors and farmers that made up the convicts crowding the street. His jaw tightened. Of course that witch-fucker Reminas would not credit him with any marketable skills. Indignation blazed anew through his chest.

That's right, he recalled. *I was to be sent to the mines.* Unskilled labour for an unskilled man—a final parting insult.

'Little Prince.'

Kio looked up, recognising Polk's voice. The mate strolled towards him, flanked by another two Qhoraakese crewmen from the *Leviathan.* They were dressed in cleaner, more relaxed linens than their usual uniform, and Kio remembered that although Polk was to lead the ship on to Xant in Emanais's absence, they were to enjoy a few days' liberty in port before setting out again.

'What is it?' Kio asked, tearing himself away from the board.

'Boatkeep wants to see you. In her room at the inn. Don't know what about,' he added with a shrug before Kio could ask.

Kio's pulse beat a little faster and the familiar pangs of thirst clawed at his throat. He didn't want to face Emanais sober. He'd been avoiding her since the charade with the guards, guilty and uncomfortable. Dhenka, he'd since learnt, was *her* consort.

And Kio couldn't stop thinking about him.

Their heated glances and playful exchanges had reignited a desire he had not felt since being held as Reminas's prisoner. Dhenka had been on his mind for days now, and memories of the man's pale gaze lingering on his lips were the only thing that banished thoughts of Rei-Hai Shaw to the past where they belonged.

But Dhenka was Emanais's consort, and Kio was just a man with a debt.

While many of the crewmen staying ashore opted for tavern rooms or boarding houses to be rented for little coin, the Boatkeep had apparently splurged on relative luxury for a suite at the inn. Part of it had been for protection—Emanais had explained that the guards would not think to look for her in such an expensive hideout—but Kio suspected the promise of privacy and comfort had also played a part. Had he any coin, he would have spent it all on a hot bath and a decent bed.

'Last door on your right up the stairs,' the girl behind the counter said after Kio asked for Nayt—the false name Emanais had been using while ashore.

'Thank you,' he said, parting ways with Polk as he made for the inn's upper level. His stomach wrapped itself in knots as he worried over what to expect, and he hesitated by the door before knocking.

'Come,' Emanais called, her voice hoarse and breathy.

Sickness take me—she's drunk, Kio groaned inwardly, knowing how erratic she could be when intoxicated. Taking a deep breath to steel himself, he opened the door.

Emanais was caught in a tangle of undulating bodies, naked limbs and flesh slick with sweat. Kio stumbled back out of the room reflexively, having seen little more than a naked arse pounding between open thighs. His skin burned.

She wanted me to see that, he concluded. It was a power play. A demonstration of dominance—of ownership. Kio felt every bit the fool she'd made him out to be. To have offended the one person capable of helping him ...

Kio was about to leave when the door swung open. He turned to find Dhenka, naught but Emanais's leather jacket draped about his shoulders, coming to greet him. Kio fought to look anywhere but where his eyes were instinctively drawn, choosing instead to stare at the rusting hinges in the doorjamb.

'She told you to come, did she not?' Dhenka said casually, that mischievous grin splitting his invitingly plump lips.

Kio looked past his shoulder to where Emanais sat on the bed, shoulders now resting against the headboard. She gave a little wave, bidding him enter. Dhenka stepped back to welcome him in.

'Dhen told me all about your little spark,' the Boatkeep said with a catlike grin. 'Even if he didn't, the walls were not so thick that I couldn't hear the flirting.'

Kio cleared his throat with a dry cough. 'I don't—'

'I'm not sure how you were raised, Little Prince, but I've always been encouraged to *share.*'

Before Kio could formulate a response, warm hands snaked up his back, over his shoulders and down into the collar of his loosely tied shirt. He closed his eyes and let out a slow, deep breath as he leant into the intimacy of the touch. Dhenka's lips were on his neck as he pushed Kio towards the bed. Kio's shins collided with the mattress and he broke from the moment, glancing up to find Emanais stalking towards him on all fours, loose locs falling over her shoulders and breasts.

Kio shoved Dhenka off him and straightened. 'I can't ...' He glanced at Emanais, then back at her consort. 'I'm not—'

Emanais withdrew with a subtle dip of her head. She clambered off the bed and sauntered silently towards Dhenka, where she relieved him of her jacket and shrugged back into it herself. Kio expected her to leave then; instead she grabbed a bottle of wine from the table along with a single glass and took a seat in the high-backed armchair across the room.

'I'll just watch, then,' she said, pouring herself a glass as she crossed her legs.

Dhenka stepped between their eyeline, pushing Kio back until he sat on the bed. Now Dhenka was free of the heavy leather jacket, Kio was painfully aware of his nakedness, of his hard arousal as it pressed into his belly when Dhenka came to straddle his thighs. He continued kissing up Kio's throat, his jaw, trailing towards his ear, where he sucked the lobe between his teeth.

Pain shot through Kio's chest like a bolt, hot and sharp.

'Get away!' he screamed, sending Dhenka sprawling to the floor with a fierce shove. Everything felt tight. His muscles, his chest, his throat. Kio rolled to his side, dragging his knees towards his chest, cradling them like a babe. His clothes had grown damp with sweat. He trembled all over.

'Leave us,' he heard Emanais bark over the sound of his wails. Dhenka shuffled from the room and the door clicked closed behind him. Kio felt no safer.

The bed dipped slightly as Emanais came to sit beside him. She did not move to touch him, and Kio was glad; his nerves were too raw, too exposed.

'You're suffering from terror, love,' she said softly. 'I've seen it before. Far too many times. Not a single Siephymn I've rescued has been spared its claws.'

'And ... how do I ... stop it?' Kio managed in between his choking sobs, his tears forming a damp puddle on the mattress beneath his face.

'Just breathe,' Emanais coached. 'In and out, nice and slow. There you go.'

She let silence and space pass between them. Slowly the vice-tight grip on Kio's muscles began to relax, and his pulse reclaimed its normal tempo as he focused on his breathing like Emanais instructed. Soon, even his sobs subsided.

'Time is the best healer,' Emanais said sagely. 'Failing that, distraction. I could see terror's talons in you and had hoped Dhen would be a better balm than booze. I need my soldiers sharp, not drunk.'

'And yet you drink,' Kio said pointedly, still curled in a ball with his back to her.

'I am the exiled captain of a convict trawler—of course I fucking drink.'

'I watched my son die. And my wife. I sat in the company of my mother's severed head for weeks and drank from the skull of a boy who was once my friend. And then, on top of all that, I learnt that the truest love I have ever felt was a lie. What the *fuck* am I supposed to do if not drink?'

Emanais did not speak. And neither did Kio, for a time. He'd never given voice to his pain before. Never verbally acknowledged all the trauma and loss he'd endured. Naively, he'd thought he'd gotten through Reminas's torture relatively intact. But the bastard had broken him after all. There was no coming back.

Kio sat up, resting his elbows on his knees as his legs hung over the side of the bed. He looked over his shoulder at Emanais, eyes red and swollen. 'What am I supposed to do, Ema?' he asked desperately—hopelessly.

Emanais shook her head softly and slipped off the bed. She placed a gentle hand on his shoulder.

'Rest,' she said. 'And rest well. Have this suite—I'll book another. Sleep, and regain your strength. We will rendezvous with the army to-morrow.'

She headed towards the door, leaving the bottle of wine open on the nightstand.

Kio awoke with a pounding head and a tongue itching with thirst. He wasn't exactly hungover—he needed much more than a single bottle of wine for that—but more so dehydrated from the previous day's tears. Despite the soft bed and crisp, clean linen, he felt no more rested than if he had spent the night in a pile of mouldy straw. At least a hot morning bath would start the day right.

Clean, Kio tied his growing hair back with a length of cord pulled from his shirt collar. It was rushed and sloppy, with many strands falling free, but it was the best he could manage. Although there was a wash-basin and looking glass in the grand suite, there was no razor he could use to rid himself of the beard thickening across his face. At least, he thought bitterly, it would disguise the way his cheeks had hollowed from stress and starvation.

Emanais was waiting outside in the street, Dhenka and several other trusted crewmen at her side. He recognised Ylan from his mess, and although the others had familiar faces, Kio could not name them. In total, it seemed Emanais had recruited ten former prisoners to make the trek across the wasteland to join her rebel army.

'Where are your supplies?' asked one of them—a man of perhaps forty years with a long, hooked scar down his face—when he noted Kio's empty hands.

'I don't have any,' he shrugged. There was no point in lying, or making some boastful claim about not needing them; Kio simply had no coin to purchase anything of use—for himself *or* the group. It occurred to him now what a burden that would be.

'The Little Prince will share with us,' Dhenka said, tossing a well-stuffed leather satchel in his direction. Kio caught it awkwardly, surprised by its weight, but hoisted it over his shoulders nevertheless. A few sparse chuckles broke out among the group; Emanais silenced them with a sharp glare.

'Yeni is to meet us at East Camp,' Emanais announced, pointing off towards the stretch of red earth before them. 'That was the plan before I set off, and my sister is a woman of her word. She has worked hard to lead the troops in my absence, even securing information on our next target.'

She pulled a folded square of parchment from the breast pocket of her vest, which she now wore over a billowy linen shirt in place of the long leather jacket she'd donned upon the ship. Kio assumed this to be the charcoal etching she had shown him in her cabin—the one delivered via the elkaven, Svern.

'We'll reach East Camp in four days,' she said, starting to walk. 'I suggest you keep pace.'

Kio had never been one for long journeys on foot, always having the luxury of a horse or even a carriage when travelling out of Adria. The ill-fitting shoes he'd been given to wear upon the *Leviathan* left his feet blistered before their first break for lunch, and his whole body ached head to toe by the time camp was pitched for the night. The weeks spent in Cirahk's dungeons and upon the ship had weakened his body far more than he wanted to admit. As the others shared stories around the campfire, Kio found himself struggling to keep his eyes open, let alone follow the conversation.

'You should rest,' Dhenka said, gently nudging Kio's shoulder with his own.

'And give them another reason to shit all over me?' Kio scoffed as he picked at the lumps of vegetables in the stew. The travel rations were a veritable feast compared to his meals of late, but he was so tired he could barely eat.

'I doubt that.' Dhenka smiled, pointing off to a flat separated from the camp by a rocky mound, where Emanais was working to erect a canvas tent—with great difficulty, too, judging by the foulness of her mouth. 'Ema will summon you when she's ready. No one will question it if you join us. Not if they want to keep their tongues, that is.'

Kio glanced across the campfire at Ylan and the others, who drank and guffawed over jibes at each other's expense. What was more degrading? Their endless sling of insults or the assumption that he was some woman's whore?

Kio set down his half-finished meal and strode off to where Emanais wrangled the long length of canvas. She greeted him with what was no doubt some sort of Qhoraakese curse. Regardless, he went in search of the other end of the fabric.

'Can't imagine you've put up many tents in your life, Little Prince,' she said sharply, eyeing him with caution.

'No,' he admitted calmly, 'but surely it's easier with two people.'

She did not respond, instead spearing one of the support poles into the rock-hard earth. The ground cracked and chipped with her efforts.

'Why don't you order the men to do this for you?' Kio asked, watching her struggle. 'Generals hardly erect their own shelters in a war camp.'

'Because,' she panted, giving the earth another stab, 'I'—stab—'am not'—stab—'a general.' She stopped to wipe her brow, pole sufficiently wedged in the parched earth. 'I'm not a queen or a chieftain or even a captain—not here, anyway. I'm a leader of rebels. And in my army, we pull our own weight. Don't expect anyone to fluff your pillows or wipe your arse, Your Highness.'

'Servants never wiped my—' Kio bit off the last words. He kept silent as he continued to help with the tent, stretching the length of canvas across the poles until it draped down to the ground, blocking the sharp wind that was beginning to pick up as night fell.

'But you do look out for me,' he said after long deliberation. 'I hardly contribute. If you're doing this out of pity—'

Emanais stalked towards him. 'I don't pity you,' she said, holding his gaze. 'I'm just trying to get you into bed, love.'

She tapped his cheek with her open palm, then pulled back the tent flap and gestured him inside.

Emanais did get him into bed, and on the third night, Kio finally realised why.

His nightmares.

They had stopped. Curled up between the Boatkeep and Dhenka, Kio never once woke screaming or covered in a cold sweat. There was nothing intimate about their evenings—since the incident at the inn, Kio couldn't even *think* about sex—but the simple fact of having not one but two living beings breathing beside him brought unspeakable comfort. Had Emanais known? Was that why she had brought him to their tent?

Kio wondered how things might change when they reached East Camp, a concern that only strengthened as they approached the rebel base not long past noon on the fourth day. The base was larger than he'd expected—not so much a temporary campsite as a stronghold encased in a ring of mudbrick walls, complete with watchtowers and a patrolled gate.

'Pretty elaborate for a ragtag bunch of rebels, wouldn't you say?' Kio remarked to Dhenka, who walked with him at the back of the group.

'East Camp was once a farm. Liberated and then occupied by our forces,' Dhenka said with a proud smile. 'A portion of the army resides here when Ema is at sea and waits to escort her back to our main base in the mountains. I always like coming here,' he added as a horn erupted from the watchtower. 'Always get the hero's welcome.'

The iron gates groaned open at their arrival and scattered cheers and applause greeted them when they passed into the square. Two dozen or so men and women with mismatched armour and weaponry had gathered to welcome Emanais and her new recruits, but there was something decisively odd about the base.

There were no buildings. No tents. No shelters of any kind. Kio could discern a large well at the centre and several stone-ringed fire pits straddled by spit-roasting meat, which certainly indicated people were living here, but nothing seemed to offer lodging for the night. Did they all just sleep out under the stars? It wasn't exactly *cold*, but ...

'My friends,' Emanais said, coming to a halt in the middle of the encircling crowd. She raised her hands to shush their cheers. 'Dhen and I have once again returned from a successful voyage, bringing back to you new members to fight for our cause! With strong arms and sharp minds, they will serve us well in our skirmish on the next farm. I've studied the plans that Yeni provided and, after a debrief with my war council, I believe we can make our move before the rise of the next Hirathi Moon!'

Kio glanced at the reddened sky, where he could just make out the Skrevaar Moon as it waxed in the shadows of the setting sun. It would be almost three weeks before they set out again.

A small, milky-skinned child with a shock of crimson hair broke away from the crowd encircling Emanais and clung onto her leg. Kio's pulse rampaged at the sight, sending ice-cold shock shooting through his veins, paralysing his limbs. But, despite the fleeting resemblance, this child wasn't Rei; taking a deep breath, he pushed the memories aside along with his grief.

Emanais scooped the boy up into her arms and gave him a tight squeeze. Smiling, she surveyed the crowd. 'Yeni?' she called, grin fading. 'Yeni?'

Panic rose in her voice, on her face, and Kio too found himself frantically scanning the onlookers, despite not knowing who he was looking for. Their expressions were grim—guilty, even—with many averting their gaze when Emanais's eyes washed over them.

'Where is Yeni?' the Boatkeep screamed. 'Where the *fuck* is my sister?'

13

REI-HAI

Rei awoke to gentle lips on his forehead, fingers in his hair. He opened his eyes to find his vision a little less blurred and the light less painful. Kio was beside him on the bed, head propped up on his hand as he withdrew from the tender kiss. His sapphire eyes were hooded and dark-ringed. Despite Rei's protests, the prince had no doubt kept an attentive vigil over the last few days, ignoring royal duties and drawing unwanted attention to his absence.

'You slept,' Kio noted with a warm smile. 'I knew the mandrake tea would help.'

Rei grimaced. That explained the bitter taste in his mouth. The concoction had certainly numbed his mind and body enough to find rest, but now its effects were waning and the hurt crept back into his muscles.

With a groan—and instinctive help from Kio—Rei managed to sit up against the quilted headboard, his head swirling at the movement. When the nausea passed, he looked down to find himself naked from the waist up, strips of clean, gauzy linen wrapped around his many wounds.

'Who dressed these?' Rei demanded wildly, panic swelling in his chest.

'I did,' Kio said, looking a little wounded himself. 'I'm not entirely useless, Rei-Hai. I know how to clean and dress a wound. Mostly. It can't be too hard, right?'

Rei's eyes narrowed. 'And where did you get the dressings?'

'I told Moyna I had an accident in the training hall and was too embarrassed to see the chirurgeon so she would get some supplies for me.' He held up a neatly bandaged hand.

'And *did* you have an accident in the training hall?'

'Of course not!' the prince scoffed. 'I've barely left your side.'

'Well, that lie is going to come unstuck fast.'

Rei regretted his sharp tongue the moment the words left his mouth. As always, stress made him savage. Coming here had been a mistake—not because Kio was a mistake, but because of the danger Rei brought down on the both of them. Regardless of his fear and regret, though, he couldn't deny that he felt better just for being here.

'Moyna won't say anything,' Kio assured him, reaching out to clasp his knee beneath the sheets.

Rei recoiled at the touch. Kio pulled his hand away, leaving it to hover with uncertainty above Rei's leg. The rejection had shocked them both, Rei unable to identify *why* his body had reacted in such a way. His nerves were so raw that Kio's touch set his senses alight in a way that induced more panic than comfort.

'S-sorry,' Rei muttered, and reached for Kio's waiting hand, squeezing it tight. Fear uncoiled its grip.

Kio's face softened. 'What happened to you, my love?' he asked, reaching out to brush the long red hair back from Rei's face. 'What did they do to you?'

But Rei would not answer that. He wouldn't relive the events of the last few months by speaking them aloud. Instead he leant into Kio's touch, closed his eyes and waited for it to pass.

Rei groaned as he woke, eyes sticky and limbs heavy. The floor beneath him was hard, damp and cold—a far cry from the comfort of Kio's bed.

Why *was* he dreaming of the past? He hated dwelling there. Was this his mind's way of ensuring he saw Kio before he died?

It could have picked some happier memories.

Amika was asleep beside him, leaning against the wall of the cave, no doubt having intended to keep watch. There was blood splattered across her clothes—*black* blood. Rei was sure for a moment that it must be his, but then he recalled the ambush by the skampils and how he—

Rei looked around the cave, catching at last a glint of light reflecting off the discarded glass syringe.

Fuck.

The last of the decoctions—Ka'ella's devolution-stemming elixir—was gone.

Next time she'd have to kill him.

'Amika,' Rei rasped, his throat dry and hoarse. The princess's eyes snapped open immediately, her hand stretching towards her blade. Her gaze met his and her expression softened.

'Hey,' she smiled. 'Welcome back.'

'How long was I gone?'

Amika glanced out the mouth of the cave, where a morning sun rose in a blood-red sky. 'Two days. You must be starving.' She began rummaging in her supply pack, but Rei shook his head.

'Just thirsty,' he lied. He *was* hungry—just not for stale bread and old jerky. He needed meat. Fresh meat. *Living* meat.

Blood.

Amika nodded, her hair dancing against the slope of her neck. She handed him a waterskin that was worryingly shrivelled. Rei drank sparingly, the restraint only making his thirst more pronounced.

'I hadn't expected to encounter demonspawn so soon after crossing the border,' Amika said, gnawing on a strip of salted meat so dry now that it looked like leather. 'Certainly not on that scale.'

'No, me either,' Rei muttered. 'I barely saw any the last time I was here.'

'Is it because of us? Opening the Tear, I mean.'

Rei gave a noncommittal, one-shouldered shrug. 'Could be. They've certainly been more active since the first seal was broken.'

Just like the curse in my blood.

'Makes me question if we're even doing the right thing,' Amika muttered, biting off a chunk of jerky.

'Bit late for that now.'

Rei hadn't meant for the words to come out so sharp. After a lifetime of poor decisions, he was hardly in a position to judge others. Before he could open his mouth to apologise, Amika changed the subject.

'We're going to need more water. It looks drier than an old crone's skin out there.'

'There are rivers,' Rei said. Groaning to his feet, he staggered towards the mouth of the cave, using the wall as support. Deities *dead*, his body hurt. From his head right down to his toes, not an inch was spared from that bone-deep ache—or the now-insatiable hunger that clawed at his gut.

'... Are they close to here?' Amika prompted.

Rei glanced back at his friend, expression sharp. 'I don't remember. My memories of Qhoraak aren't exactly clear—or fond. Piren-Ha will lead us to one.'

Stumbling slightly without the support of the wall, he wandered out of the cave and into the fresh morning air. The desert heat would rise steeply with the sun, but for now it was cool—comfortable, even. Strange, considering the ominous red aura that befell them from the sky, making the world glow crimson like hot coals in a fire.

Rei took a seat on a large boulder, almost moaning at the relief. He worked a clean needle from the canister on his thigh and pressed the sharp tip into his thumb until a bead of black blood pooled at the wound. Smearing the blood across his tongue, he whispered the name *Piren-Ha*, then waited for the creature to arrive.

Within moments, the elkaven was streaking overhead, her great wings beating slow and steady as she glided down to greet him. Rei raised his arm for her to perch upon and the bird cooed when he gave her a scratch beneath her beak in welcome.

'Hey, girl,' he croaked, throat still raw. 'You seen Kio?'

Piren-Ha gave a series of clicks expressing her distress.

'All right, all right. We'll still look for him, but we have to find some water first. Can you take us to some?'

The elkaven squawked, fluffed her inky feathers, then took flight with a thunderous flap of wings. She headed east, towards the coast, and Rei hoped that the water she made to lead them to was not the ocean.

'How long until she finds us water?' Amika asked as she approached, adjusting the straps of both packs slung about her shoulders.

Rei shrugged. 'A day. Maybe two.'

Truth was, he had no idea. Last time he was here, he'd been captured by the Siephymn farmers not far from the caves. He'd hung close to the ranges that time, following them south. The Crags traversed Qhoraak top to bottom like a spine, and his intel had suggested tunnels—old mining shafts—cut through them towards the capital. Rei would be happy to take the long way around, but …

'We'll double back towards the mountains once we've refilled our skins,' he told Amika in huffy breaths as they carefully descended the rocky path down from the cave. The terrain was steep and unstable, all broken slate and sharp red pebbles. 'It will be the quickest way to Xant. If anyone has information about Kio, then—'

Rei turned abruptly at the sound of Amika's scream.

He expected to find her set upon by some horde of demonspawn that had escaped his awareness; instead, he found her half screaming, half *laughing*, as she slid down the steep mountainside on her arse.

'You alright, Princess?' he asked when she came to a stop, offering a hand to help her stand.

'Phew, what a thrill! Who would have thought dry land to be so slippery,' she said wryly, wiping palms dirty with dust and blood clean on her thighs. She took Rei's hand and he hauled her back upright, groaning under the strain of the weighty packs.

'No wonder you lost your balance,' he muttered, gesturing to his own supplies that she also carried. 'Let me take it for a while.'

Amika scoffed, swatting away his hand. 'You can barely stand as it is.'

Rei did not press it further. It had been a hollow offer, anyway. He knew he could no more shoulder his own pack down the mountain than he could sprout wings and fly to Kio's side. It was only dumb luck that *he* wasn't on his arse in the dirt.

Could I even get up if I fell?

Amika must have sensed his musings. Her hand closed around his with a comforting squeeze. 'How about we both just take it slow?'

With their joined hands and careful pacing, it took two hours to descend to a plain even enough that Rei didn't feel like his feet were constantly sliding forward in his boots, crushing his toes. His thighs burned and his head pounded from thirst, but he didn't ask for the waterskin; he couldn't take the last of their precious stores—not when he was going to die anyway.

It was unbearably hot now the sun was high above them. Rei had sweated through his shirt, and the cloth clung damply to his skin and chafed with every move. While he was used to travelling under the shroud of his black shawl and leathers, his waning health now made the feat seem impossible. He was feverish, he could tell; sweating rivers one minute then racked by bone-shaking chills the next. His head pounded so badly it felt like his skull was caving in on itself.

Rei cleared his throat to speak. 'A-Amika ...'

The princess shook her head, swallowing the salted meat she chewed while they caught their breath. 'If the next words out of your mouth are *kill me*—she imitated his raspy voice—'save it. I don't want to hear it. We're getting you to Kio.'

It hadn't been what he was going to say, but the thought was there, lingering in the back of his mind like a thick miasma that refused to dissipate. With each turn of the moon the situation seemed more hopeless. Not just finding Kio, but getting to him before—

Piren-Ha cawed in the distance. Rei looked to the bruised and bloodied sky, at last spotting a black streak approaching from the south.

'She's back!' He pointed skyward for Amika to see. He smiled at the elkaven's approach, wider and more genuinely than he had in a while. For a brief moment, hope dared to shine.

Thunder cracked through the mountains.

Piren-Ha burst into a spray of smoke, feathers and blood. Rei screamed, throat raw.

Piren-Ha! His pet. His companion. His only connection to Kio all these years. She couldn't be gone. She *couldn't*. Not like this. Not when—

Rei clutched at his skull, pain ripping through his body. Pain so bright, he couldn't see—couldn't breathe. With a final spasm, he dropped to his knees and broke.

14

AMIKHARLIA

Piren-Ha's remains fell to the ground like oily, ashen snow. Rei writhed in the dirt, black spittle on his lips.

'N-no,' Amika breathed, shrugging off the supply packs to rush to his side. 'No, no, no. Hold on, Rei. You can do it.'

But his back was arching off the ground, bones bending at angles they shouldn't have, and that scream ... That scream just wasn't human.

Amika froze. From her fingers to her toes, nothing moved. Even her breath stilled. She was utterly helpless as her oldest friend kicked and flailed like a wild animal against a master's restraints, vomiting ink and tearing strips of his own flesh with his claws.

She couldn't watch Rei succumb to his curse. But she couldn't draw her blade, either.

Tears welled in her eyes. She reached for her *khe'torla*, but it was soft and distant, hard to grapple with. The desert around them was barren and lifeless. Even the earth beneath her feet was silent and dead. She'd exhausted herself blasting away the skampils, but she had to do something.

Gritting her teeth, she stretched her hand towards the sword that hung at her hip. She might not be able to strike first—but she could defend herself.

'Come on, Rei,' she choked, tears spilling down her cheeks. 'Come at me. I'll do it.'

Rei growled as if in response. He flipped over onto his stomach, clawed hands gouging at the dry red earth as he scampered on all fours. The blackness had stretched further up his arms now, up over his elbows and partway up his biceps. His muscles bulged abnormally; his shoulders and elbows cracked and dislocated and bent back on themselves, grotesque and horrifying.

Amika widened her stance, softened her knees and prepared for an attack. *This is a demonspawn,* she told herself, staring into the luminous golden eyes of the creature she had once called friend. She didn't want to remember him this way, but a part of her feared this was the image of Rei that would remain with her forever—some man–beast hybrid instead of the soft-featured boy he'd been. She knew now why he'd not wanted Kio to see him like this.

The beast closed in on her, and Amika took a strategic step backward—only to feel something hard and metallic press into the small of her back.

Fear seized her. She'd been so focused on the threat in front of her, she'd forgotten about the attack on Piren-Ha. Fighting the instinct to spin around and face this new enemy, Amika turned her head only slightly and managed to catch something in her peripheral vision.

Two figures stalked towards her from behind, a third holding a weapon at her back.

'Drop your sword,' barked one of them—a woman—in thickly accented Meytaran.

'I'd rather not,' Amika forced through clenched teeth. She expected a blow to the head or some other move to disarm her; instead there was a *click* and a *boom*, and the earth before Rei exploded in a shower of splintered rock.

With a squeal, he scampered off like a frightened dog. Two of their assailants gave chase.

'Don't hurt him,' Amika cried over the ringing in her ears. She had to make a conscious effort not to run after him. If they discharged that *thing* into her back …

She was almost certain it was a pistol—a Qhoraakese firearm. It had been years since she had seen one, but she could still remember the indiscriminate way it tore through flesh and armour alike. She let her sword clatter to the ground.

Amika swallowed a sob as she watched helplessly, weak and unable to focus her *khe'torla* in such distress and deflation. She had failed Rei. Now he would die at the hands of strangers.

Two men set upon him and tackled him to the ground. They wrestled in a comical scrap of limbs, a tangle of cats quarrelling in an alley. Eventually they stilled as one of them—a large man with a bundle of braids atop his half-shaved head—subdued Rei in a chokehold. The Siephymn's legs thrashed wildly in the dirt, kicking up clouds of dust as his claws sliced into the thick leather braces about the man's forearms.

'D-don't,' Amika pleaded pathetically as the second man pulled something small and sharp from his belt and sauntered towards her restrained friend. He gripped it in two hands, raised it high above his head, then speared it right into Rei's gut.

'No!' Amika screamed.

Rei kicked and spasmed and grew still.

Frozen with the firearm still pressed menacingly to her back, Amika watched in horror as the weapon was wrenched free, expecting to see a blade dripping with Rei's inky blood.

Instead she glimpsed a long, thin needle slipping from a wound no larger than a pinprick.

Rei fell limply from the relaxed chokehold, his body reverting to its natural state. But the black stain stretching up his left arm did not recede, now lapping at the edges of the Tower's tattoo. Amika glanced up at their assailants.

They had saved him.

'Th-thank you,' she stammered, racking her brain for the Qhoraakese word, but it came up blank. If the men understood the Meytaran tongue, they did not show it, and the woman who had spoken earlier now seemed to ignore her.

The threat having passed, Amika made to join her friend—but a prod in her back demanded otherwise. Wordlessly, the pistol-bearer pushed her in the opposite direction. Having encountered the devastating weapon during her years in Ciraselo, she knew better than to disobey—especially without her *khe'torla* easily within reach.

And so she followed the silent command, glancing briefly over her shoulder to see the shaven-headed man flopping Rei over his shoulder like a sack of grain. The other man brushed Rei's long hair aside to inspect the back of his neck. Amika caught a glimpse of a silvered scar; it was apparently of interest to the Qhoraakese as well, as he pointed it out to his companion. They exchanged words that Amika could barely hear, but she could hazard a guess at their meaning.

Siephymn farmers.

Amika stopped and earnt a clip around the back of the head for her dallying.

'*Kaeya magh,*' she swore—of course *that* she could remember—and got a pistol butt to the ribs.

'Keep move,' the woman with the pistol growled in her broken Meytaran. She stepped closer, allowing Amika to catch a glimpse of her captor. Russet-skinned and younger than the others, she had braided locs that had been bleached ochre by the sun. She studied Amika with pale green eyes before nodding at her companions to keep walking.

So she's the one in charge here…

They walked for the better part of the day without stopping, traversing the gravelly descent from the mountain with more care than urgency. When they did stop it was nightfall, and they had reached the gentle slopes of the coast. Amika had thought they were further inland, having not seen the ocean when they exited the caves. But looking back upon the dark path they had descended, she saw now that the curve of the mountains had blocked her vision of the coastline.

Amika relished the refreshing scent of salt spray and the steady crash of waves on the beach as they stopped to make camp. She hadn't been by the ocean since she was a very young girl and visited southeastern Bararn with Tallas, when their families had been trying to determine the suitability of their betrothal. The beach she sat beside now was nothing like the white expanse she remembered; it was an unsteady patch of pebbly grey sand penned by a ring of jagged red stone. The waves of the ocean, black under the dusk sky, broke across the rock, depositing weed and other debris from the depths onto the shore.

The men propped Rei against a rock and set to work starting a fire, a task made shockingly simple thanks to a sprinkling of powder. Amika's memory prickled; she'd seen this before. Firesand—the expensive Qhoraakese export they used to fire their pistols and fuel their iron forges. It had seemed magical to her, the first time she saw it, but having come to understand the true power of *khe'torla*, she found firesand to be no more exciting than a parlour trick.

Her listless gaze was pulled from the ocean when someone spun Amika around by the shoulder. Behind her, the woman holding the pistol dipped the weapon at the ground by the sputtering new fire.

'You sit,' she growled.

Amika stood defiantly for a moment until a click from the firearm forced her to acquiesce. The woman set about unloading her pack, iron barrel still levelled at Amika, and took a seat opposite her. She dropped Amika's sword from where it had been hitched to her belt, the blade dinging dully on the pebbles as it fell. Amika flinched; it better not be damaged.

The men left Rei where he had been placed and came to sit beside the commander, chatting away in their native tongue as they rummaged through their packs for the evening meal. Amika's Qhoraakese had grown shamefully rusty in the months away from Ciraselo—not that she'd been fluent to begin with. But perhaps her diminished confidence was a blessing; if they thought she knew little more than curses, maybe they would carelessly reveal something she could use to her advantage.

'Amika,' she said, pressing a splayed palm to her chest. 'I'm Amika.' Pointing at her unconscious friend behind them, she added, 'Rei-Hai.'

'Siephymn,' the man with the piled braids corrected.

'Rei-Hai,' Amika insisted, struggling to keep her indignation at bay. 'He's a *person*, damn you! Like me.'

'You *yarltok*,' he sneered.

Now that was a word Amika recognised. And it sent fire roaring through her veins. 'I'm not a slave, you witch-fucking—'

Something hard bounced off her chest and into her lap. Amika glanced down to find a heel of bread, so dry it felt like a porous scrubbing stone from a bath house. She turned it over in her hands.

'You eat,' the woman said. 'Walk lots.'

'I suppose you can't have your merchandise collapsing before you get a good price,' Amika muttered bitterly under her breath. She took a bite, all but chipping a tooth on the crusty loaf. 'You could at least tell me your name.'

The Qhoraakese slave traders exchanged a glance before the woman spoke, her lip curled back in a snarl. 'You not worth our names, *yarltok.*'

Khe'torla stirred beneath Amika's skin, but she breathed deeply to calm it. Her strength had returned in the presence of a fresh source—the crackling fire—but now was not the time. These slavers didn't mean her harm. Not yet, anyway. And with Rei unconscious and on the verge of turning, she would die in the Waste without a guide.

They would have to march her to a city to be sold—Xant, if she were lucky. There, she could get her bearings. Formulate a proper plan. The Sickness would take her before she allowed herself to become a slave, or saw Rei sent back to a farm to be bred like livestock.

She would make them burn before that happened.

She just had to bide her time.

15

KIOKHAREN

Emanais had gone to ground. After several laps around the sparse complex and broken conversations in Meytaran with her misfit army, Kio learnt that these words were, in fact, quite literal. She had taken off in a rage following confirmation of her sister's disappearance and Kio had lost sight of her in the confusion. The small child had also vanished.

From what he had deciphered from the fractured exchanges, the majority of Qhoraakese dwellings were underground to protect them from the harsh sun and dry, windswept wasteland. These caves and tunnels beneath the earth also offered security. With few visible structures topside, the camp looked little more than a ruined, abandoned outpost—a perfect hideout for an army of rebels.

Kio descended the steps carved into the stone that led him down the dugout where Emanais was said to be holed up. The underground complex was strange, and not just because of its red earthen walls and lack of windows or natural light; it was the rooms spanning off the central passage, hidden behind barred doors, each identical with a raised iron slab for a bed. It was the old stench of blood long since drunk dry by the parched earth. No matter how you looked at it, this place was a prison.

And Emanais had chosen it for solace.

At the end of the dark tunnel, one of the doors was ajar, a warm glow emanating from within. Kio peered around the doorway to find this chamber furnished with homely fittings: a straw mattress and blankets on the iron pallet; a fur rug on the floor; a number of trinkets and what Kio assumed to be sentimental items displayed in the niche shelves carved into the stone walls.

Emanais sat on the bed, knees pulled to her chin with a pillow pressed tight against her chest. The child played on the floor in the corner, hands busy with a block of grey wood carved into the shape of a horse.

Kio knocked on the door to announce his presence, a cold, hollow *ding* echoing around the room. Despite it already being open, he lingered on the threshold, waiting for her to bid him enter. He felt oddly unprepared to comfort her; his hands and pockets were empty of wine or flask, and the distress on her face told him words alone would soothe nothing.

'Can I come in?' Kio prompted after a moment without acknowledgement.

The Boatkeep looked up at him, hazel eyes rimmed red. Her locs fell limply about her shoulders, as hopeless and dejected as she looked. The nod she gave was barely visible, but Kio took the slight movement as permission and stepped into the room.

He took a seat at the end of the bed, profile turned to Emanais as he observed the little boy. He must have been three, maybe four—slightly older than Kio's own son, had he lived. He reached out to pat the child's shock of red hair, bright against the milkiness of his skin. The boy looked up at Kio, smile reaching his pale brown eyes as he proffered the wooden horse.

'Ah, what a fine stallion you have there,' Kio said, taking the toy. He turned it over in his hands, inspecting it with an exaggerated scowl as if he were a peddler. 'Very fine indeed. I'll give you two bronze for it.'

The little boy shared a wider grin and reached for the horse. Kio placed it in his hands and patted his soft red hair, pretending for a moment that he could still see through his blurred vision as hot tears filled his eyes.

'Sylar,' Emanais said, voice sandpaper-rough.

Kio sniffed and blinked away his grief, turning to the woman huddled on the bed.

'His name is Sylar. My nephew. If we don't get her back, then I'm all he has. They took her, Kio. When she was out scouting our next target. The witch-fuckers took—'

Her words drowned in a flood of choking sobs. She dropped her face into her war-calloused hands and wept like a child. All the while the boy watched on in silence, pale eyes wide.

Kio scooted up the bed and pulled Emanais into a tight embrace. A part of him expected her to baulk at his comfort, to shove him off as if he were a lover whose appeal had gone cold. But she didn't. She fell into his chest, fists grabbing handfuls of his rough linen shirt. Kio leant his cheek atop her head and rubbed soothing circles across her back.

'We'll get her back,' he said, confident even as uncertainty gripped his heart. 'I promise. We'll bring her home again. You just have to stay strong.'

Kio had gleaned enough from campsite chatter on the road to piece together the horror of the Siephymn farms. If that was where Yeni had been taken again, it was little wonder Emanais was so distraught. So few survived their first imprisonment. Was there any hope for a second escape?

Not wanting to share his doubts, he remained silent until Emanais calmed. Eventually she pulled away from him and wiped her eyes with the balls of her hands.

'You're right,' she said. 'I will be strong—strong like her. This was her room, you know.'

'I figured as much,' Kio said, following her eyesight as she surveyed the meagre attempts at decoration.

'No, I mean this was her *room*. Back when it was a farm. This is where she was kept.'

Kio's gut hardened, his blood flowing cold. *But why?* he wanted to shout. How could anyone choose to live in a place of such torture? He thought of the Cirahk dungeons. Of the cold and the damp and the shit and the blood and the bone—

He swallowed and drew a deep breath. No. He could not return there. Not even in his mind.

'She *is* strong,' he mumbled, though the word felt inadequate.

Emanais nodded. 'She didn't want the experience to own her, so she decided to own *it*. That's why we took this place as our base. To draw strength from the suffering of those we liberated—and rage from those we didn't.'

Kio's eyes continued to wander around the room, pausing at a splash of spilt ink on the floor by his feet. *Not ink*, he remembered sickly—*Siephymn blood*.

'I couldn't do it,' he said, a chill prickling his skin.

'You're not alone there,' Emanais agreed, setting a hand on his forearm. 'There are tents for those of us who prefer to bed down above ground. Mostly those whose loved ones did not survive, but not all. Some come down here to be close to what they lost. We all grieve in our own way.'

Kio considered the alternative, but then remembered it might mean sleeping alone. If the nightmares were to come in a place like this ...

'Dhenka prefers it,' she said, as if reading his thoughts. 'Can't stand the stale air.'

'How do you stand it? Not just the air, I mean. How do you—'

'It gave Yeni strength, which in turn gives *me* strength. And Hirathi knows I need that now.'

Emanais looked down at Sylar, who had wandered up beside the bed to cling onto her leg. She ran her fingers through the boy's hair with all the warmth and affection of a mother. He smiled softly, but did not make a sound; in fact, Kio realised, he never had.

'I don't think they knew Yeni was pregnant when we took the farm,' Emanais said, still gazing upon the boy. 'Witch-fucking cowards, the lot of them. We broke into the cells only to find the captors lying dead beside their prisoners—many of the women slashed through their swollen bellies.'

Kio's jaw cracked as he clenched it tight. The blood on the floor ...

Blood on the sheets. On the floor. On his hands. Moyna's blood—

'Sylar can never fall into the Allchief's hands,' she said gravely, turning her hazel gaze towards Kio and bringing him back to the present. 'He can never have what he wants. Whether that's Sylar or any other child bred from those awful farms.'

Shaking his head to rid it of the unwanted memories, Kio looked at the boy, and then to Emanais. He'd promised to help her in exchange for his freedom; now, he would help her because he *wanted* to.

'I gave you my word,' he said, putting as much steel in his voice as he could muster. 'Use me however you need.'

There was silence as Emanais let the reality of his pledge sink in. 'I may need you to kill,' she said at last. The words were flat, emotionless.

Kio's hands curled into fists as he let out a long, steadying breath. 'Then I'll kill.'

Kio couldn't return to the tunnels. Instead he slept in one of the many tents that were erected at nightfall, only to be packed away at dawn to help the camp seem uninhabited should the Allchief send demonspawn scouts from the air. Kio hadn't really understood what was meant by that, but he did not ask questions. Every answer he got only horrified him more. Ignorance truly was bliss, it seemed.

Emanais had stayed below ground, leaving Kio to share the tent with Dhenka alone. On the third morning since their arrival at camp, Dhenka returned to the tent from a meeting with Emanais, his arms laded with a washbasin, looking glass and razor. Kio sat up sleepily, rubbing at his heavy eyes as he pushed back the blankets. He hadn't slept well since arriving here; even though he had Dhenka for company, the truth of the tunnels beneath his feet left him uneasy and anchored to memories he'd been trying to forget.

'Ema has a job for you,' Dhenka said, placing the tray of washing supplies at the end of the bed pallet.

'... and it requires that I shave?' Kio asked slowly.

'It requires—and these are *her* words—"Someone who commands fear and respect, not someone who looks like an *ekrogam*".'

'A what?'

'A, um ...' Dhenka's slender hands turned as he thought. 'Street tramp.'

Kio snorted. He'd gotten so used to the grot and the grime that he hadn't even realised he'd not washed since they'd left Convict Cove near ten days ago. The thought of it made his skin crawl now, his scalp itching uncontrollably.

Suddenly eager, he pulled off his shirt and scampered towards the steaming basin. He paused as he caught a glimpse of his reflection in the looking glass, his thick dark hair askew, having escaped from the cord he'd used to tie it back.

'Deities dead,' he muttered, submerging the towel under the hot water. He pressed it to his face, almost moaning as the steam soaked into his pores. When he wiped away the grime and opened his eyes, he saw Dhenka still standing at the entrance of the tent, a strange half-smirk on his lips.

'What?' Kio asked, eyebrow raised warily.

'I wonder if the Little Prince knows how to shave?' His smirk grew into a wide grin and Kio was as irritated as he was charmed.

'Of course I know how to—' he stopped abruptly, knowing the lie would soon unravel if he left the tent covered in nicks and blood. He picked up the razor and held it out to Dhenka handle-first. 'Would you?'

The young man stepped forward, took the razor and knelt behind Kio on the mattress, still smiling as though he'd gotten what he wanted after all. Wordlessly, and with the finesse of a trained barber, Dhenka lathered the soap into a foam across Kio's cheek and throat and guided his head back to rest against his shoulder. Despite Kio once having had a similar ritual performed every other day, he found it a strange and vulnerable thing to have a man hold a blade to his throat.

'I have five brothers,' Dhenka said in that deep, smooth voice of his, as if he'd sensed Kio's unease. 'I am the youngest.'

The blade slid along his jaw like boots on ice. Dhenka's fingertips were soft, warm, and Kio felt his skin come alive beneath the touch. Heat prickled down his neck, down his back, and his eyes fluttered closed as he listened to the melodious drawl of Dhenka's voice.

'And once I was old enough to hold the razor,' he continued, 'it was my job to keep us well groomed. A custom in my family. Closely shaven face. Closely shaven head.' Dhenka brought his lips close to Kio's ear. 'And closely shaven balls, too.'

Kio burst into laughter. He couldn't help himself—even with the threat of an exposed blade at his throat. Gods, how long had it been since he'd *laughed*? He twisted around to Dhenka and saw that the other man's impish grin had sharpened to a sultry edge.

One breath was all it took for their lips to be joined. They were hungry for each other—restraint, caution and fear forgotten after a single, lingering touch. Kio had Dhenka below him on the bed, eager in a way he had not been for months and thought he never would be again. Dhenka's roaming hands were inside his shirt, wandering the plains of his back and belly until his fingers found the laces of Kio's pants.

Kio's chest tightened and he froze. Throat closing, he struggled to breathe—and not because Dhenka's skilled hands left him breathless. The terror was returning. Racing down his spine like a cold chill, it squeezed his heart, his lungs, his neck.

He pushed off Dhenka, turning away, hand to his chest as he tried to reclaim his breathing. With time and space, his pulse began to slow, all while the other man sat silent and forgotten on the bed. He opened his mouth to apologise, but no words came. His tongue throbbed with a thirst for wine; he glanced around the tent, but saw naught but the toppled carafe he'd drained the night before.

Sickness take me, Kio groaned inwardly. Was this his life now? Cursed to never touch or be touched again? He would have thrown himself overboard had he known. Better to drown in the depths than die of a thirst he couldn't quench.

'Let me finish for you,' Dhenka said, reaching for the razor Kio realised he now clasped in his own hand. He stared at it for a moment, unsure of how it got there or what it meant. He loosened his grip and Dhenka slipped it free, drawing no further attention to the moment.

They didn't speak for the hour Dhenka spent on finishing his grooming. Kio was numb and no longer registered the scrape of the blade up his throat, or even the warmth of the other man's hands upon his neck.

Dhenka gave him a nudge to wake him from the strange trance he had slipped into and held the clouded looking glass to his face. 'Not bad, no?'

Kio took the glass and ran a hand along his now-smooth jaw. Dhenka had done a good job—not a nick in sight. His hair had been trimmed significantly, and was similar to, if not tidier than, how he used to wear it back in Adria. Kio ran his hand through the thick black waves, pushing them back off his face.

'Thank you,' he said, handing the looking glass back to Dhenka. 'I feel better.'

Well, I look *better, at least.*

Dhenka smiled his infectious grin. 'Wonderful. We'd best not keep Ema waiting. She is in a mood.'

Kio was about to grumble that she was *always* in a mood, but Dhenka was already up and on his way out of the tent. Reaching for his shirt, Kio quickly followed, squinting as the bright sun of the day assaulted his sleep-deprived eyes. The slight breeze felt extra chill against his now-naked face, but even though winter had well and truly fallen, Emanais's rebels sweated under the red sky, shirtless and glistening as they went about their training drills.

The Boatkeep stood on a steel shipping crate at the head of a squadron, shouting commands in Qhoraakese as the soldiers twirled and thrusted their wooden spears with rhythmic precision.

'Ah!' Emanais called in delight when she spotted Kio and Dhenka across the crowd. She hopped down from her box and ran towards them, beaming. 'Look at you!' she cooed, stretching up to tousle Kio's freshly cut hair. 'And to think we thought you handsome before! Now you look every bit the prince you claim to be.'

'I *am* a prince,' Kio grunted, swatting her away like a fly. 'Maybe not here. Maybe not now. But it's still who I am, Emanais.'

'Well, whatever, Your Highness. Unless you can use your princely charm to whip some discipline into these bastards, I care not who wears your crown.' She gestured flippantly towards the group of rebels, who had ceased their drills once Emanais's back was turned. '*Kaeya magh*!' she swore, shouting at them before turning back to Kio. 'Useless lazy witch-fuckers. No skills. No talent. This is why I need a strong trainer.'

Kio snorted incredulously. 'What exactly do you want me to do?' These men didn't respect him. He could shout until his lungs burst and they'd not raise a finger. 'I'd be of more use if you gave me that.' He pointed to the firearm slung over Emanais's back.

'Absolutely not,' she said, clinging to the weapon possessively. 'You'll get frustrated with them and shoot someone.'

'Like you've never done that before?'

'*Exactly.* No. No guns. Earn their respect another way.'

Kio looked beyond Emanais to the rabble. Many had dropped their spears or leant against them like canes as they gossiped and guffawed while their commander was distracted. If old Geraad Shaw had seen his recruits doing that between lessons, he would have—

Clenching his fists, Kio strode towards the group. 'Ylan!' he called, certain the Bararnite thief was among them. Sure enough, he spotted him at the heart of the dissent, snickering at Kio's approach.

The prince plucked a spear from the slack hand of a rebel and brought it down on Ylan's head so swiftly the man barely had time to defend himself. The crowd dispersed at the sudden attack, leaving them with ample room to swing their weapons.

'I don't believe your training is over,' Kio said. He raised the spear again, ready for another offensive.

'I don't believe I give a shit, you pompous little prat,' Ylan mocked. 'Piss off back to yer tent, boy. The men are talking here.'

Kio aimed a weak thrust at Ylan's chest, who parried out of instinct rather than skill. His own muscles were out of practice, but the sloppiness of the Bararnite's movement caused his confidence to swell. He teased again, batting clumsily at the wooden shaft to bait Ylan into an attack. The other man sneered wickedly before unleashing what he expected to be a disarming lunge; Kio pirouetted aside.

An impressed murmur rumbled around the crowd as their dance gained momentum, dust bursting from beneath their feet. Ylan was every bit the undisciplined brawler Kio expected. His ill-timed thrusts were followed by attempts to kick or knee his groin; any parry he managed was little more than dumb luck. Ylan's temper rose with every missed strike, every powerful lunge Kio glided away from. A smile broke his lips as he taunted the man—an arrogant gesture that would have earnt him a clip around the head from Geraad.

But he didn't care. It felt *good* to be in control again. It felt like being himself—like being *free*.

He upended Ylan with a sweeping kick to the ankle. The Bararnite fell on his arse in the red dirt to the sound of mock applause. Kio stood over him, feet planted either side of the stocky man's wide ribcage. He thrust the rusted speartip into the earth, so close to Ylan's head it almost shaved the whiskers from his cheek.

'Next time I tell you to train, you fucking do it,' Kio growled. 'Understand?'

Ylan sneered. He clamped his arms down against his flank, trapping Kio's ankles, then sat up sharply, knocking the prince off balance. They wrestled around in the earth, dust and fists flying as they both struggled to find purchase. Shielding his face with his forearms, Kio waited for a pause in Ylan's volley. He seized the brief moment of hesitation in the other man's blows and flipped Ylan beneath him in the dirt.

A cheer went up from the crowd. Kio slammed his fist into Ylan's unprotected face, again and again and again. Skin split on his knuckles, but still he kept punching, feeling bone crunch with every strike—

Thunder cracked through the camp.

Kio cowered. He turned to see Emanais in his shadow, pistol raised to the sky, smoke billowing from the barrel.

'That is enough,' she hissed. 'Let him up.'

The crowd that had encircled the brawl backed away, silent and slow, as she stalked towards Kio, offering him a hand. He took it, fists slick and bloody, and clambered off Ylan's groaning form. Kio glanced down at the mess of the Bararnite's face. His nose was surely broken. Cheek and eye socket too. But he was still conscious. Somehow. Kio's hands started to shake.

'Get him out of here,' Emanais said, gesturing at two shirtless recruits. 'Clean him up. And let this be a lesson to you. This man speaks and you listen. Understand?'

A fractured, noncommittal chorus of 'Aye' mumbled from the crowd.

'Understand?' Emanais screamed, and the response came in unison.

As they dispersed, returning their training spears to a barrel and helping Ylan down to the tunnels, the Boatkeep turned to regard Kio, her expression unreadable. 'Feel better?'

Yes, he wanted to say, but instead remained silent. Kio looked down at his hands, at his trembling blood-smeared fingers. He should have been disgusted, but he wasn't. He felt strong—stronger than he'd felt in years.

'Try not to make a habit of it,' Emanais said, clapping a hand on his shoulder. 'Soldiers are in short supply, and I can't afford to have them all—'

A slow, droning horn sounded from the watchtower by the compound's gate. Emanais turned towards the noise, hope rather than panic painting her features. She'd sent a dozen or more scouts out to search for Yeni—more than they'd had to spare, she'd confessed to Kio. This must be the first to return.

Kio followed as she raced towards the gates, gesturing wildly for the guards to pull them open.

'Stop prodding that thing in my fucking back—I'm not going to run,' a woman's voice barked in Meytaran. Kio's ears pricked at the Holanian lilt to the words.

The scouting party rounded the corner of the mudbrick walls, herding their grubby female captive through the opened gates. She was taller than the Qhoraakese woman who shoved her inside, her chestnut hair cropped in a bob at her shoulders like a commoner, but she had the most piercing blue eyes Kio had ever—

His heart stopped. Actually *fucking* stopped. The whole world stood still as recognition warmed his entire body the second their gazes met across the camp.

'Amika!'

Kio raced across the compound, knocking Emanais from his path. He took his sister in an embrace so strong it knocked them both off their feet and into the dirt. He clung to her like life itself, burying his face in her neck.

'Deities dead, it's really you,' he sobbed. 'Oh, *fuck*, Amika. It's really you.'

Kio could feel his sister's tears on his cheek, her own sobbing breaths. He sat back on his heels to give her space, his bloodied hands clamped either side of her face to admire the sight of her.

'K-Kio ...' she sobbed, tears falling harder. She glanced back over her shoulder at the rebels who'd brought her in. Kio followed her eyeline, heart filling his throat.

There, slung limply over the scout's shoulder like a hunter's fresh kill, was Rei-Hai Shaw.

16

KRIAH

Nell's plan was to follow the coastal road south towards Cirahk. Faster than the merchant highway, he insisted, though the trail was known to be rough. The horses he had bought using the coin his parents kept stashed in an old urn for emergencies were solid, healthy creatures and handled the poor terrain well. Kriah rode his mount—an ashen mare named Star—like there was a beast at their backs, slowed only by Nell struggling to control his own.

'She ... just ... won't listen ... to me,' Nell panted after they dismounted for their midday meal and brief rest. He wiped the glistening sweat from the mare's flank, muscles rippling under her short chestnut coat. Maiden, she was called, named for her mild temperament—or so the man had told them when they bought her. 'Nothin' sweet 'n' demure 'bout the thing,' Nell grunted, pulling his rations from the saddle bags—dried fish and strips of kelp.

Kriah unpacked too and was sitting on one of the many boulders dotting the landscape by the time Nell had finished tending to his horse. 'She knows you're scared of her,' he said, mouth full of food. 'Horses are clever like that.'

'I'm a sailor,' Nell said gruffly, sweeping his pale hair from his eyes as he turned towards the stretch of ocean on the horizon. 'Don't do so well travellin' by land.'

Kriah followed the boatswain's wistful gaze. The coastal road they followed was perched atop sheer, high sea cliffs, making the ocean feel further away than it actually was. He too felt out of his element. Having grown up in the depths of the Li'Nea Wood, surrounded by thick forest rich with *khe'torla*, he found this treeless, stony landscape every bit as barren as a wasteland. And with the bloody, battered Tear stretching further across the sky ...

Surely Azet'haal must struggle here. Cut off from the forests of Kherunis, with the Tear sucking *khe'torla* into its void. Could that be their advantage over him? He certainly didn't seem to be suffering. Kriah recalled Azet'haal's gaze piercing through that eerie, featureless mask and shivered.

'Kriah?' Nell said, voice raised slightly.

Kriah blinked, dazed as if waking from a dreamscape. Had Nell been talking this whole time. 'S-sorry?'

'Is there any hope fer me sister?' he asked. 'And all the others enthralled in Gerrick Port?'

It was the first time Nell had mentioned Vynalla since they'd left her and his home behind days ago. Truthfully, Kriah had been suspicious about how quickly Nell had wanted to leave, how accepting he had been of all Kriah had shared with him through that impromptu dreamscape. A Second Born should have cowered, should have cursed the magic and he who used it. But Nell ...

Kriah chewed thoughtfully on his strip of dried fish, watching the one-eyed boatswain tighten the leather laces on his boots. 'I don't know,' he admitted softly. 'In fact, there's very little that I *do* know. That's why I'm so shocked you believed me.'

Nell looked up from his boots and out at the vast sea so far below them. The wind blowing off the ocean was icy, but he didn't seem bothered by its touch, even as Kriah's skin prickled beneath the thick wool cloak borrowed from the Ylesses' old wares.

'I know that,' Nell said. 'And that's *why* I believe yer.'

Kriah raised an eyebrow.

'More than just yer memories passed between us when yer ... did what'ver yer did.' The boatswain knocked a fist against his chest, his face turning solemn. 'I felt it. Everythin'. Yer pain. Yer grief. Yer love.'

Kriah shifted uncomfortably on his rock.

'My head tells me to be mad,' he continued. 'Yer messed with our minds. Slept with me sister. But now I can't even *feel* how I want to feel because yer guilt and yer justification and yer desire to fix everythin' pushes my thoughts aside. I can't grieve me da because I grieve yer grand-pap, even though he was the one who took Da from me.'

Nell closed his eyes and took a deep breath. The tightness in Kriah's gut grew painful. He felt exposed—violated—but mostly horrified. He'd manipulated Nell, robbed him of his chance to respond however he needed to respond to such overwhelming loss.

He was no different to Greist'hal.

'I'm ... sorry...' His words were pathetic. *He* was pathetic.

'Aye, I know,' Nell said simply. 'Same as I know yer *not* sorry. Not really. Not for what yer did, only the damage yer caused doin' it.'

Nell's words were sharp, but he spoke without emotion, without venom. It was just a list of indisputable facts; Kriah could do nothing but nod in agreement like a berated child who knew he was wrong.

'I was yer *friend*, Kriah. I would have listened. Maybe not at first, but in me own time, I would 'ave. Yer took that choice away from me.'

Was. It was the simple suggestion of the past that stung Kriah the most. His appetite left abruptly, the half-eaten strip of salt fish now discarded and crushed beneath his boot in the dirt.

'I'm sorry,' he muttered again, tears stinging hot in his eyes. He blinked them back.

'Kriah, I *know*,' Nell said, voice a little firmer. He reached out and clapped a hand over Kriah's forearm. 'I told yer already—I know everythin'. And that's why yer need to know how *I* feel. I don't hate yer. Even if I wanted to, I don't. I *can't*.'

'That ... doesn't make it sound any better.' Kriah's throat was tight, but he somehow managed to stem the tears.

'Maybe not.' Nell shrugged, stood, stretched out his back. 'But it is what it is. C'mon. The quicker we get to Cirahk, the quicker we can stop this thing from spreadin'.'

The ride to Cirahk was a hard trek, made all the more difficult under the weight of Kriah's heavy shame. Nell assured him that he bore no ill will; now that he had said his piece, he was content to accept the situation and move on.

But Kriah was not.

His thoughts spiralled like leaves caught in an updraft. Was Nell helping him because he wanted to? Or because Kriah had forced it upon him? It would forever play on his thoughts, undercutting every decision Nell made, every kind gesture of friendship.

Is it real or is it pity?

'There it is,' Nell announced, pulling on Maiden's reins to slow her pace. He pointed to the dark monolith breaking the horizon. 'Cirahk.'

Kriah's books described Ciraselo, the ruined capital of the once-prosperous Meytaran Empire, as the most magnificent city in all of Whyt'hallen, and even though Kriah had seen it well past its glory, it had still been an impressive sight. But this ... this made Ciraselo seem a speck no larger than Gerrick Port. Buildings spread as far as he could see, no longer encased by the city walls. They were all different heights and shapes, making the horizon as jagged as a row of broken teeth. Smoke billowed from chimneys; gulls swarmed over the coastal fringe above clusters of white sails; and a huge dark castle rose in the centre of it all, spires like speartips piercing a hazy, blood-red sky.

'We'll head straight fer the docks,' Nell said. 'Quickest way to pick up a rumour—or start another. Whisper Kohle Mak's false salvation into a few deckhands' ears ... Suddenly the whole city will know.'

'Do we have enough coin to get through the gates?' Kriah asked, recalling how Amika had bought passage into Ciraselo. His own pockets were empty.

Nell cocked his head, confused, then chuckled to himself. 'No need to pass through any gates in Cirahk. 'Less yer want an audience with the prince!'

Kriah blanched at his foolishness. He could see now, as they drew closer, exactly how far the city spread beyond the imposing central walls circling the castle. The buildings were carved of brick and stone, with roofs of clay tiles, far sturdier and more opulent than the thatched-roof shacks of the Port. Most were taller too, some standing two, three levels above the rest. But despite the densely packed structures, the streets were empty, and a shroud of smoke hung heavily above the city.

Kriah's stomach dropped to his knees.

'It's here …' he breathed. He turned to Nell. 'I don't understand. I thought Nalla said the rider first brought news from the north?'

'She did,' Nell agreed soberly. 'Let's keep our distance. Enter the docks from the south, rather than cut through the city. Somethin' tells me it isn't safe.'

It was dusk by the time their detour brought them to the streets of Cirahk. They disembarked their horses at the city's edge, leading them towards the southern docks, where the buildings and smoke grew thick. Kriah had hoped to find his fears misplaced, that they would instead arrive to find festivities afoot, food carts heavy with roasting meats like he had seen in the markets of Ciraselo.

But that was not to be.

A mound of corpses piled high on the cobbled square opposite the docks smouldered like coals at the bottom of a day-old campfire. A man in a beaked mask with a cowl pulled low over his eyes hauled a wagon laden with more dead for the pyre.

Kriah followed Nell's lead and raised his scarf around his mouth and nose, like those without the birdlike masks already had. Many held pomanders to their faces, and although the herbs were useless, Kriah wished he had one to combat the stench of burnt, rotten meat.

'The Goddess has forsaken us,' an old man droned, sitting on an abandoned food cart and slowly ringing a brass bell, long white hair spilling down over his shoulders from beneath his hood. 'The Sickness has returned!'

Kriah made towards him, overcome with the need to shake sense into the destitute old fool. Nell grabbed his arm and held him back.

'Best not draw too much attention to ourselves,' the boatswain cautioned.

They left the square behind, turning away from the black water lapping at the abandoned docks to a tavern perched three streets back. It was a gloomy building, not full of light and liveliness like the public houses in Ciraselo. The walls of the lower level were built of an irregularly cut grey stone, the upper floors coated in a white wooden facade beneath a roof of dull brown shingles. A placard carved with the words *THE DRIPPING BUCKET* hung above the door.

'There's nowhere to keep our horses,' Kriah noted, unable to locate any pens or stalls to water and feed their mounts.

'Aye, this is a sailors' tavern for men to enjoy the comforts of land away from the ship fer a night or two,' Nell explained. 'Not too many of 'em have horses or any need for 'em.' He tightened Maiden's reins about a veranda post and gestured for Kriah to do the same. 'I'm sure they'll be fine here anyway.'

Kriah fixed Star alongside Maiden and gave her a gentle stroke down her muzzle before following Nell inside. The door creaked as it opened, and the face of every patron turned towards them before it even swung closed. They were greeted by air thick with smoke, but unlike the street outside, it was scented with tobacco and not flesh.

Nell coughed awkwardly at the attention and tightened the scarf around his face; Kriah did the same, realising now it had slipped slightly, exposing his face, much to the ire of the crowd. They were all covered in veils of thick fabric, slitted only at the eyes, which couldn't have made breathing very comfortable. Some donned the strange beaked masks like those he had seen outside at the pyre, and most wore pouches of herbs tight about their throats.

'What brings yer to The Dripping Bucket?' a veiled woman called from behind the bar, face covered but breasts prominently on display over the tight cinch of her corset.

Kriah fumbled with his words.

'After a table and bed fer the night,' Nell said, confident where Kriah had failed. 'Are we welcome?'

'Aye,' the woman said. 'Not in a position to be turnin' down coin, what with ships being banned from port and all. But I don't know who yer are or where yer came from, so you can sit up back in that booth. And I'll get back to yer about that room.' She pointed a long ringed finger at a secluded table in the back corner of the hazy tavern, away from the other patrons, few that there were.

They trudged through the layer of straw coating the hard dirt floor and slipped into the booth, which barely received any light from the dying candles of the low-slung chandelier in the centre of the room. Nell clamped the scarf tight over the bridge of his nose and leant in close across the table.

'I don't understand,' he said. 'The Sickness is so much worse here. How could it already have covered the whole east coast?'

Kriah didn't have an answer; instead he brooded in silence.

'Are you *sure* it's not coming from the Tear?' Nell pressed.

'It's not coming from the Tear,' Kriah confirmed, hoping his words came out more resolute than he felt. 'There was no evidence of it in Ciraselo when we left. The people feared it, but it was not there.'

'But the Tear wasn't *open* then.'

I broke the first seal in Kherunis, Kriah realised. Panic crept up his spine, freezing his limbs at each joint. Had he done this? Had he unleashed the plague?

'No,' he said. 'No. The Sickness appeared in Mey, long before the sky was torn. This is something else. This is ...'

It was Azet'haal's doing, he was sure of it. A means of tapping into the Second Born's generational fear so they'd embrace salvation wherever it appeared.

'Do you think he'll go after Amika?'

Kriah startled at the sound of her name on Nell's lips. It was so easy to forget he knew everything. Kriah's past. His thoughts.

His feelings.

Kriah rubbed his hands together, wishing he had a drink with which to distract himself. He tried not to think of her, yet she was *all* he thought about. Holania wasn't far from here, but he had no way of knowing if Amika was still there—or if she'd ever arrived.

'Do you think—'

Kriah's question was cut off as two mugs of flat ale slammed onto the table between them.

'Four silvers for a room,' the masked woman from the bar announced, wiping her wet hands on an already grubby apron. 'Another bronze each fer the drinks.'

'We didn't order these ...' Nell grumbled, rummaging in his jerkin for his coin purse nonetheless.

'Table fee,' the woman said. 'I wouldn't get too excited. Got more water in it than me nan's tea. Haven't seen no trade ships since the last Nirhana Moon. Don't ask what's in the bread if yer think sawdust will turn yer off yer meal.'

She took the coins from Nell and was turning away when Kriah spoke.

'Wait. There's been no trade ships? What about riders? Messengers from outside the capital? Is Holania like this?'

The woman spat a wad of saliva into the straw by her feet. 'Don't much care if it is. Good enough for 'em. First their hateful heir tries to kill Prince Reminas, then their bitch princess goes 'n' burns herself alive in their marriage bed, taking our liege with her.' She spat again. 'You ask me, this is their doing. Sickness take the bloody lot of 'em.'

The woman stomped off, hand clenched around the fistful of coins, before Kriah could question her further.

The cold fingernails down his spine gouged even deeper. His mind raced with hundreds of possibilities, all leading to *What if Amika is dead?*

He downed the watery ale. The bitter tang did nothing to quench his thirst, or alleviate any of the swelling dread. She had to be alive. None of this meant anything if she was—

'I know yer worried about yer girl,' Nell said softly, although his gaze was fixed across the tavern. His good eye followed something about the room, moving erratically, as though chasing a moth flitting around a flame. 'But we have to do somethin' for the people here. If Kohle Mak—Azet'haal—hasn't been here, then we still have a chance to stop 'em fallin' for his cure.'

'If he hasn't been here, why is the Sickness so strong?' Kriah muttered through a clenched jaw.

'Could other Meah-Hyren be spreadin' the curse? Whatever it is.'

Kriah straightened. The silver-haired man with the bell.

He wasn't old at all. He was—

'They could have infected the whole Bararnite coast by now,' Nell concluded grimly. It was his turn to down his drink, which he did while keeping his focus distinctly elsewhere. Kriah let the silence grow between them and thicken like cornstarch in a stew. He wanted to solve the problem in front of them, but his mind kept drifting to Amika and her rumoured murder-suicide.

She has to be alive.

Nell stood abruptly, the rickety table shuddering at the sudden disturbance. 'Let me investigate things here,' he said, gaze still preoccupied. 'Yer need to get some sleep. I know you haven't done so in days.'

With that he was off, shouldering past a roving waitress towards a Qhoraakese woman disappearing into a back room. Kriah blinked to test his eyes, then saw Nell exit through the very same door.

'I had a girl once,' Nell had said back on *Amikharlia's Tears*, before Greist'hal's magic ruined Captain Yless's mind. When Nell still thought of him as an orphan called Kry, a simple nomad's boy seeking honest work and purpose. Kriah still sought that, even if Nell would never see it in him now.

I'd run away from me the first chance I got too, he thought bitterly, taking one last hopeless swig at his empty mug before asking for the key to a room upstairs.

It looked like a brothel. At least, it looked like what Kriah *imagined* a pleasure house would look like, having never stepped foot inside one himself. There were far too many pillows on the bed, although none of them looked overly inviting. The large bed had posts at each corner, but no canopy as he supposed more opulent chambers did, and there was additional seating—a faded chaise longue, a patched footstool—dotted about the ambiently lit room. A three-stemmed candelabra was set on a writing table against the wall, deliberately placed to create a more intimate mood, or perhaps out of caution of wayward limbs.

It was luxurious in a derelict, unclean sort of way. The sort of luxury a sailor long at sea was like to love as vigorously as the girl he tumbled into bed with. But Kriah found no comfort in it. It was much too large and far too empty to be in any way inviting. Not like the cosy intimacy of the Yless shack or even Ka'ella's rundown place in Ciraselo; they had been homes—not temporary places to board, but lived-in, comfortable places. Nothing he would likely experience again.

Kriah discarded his pack at the foot of the bed and flopped heavily on the mattress to remove his boots. He was tired down to his bones, and had been nursing a dull, throbbing headache for hours. It had been at least ten days now since he'd last slept or dreamscaped, and he certainly seemed to be pushing the limit of what was sustainable.

He reclined on the bed ... and was out before his head hit the pillow.

Kriah did not dream. Unlike his conjured dreamscape—a white expanse he could alter at will—mortal sleep was a cavernous black void, silent and consuming. But tonight, there was a force. A whisper. A gentle scratch in the wall by his head.

'—alf—d.'

'—lfblo—'

'—lood.'

'Halfblood.'

Kriah sat up, opened his eyes. His heart hammered in his chest. He was in the room where he'd gone to sleep, but a fire crackled in the hearth that had not been there in the waking world. A robed figure watched the flames. Kriah swallowed hard. The figure turned.

'Ah, there you are.' The words resonated from behind a featureless mask, lips unmoving and eyes solid.

Azet'haal.

Kriah's hands tightened to fists. 'How did you get inside my dreamscape?' he growled.

'Dreamscape?' Azet'haal chuckled, low and menacing. 'This isn't your dreamscape, you silly little halfblood. You *are* asleep. Quite the vulnerability you have there.'

Kriah glanced around the room, looking for other abnormalities that would confirm Azet'haal's claim. Aside from the fire, everything looked as he had left it. He was still in the bed where he had collapsed, wearing the same stained clothes ... but when he looked down he saw another set of hands, solid where his were incorporeal, protruding grotesquely from his wrist. He twisted to get a look behind him and saw his own sleeping form immobile on the bed.

Turning back to Azet'haal, he demanded, 'How have you done this?' His voice lacked the sharp edge he'd hoped for.

'It was a foolish thing you did,' Azet'haal cooed, 'opening yourself up to that boy. Made it very easy for others to slide right in.' He clasped his hands behind his back and took slow, confident steps towards the bed. 'I know everything he does now. I know that Nirhana's Chosen has gone to Adria to find the key, and I know that you fear her dead. One less thing I have to worry about, now that I'm tied up here, puppeteering the people of Bararn.'

Azet'haal raised a hand to inspect his fingernails for dirt. 'Of course, I can only pillage your little mind when your defences are down. Which they are'—Kriah *felt* the smile form behind the mask—'when you sleep.'

A cold breath whispered across Kriah's skin as he glanced down at the unconscious body beneath him. He couldn't stay awake forever. Couldn't stop Azet'haal entering his mind. He had to make this connection worth it.

'How did you bring back the Sickness?' he demanded.

Azet'haal scoffed. 'What does it matter? Your filthy diluted blood will never command the *khe'torla* necessary to stop me. Not now that your grandfather has given me the power and knowledge to rival Miatha herself. And that is what I am to these creatures now—a *god*.'

Kriah swallowed the wave of grief swelling up his throat. He felt the *khe'torla* in the room swirl at the mention of Greist'hal. Was he here, somehow? With Azet'haal? His *khe'torla* had been absorbed by the other Meah-Hyren when he died. Could he ...?

He searched for any semblance of his grandfather, any piece of Greist'hal he could reach out and touch for support. There was the faintest of sparks—an ember. Kriah stretched towards it with his *khe'torla*.

A flash of light blinded his vision. Images cycled rapidly through his mind: Kherunis and *kha'nini* fruit. Puffs of pollen and dark storm clouds. A robed figure walking through a sea of flowers, which turned black and wilted as he passed. People coughing. Blood, blood, *blood*—

They stopped abruptly and Kriah was back in the room, Azet'haal standing over him.

'You created it ...' Kriah breathed, piecing together the visions that had bled into his mind. 'You created it and now you're healing—'

'They will submit to me or die!' Azet'haal screamed. 'I am their god now!'

Kriah sprang from the bed, hands splayed outward like a pouncing cat. He fell through Azet'haal's form and hit the floor behind him.

The jolt shocked him awake. He sat upright in bed, breathing hard, sweat coating his body. The room was empty, the fireplace and Azet'haal gone.

He rubbed his hands down his face, fingers caressing the depressions of his eyes, which continued to sting with lack of sleep. He looked out the window at the moonless night outside, still tinged faintly crimson from the Tear in the sky, and wondered what the fuck he was supposed to do now.

17

AMIKHARLIA

Amika was in chains.

Moments after her reunion with Kio, she'd been clamped in irons and led to an underground bunker, where she had been left to wait alone. The room smelt like old blood. Like earth and rust and grease from recently oiled hinges. She sat on what she assumed was a bed, though nothing about it suggested it'd been designed for rest.

Closing her eyes, Amika breathed deeply, searching for *khe'torla*'s pulse—for anything she could tug to leverage herself free. But the land here was silent. Cold.

Dead.

The door creaked as it opened, despite its recent maintenance, and Amika turned towards the sound. The woman who had ordered her imprisonment entered, walking like she was ten feet tall; Kio followed in her shadow, slinking into the room like a downbeat hound. Amika baulked at the image.

Oh, my brother ... What happened to you?

Kio closed the door and stood by the entryway, arms folded. Wordlessly, Amika passed her gaze back to the woman.

'The Little Prince tells me you're his sis—'

'I *am*—'

The woman raised a hand sharply. 'You will not interrupt me.'

Amika bit back her words. Not out of obedience but self-control; saying something impulsive would serve neither her nor Kio any favours.

'He also tells me you have been missing almost five years. That no one knows where you've been, what you've been doing. And yet, here you are, battling a Siephymn mere moons after *my* sister—'

'Emanais, you can't think—'

'Shut up, Kio,' the woman, Emanais, growled, her gaze never leaving Amika's face. 'Zhayar told me that you were trying to kill that Siephymn boy. That you speak in our tongue.'

Amika felt her brother's gaze shift, saw the doubt and confusion in his eyes. 'I promised him I would.' She directed her words at Kio, not Emanais. 'It's what he wanted.'

Her brother looked away, fighting tears.

'And what do you know of a Siephymn's wants? You, a missing princess from the Middle Kingdoms, who shouldn't know a demon-spawn from a feral dog!'

'Because that's what I've been doing for the last five years.' It was a struggle to keep her tone even and not succumb to her emotions like Emanais, whose accusations dripped with barely contained contempt. 'Hunting demonspawn. Selling their pelts to pay for my board in a Qhoraakese tavern in Ciraselo. *That* is why I speak your tongue. *That* is why I know a Siephymn would rather die than devolve.'

Emanais's hard facade showed no sign of cracking. Kio kept his gaze averted and Amika could tell from the taut muscles of his cheeks that his jaw was fiercely clenched. She wanted time alone with him, to explain herself—to apologise—but she couldn't do that while she was in chains.

'What is your connection to the Allchief?' Emanais demanded out of the silence.

'I have no connection!'

'Then why are you here?'

'*Enough!*' The sound of Kio's fist colliding with the steel of the door echoed around the small earthen bunker. 'Emanais, this is my *sister*. I will not have you interrogate her like a criminal.'

He snatched the keys from the loop of her belt and knelt before Amika to loosen the manacles. The irons dropped free and she instinctively rubbed the reddened skin, though she had not been imprisoned long. She looked up at her brother to thank him, but found no warmth in his features.

'What are you doing here, Amika?' he rumbled. 'Why now? And why ... with *him?* He works for Reminas!'

'Reminas is dead,' she said coolly.

A shiver broke out across her skin as she spoke those words. She hadn't thought about him since that night. Since she'd burned through his throat and left him wheezing for air—before Rei had burst through the window and slashed his face to ribbons. Nausea rolled through her belly as the sight, the *smell*, came crawling back. She swallowed the memories down so she could speak.

'We were in Ciraselo when we heard what had happened to Adria. To you. To Moth—' Amika clipped the word to stop a sob. 'Rei insisted we go home to help. To set things right.'

'He works for the Tower, Amika.'

Amika shook her head vehemently. 'Not anymore. I watched them try to kill him, Kio. In Ciraselo, and then in the tunnels on our way here. He's not with them. He's loyal to us. Loyal to *you.*'

Kio rubbed his hands down his face. 'But Reminas—'

'Reminas lied, Kio. He's always lied. He lied to me, saying he'd release you if I married him. Look how that turned out.' Amika flicked her gaze to Emanais, whose turn it was to stand wordlessly, arms folded. 'And *that* is why we're here.'

Emanais gave a dissatisfied sneer, but raised no protests. Kio slumped on the iron cot beside Amika, head falling into his hands. This brief conversation had barely touched the surface of all that needed to be discussed. There was five years of damage between them. But something told Amika the greatest pain had been inflicted far more recently than that.

'Kio ...' she began, placing a delicate hand on his shoulder.

Before he could shrug her off, footsteps sounded, rushing down the hall outside the room. A hollow knock announced the visitor's presence.

'What is it?' Emanais barked, almost tearing the door from its hinges.

The man, who Amika recognised from the scout party that brought her in, looked from Amika to Kio, before setting eyes back on his commander. 'The Siephymn they brought ... He's ....'

Kio was on his feet, bursting out the door before the scout even finished speaking. Amika made to follow, but Emanais intercepted, challenging her with a glare.

'He's my friend,' Amika insisted, palms open before her. 'I just want to know he's alright.'

The hard woman relented and allowed Amika to pass through the door before her. *She means to make sure I don't run,* Amika realised as she was pinned between Emanais and her scout.

Outside the room, Kio hadn't gotten far; he deliberated at an intersection in the labyrinthine corridors, fingers rubbing at his knuckles anxiously. How anyone found their way around here was a mystery to Amika. She had been led through so many twists and turns on her way to the holding chamber that she could no longer tell which way was north, or where they had entered this peculiar underground complex.

From above, the enclosed facility had looked more like a training ground for soldiers to practise their formation drills. There was little in the way of buildings, save for the mounds of dirt that served as entry to the base below. It was cooler down here, that was certain—a welcome relief from the stifling Qhoraakese heat that persisted despite the winter; Amika hoped it retained warmth at night, too.

Following the lead of Emanais and her scout, Kio walked at a brisk pace. Amika struggled to keep up, fatigue finally catching up with her now she had sat for a few hours. Despite being given a share of rations when she was captured, she and Rei had been travelling close to two months now, and had spent the recent weeks half-starved and half-parched.

After rounding a final corner, the guard stopped before another nondescript steel door. Unlike the other corridors that were lined with row after row of cells, this was the only chamber in this particular stretch of red rock wall. As they lingered outside, the man spoke to Emanais in Qhoraakese, low and fast so Amika could not overhear. All she managed to interpret was *uncertain* and *up to him*.

Emanais nodded, dismissing the guard. 'We've done what we can to stabilise him,' she said. 'But the curse is advanced. It may not be enough to stop him turning. Be prepared to say goodbye.'

Kio kicked the door open and burst inside. Amika followed, pushing past Emanais after her brother.

The room was some sort of chirurgeon's infirmary, but significantly more advanced and better equipped than any Amika had ever seen in Adria. Rei lay in a cot stretched in white linen, all manner of tubes plugged into his arms and down his throat. She caught a gasp with her palm when she saw him.

Kio all but collapsed beside Rei's bed, wailing like a babe. He bundled the unconscious man's blackened hand tightly between his own and brought it to his lips before resting it against a tear-stained cheek. Amika felt his anguish in her chest and fought back tears of her own.

'I'll leave you for a moment,' Emanais said gently. It was the first note of warmth Amika had caught in her words. The softness withered as her gaze turned to Amika. 'We will speak more later.'

Now alone, Amika went to her brother. She dragged a wooden stool across the stony floor for him to sit on, which he did without releasing Rei's hands or breaking his unflinching stare at Rei's face.

It was a confronting sight: their childhood friend lying there like that, skin the colour of bone stretched over sunken cheeks. The long tube shoved into his slack, open mouth hung limply between his pale lips. His eyes were so dark they looked bruised; and then there was the blackness stretching like ink up his left arm, which Kio clutched hopelessly against himself.

Amika placed her hand on her brother's back and rubbed it in slow, soothing circles. 'He didn't want you to see him like this,' she croaked, finding herself unable to hold back the tears. 'But at the same time, all he wanted was to see you. See you before he—'

She could not finish the sentence.

Amika let the moment sit with Kio awhile, silent and still. She found herself another stool and took a seat on the opposite side of Rei's bed, picking up his other hand. His skin was cold and clammy, puckered at the site where the tubes entered his arm. A deep red liquid swirled within the semi-translucent pipes.

The decoction, Amika thought, remembering the remedy of virgin's blood—*her* blood—that Ka'ella had brewed in Ciraselo. A temporary fix, she had warned them.

But it still seems to be working…

She watched her brother as discreetly as she could, stealing glances across the bed during their silent vigil. He was practically asleep on his feet; his eyes fluttered closed intermittently before snapping open to stare at Rei with renewed intensity. Amika summoned the courage to speak.

'I always thought you loved Moyna,' she said lightly, trying to ease the tension.

'I did love Moyna,' he returned hoarsely. His grip on Rei's hand tightened. 'But not like this.' He rubbed his red, swollen eyes. 'I don't expect you to understand.'

His tone was not venomous, but it stung all the same. She *did* understand. She loved Rei deeply. She would die for him—*kill* for him. Just as she would for her brother. Was the power of her love somehow diminished because it wasn't sexual? Wasn't *romantic*? Love was more than taking someone to your bed… wasn't it?

Amika suddenly felt awkward in the couple's presence, like she was intruding on something she shouldn't be privy to. Dropping Rei's hand, she stretched across the bed to give Kio's forearm a brief squeeze.

'I have to speak with Emanais,' she said softly. 'I want her to trust me.' *I want you* both *to trust me.*

'Good luck with that,' Kio snorted, and Amika caught the first glimpse of his old self, no matter how fleeting.

'Where is she?'

'Two doors down from where you were held,' he said, jerking his head in a vague direction. He was clearly distracted, and Amika didn't press him for more details. She would find her way back on her own, even if it meant wandering with her thoughts for a moment.

She only remembered turning left during the race through the tunnels to Rei's room; by that theory, if she only turned *right* she should eventually make it back to Emanais's chamber. With few features distinguishing one corridor from the next, it would be very easy to become disorientated. Had it been designed like this on purpose?

After rounding the third corner, Amika turned into a hall with one open door. The faint sound of laughter rumbled from within, jarring against the oppressive gloom of this place. She crept towards the room like a cat.

Emanais was seated cross-legged on the bed, a child thrashing about in front of her as she tickled him mercilessly. She was smiling broadly, a warm, motherly figure in place of the mercenary who had presented herself to Amika. When she noticed the princess lingering by the door, she stiffened like a board, expression stony.

'You wanted to talk?' Amika prompted. 'Or would you prefer I be in chains?'

Emanais reached down beside the bed and lifted a long firearm. She cocked the barrel and squared it at Amika's chest. 'I'll take my chances,' she said flatly.

Amika sighed and leant back against the wall carved of hard, red earth. There was no easy way to explain the rest of her story. It was unbelievable, even to her own ears. But if she had any hope of finishing what she'd started, she'd need Emanais's help—and her brother.

'Rei-Hai and I came to Qhoraak looking for Kio,' she said, folding her arms. 'But it's not the only reason I'm here.'

A faint, satisfied grin bled across the other woman's face. She steadied her weapon.

'I'm looking for the Hirathi Blade, and someone to wield it,' Amika continued. 'Do you know of any shrine or significant place of worship? Somewhere the blade might be kept, along with Hirathi's seal—his sigil?'

Emanais gave a brief laugh. 'This is Qhoraak, love. Places of worship everywhere.' Her expression hardened as she continued. 'But what you're looking for is in Xant. The Allchief sits on the Seat of Hirathi. The blade hangs above his throne as a symbol of his power. These things are sacred to my people. Why do *you* want them? You abandoned your Deities.'

Amika exhaled heavily. *Here goes nothing.* 'Because I'm trying to resurrect the Goddess.'

She braced for the mockery that would inevitably follow, but it never came. Emanais's weapon wavered slightly. When she did not speak, Amika persisted.

'There is a prophecy,' she said, recalling the words Grey had spoken to her what felt like an eternity ago. 'When a daughter of power is born to a line of men, the Goddess will be reborn—or something. That daughter is me. The first Holanian princess born to our kingdom since the Great King Kiokharen forged our house. I have the power to revive the Goddess, to break the seals on her soul. A friend of mine, Kriah, has already started. He broke the Skrevaar Sea—'

Emanais straightened. 'Skrevaar walks among us once more?'

'What? No! I don't ... think so?' Amika stumbled. Greist'hal had never mentioned anything like that. But then again, he failed to mention a lot.

Since blindly setting the Prophecy in motion, Amika had never stopped to think what breaking the seals actually meant. Her skin grew cold.

Were they bringing the Deities back, too?

'We have long thought our Deity to be trapped in the sky with Miatha,' Emanais said, cautious, as though sharing a great secret. 'Not dead and gone, simply ... trapped. But we never imagined he could be freed.'

'I wasn't there when Kriah broke the seal,' Amika admitted. 'I don't know if it freed Skrevaar, or what will happen when the Hirathi seal falls. But if you take us to it, you'll have the chance to find out.'

It was a bold claim, Amika knew. Risky and perhaps undeliverable. She didn't actually believe the Deities would walk free of the seals—they were *dead*, after all—but if pious hope was the only way to earn the woman's trust and cooperation, she was not about to throw it away.

The aim of Emanais's firearm was decisively lower now, as if she had forgotten to keep it raised in threat. She studied Amika like a lord appraising a new attendant; her other hand patted the boy intermittently on the belly as she thought. Amika looked at the child properly now, noting the paleness of his skin and shocking red of his hair. A Siephymn, she realised—just like Rei. He even looked a little like her friend.

'What did your brother tell you of *our* mission here?' Emanais asked, hazel eyes narrowing.

'Nothing. You were too busy interrogating me—I never got the chance to ask.'

Emanais's smirk was fleeting. 'Kio is one of my soldiers. This is my army. We're going to destroy the Siephymn farms.' Her gaze slid to the boy on the bed, whose golden eyes were slipping closed with sleepiness. 'Don't suppose you know what those are?'

Amika recalled the woman in the caves. The blade stuck in her neck. The look on Rei-Hai's face when he discovered the brand on her skin. 'I do,' she said sombrely. 'Rei was held in one of them.'

The woman released a rumbling sound from deep in her throat; Amika couldn't tell if she was surprised Amika knew about it, or impressed Rei had survived one. Emanais nodded slowly, a new plan seeming to form in her mind.

'Are you as good with a blade as your brother?'

'Better,' Amika announced confidently. 'We received the same tutelage in Adria, and I've had five years hunting demonspawn to sharpen my skills even further. And—'

She bit off the words, stopping herself from blurting out all her secrets. In her months travelling with Rei, she had grown complacent. Manipulating *khe'torla* without reserve had become second nature to her now; she was bound to slip up eventually.

'I'm a prophesied daughter of power,' she said carefully. 'One of Miatha's Chosen. I can do more than swing a sword.'

A broad grin crept across Emanais's face 'Is that so?' she laughed, though the expression was mocking—*doubtful*. 'Go on then, love. Show me what you can do.'

Amika scanned the room for a source, nerves roiling in her gut. Exposing her gifts would either condemn her to execution—or convince Emanais there was more than madness in her words.

The earth in this camp was depleted, too old and exhausted to draw upon; this deep underground, the air was stale and weak. Amika spied a glass pitcher filled with water on the stand beside the bed. She could shatter it, she supposed, but water was a pulse she was yet to harness. Fail, and she might not get a second chance.

Finally, she noted the three candles flickering about the room—one beside Emanais and two in a sconce on the wall behind herself. *That* would be her source.

Closing her eyes, Amika reached for the flames. All three of them, simultaneously. The barrenness of Qhoraak meant there wasn't much *khe'torla* vying for attention; she wasn't trying to pick the flute from the cacophony of the orchestra. Holding all three sources was easier than she thought—or maybe she was just getting better.

While it wasn't necessary for the success of her cast, Amika raised her hands slowly, palms facing up, in a theatrical display of her gift. The candle flames rose with the gesture, sputtering into towering pillars of fire that licked the earthen ceiling. The Siephymn boy shrieked and burrowed into Emanais's chest. She held him tight, jaw wide, but not in fear.

'*Hae ante Hirathi*,' she breathed, eyes almost as round as her gaping mouth. 'Nothing to fear, dear Sylar. The flames are Hirathi's to command. He calls out to us to set him free.'

Relief flooded Amika's veins as she snuffed out the candles and exhaled deeply. Drawing from simultaneous sources had left her a little faint, and she reached out for the wall to steady herself, shaking her head to clear her vision.

'Your brother never told me,' Emanais said pointedly.

'My brother didn't know.'

Didn't want *to know*. He had been there that night on the plains when Amika had first expelled *khe'torla*, but they'd never spoken of it again. Kio had never been one for monsters or magic tales—how must he feel being surrounded by them?

'I'd like to keep this between us,' Amika said to Emanais. 'At least for now. He's been through a lot, and now with Rei as he is …'

Emanais nodded. 'Yes, I agree.' Stroking the child's crimson hair, she sighed. 'I told him to say his goodbyes and prepare for the end, but … Well, these things are easier said than done.'

She seemed to drift away then, and Amika wondered exactly what was between her and Kio. How he ended up here and not at a slaver's auction house in Xant …

'What is my brother to you?' she couldn't help but ask. 'Why do you care so much?'

'Because he reminds me of *me*.'

Amika's head cocked to the side in piqued curiosity but remained silent, bidding Emanais to elaborate when she was ready. She took longer than Amika expected and sat chewing on her lip in a vulnerable manner so strikingly at odds with the facade she presented.

'I was someone who lost everything,' Emanais said, looking at the boy instead of Amika. 'Someone who watched her family slaughtered and her throne usurped. It had been my destiny to win the Seat of Hirathi from my father once he grew too old to lead our people. Waqar stole that from me.' She trailed off, voice hardening as her eyes rose to meet Amika's gaze. 'I'm not the selfless hero I claim to be, Amika. I don't want to kill him just because he enslaves Siephymn—I want to kill him for revenge.'

The Prophecy returned unbidden to Amika's mind. *Pure blood. Tainted blood.* Royal *blood…*

'The Hero,' she whispered, so quiet the words touched her ears alone. 'Emanais, I …' Amika gave a bitter laugh. 'I was never one to believe in fate and design, but the more I unravel the Prophecy, the more inevitable its truth becomes. Our lives have crossed paths for a reason. There are four Chosen destined to break the Deities seals. I think you're one of them.'

Amika recalled her own guffawing cynicism when Grey had presented her with a similar conclusion. Emanais had not held back her scathing judgement previously but she was now silent in her contemplation. Her gaze was unfixed as she stared off in thought, fingers stroking the boy's belly as though he were a cat. Apprehension clawed at Amika's gut. Had she said too much? Pushed beyond the realm of plausibility?

'Fulfilling this Prophecy ...' Emanais began, still distant, 'will it help me win back my throne?'

Amika swallowed, choosing her words with care. 'If Waqar holds the Hirathi Blade, then I see no choice but to take it from him.'

A slow smile crept across Emanais's face and she paused her absent-minded patting of the boy to stretch her hand towards Amika. 'Welcome to my army, fellow Chosen.'

18

REI-HAI

Rei was choking. As he fought to expel the foreign object from his throat, all he seemed to do was suck it deeper.

Hands on his chest, holding him down.

'*—ng on, Rei! Hold still.*'

A woman's voice—*Amika?*

Rei screamed as the object was pulled from his throat, scraping the inside as it went. It left his mouth with a great gasp. He bent forward and gagged. Catching his breath, he rubbed the blur from his eyes, flinched at the pinprick pain in his arms. Several tubes bit into his flesh. In a panic, he plucked them free. He ran his hands over his face, through his hair, expecting to find horns or other deformities.

But there was nothing. He was ... normal.

Except for the black stain running up his left arm.

'Oh, Goddess,' Amika gasped, smiling despite the tears filling her eyes. 'Kio's going to kill me.'

'K-Kio ...?' Rei breathed. He looked around the room. At the earth-and-stone walls, the iron door. His pulse spiked. Chest tightened until he couldn't breathe. 'Amika,' he croaked, 'why are we in a farm?'

'No, no.' She gripped his face to hold his gaze. 'We're not in a farm. Not anymore. You're safe here.'

He felt himself mimic her reassuring nods until she dropped her hands to squeeze his forearm instead.

'It's alright. You're alright.'

She turned her head suddenly towards the sound of breaking glass. Rei followed her gaze.

Kio stood in the doorway, a bottle of wine in shards at his feet.

Neither spoke for a moment. Joy and relief and shock and heartache fought for dominance in Rei's chest. It was Kio—alive, strong and deadly handsome. But it was also Kio—broken, grief-stricken and empty.

'Hello, my p—'

Kio's arms swallowed Rei in an embrace before the weak words could leave his mouth.

Rei lost himself in the expanse of his chest—in the scent of him. His hands clung to the prince's back, fingers grasping fistfuls of fabric. For a moment he forgot himself—forgot everything. He forgot the pain that reached down to his bones. The insatiable hunger. The thirst he couldn't quench. His blood no longer felt like acid in his veins. He was strong. *Whole*.

'I sat by this bed for five fucking days,' Kio croaked, cheek rested atop Rei's head. 'Why did you wake when I was gone?'

Rei did not answer. Kio had withdrawn from the embrace and now held him back at arm's length, hands gripping his shoulders. They smiled at each other weakly.

'Get Emanais. The chirurgeon—whoever.' The fingers of his left hand combed through Rei's hair as he spoke; Rei leant into the tender touch. 'I'm not going anywhere.'

Irritation flickered across Amika's features at the order, but she did as her brother wished, boots crunching on the broken glass as she left. Kio reached out for the stool she was using, dragged it close so he could sit at eye level with Rei.

'Deities dead,' the prince breathed, thumb stroking the length of Rei's jawline. 'Oh, my love, you're alive. You're *here*. And you're just as beautiful as I remember.'

The words were a reflection of everything Rei held, silent and hidden, in his chest. He threw himself at Kio, practically tumbling off the bed and into his lap as he hooked his arms around his neck to kiss him deeply. The prince tasted of wine—no doubt all he'd consumed of late—but Rei didn't care. He just wanted to touch him, *feel* him. Every inch across every plane of his body.

His desire grew as their tongues danced, bodies pressing into one another. He felt Kio respond in kind, but instead of hands fumbling with their cumbersome clothes, Rei was being pushed away.

'No. No, no no no no,' Kio chanted, shaking his head as their lips parted, foreheads joined and eyes still closed in bliss. 'No. You need to get well.'

'I *am* well.'

Rei stretched for another kiss. Kio turned his head away; the rejection stung.

'I'm serious,' he insisted. 'I feel stronger than I have in months. Whatever they pumped into me worked.' He glanced at the tubes that had been embedded in his arms, now lying limp on the bed, and the little black holes they'd left in his flesh.

'Of course it did,' a heavily accented female voice said from the door. 'Qhoraakese medicine is second to none, especially when treating Siephymn. Whatever tonics our deserters took with them to Meytar have nothing on what we can produce here.'

She strode right up to Rei's bedside, locs braided together in a thick rope down her back. 'Excuse me,' she said perfunctorily, sweeping aside Rei's long hair to get a look at the nape of his neck.

'*Hey,*' Kio growled, batting her away.

'How did you escape?' the woman demanded.

Rei's jaw tightened. He didn't need her to elaborate. She recognised the brand on his neck—the mark that indicated registration at a farm and by whom. He'd asked Xenae, the tattooist at the Tower, to remove it after his escape, but the Yaian master refused; Rei tried to burn it off himself with a dagger blade, heated over a candle in his room, but the attempt had been poor. Anyone with knowledge would still recognise the symbol beneath the bubbled flesh and what it meant.

He felt Kio's fingertips inspect the area, but Rei held the Qhoraakese woman's commanding gaze. 'Through my own sheer determination not to die,' he said in answer to her question. 'Ironic that I find myself back here on death's doorstep.'

'And you never thought to liberate those imprisoned alongside you?'

'No,' Rei said simply. Indignation registered on the woman's face immediately. 'I was selfishly preoccupied with saving my own arse.'

For a moment he thought she might strike him. It wouldn't be the first time his mouth had earnt him a blow to the face, and he was already bracing himself for it. But the woman seethed silently, pinched the bridge of her nose instead.

'You are lucky to be sitting there alive,' she hissed between clenched teeth, eyes closed. 'Not many escape the farms. Fewer still return from so deep in their curse. It seems you are rather difficult to kill.'

'Indeed—like a cockroach,' he quipped. He was about to make another joke about *cock* when he caught Amika rolling her eyes from across the room.

At least I feel myself enough to jest, Princess, he said inwardly before turning his attention back to the needlessly aggressive Qhoraakese woman. She was looking at Kio.

'He is well,' she said. 'Better than expected, actually. He still needs his rest—but he does not need you by his side for that. Come. We are long overdue for our war council.' As she was turning for the door, she added, 'Do not forget why you are here, Little Prince.'

She pushed past Amika and left. Kio sighed and pressed a simple kiss to Rei's forehead. 'I'll be back,' he said. 'Rest.'

He exchanged a look with Amika on his way out, but with his back turned, Rei could not tell what it said. Thankfully, Amika lingered after the others left.

'Care to explain why that woman is wearing your brother's balls, Princess?' Rei asked.

Another eye roll, this time followed by a humourless chuckle. She moved towards him and placed a hand on his forearm, giving it a sympathetic squeeze. 'She was the one who saved him, Rei. Saved him from a life of slavery in the capital. He's indebted to her.'

'And that means we should trust her? This is a fucking *farm*, Amika.'

'A repurposed farm,' the princess insisted. 'Emanais told me what she's doing here. She fights to save Siephymn—to save her sister. Kio wants to help her. And so do I.'

Rei wanted nothing more than to see Qhoraak burn. Being here made his skin crawl, and not because of the curse in his veins. There were memories here he could never erase; pain that was a part of him now, just like the blood soaked into these walls. He closed his eyes and exhaled heavily, calming his fears as much as his rage. If Kio was here, then so was he.

He made to stand.

'No, no,' Amika pleaded, pressing down on his shoulders. 'Please, Rei—just rest. We'll be back soon.'

Defeated, he flopped back on the hard bed and stared at the stony ceiling overhead. Within minutes, he was asleep.

When he woke again, annoyed he'd needed the rest he'd so fiercely denied, the room was dark. The lantern that had lit the chamber had gone out. Rei's skin prickled; he could hear breathing.

'Kio?' he asked hopefully.

'Amika,' the princess responded sleepily. The lantern sputtered back to life, ignited by her magic, and he saw her slumped in the chair in the corner, rubbing her eyes. 'Thought you didn't need rest?' she mumbled.

'I'm a compulsive liar. Where's Kio?'

'With Emanais.' Amika sat up now and stretched out her back, grimacing as she did so. How long had she been sleeping in that chair?

'I need to get up,' Rei insisted, pulling back the blanket to find himself stripped to his undergarments. 'Where are my clothes?' *And my weapons. Knives. Needles ...*

Amika reached behind her and passed him his shirt and leather breeches, which had been laundered, mended and folded across the back of the chair. As he shrugged into his shirt, he noticed that his shoulder was not as stiff as it had been. He loosened the collar to inspect the wound Jahaanya Yai had inflicted in Ciraselo; it was healed now, restitched into a neater, cleaner line, and no longer inflamed with mild infection. Qhoraakese medicine really was impressive.

As he slipped from the bed to lace his breeches, Amika had to steady him. He was weaker than he thought—slimmer, too. Even pulling the laces as tight as they would go, his pants still hung loose on his hips. He looked for the bindings he used to conceal the tattoos of the Tower, but could not find them among his things. He turned to Amika, but the princess only shrugged.

Rei glanced at his hand, at the inky stain stretching from fingertip to bicep, at the blackened nails, sharp and ridged like claws. He curled it into a fist and squeezed.

Guess their medicine can't reverse everything.

Amika led him through the winding tunnels of the underground camp, his hackles rising with every step. The red earthen walls, the stale air and the lingering scent of blood left his pulse raised and breath shallow. This place was too familiar. When Amika stopped at a rusted door, he almost forgot to breathe altogether. Despite an attempt to scratch the markings from the door, Rei still recognised the number etched into steel—and a symbol that matched the brand on his neck.

'... not there,' he heard Amika say as she returned from inside the room. He hadn't even seen her leave.

'Sorry?' he said, rubbing his eyes to clear his head.

'They're not there,' she repeated, eyebrow raised as she studied him. 'Must be in his tent. Are you alright?'

'Fine. Still tired, I guess. Tent, you said?'

'Yes ... Kio sleeps above ground. He won't stay down here. Can't say I blame him.'

Rei's muscles relaxed the moment they were out in the fresh air. It was colder than he expected after the insulated warmth of the tunnels, but that didn't stop Emanais's troops going about their tireless training under crackling torchlight. A drill master stood atop a crate at the front of the cohort, shouting orders in Qhoraakese. Rei shivered as he recalled being on the receiving end of such commands—and the vicious blows that followed when he didn't obey. He hadn't understood Qhoraakese, and his refusal to conform was rooted in genuine misunderstanding. Not that it made much difference *why* he defied the masters of the farm—only that he did.

'That's Kio's tent,' Amika said, pointing to a conical canvas structure by the external walls. It was the third tent in a long row of identical dwellings, each large enough to accommodate several cots. Rei hoped Kio was alone.

'I'm in that one,' Amika said, pointing to the first tent. 'For women,' she added with a shrug.

'Suppose I won't have much business there,' Rei said, grinning wickedly.

The princess smiled awkwardly. 'No, I suppose not. Goodnight, then.'

She disappeared inside her tent and Rei headed towards Kio's, hope dampening slightly at the light flickering through the half-open flap. Nerves alight, he peered inside.

Kio sat on a low wooden bench beside a coal brazier, its red glow more for warmth than light. Several lanterns flickered around the expansive tent, which, as far as he could tell, was furnished with a single wide, heavily blanketed cot. Rei let the canvas flap fall audibly closed behind him; Kio glanced up from the sheaf of parchment he was inspecting.

'Rei-Hai,' he said, jumping to his feet, his expression a mix of surprise and concern. 'What are you doing out of bed? You should be resting.'

'I'm getting tired of hearing that,' Rei muttered, closing the distance between them. 'I'm fine.'

'You do look better,' Kio admitted, brushing loose hair back from Rei's face. 'Deities dead, I actually don't believe it. I'd given up. I thought ...'

'So did I.' Rei closed his eyes and leant into the taller man's touch. 'I'm sorry I couldn't save you, my prince,' he whispered. The guilt that had gnawed away at him ever since he'd failed to break Kio out of Cirahk had only strengthened when he learnt another had succeeded where he had not.

'Don't say that,' Kio said, voice equally low. His head bowed to meet Rei's, where it stood just shy of the prince's shoulder. Rei savoured the warmth of Kio's cheek against his temple, the hot breath tingling his skin. It had been so *long*—a year, almost two—and Kio had been deep in his grief for Moyna and his son when last they met. And now ...

Rei opened his eyes to find the prince looking down at him, a soft, warm smile on his lips. Rei's body *burned*. Stretching up on his toes, he hooked his arms about Kio's neck, bringing him close enough to kiss. But Kio was slow, hesitant, and it only made Rei more eager, more desperate to let him in.

When Kio finally complied, Rei felt his arms enclose around him, hands groping at his back, his hips, his arse. Rei moaned into the kiss and let his own hands travel the expanse of Kio's body, down his broad chest, his taut belly, to the ridge of his belt, where he felt the prince's arousal stirring behind his trousers.

Kio pulled away. His hand crushed Rei's wrist, prying it back from the buckle he had already begun to loosen.

Rei felt cold. He looked down at the hand Kio had shunned. At the leathery coarseness of his skin. At the claws. And he knew.

He was hideous.

Kio knew what he was now, and it repulsed him. Of course it did. He wasn't *human*. Wasn't worth the effort it took to love him.

Rei gritted his teeth. Snatched his deformed hand away. He spun towards the exit. He would not cry here. Not where anyone could see it.

Kio seized his elbow. 'Wait. Stop,' he said, voice equally choked. 'It's not you. It's ... I can't ...'

His hands gestured hopelessly, searching for an explanation he couldn't find—or words he couldn't say. It was Kio's turn to retreat now, and he withdrew to the bench by the coal brazier, head falling into his hands.

'Every time I close my eyes, I'm back in that fucking cell. I can't eat. I can't sleep. And now I can't even fucking touch the one person I so desperately want to, and I can't—'

He choked down a sob, burying his face again. His curled fist pounded on the side of his head in frustration as he screamed.

Rei said nothing. Words wouldn't help here. He knew that because he'd been there himself. Years ago, when he'd escaped the torment of Qhoraak. He'd run to Kio for comfort, but he'd wanted nothing more than to *be* with him—to simply exist in the same space. It had been a while before he'd felt ready for anything more. Longer still before he'd been able to talk about it.

'Can I ...?' Rei gestured at the seat next to Kio. The prince nodded; Rei slid beside him. 'So,' he said, puffing out a deliberate breath. 'What has our demanding leader got you so preoccupied with?' He settled his head against Kio's shoulder and pointed to the stack of parchment the prince had been perusing when he arrived.

'Battle plans,' Kio said, picking up the papers. He leafed through them. 'Terrain maps. Base schematics. Known captives we need to rescue.' He paused on a charcoal etching of a young woman, Qhoraakese in features save for the slitted pupils of her eyes.

Rei straightened, lungs paralytic. He knew that face. He knew it like he knew his own shadow. A face he had seen in pain. Screaming. Begging. *Hating.* A face he saw every night he dreamt, and one that he *never* wanted to see again.

'Ema's sister,' Kio was saying, though Rei barely heard the words. 'They saved her from this farm. But not before she was raped repeatedly. Luckily the slavers never knew she was with child or they would—'

'She was ... pregnant?' Rei managed to squeeze the words out of his constricting throat. He held his chest. He couldn't breathe—couldn't *move.*

'Yes, with a little boy. He's—*gods*, Rei-Hai, what's wrong?' Kio turned to him now, tossed the parchment aside and gripped his shoulders desperately.

'I was ... She was ...' he stammered brokenly. 'The farm ...'

'No,' Kio said sharply as everything fell together. '*No.* Rei, did you ...'

'I did not!' Rei screamed, hot tears bursting from his eyes. '*I* was raped. That's what happened at those farms, Kio. To each and every one of us. I was pumped full of so many fucking drugs I couldn't move. I couldn't think. I was strapped to a bed for *months*, trapped inside my own fucking head while they made sure the only part of me they needed performed for them at will.'

He clenched his fists. The claws of his left hand speared into his palm and drew blood.

'If the drugs didn't work, they found other ways. Hands, mouths—depended on the guard. And then they brought her to me. My *mate*. Thrashing and screaming, but every bit as drugged and useless as I was. But still they forced us on each other. Over and over and—'

Kio crushed Rei to his chest. The jolt knocked the memories from his mind, silenced the horrors spilling from his lips. It was only now he realised how badly he was shaking. How ferociously the tears spilled from his eyes. Kio's shirt grew damp in seconds, but he did not let go.

Rei hoped he never would.

19

KRIAH

Kriah wasted away the small hours of the morning staring out into the street. A bird-masked man wandered from house to house with a wagon, collecting corpses for the communal pyre in the square. Smoke made its way persistently through the battened glass window of Kriah's second-storey room, filling the space with a visible haze. The Sickness had taken hold here in such a way that it was no longer possible to determine the source.

Had Azet'haal tainted the *khe'torla* in the earth? In the air? The city lacked the natural vegetation of the plains, but with the densely packed buildings and population, it would not take long to jump from person to person.

'How am I supposed to stop this?' Kriah whispered to the empty room. 'What would *you* have done?'

His grandfather had kept so much from him. The truth of Kriah's birth, his plans for the Prophecy. But most regrettably, his knowledge of *khe'torla*. Grey had taught him the basics—how to resonate, manipulate and expel—but he never shared any indication on the First Born's breadth of abilities. Or was Azet'haal's power only possible due to the vast amounts of *khe'torla* he had inherited through the murder of his kin?

By the time the sun crept through the smoke clouds, Kriah's head was aching along with his eyes, starved of sleep. The whole night had passed without Nell returning to the room. Kriah wasn't really surprised, though. He'd seen the boatswain leave with a woman and remembered the story Nell told when they'd first met, about a lover he had in Cirahk. Kriah couldn't blame him for pursuing her now, knowing what he did about the fate of the world. If Kriah had his time over, he wouldn't have sent Amika off to Holania without telling her how he felt. It might not have changed anything, but at least she would have known.

Amika.

His heart ached at the memory of her. He didn't believe she was dead—she couldn't be. Whether through the spread of Azet'haal's sickness or at her own hands in a murder-suicide, there was no way she could be gone. She had to be alive. She just *had* to be. And he would go to Adria to find her.

Kriah slipped on his boots and trudged down the stairs into the bar of The Dripping Bucket, where he quickly located Nell in the booth they'd been seated at the night before, crunching on a dry roll of bread. The boatswain dropped it as he saw Kriah approach, mouth agape.

'Yer look ... terrible,' he offered grimly. 'I thought yer'd sleep well here. Not having to keep watch 'n' all.'

Kriah slid into the chair opposite and ran his hands through his curls. 'Too noisy,' he said, reaching for the most plausible excuse he could find.

Nell's grin widened. 'Aye, these places tend to be. Can't say I did much sleepin' meself either.' He took a drink awkwardly when Kriah didn't respond to his loaded suggestion. 'Anyway,' he continued with a cough, 'I learnt a few things about this plague. Told yer the docks were the best place for catchin' rumours. Seems the first people got sick at the turn of the Nirhana Moon before last—aye, some two weeks before we first heard of it in Gerrick Port. Either way, people here are all convinced it's got to do with the Tear in the sky. That the Goddess is cursin' us for abandonin' her or somethin'. Some even think it's she who abandoned *us*. No doubt it's Meah-Hyren sowin' them seeds about.'

Kriah nodded vaguely. After his visit from Azet'haal, he'd drawn the same conclusion. The plague was more than a way to enthral the Second Born—it was designed to thin the herd, to cull them to numbers more manageable for the Meah-Hyren to control. Azet'haal didn't need a whole continent of disciples—just enough to seize Whyt'hallen for his own.

'What did Stelaya have to say?' Kriah said, finally recalling the name of Nell's lover.

The boatswain smiled coyly and popped a lump of bread into his mouth. 'Quite a lot, actually.' He paused to swallow. 'She has a sister who works as a pleasure girl over on Lily Crescent. The Sickness is worse in that part of the city—livin' in close quarters 'n' all. Well, Stel received word some four days ago that her sister's come down with fever. Madame told her she knows of a healer who can save her sis, but she needs to front ten gold coins b'fore she'll take her.'

Kriah didn't know if that was expensive or not; judging from the grey expression on Nell's face, he could only assume it was well beyond the wealth of a bar girl.

'Stel plans on payin' the fee,' Nell said, lowering his voice. 'Been savin' 'n' borrowin' these last few days. She's to meet a man outside her sister's workplace in the Crescent when the town bell tolls Sixth Hour tonight.' Dropping his voice even further, he leant in and added, 'A man with silver hair 'n' black eyes.'

Kriah's fists tightened and his heart raced. He was sure Azet'haal himself was not in the city, but what was to say the other Meah-Hyren weren't capable of enthralling the Second Born as well?

'We can't let her go,' Kriah said.

Nell relaxed back in his chair. 'Of course not. I told her to take her coin and leave the city. Head for an inland village like Trendon. She left before dawn. I plan to follow her—after I see yer to Adria.' He paused before adding, 'I trust that's agreeable?'

Kriah nodded emphatically. Although his heart stung at his only friend being so eager to leave, he could hardly begrudge him that. Nell deserved a chance to live happily with the woman he loved; Kriah would not rob him of that, too.

'Of course,' he said, throat dry. 'I appreciate you coming this far.'

Nell clapped his hand over Kriah's forearm and flashed a half-smile. 'Thank me once we find yer girl alive.'

They waited out the day resting as much as they could. Replenishing supplies proved harder than expected, given the rarity of rations within the city now the ports were closed. Butchers sold game meat of questionable freshness; fishmongers hawked their undersized catch, pulled in from nets thrown off the docks themselves.

The farm produce was just as poor—plucked from the earth too early or left to wilt too long in the stall, it was still sold at a price higher than peak harvest season. Even Kriah knew he was being robbed, paying four bronze for a handful of potatoes that had gone soft and started sprouting roots. He wasn't really sure what to do with them, but perhaps they could bulk out a stew made from the strips of salt fish still held in Nell's supplies. If he only still had the water-lined satchel he used to use for trade, he'd be able to purchase *fresh* fish to poach instead; but that bag was lost to the ocean off Kherunis along with everything else he owned, and without the ability to turn it into a portable icebox with the help of *khe'torla*, they had no way of stopping the spoilage.

Dried bread and cheese it is, he thought sadly, tightening the straps on his travel bag before meeting Nell downstairs.

It was late afternoon now, and after scouring the markets for their pitiful rations, they'd retired to their rooms to rest. Kriah, of course, had not slept—not even dreamscaped. He was still reeling from Azet'haal's invasion, and the mere thought of closing his eyes sent red-hot anxiety ripping through his chest to seize his heart.

'It's a bit of a trek across the city,' Nell said as they stepped out onto the wintry street. A misty grey rain descended on the Bararnite capital, adding another layer of gloom to the thick, smoky air.

'Which way?' Kriah adjusted the straps slung over his shoulders before fixing his scarf around his face. Nell did the same and pointed towards the sharp spires of the castle looming to the west.

They crossed the city without incident, although the looks they received were anything but welcoming. The suspicious glares bored into Kriah's back like knives. He ignored the feeling as best he could, following Nell over arched bridges across canals until they reached the heart of Cirahk. A warm glow pulsed through the streets here, but from lines of torches and not the great flame of a funeral pyre like they'd seen at the docks.

'Deities dead,' Nell breathed, slowing to a halt in the shadow of a multi-level building. 'What're they doin'?'

'Praying,' Kriah said, swallowing dryly.

The townspeople were on their knees in droves, heads bowed and hands clasped in front of their chests as they chanted, low and guttural. A hooded and robed man stood on a recently constructed wooden platform before the masses, arms outstretched towards the sky, white hair peeking from the shadow of his cowl.

'Kohle Mak hears your devotion!' the Meah-Hyren shouted. 'See how he blesses this part of the city!'

He was right; none of the enthralled citizens wore masks against the plague. Had they lied about Stelaya's sister to draw others into the horde?

A shiver ran down Kriah's spine, sending a tremor all the way to his fingertips. *Khe'torla* swirled in the square around him. What could he do? What could he *possibly* do to save these people?

He felt the Skrevaar Blade stir in his veins. The great sword had lain dormant within him, fused with his own *khe'torla*, since he'd broken the seal in Kherunis.

That's it, he realised. The Second Born feared magic; Amika had been left to die in the woods when she expelled *khe'torla* before a bunch of mercenaries from Ciraselo. If Kriah could force one of their *prophets* to display the same demonised skills, they'd shun him.

At least, he hoped they would.

Kriah flicked his wrist. The Skrevaar Blade shot from his palm in a bolt of light. His muscles bulged as he caught the sudden weight of the claymore coalescing in his grip.

Nell gasped and recoiled.

'Wait here,' Kriah said quietly, slipping the pack from his shoulders. 'And get ready to run.'

Nell nodded, taking the supplies. Kriah stalked towards the dais, hidden in the shadows cast by the many torches crackling around the square. The Bararnites' eyes were closed, heads bowed, and they did not notice his approach; the Meah-Hyren cast his gaze in Kriah's direction and smirked, but did not move. He continued to lead the enthralled citizens in a prayer to their new god.

Kriah ascended the stairs. Blade outstretched and levelled with the Meah-Hyren's neck, he growled, 'I know what you're doing. It stops now.'

'Does it?' the Meah-Hyren replied with infuriating lightness. He lowered his arms; the chanting from the crowd fell away in fragments until it ceased altogether. In its place, isolated gasps filled the silence. 'What will you do now?'

Panic flooded Kriah with adrenaline. Instead of running, he tightened his grip on the Skrevaar Blade and let the crystalline edge kiss the soft skin of the Meah-Hyren's neck.

'This man is not a god!' Kriah shouted at the stunned crowd. 'Nor does he serve the Deities. He is Meah-Hyren, from the Kherunis Isles, come to enslave you. They're responsible for this!' He pointed his free hand towards the docks. 'And the cure they offer is false. Just like Kohle Mak.'

Murmurs rippled through the congregation. Shadows danced across their faces in the dark. Confusion had them rattled.

'*This* man is a zealot,' the Meah-Hyren retorted calmly. 'Still clinging to the past, he would see you all die to appease the old gods—the ones who abandoned *you*. Sickness has come to Whyt'hallen! What has your Goddess done?'

Kriah ground his teeth, driving the sharp edge of the blade further into the Meah-Hyren's flesh. The man hissed.

Come on, Kriah urged silently. *Make me stop hurting you.*

But the Meah-Hyren did nothing. Did not even flinch. Blood trickled down the blade.

'I watched my mother die,' a voice from the crowd said. 'I called for Miatha and she did nothing!'

'Miatha is dead.' A young man got to his feet. 'My wife developed the bleeds. But instead of Miatha's name, I spoke the Blessing to Kohle Mak and *He* answered.' He stretched his hand to the woman beside him and hauled her up. 'She is saved!'

Awe and joy sang from the crowd, and Kriah felt his chance slip away like rope through wet fingers.

'Break whatever spell you've cast here,' Kriah growled. 'Or I'll kill you.'

The Meah-Hyren turned his head, smile stretching across pale lips as he regarded Kriah from the corner of his eye. 'By all means, please try.'

That was it. The arrogance Kriah had been goading. All he need do now was attack and watch the Meah-Hyren expel *khe'torla* to defend. He wrapped both hands around the hilt and drew the great blade back in an arc over his own shoulder. With all the strength he could muster, Kriah unleashed the Skrevaar Blade on the Meah-Hyren in a sweeping horizontal swipe. He braced himself for the rebound of the blade colliding with a shield or a weapon summoned to defend him.

But it did not.

The Skrevaar Blade sliced through the Meah-Hyren's neck. Through muscle and sinew and bone like fire through ice. A wave of blood sprayed across Kriah's face, red, hot and thick. The Meah-Hyren's head hit the deck before the body crumpled, rolling across the platform to the edge, where it stopped, staring at Kriah with unseeing eyes of obsidian, smirk still curling partially open lips.

He ... he didn't even try ...

The Skrevaar Blade slipped from his sticky hands, shattering on the ground like a crystal goblet. The shards melted into the earth and dissipated; Kriah felt the buzz of *khe'torla* as the blade returned to his body.

'He didn't ...' he stammered aloud. 'He didn't ...'

'Miatha's followers would rather see us dead than unfaithful!' a voice from the crowd trembled.

'Kohle Mak was right!'

'Zealot!'

'The Deities are dead!'

'Miatha abandoned us!'

'Get out of our city!'

A sharp blow to his forehead brought him back to the moment. A rock, thrown from the crowd, grazed the side of his head, splitting the skin through his left eyebrow. His own blood was indistinguishable from the sticky sheen already coating his face like war paint. Another came hurling towards him; he ducked at the last minute.

'Kriah!' Nell shouted from the alley—a warning.

A man with a plank of wood charged towards him, ready to swing. Unable to dodge this time, Kriah stretched out his hand and reached for the *khe'torla* crackling in the torches around them. The wood exploded into flame. The man shrieked as the fire engulfed him too, hands bubbling with blisters by the time he dropped the plank.

The mob swarmed Kriah, enraged rather than cowed by the magic. Kriah leapt from the platform, shouting and waving his arms wildly towards Nell to get him to start running too. His pulse was in his ears, blood in his eyes, as he ran at a speed he'd not thought possible.

But Nell was lagging behind. Although possessed with the strong upper body of a seaman, the boatswain had had little opportunity for sprinting on the confines of a ship, and his lack of athleticism showed. Kriah glanced back over his shoulder to see his friend stumble and skid on shredded palms across the cobbled streets. The mob was gaining.

'Go, *go!*' Nell screamed, waving Kriah on. There was blood on his chin where he'd scraped it across the path. He was slow to get up. Panic rose in Kriah's chest, up his throat, where it blocked his airway along with his words.

He would not let Nell be swallowed by Azet'haal's heretics.

Kriah reached down into the earth, *khe'torla* flowing from his feet and beyond. The pulse was weak—*distant*—or maybe he just wasn't concentrating. He gritted his teeth and groped for purchase, hands clawed and twisting as though he were turning invisible cogs.

The ground between them splintered.

The Bararnite throng lost their balance as the fissure widened with a thunderous crack. Kriah *pushed* a little further, groaning, sweat beading on his forehead. He'd only meant to nudge it another five, ten feet, but the whole world shuddered—a rusted lock finally snapped free.

The city of Cirahk split apart to the sounds of escalating screams. Kriah's *khe'torla* thrust the central district from where they'd fled some hundred feet into the sky. Buildings slipped into the chasm it wrought, fearful voices growing faint as they disappeared into the rift.

Kriah fell to his knees. Had his cast been unstable? No—he'd matched the resonance perfectly, despite how faint it had been. But that power ...

Wiping the sweat and blood from his eyes, he staggered towards Nell, who had rolled over to watch the destruction. The boatswain's mouth was wide in horror—a look that remained even when his gaze fell on Kriah.

Wordlessly, Kriah stretched out his hand, offering to help Nell back to his feet. Nell hesitated, and for a moment he thought the boatswain might shun him; but Nell clamped his hand around Kriah's wrist and groaned back to his feet.

'The sooner we get to Holania, the better,' he said, clapping Kriah on the shoulder before taking off in a limping jog. Kriah trotted along after him and tried to block out the wails and the rising smoke from the ruins around them.

But he could not ignore the sight of the slain Meah-Hyren running along beside him like a shadow.

20

KIOKHAREN

Kio felt Rei tense beside him. He'd been sleeping peacefully up until now, still as the dead, content and safe entangled in Kio's arms. But now he thrashed about, groaning, hands clutching his head.

'Rei-Hai.' Kio shook him by the shoulder, hoping to wake him from whatever nightmare had invaded his dreams. 'Rei, I'm here. Tell me what's wrong.'

His lover sat up, awake but groggy, fingers massaging his temple as though he fought a terrible hangover.

'Demon ... spawn,' he panted between clenched teeth. 'Get Amika.'

Kio hesitated. Was this it? Was this the end? If he left, would Rei ... be here when he came back? Emanais's medics were supposed to help, buy them more time—

Rei shoved him in the chest. '*Go*,' he urged impatiently. 'I'm alright. I just ... need a second.'

He squeezed his eyes shut against another shard of pain and this time Kio sprang from the bed, stumbling into his boots. After grabbing his leather jerkin from a stand of clothes, he hastily laced it closed and burst from the tent.

The camp was chaos. Panicked soldiers hurried to arm themselves with spears, rifles and swords. Horns sounded from the watchtowers in low, frequent blasts.

From the confusion, Kio plucked a soldier by the elbow. 'What's going on?' he demanded.

The young man's pale brown eyes went wide as he stuttered something in Qhoraakese. Kio dropped his grip on the boy's arm and watched helplessly as he scrambled off.

'Kio!'

He turned at the sound of Amika's voice and saw her bounding towards him, hurriedly fixing a sword belt about her hips. 'Is the camp under attack? By who?'

'Demonspawn,' Rei said, approaching silently through the scramble. He was dressed in his leathers, daggers strapped to his thighs. A flicker of pain and discomfort was still visible around his eyes. 'A *lot* of fucking demonspawn. I can't get a handle on how many.'

'Then you should get down into the tunnels,' Kio urged, and made to usher them both below ground. Rei laughed sharply as Amika shoved him off.

'I don't think anyone has the luxury of hiding, least of all us,' she said, gesturing to Emanais across the camp.

The Boatkeep stood atop a stack of iron crates, barking commands at the newest recruits in her ragtag army. Anxiety swelled within Kio. Amika was right; whatever onslaught approached them from beyond the gate would require every skilled fighter they had. His sister and Rei-Hai were both castle-trained and worth ten of the undisciplined brawlers Emanais had liberated from the convict trawler.

'The Little Prince will hold the central gate,' Emanais said, addressing the herd of ruffians in the common Meytaran tongue as Kio and the others approached. Sweat beaded on her forehead despite the cool night; the fierce grip on her spear turned her knuckles white as she waved it about to punctuate orders. 'Amika and a platoon of my finest spears will support you. The Siephymn will join myself and the riflemen on the wall.'

Rei folded his arms. 'My, how fun for me,' he muttered. 'The teacher's little pet.'

He turned to follow the dispersing troops to take his place among Emanais's ranks, but Kio caught his elbow.

'You haven't recovered,' he whispered, pulling Rei close. 'I'm serious—go below with Sylar. I can't fight if I'm worried for you.'

Rei shook himself free. 'I'm not a child. Why do you think your commander wants me at her side? I'm *useful*, Kio.'

It was hard to reconcile what Kio had learnt about Siephymn with the man he loved. Rei-Hai was precious—capable of protecting himself, yes, but something Kio wanted to shield all the same. But the Siephymn were powerful, otherworldly, bonded to demonspawn. Kio suddenly felt foolish for never suspecting that Piren-Ha's obedience was anything other than training.

'Stay safe,' he said, nodding defeatedly. 'And be careful.'

A faint smile graced Rei's lips. 'I'm always careful,' he said, just as he always did before slinking out Kio's window into danger. Only this time he hastened towards Emanais and her battalion instead of the masters of the Tower.

As Kio watched him go, Amika stepped into his eyeline. Her hand was curled around the sword at her hip and she held herself like a captain addressing a general rather than a baby sister speaking to her brother.

'It's not normal for demonspawn to congregate in such large numbers,' she said gravely. 'I've seen ukarat hunt in packs, and Rei and I encountered a swarm of skampils on the road here, but word from the scouts is that this is something *more*. Hordes of them, all heading this way.'

Kio's skin quivered as memories of the assault off the Dread Isle played on his mind. The drumbeat flap of wings. Harpy cries. Screams of a boy pierced by talons and dragged skyward as though he were little more than a lump of meat on a butcher's hook.

'But they're beasts,' he said, voice breaking slightly. He cleared his throat before continuing. 'How can they launch a coordinated attack?'

Amika shrugged one shoulder as if trying to dislodge an irritant from her neck. 'Everything's been weird since we opened the Tear.'

A story for another time, Kio reminded himself, swallowing the questions racing to his lips.

Around the camp, the faces of his charges grew anxious with idleness. Emanais and her rifles had already taken their places along the wall, Rei joining her in the watchtower above the gate. Kio exhaled uneasily. For all his training, he was a peacetime prince. He'd never led anything more than a parade—a ceremonial display of troops to give the Adrian populace a sense of security.

Little good that did.

Kio never saw the sacking of the Holanian capital, though Reminas took great delight in relaying the events in graphic detail. Hot oil. Flame.

Indiscriminate slaughter. A footpath of charred bones and melted flesh to pave the road for occupying forces.

And he'd done nothing—*known* nothing. Nothing but the darkness and rot of the Cirahk dungeons, and the blank stare of his mother's—

'—can use as shields? Wooden boards, broken crates … Yes, good. That will do.'

Amika directed the squadron into a rigid square formation inside the gates. Kio blanched at how effortlessly his sister had assumed control—and how quickly he had spiralled into panic. Gods, he needed a drink.

'Those with spears and shields come to the front,' she called, ushering a couple of men who'd equipped themselves with the curved and splintered side of a barrel to take their place in the wall she was constructing. 'Swords fall in behind. Be ready for any beasts that jump the barricade.'

The men muttered among themselves, but fell into line. Fear made them pliable, just as it had when Kio pounded Ylan's face to a near-unrecognisable pulp. His fist ached at the memory of it, fingers trembling—or perhaps it was his own fears rising up to consume him.

He plucked a broadsword from the racks of weaponry, buckled it around his waist before also reaching for a spear. He favoured the sword, that was no secret, but the staff and the pike were more common in Qhoraak, and he couldn't help but wonder if there was reason behind that. Going into the unknown, it couldn't hurt to be *too* armed.

Amika stood at the front of the squadron, hands on hips as she observed the formation.

'Learn strategy on the road as well, did you?' Kio muttered gruffly as he joined her.

'It's not strategy so much as it is common sense,' she said, turning away from the troops to face him. 'We're fighting demonspawn, not armies of men. We won't know what we're up against until they're atop us. All we can do is defend until then.' She clapped a hand on Kio's shoulder. 'Had you not been so tangled in your thoughts, you would have seen it. Get out of your head, brother.'

There was no parry for her criticism; he allowed the blow to land unmitigated.

'Wine tends to help with that,' he mumbled. The thirst was extreme now; his dry tongue felt too big for his mouth and his throat was as rough as sandpaper.

Amika glanced over her shoulder as if preparing to share a secret, then released a heavy sigh. She reached into her tunic and produced a watertight leather pouch no larger than her fist. Kio's heart raced at the sight of it.

'Here,' she said reluctantly, proffering the wineskin. 'Emanais gave this to me. Said you might need it.'

Kio snatched it from her and pulled the cork stopper free with his teeth. He drank voraciously, gagging slightly when he realised it wasn't wine but Emanais's strong and fiery Qhoraakese whiskey. He gulped it down regardless.

'She understands me,' he said in response to Amika's narrow-eyed gaze upon him. He wiped his mouth with the back of his forearm and handed the empty skin back to his sister. She tossed it into the dirt at her feet.

'I know,' she said evenly. 'But enabling another's vices is never kind.'

Kio bristled at his sister's judgement. 'Then why give it to me?'

'Because you can't swing your sword with that tremor in your hand.' Her head dipped towards his right arm, now relaxed and still as the night.

'It might just be ointment on a sword wound, but if it sees you survive this battle, then so be it. We've been through too much for you to die because you can't keep yourself in the present.'

The words hung between them, heavy as the black-and-scarlet clouds above. The pulsating, infected gash in the sky had been with Kio since he emerged from the bowels of the *Leviathan* and he no longer thought too much of its presence. But he felt it tonight. Felt the *weight* of it. Oppressive and empty all at once.

It cast its crimson glow upon the soldiers in his squadron, the red shadows making their faces gaunt, distorted and utterly grim. Most of them were Meytaran—criminals from Cirahk or the Bararnite Coast—and would never have encountered demonspawn. Had Kio not been on deck when they passed the Dread Isle, he too would have remained oblivious to the hordes of beasts still roaming Whyt'hallen; he'd always thought Piren-Ha an anomaly, a relic from a blight long banished from the Middle Kingdoms. Cold fingers waltzed down his spine.

'I thought the demonspawn must have been close, given how Rei reacted,' Amika said softly. She was looking up at the tower, where Emanais and Rei held watch. 'Maybe there's just that many of them.'

Kio swallowed. Rei was hunched over the railing, fist at his temple and Emanais's soothing hand on the small of his back. He couldn't fight like that. No more than Kio could with his unsteady hands and wandering mind.

That's why she has him up there. To keep him safe. To keep him useful.

Rei suddenly lurched forward, air exploding from his lungs as if he'd emerged from underwater. He turned away from the wasteland, glancing down at Kio and the others with panic in his beautiful golden eyes.

'There's hundreds of them,' he said, more to Amika than anybody else. '*Hundreds*. Multiple subspecies. All running together.'

Kio saw the terror sweep across his sister's face, watched as she battled to rein it in. She managed to keep herself calm, stoic—everything Kio himself never managed to be.

'Princess,' Emanais called, drawing Amika's attention. She had taken a bow from one of the archers who had joined her marksmen on the wall and dipped the arrowhead into the crackling flames of the brazier. 'Let's light up the horizon.'

His sister nodded and closed her eyes, and Kio swore the fire consuming Emanais's arrow flared brighter. The Boatkeep shot the burning bolt out into the wasteland, but instead of the light weakening in the distance, it grew hotter—*stronger*—igniting the horizon like a torch. She shot another and another, each arrow a blazing bonfire instead of the single wooden stick that it was.

Kio glared at his sister, at her closed eyes in concentration.

'Deities *dead*, Amika!' he growled. It all came back to him now. The night on the plains. The beast—no, the *demonspawn*—that Amika could have only killed by exploding it with her mind. 'Oh, *fuck*.'

Amika's eyes snapped open, sapphire glinting in the light. She gripped him firmly by the elbows. 'I know you have questions, but now is not the time. I'll tell you all when we survive this.'

Kio wanted to scream, bemoan all he didn't know and couldn't understand—*Simple* fucking *Kio*—but he looked past his sister's shoulder, at the flickering pyres in the distance, and the black smear it now illuminated, spreading and stretching towards them like a slow-rising flood.

'They're coming,' he breathed.

Amika whipped around. 'Get these gates closed!' she shouted at Emanais, and the general gave the order to seal them in. Amika squeezed Kio's arms once more, and drew her sword.

Kio could hear nothing but the pulse drumming in his ears. His gaze found the trampled wineskin in the dirt beneath Amika's feet and his thirst rose anew. If he couldn't numb his senses with liquor, he'd have to find another way to wrest control.

He had to get angry.

Kio reached down deep into that well of hatred and rage, that dark pit of fire whose flames made him feel powerful, if not blind to everything beyond its veil of smoke. The acidic fuel that sustained him in the Cirahk dungeons, on the *Leviathan*, pounding the life out of Ylan's contemptuous face.

Hate was all he had to make him feel strong.

'Keep inside the shield wall and be prepared for attacks from above,' he said. 'Some of these things can fly.'

Sceptical mumbles rippled through the ranks; he was about to silence them, but a distant shriek did it for him. Complaints turned to gasps and hardened to resolve. Swords were drawn. Spearhands lowered their pikes between the shields.

They waited.

Thunder cracked through the night—bright explosions from firearms atop the wall. Flame-tipped arrows streaked across the sky. A cacophony of beastly roars and guttural howls followed in their wake. The marksmen reloaded to the beat of Emanais's command.

Kio's grip was sweaty on his sword as he heard the beasts cry out and then die. He pictured them falling in scores, flesh shredded and scorched by the hot lead pellets. His chest contracted. They were monsters; it shouldn't matter how they died. But demonspawn had once been more than just beasts.

'Amika,' he rasped, throat dry and tight. 'What if these were people?'

'You can't think like that,' she said, keeping her eyes fixed on the locked gate. 'They're not people. And even if they were, they are not Rei. They will *never* be Rei.'

His sister looked at him now, her gaze as shaken as he felt. But she was right. Rei could never become this—*would* never become this. Not while Kio still lived.

The prince glanced towards his lover in the watchtower—just in time to see it burst into splinters.

Screams pierced his ears. Bodies fell from the wall. A winged beast careened through the cloud of shattered wood and stone, the sheer size of it slicing the tower's canopy clear off.

'Breach!' someone cried. Emanais. There, emerging from the rubble of the spire. Rei popped up beside her, and Kio found his breath again.

But the relief was short-lived. Shadow after shadow shot over the wall, each creature the size of a bull, talons outstretched and lightning-bright in the dark. They fell as quickly as they passed overhead, their paper-thin leathery wings pierced full of holes by arrow tip and bullet alike. One cometted into the scattering shield wall; another crashed into the dust at Kio's feet, shrieking and writhing under the weight of its broken, crumpled wings.

It was similar to the draconic beasts that had attacked off the coast of the Dread Isle. Instead of scales, it was coated in sparse, wiry hair like a rodent, but its head and clawed feet were decisively reptilian. A forked grey tongue flopped out from its maw, thick with inky saliva. Its golden eyes locked on Kio, slitted pupils narrow and piercing. He hesitated.

It's not Rei. It will never be Rei.

With two hands on the shaft, he thrust his spear through the demon-spawn's long, thick neck. Anchored to the ground, its head lay still while its lower half flopped and thrashed like a fish. Another came gliding overhead; Kio abandoned the spear and tumbled out of the way, drawing his sword as he rolled. Rising to his feet, he hefted the blade skyward, sundering the creature in two. Blood, viscera and entrails rained down in a heavy black shower.

'Keep your eyes on the gate!' Emanais screamed between the relentless crack of pistol fire.

Kio turned back to the portcullis and saw that the ill-trained squadron had dispersed, leaving Amika to defend the threshold alone. His sister held her ground, fingers splayed and stretched towards the gate, which trembled and quaked with the demonspawn onslaught. Whatever she was doing seemed to be working, however inexplicable and unnatural it may be.

The strong wind that had been blowing at their backs suddenly calmed; Amika dropped to her knees in the dirt.

The wood began to splinter.

'Amika!' Kio dashed towards his sister, sweeping her out of the way just as the gate gave way like a dam.

Demonspawn burst through the opening, wriggling and writhing through the crack—maggots spilling from an infected wound. Kio landed heavily on his shoulder, Amika wrapped in his arms. They both had the air knocked from their lungs; blood trickled from his sister's nose. Her eyes were closed.

'Amika ...' Kio groaned. 'Amika, wake up—'

She didn't stir.

Kio pushed himself up on his elbows. A wayward demonspawn bounded towards them, having separated itself from the desperate herd scampering through the wall. He searched for his sword, but it had careened beyond his reach. There was no stopping the beast's trajectory. Kio threw himself over his sister like a shield and waited for the searing pain of claws shredding his back.

It never came.

Daring to glance back, Kio saw the dog-like demonspawn skidding to a halt at their feet. It thrashed and howled, tethered by an invisible leash. Amika's head lolled to the side and she moaned in discomfort as she slowly woke. But she wasn't the one doing this. How was—

'Kio! Fucking *move!*'

He turned to the ruined watchtower to find Rei screaming his way, one hand clutching his head, the other stretched towards the demonspawn frozen in his attack.

'I can't ... hold it ... forever!'

Despite the questions weighing him down, Kio rolled and reached for his sword. Still on his back in the dirt, he swung the blade, hack, hack, hacking at the beast's meaty neck until sinew and stubborn cords of muscle finally gave way to steel. The head fell with a heavy thud. Blood sprayed in a thick black torrent, drenching Kio with its warmth.

'Are you alright?' Rei was at his side now, hands on Kio's shoulders, dragging him back from the gore. Amika too was sitting up, looking dazed and disorientated at the death around them ... or rather, at the lack thereof.

The demonspawn overhead flew on without attacking the soldiers behind the wall. Those pouring through the breach lashed out at their assailants but mostly they raced to escape the fray, speeding across camp to scamper up the opposite wall or frantically try to break through it.

'What did you do?' Kio asked Rei, wiping the blood from his eye with one hand and pushing himself to his feet with the other. 'Why are they retreating?'

'They're not,' Rei said, helping Amika up. 'They were never attacking to begin with.'

Amika's eyes widened. 'They're running,' she breathed. But it was not a sigh of relief. It was fear. 'Rei, what are they running from?'

Before Rei could speak, horns blasted from the towers, low and thunderous, in three long bellows.

'Get the fuck off the wall!' Emanais screamed.

The crack of firearms ceased. Flaming arrows no longer streaked across the crimson sky. Marksmen jumped from the wall like rats abandoning a sinking ship.

A great roar pierced the night, so strong it shook the ground beneath their feet.

'Deities dead, what was that?' Kio asked, unable to restrain the fear shaking his voice.

Still silence enveloped the camp. The soldiers froze in their attack and the demonspawn, rather than pouncing on the distraction, scrambled in the opposite direction. Everyone turned to the sky.

A piercing cry ripped through the night. Kio almost dropped his sword to cover his ears, stumbling against the gale-force wind that followed. Wresting back composure, he straightened—and laid eyes on the beast that had demonspawn on the run.

He only saw its head, but that was enough. A giant, serpent-like skull, sharp and angular; a great spined ruff fanned from a strong, sleek neck.

Luminescent scales ran the length of its body and it might have been beautiful if not for the sheer, devastating size of it.

'Run, you daft witch-fuckers!' Emanais screamed, waving her troops towards the entrance to the tunnels. 'Get the fuck underground!'

Kio grabbed her as she passed. 'What is it, Ema? What *is* that thing?'

Emanais's eyes widened, more white than hazel in her fear. The demonspawn's giant head lingered over the wall, smoke streaming from its nostrils. Slowly, it opened its great maw, exposing row after row of vicious sharp teeth. A low rumble resonated deep from its throat as it regarded Kio and the others.

'It's a fucking *khaaja*, Kio,' Emanais breathed, shaken. 'It's one of the First.'

21

KRIAH

Kriah ran for hours. Maybe even days. Only stopping when he collapsed from exhaustion. He didn't get up. Not even when the stubbly dry grass of the plain cut into his skin, or when a misty rain began to fall. He was back on the boat. Aimlessly floating between Kherunis and the mainland without so much as a flicker of hope.

The clothes on his back grew damp with the rain. They clung coldly to his back, but still he did not move. He had destroyed a city. A good part of it, anyway. He hadn't turned back to see if the land he'd fractured ever came back to the ground. If it did, they'd all be dead. Trapped in the rubble and the dust, unable to breathe. No, he hadn't dared turn back.

'Kriah.'

A hand on his shoulder. It rolled him over to stare up at the sky. He blinked as raindrops fell into his eyes.

'Kriah, we'll catch our deaths if we stay 'ere,' Nell was saying, though Kriah's gaze was so distant he could barely see his lips move. 'Trendon's not far. We have to push on b'fore we freeze.'

Cold.

Kriah felt it now, the icy weight of the rain burrowing into his bones. He groaned to his feet. Pain seared from blisters rubbed so raw the skin adhered to his socks. Nell too hobbled along with a slight limp—a rolled ankle, perhaps? But still they kept walking.

Trendon was further than they anticipated, or perhaps they had just grown slow with exhaustion. Either way, they would not reach the town by nightfall, and the steady rain was quickly developing into a bitter winter storm. Any shelter was better than none; they could forego food and bedding for the night if it meant a dry roof over their heads.

Despite hailing from the eastern coast, Nell was familiar enough with his kingdom to know the plains surrounding the Faethou River were dotted with farmland and managed to find a long-abandoned shack on what must have been a large homestead's property. It was too small to be a cottage, or even a barn, and when Kriah shoulder-barged the door open, he found the old shed to be filled with tools, rusted and neglected.

'This'll have to do,' Nell said, all but collapsing between two blunt ploughs. He was pale and trembling as he leant back against the wall.

'It's dry enough for a fire,' Kriah said as he looked around for something to burn. 'And there's a window for smoke. I'll try to warm things up.'

Nell gave a faint groan in response and fell asleep the moment his eyes drifted closed. Watching his friend succumb to his exhaustion only reminded Kriah how long it had been since he'd enjoyed restful mortal sleep; but with Azet'haal able to haunt him whenever he drifted off, he dared not close his eyes again.

And so he made himself busy, body and mind, snapping the brittle handles off old axes and hammers to build a pile of kindling for their fire. Stuffing the cone of sticks with straw scratched up from the floor, he went in search of something to spark flame. It was a pointless exercise, he knew, mostly because he had the ability to light it without flint, but the habit of keeping up pretences was a hard one to break. That, and Kriah was hesitant to cast *khe'torla* with so many Meah-Hyren on the mainland—and on his tail.

'They won't notice, you know,' a voice said from across the shack. 'They're deafened by the disaster you left behind.'

Kriah raised his head towards the sound, towards the Meah-Hyren leaning against the wall, arms folded with a long silvery-white braid cascading down his back. Hair prickled at the base of Kriah's neck. The man was without doubt the Meah-Hyren from Cirahk, no longer shrouded by the deep cowled hood.

'I killed you,' Kriah said evenly. 'You're not real.'

The Meah-Hyren laughed, a short and bitter burst. 'Believe me, no one is more shocked I'm standing here than me. Azet'haal thought you too weak to be afflicted by our curse.' A smile broadened across his pale face. 'I wish I could be the one to tell him he was wrong. I suppose his face might look something like yours.'

Kriah caught the slight flicker of malice burning in the Meah-Hyren's eyes before his mind started spiralling at the words.

Afflicted by our curse.

'No,' he breathed. He didn't want to believe it, but it explained so much. The sudden, devastating power of his *khe'torla*. The spectre standing before him ...

Kriah had absorbed the Meah-Hyren's life force, and would carry the dead man's consciousness with him until the end of days—or until it drove him mad.

Just like Azet'haal.

Just like Grandfather.

'I didn't ...' Kriah swallowed dryly. 'I didn't mean to ... kill you.'

'My severed head suggests otherwise.'

Tears prickled Kriah's eyes as he remembered the thud of the head hitting the deck, the hot spray of blood. 'I wanted you to defend yourself. To use *khe'torla* to stop me.'

'Yes.' The man pushed off the wall he'd been leaning against, stalking towards Kriah in rage. 'The *one* thing we were forbidden to do. Spread the Sickness. Enthral the Second Born. But defend ourselves? No. That was out of the question!'

He's not angry at me, Kriah realised, stunned. *He's angry at Azet'haal.*

'If Azet'haal hadn't ordered you here, you wouldn't have died,' he surmised provocatively.

'I *died* because you cut my bloody head off, you *vesk'raati!*' the Meah-Hyren swore savagely in their native tongue—such a rare occurrence that Kriah couldn't even attribute an accurate translation to it. His disdain was palpable, and yet ... Kriah never really felt threatened.

He almost laughed, then, at the absurdity of it all. He and the man who was to haunt him for eternity shared a common enemy, even if he didn't openly admit it. How many others among the Meah-Hyren army had marched into a war in which they held no interest? Could they be persuaded to simply ... go home?

Kriah really did laugh now, a transient delirium born of mental exhaustion, anguish and fatigue. When it passed, he felt numb—empty—and sat poking the little fire with no real purpose. Nell continued to sleep. Deeply, though his breaths were slow and shallow. Kriah had managed to take the chill from the air, but their clothes would take longer to dry.

Too long, he thought. The concerning rattle of his friend's chest bothered him. *Could he ...?*

The Meah-Hyren hadn't spoken since his outburst, but Kriah was aware of his presence in the same way he was aware of his toes at the ends of his feet.

'Do you know how to cure the Sickness?' he asked the spectre.

'No.'

He was sitting cross-legged on the ground, chewing at a fingernail—a peculiarly immature act for a being Kriah always believed to be innately stoic and wise.

Am I stuck with an actual child?

Nell coughed in his sleep. Softly at first, but it soon escalated into a violent, hawking fit. Kriah turned towards his friend to see his chest convulsing violently, blood spilling from his mouth and down his chin.

'No, no, no!'

He rushed to ease Nell onto his side, tilting his head forward to stop the blood running back down his throat. His skin was hot but coated in a cold, sticky sheen, and his colouring turned the shade of old bone.

'Tell me how to fix him!' Kriah demanded of the Meah-Hyren.

'I don't know how.' The reply was dismissive.

'TELL ME. HOW. TO FIX HIM!'

'I DON'T KNOW HOW!'

The Meah-Hyren responded with the same boiling anger, setting Kriah's cheeks alight. Hot with panic, he turned away from the spectre and sought Nell's vitals. His pulse was steady but weak, and his breathing was even now the cough had settled. Kriah splayed his hand across the young man's chest, reaching for the *khe'torla* marching through his veins. It was so faint. There had to be a way to strengthen it.

He thrust his own *khe'torla* down into Nell's chest. His mother had used infused ointments to heal the Second Born in Ciraselo—surely this way was quicker, more effective. The young man's back arched and the wind howled outside, suddenly vicious with reverberance from the unstable cast. The rafters cracked and rattled; several shingles went flying, rain now pouring through the gaps.

'You can't heal him like that—*stop!*'

But Kriah could feel the power coursing through him, bright and sharp in a way it had never been before. His *khe'torla* was inside Nell's lungs, his veins, his blood. He didn't know what he was doing, but he was doing *something*. And now he couldn't stop.

The ground began to quake, knocking Kriah off balance. His shoulder landed heavily on the cold floor. With the collision came clarity, and now he could see what a desperate fool he'd been. Attempting an aimless, unstable cast ... he could have brought the very walls down.

Or torn another hole in the sky.

He checked Nell's pulse and found him sleeping peacefully, heartbeat steady and breath strong. The blood had dried on his chin. Kriah leant against the wall, elbows resting on his knees. The Meah-Hyren glared at him from across the narrow room.

'Having fun with your stolen *khe'torla*?' he spat venomously.

Is that what this was? Stolen *khe'torla*. A power inherited from a life never meant to end. It made Kriah feel strong. So strong it was intoxicating. Euphoric. Addictive. Satisfying, like the numbing bliss of a night deep in the cups. He saw it with clarity now, the truth of the Meah-Hyren curse. It wasn't the spirits of the dead that drove the Meah-Hyren mad—it was the magic itself.

'I did not kill you with *khe'torla*,' Kriah insisted weakly. 'I used a weapon. A man-made weapon. How did I syphon your power?'

'You used the Skrevaar Blade,' the Meah-Hyren retorted with a hiss. He folded his arms. 'Besides, it doesn't matter. You are Meah-Hyren. You *killed* a Meah-Hyren. The power is yours—the *curse* is yours.'

'I don't understand.'

'Of course you don't. You were never meant to. Because you were never meant to exist.'

The room grew cold at that, somehow larger and more empty. The reminder was savage but long overdue; Kriah himself had forgotten how *different* he was—how unnatural. The only reason he drew breath was because his grandfather had made it so. A convenient solution to an impossible problem.

I'm not solving anything, Kriah thought bitterly. *All I'm doing is making it worse.*

He glanced down at Nell, who was peaceful despite—or perhaps because of—whatever he'd done. Guilt clawed at his gut. He'd already messed with his friend's mind—how could he tamper with his body, too?

'How did you know it wouldn't work?' Kriah asked. 'You told me I couldn't heal him like that. How did you know?'

The Meah-Hyren was silent so long Kriah thought he'd been ignored; but when he finally spoke his words were soft, measured. '*Khe'torla* cannot be used to heal the body directly,' he said. 'Not with any kind of stability. Our bodies are too complex, as was the Goddess's design. Did not anyone tell you this?'

'They did,' Kriah said bluntly. 'I assumed they lied.' *Like about everything else.*

The Meah-Hyren scoffed. 'Poor little halfblood,' he sneered. 'How hard it must be to be *you.*'

Kriah let the moment sit awhile, the pathetic fire hissing to smoke as rain from the broken roof dripped on the coals. He snapped his fingers and it flared to life.

But the room was no less cold.

'What's your name?' he asked the ghost. 'If we are to endure a lifetime together, then at least tell me what to call you.'

The Meah-Hyren nibbled at his thumbnail again. 'Yae'ilston,' he said quietly. 'My name is Yae'ilston.'

Nell awoke, alert but weak and deathly pale. Kriah fixed a warming meal as best he could from their dwindling supplies. They'd replenished their rations in Cirahk, but with Kriah's pack abandoned in the escape, there were now fewer than when they first arrived.

The soup was thin and lacking flavour, but Nell didn't seem to mind as he sipped gratefully from an old tin bowl while huddled beneath their cloaks. He coughed softly; Kriah's head snapped up like a hound.

'Wrong hole,' Nell rasped, tapping his throat. His eyes watered as he struggled to suppress further sputters.

'Trendon's not far from here,' Kriah said, glancing out the small, grimy window towards the west. The jagged silhouette of a township rose on the horizon. 'Half-day's walk. I'll look for Stelaya, get some more supplies—'

'Kriah.' Nell's voice was small but steady. 'Let's not be fools. We both know I have it.'

A spear of pain shooting through Kriah's chest. It was hard to hear out loud. He swallowed, throat dry.

'Whatever you tried didn't work,' Nell said. 'I'm … so cold. The fever's returning. It won't be long b'fore the bleeds set in for good.'

'But we're so *close*,' Kriah urged. 'Stelaya—'

'Stelaya can't see me like this!' A vicious cough rattled his body. Soup spilt from the bowl all down his front. 'I don't want her to remember me like this. And I don't want to give it to her.'

Regardless of how the Sickness had originally spread, it was still highly contagious. With his Meah-Hyren blood, Kriah was immune. But the Second Born were so dangerously susceptible to infection; anyone in Cirahk could have been responsible for Nell's illness—perhaps even Stelaya herself.

Kriah let the silence sit with them in the small room, soaking up the sombre truth of it. Nell was dying. Pushing his despair down deep, he inhaled a slow breath. 'What would you like me to tell her?'

Kriah engrained Nell's parting message into the very core of his memories. Leaving him alone in the shack left a foul taste in his mouth, but allowing Nell to die without closure was a cruelty Kriah would not abide.

The rain had subsided, leaving a wispy, wintry fog in its wake. Kriah shivered violently in the cold, his cloak left his cloak with Nell for added warmth. Boots still damp, his toes were ice as he squelched across the sodden plain.

'Why make yourself suffer?' Yae'ilston asked haughtily. He strode alongside Kriah, his footsteps leaving no impression in the wet soil. 'You have a way to warm yourself and you choose not to use it. Why? Does your diluted blood make you daft?'

'No, it makes me compassionate,' Kriah snapped. 'Nell deserves to be comfortable.'

'Nell is dy—'

'You think I don't know that?' He whirled towards the Meah-Hyren and groped at the collar of his robe; his hand passed through the visage. Yae'ilston laughed, inflaming Kriah's raw emotions even more. 'It's my fault he's dying. *Mine.* The least I can do is let him use my fucking cloak.'

Kriah stomped off, half slipping in the mud. Yae'ilston lingered on the edge of his awareness—a fly drawn to a corpse.

'I wasn't talking about some silly little strip of fabric,' he said as he quickened his stride to catch up. 'I'm talking about *khe'torla*, you fool. Do you not know how to regulate your own body heat?'

Of course I don't, Kriah wanted to spit. Greist'hal hadn't taught him anything beyond what he needed to fulfil his function as Chosen. Basic skills—*incomplete* skills. He could manipulate the elements to heat a room, raise a whole city into the air. But when faced with the ability of a full-blooded Meah-Hyren, his tricks were about as impressive as a child piling up blocks and calling it a castle. He couldn't defend himself with a shield wrought of energy. He couldn't delude the masses to follow his cause.

He couldn't cure his only friend.

'Well? Are you going to help me or belittle me?' Kriah asked tiredly. 'We have an eternity together; I know which one I'd prefer, but I suppose it's really up to you, isn't it?'

He expected to trudge the rest of the way to Trendon in irritating silence; to his surprise, Yae'ilston stepped before him, blocking his path.

'It's really quite simple,' the Meah-Hyren insisted, arms folded across his chest. 'You just turn the resonance inward. Towards your internal *khe'torla*, instead of dry kindling or whatever else you're trying to light. Get it wrong, though, and *you'll* go up like a torch instead.'

A cruel smile cut his face; Kriah scoffed and pushed through him.

Yae'ilston shot after him with a sneer. 'Coward.'

He was right. Kriah was a coward. He was too scared to try anything any more. After what he'd done in Cirahk, how he'd lost control with Nell ... He didn't trust himself. Not with Yae'ilston's *khe'torla* flooding his veins like a river stretched beyond its bank. It was too unpredictable, too *wild*.

Blocking Yae'ilston's remarks as best he could, Kriah continued broodily towards Trendon. A warming bud of hope bloomed in his chest as tendrils of smoke rose from the township—fireplaces heating homes against the chill. It quickened his step as much as his pulse. If Stelaya were here, she would be at the inn, and if Kriah had learnt anything about Meytaran settlements, it would be in a central location, easily accessible to locals and travellers alike.

But as he approached the town, his spirits dampened like candles in the rain. Smoke was not rising from chimneys, or even from a central pyre. It smouldered from charred corpses in the street, immolated where they had stood. Some were huddled together—families, most like—and others lay broiling alone, hands outstretched for help that never came.

Kriah's head grew light, and it was only when he was close to fainting that he realised he'd stopped breathing. It took conscious effort to shake the paralysis from his lungs.

'The Meah-Hyren did not do this,' Yae'ilston said, voice low as he pre-empted the blame Kriah wanted to hurl his way.

'I know,' Kriah mumbled, words fighting for space against the bile rising in his throat.

The fires of Cirahk had been organised—a structured and systematic disposal of bodies. This was slaughter. A frenzied and chaotic cleansing of the populace. Not even children had been spared.

Kriah approached what he thought was the tavern, its pitched roof half-collapsed, windows smashed in the heat of a blaze that now smouldered in ashes. Black, charred bodies clogged the doorway where they had become stuck in their escape. A bright smear of red paint splashed across the wall beside them.

'*It dies… with us,*' Kriah read. A body slumped against the wall, broken lantern and upturned pitcher of oil at its feet. 'Deities dead … They did this to themselves.' He turned back to where Yae'ilston lingered beneath the smoke. 'They burned everyone alive.'

Yae'ilston stepped over a body, even though his incorporeal form had no influence on the world. He squatted to observe the dry remains.

'What curious things the Second Born are,' he said, fascinated like a child watching a spider in a web. 'Throwing away such a fleeting existence, all to stop the spread of a sickness they may or may not have had.'

'You did this,' Kriah growled, jaw tight. 'You may not have sparked the fire, but you damn well fanned the flames!'

Yae'ilston clicked his tongue as he stood. 'Did you ever think that we might have stayed quietly on our islands had *you* not broken the first seal? *You* threw the first punch. *You* provoked this war.'

The accusation hit Kriah hard. There were truths hidden in that blow. Truths that stung like acid splashed across his skin. 'Azet'haal wants to be a god,' he said weakly, repeating the words Greist'hal had told him so many times. 'He wants to seize control while the Goddess is away from her throne. We had to strike first. We had to—'

'Azet'haal is mad,' Yae'ilston spat. 'He's always had ambitions, yes, but no pressing need to act upon them. Time means nothing to him. He is immortal. He is powerful. But you gave him reason to act and to act *now*. We're all here because of *you*, whether we want it or not. We have no alternative.'

Kriah tried to swallow, but his throat was too dry from the panic. 'You're ... you're afraid of him.'

'Of course we're afraid of him!' Yae'ilston shouted. 'Because he's afraid of *her*. Miatha's return challenges his power and he will do anything—*anything*—to keep it!'

He took a deep breath, closing his eyes for a moment as he fought to regain his composure.

'And that, my dear halfblood,' he continued, eerily calm, 'is why all of us will die.'

22

AMIKHARLIA

The demonspawn scattered, and Emanais's army let them. Retreating to the safety of the tunnels, the soldiers watched the beasts run wild through the compound, while those unable to scale the high walls frantically tried to dig beneath them.

The *khaaja* hovered overhead. Its immense serpentine form blocked the red glow seeping from the Tear, shrouding the camp in a darkness they hadn't seen in months. Smoke billowed out of its cavernous nostrils; blood dropped from its great maw—no, from its entire body.

'Deities dead,' Amika breathed, gripping her brother's arm as he pushed into the tunnel beside her. 'It's falling apart. It's ... it's *rotting*.'

Muscle and flesh sluiced off the *khaaja*'s long body in globs of melted skin. The ground below sizzled as it landed, steam rising as it bored craters into the earth like acid eating through parchment. Amika brought a hand to her mouth to suppress a scream as a strip of decaying flesh splashed onto a wounded soldier below. He howled briefly. Silence.

'I don't understand,' she said, swallowing the bile back down, looking back at Rei, who lingered in Kio's shadow. 'You said the *khaaja* that came through the Tear took human form. This ... this is anything but!'

'They *do* assume our form,' Rei insisted. He was paler than normal, blood seeping from a cut through his eyebrow, arms battered and bruised from the watchtower collapse. He pressed his fingers to his forehead and inspected the blood he found there as if only now realising he was wounded. His gold eyes flicked to Emanais, who stood in the mouth of the tunnel, guiding her soldiers below.

'My scouts have uncovered some disturbing rumours of late,' she said, expression grim. 'It seems some of the *khaaja* are losing the ability to sustain their guise, ever since the wound in the sky reopened.' Emanais looked out on the camp that had become a killing field, avoiding eye contact with Amika and the others. Her hands tightened to fists at her sides. 'One was even found dead. West of here, out in the Waste. He was … one of the oldest sires known to us. Uz-Arahk-Nar.'

Her choice of words took Amika by surprise. *Sire.* And she had called it by name, a familiar sentiment for a creature that was effectively raping women and condemning them—and their offspring—to death.

'The Tear is killing the *khaaja*?' Amika pressed. 'Isn't that a good thing?'

Emanais tore her gaze away from her dying comrades to face Amika now. Fear and anger burned behind her eyes. 'You Meytarans know *nothing*,' she spat. 'Sever the bloodline and *everyone* dies. Who knows how many Siephymn dropped dead when Uz-Arahk-Nar fell. How many will die with that one!'

She thrust a desperate hand towards the serpentine beast floating menacingly above them. But it didn't attack. It was looking for something—or waiting for it. The golden orbs of its eyes scanned in opposite directions, swirling in its skull like incandescent glass beads.

'Better they die human,' Rei mumbled, but the words still caught Emanais's ears. She lunged at him, grabbing the collar of his shirt; he made no attempt to evade or even shrug her off.

'You think you speak for everyone, hmm?' she hissed, dragging his face close to hers. 'If you're so afraid of becoming a monster then kill *yourse*—'

'*Hey!*' Kio intervened, shoving Emanais back so hard against the stone wall Amika heard the air leave her lungs with a huff. Her jaw was firm and strong as she held the prince's challenging stare, but Amika could see the glisten of tears in her eyes. 'No one is killing anyone,' Kio growled.

The *khaaja* roared and the ground shook. Amika blocked her ears, covered her head, as slivers of chipped rock and dust from the tunnels rained upon her. Its thrashing tail whipped up wind like a tornado as it shook its whole body, a wet dog ridding water from its coat. Globules of rotting flesh flew to earth, covering the soldiers too wounded to run in a foul, acidic sludge.

'Well, except maybe that thing,' Kio muttered bitterly. Emanais slapped out of his grip, pushing herself off the wall.

'And what if that *thing* is Yeni's sire? What if it's *his?*' She pointed at Rei.

'It's not mine,' he said.

'What makes you so sure? Familiar with your father's true form, are you?'

'No, but a regular demonspawn gives me a splitting headache; I think my *sire* might have more of an effect on me.' Rei folded his arms, fire dimming. 'Besides, my mother was raped in Kheshtarl. I doubt that thing could have crossed the ocean in its current state.'

As their argument fell silent, Amika heard the screams of the soldiers still fighting. Some had remained to help injured comrades, slashing and stabbing at the demonspawn more concerned with feeding than fleeing from the *khaaja* like their brethren. It hadn't occurred to Amika why they were even running from an alpha ... until it reared back its great head, opened its cavernous maw and lashed towards the rabble like a cobra striking through grass. It consumed demonspawn, Qhoraakese and stone alike, flicking its head towards the sky to guide the meal down its gullet.

'Well. Fuck,' Rei observed dryly.

'Guess that explains why the demonspawn are running,' Amika mumbled to herself. To Emanais, she said, 'It's eating its own kind. It's gone mad. We have to kill it.'

Emanais closed her eyes and drew in several calming breaths. Amika understood her hesitation. Saving themselves here would condemn others, maybe even her own sister. Maybe even Rei. The consequence weighed heavily on Amika, too, but she was even more aware of what would happen if *she* died, if the seals on the Goddess remained intact. Whyt'hallen would continue to decay in purgatory, unable to set itself right without Miatha's healing hand. Amika had to survive this—or no one would.

'Let's try to draw it away from the camp,' she said. 'Get it out in the open and I'll ... do something—I don't know. But I'll kill it. And you can help the others while it's distracted.'

'Absolutely fucking not,' were the next words out of Kio's mouth; Amika expected nothing less from her brother. But Emanais and Rei were silent, pragmatically considering the merits of her plan.

Amika opened her mouth to push her case further when a high-pitched keening echoed deep within the tunnels. She turned towards the sound, to the soldiers packed in the narrow space trying to shuffle aside to make room for something coming through.

A little boy pushed his way towards them, arms outstretched in search of comfort, tears wet in his amber-gold eyes.

'*Sylar!*' Emanais breathed, dropping to her knees to envelop the child in a tight embrace. She rested her cheek against his crimson hair and swayed back and forth to calm him. 'It's alright, baby boy. *Abna*'s here. I've got you.'

'Ema ...' Kio cautioned through clenched teeth. 'Get him back below.'

'Give me a minute, will you?'

But they did not have a minute. Amika saw the reason for Kio's urgency.

The *khaaja* had spotted the tunnels and was headed right for them, slithering through the sky as easily as it would have moved on land.

'Go, go, go!' Kio shouted, pushing everyone back as the beast lunged at the entrance. The ground trembled and Amika lost her balance. Screams echoed in her ears—human and *khaaja* alike.

The creature's colossal head had no hope of fitting past the threshold, but she could feel its hot breath streaming in on them, drowning out the air in the narrow space. It nipped and scratched at the rock, desperately digging with its comparatively short forelegs like a fox at a rabbit warren. And that was exactly how Amika felt—small and feeble and trapped in a hole. Cornered by a predator she had no hope of besting.

They retreated through the tunnels, the soldiers dispersing down the many different corridors, Emanais leading Amika and the others to that homely, furnished room. She guided Sylar towards the bed and wrapped him beneath the furs and quilts to keep him safe and calm. Amika and Kio filed in after her; Rei lingered at the door.

'What is it?' Amika asked, noticing his hesitation. He scanned the room with caution but said nothing, feet firmly planted beyond the threshold.

'Rei?' Kio pressed.

'I'm fine here.'

The ceiling overhead shuddered, dust and rubble sprinkling down like crumbs from a good pie crust. Sylar wailed beneath the cocoon of blankets. They must have been ten, fifteen feet underground. But with the *khaaja*'s immense size and strength, its relentless gouging at the earth, it wouldn't take much to cause a breach.

'Is there another way out of the tunnels?' Amika asked Emanais. They'd only ever used one entrance to the facility, though it seemed impractical for such a large base. But the Qhoraakese woman's face only paled, expression growing stony as she shook her head.

'This place was a prison,' she said grimly. 'Only one way in or out. We've been working on digging our own escape routes, but we've yet to break the surface.'

The air in the room suddenly felt sparse. Amika never thought herself claustrophobic, but the realisation that they were trapped below ground with no windows or doors to the outside sent her heart thumping, her chest growing tight.

'There is another way.' Rei's voice was small from the doorway. His arms were folded so tightly across his body it was as though he were wrapped in his own embrace. 'A narrow shaft heading straight up. Easily mistaken for ventilation, unless it's been filled in.'

'Impossible. We would have found it.'

'I escaped a farm, Emanais. *This* farm. You think I'd forget how I did it?' Rei snapped. Then, relaxing his posture with a breath, he added, 'But seeing as we're not going anywhere, I guess I'll go check.'

Kio made to stop him, but Amika called him back; she remembered how Rei looked when they passed this room yesterday. Keeping him here would help no one.

Instead her brother moved towards the bed and rubbed a hand over the keening pile of fabric that was Sylar. He tried to shush the little boy, but even the combined efforts of Kio and Emanais did little to soothe him.

'Do you think ...' Amika began, then cleared her throat to gather her thoughts. The *khaaja* had only turned on the tunnels when Sylar came to find them at the entrance, screaming and distraught. Rei told her once that demonspawn were drawn to him, and he suffered in their presence; for a full-blooded Siephymn—a child, no less—to come face-to-face with a *khaaja* ... The pain must be extraordinary.

'Could it be after Sylar?' she said at last. 'You said the Allchief was breeding Siephymn for a reason. Perhaps what he's really after is a way to trap *khaaja*.'

Emanais's hazel eyes grew hard and narrow; Amika braced herself, half expecting to find a firearm levelled at her chest. But instead Emanais's rage turned inward as she considered what Amika hypothesised.

'That may be,' she said, 'but what exactly are you proposing? That we use the boy as *bait?*'

There was a challenging hiss to her words, but before Amika could defend herself, Kio leapt to the attack as well.

'You can't be serious, Amika! The boy is Rei's son!'

'*What?*'

Amika and Emanais's voices both echoed around the chamber. Amika wasn't sure what shocked her more—the assumption that she'd use a child to lure away a monster, or that Rei had fathered the boy. For Emanais, it was definitely the latter. Pandemonium descended upon the room. Indignation. Accusation. Fear. Disgust. It all swirled in a maelstrom of raised voices and stabbing fingers.

'He fucking *raped* my sister—'

'—it's not like that, he—'

'How could you think I'd sacrifice a—'

'The escape shaft's still there.'

Silence fell, heavy as a hammer. Rei stood in the doorway, face impassive. Amika looked at her brother, at his closed eyes and slow exhale, regret pouring off every inch of him. No one could bring themself to speak; even Sylar had hushed.

'I suspect Amika is right,' he said. 'The *khaaja* probably is drawn to the boy. Well, his blood, anyway. We should be able to use it to lure the beast away. What we do with it then—well ...' He shrugged. 'At least you'll have time to evacuate.'

Amika nodded, digesting the plan. 'So, we climb out this tunnel of yours and draw the *khaaja* away from the entrance.'

Rei shook his head. 'There's no *we*, Princess. I barely fit through that hole. You might get out by shredding that pretty skin of yours, but those two'—he gestured at Kio and Emanais—'not a chance.' Sighing, he rubbed at weary eyes. 'I'll take the boy's blood up the shaft and lead the *khaaja* away from the compound. I'm small, agile, fast on my feet—I should be able to outrun it. Once the entrance is clear, you can come after us and, I don't know, Amika can blast it with her powers or something.'

His tone and body language were flippant, but everyone in the room understood the desperation of the plan. There was little space for error; even less hope of success. But if they didn't do something, everyone here would be crushed to death. What was a little bit of child's blood compared to that?

Emanais evidently drew the same conclusion. Her frown was as sharp as a razor blade, but she nodded. She stood and pried open the creaky iron door of a tall metal cabinet running the height of the room, built directly into the stone wall. She produced a long, slim firearm with a polished wooden grip the colour of rich mahogany. The barrel gleamed like a mirror.

'Here,' Emanais said, thrusting the weapon into Kio's chest. She dropped a sack, heavy with iron pellets, into his hands. 'You wanted to shoot a firearm; now's your chance. Hope you can handle the kickback, Little Prince.'

She returned to her spot on the bed next to Sylar and placed a comforting hand on the mound of blankets.

Kio looked around, bewildered. 'Amika, you can't be seri—'

'The sooner we get it over with the better,' Rei mumbled. He produced a dagger from somewhere and drew a slow breath as he stepped into the room. Stopping beside Sylar's cocoon, he knelt down to what would be the child's eye level. 'I need his arm,' he said, thrusting his own under the mound of furs.

The boy wailed in panic; Emanais seized Rei's wrist, fire in her eyes. Kio jumped to his feet in his lover's defence.

'I'm going to give his arm a little nick, not cut it off. Deities fucking dead,' Rei hissed, ripping himself free. If he felt troubled slicing the flesh of his own son, he did not show it; his expression was as unreadable as ever, though Amika might have imagined a slight clenching of his jaw. He tenderly ran the blade across the boy's forearm, like a hot knife kissing a block of butter. A high-pitched shriek erupted from the blankets as blood beaded on the wound, black and pearlescent.

Rei smeared the inky substance across the blade and tucked it into his belt. 'I'll head east,' he said, turning to Amika. 'Take it down as quickly as you can. I may have my strength back, but I can't run forever.'

He slipped away without any form of goodbye, not so much as a glance at Kio. Her brother immediately gave chase but Amika lingered a moment. Fear hung from her chest, as hard and heavy as armour. But if its weight was tangible, she could use it. Twist it, temper it, wield it like a blade. Anything to help them survive this.

'Once the camp is clear, retrieve your men,' Amika instructed Emanais. 'Some of them might yet be saved. Don't waste our distraction.'

'I won't,' the woman said, giving a solemn dip of her head. 'Don't get yourself killed, Chosen. How can I fulfil my destiny without you?'

Amika returned a stiff nod, unsure if Emanais was mocking, and made her way out into the meandering tunnels. Bodies filled the narrow space wall-to-wall. The air was heavy and clouded with dust, thick with the stench of blood and piss. Amika pushed against the flow of soldiers edging away from the entrance as she tried to catch up to her brother, whose head she followed above the crowd like a beacon. He moved quickly, shoving people aside as he cut through the throng. Amika finally reached him as he approached the stretch of corridor leading to the surface, where the *khaaja* thrashed against the stony earth.

'Hey,' she said, gripping Kio's elbow. 'We'll come through this. We have to.'

Kio shook her off. His posture was rigid, broody, as he stood before the mouth of the tunnel, Emanais's long firearm cradled against his chest. They were beyond the *khaaja*'s reach. Its great snout may have been too large to breach the entranceway, but its claws were long and desperate and had already carved several deep runnels into the stone. Her brother let the silence grow and Amika floundered; the last thing she wanted to do was let time pass wordlessly between them.

'Rei's fast,' she said. 'And stubborn. He dragged himself here half-dead just to see you again. He's not going to throw that away in a hurry.'

'Don't, Amika,' was all Kio said.

She opened her mouth to protest when a sudden silence drew her attention. The khaaja's assault had stopped, its head turned elsewhere. There was a moment of stillness before a piercing cry ripped through the underground labyrinth and the beast withdrew, swift as smoke.

'This is it,' Amika breathed. 'Let's go.'

Kio nodded and waited for her lead. She clambered over the ruins of the tunnel's entrance and up into the camp. The air was hazy from smouldering fires; moans and cries of wounded soldiers filled her ears. She blocked them out, looked to the east. A dark streak burst from the breached walls, the immense serpent on its heels.

Amika ran. Her body was battered and bruised from the earlier battle, fuelled now by adrenaline and little more. Kio struggled to keep pace, but with the long-range capabilities of the firearm in his hands, he could afford to fall behind. Amika glanced over her shoulder to see him load a bullet into the chamber as he ran, leather satchel gripped in his teeth.

'Not yet!' she screamed. They couldn't afford for it to turn on them—not before she had a plan. But the land here was barren. Not just infertile soil but earth devoid of *khe'torla*, a shrivelled husk left too long in the sun. She found nothing to draw from, no clear resonance to grasp.

The *khaaja* dived. Splinters of rock shot into the sky, swallowing the beast's long form in a mushroom-shaped cloud. Amika slid to a halt; Kio raised the firearm. Fire crackled through the air.

A hollow thud. A guttural shriek.

The rifle belched smoke and steel. Kio cursed, the force of the blast having sent the weapon careening back into his face. He spit blood from a split lip and prepared to reload, but they were blind in a rain of dust and debris. He'd been lucky to hit anything with his last shot, Amika knew, and he'd only waste bullets if he continued firing wildly into the plume. But at least he was doing *something*—more than she could say for herself. Doubt spread like a noxious weed through her chest, furling its tendrils around her heart, her lungs, her throat. This plan was foolish—suicidal, even. Why had she agreed to this? Why did she—

A shadow burst from the collapsing dust cloud, small and thin as a needle in the distance. Hope dared to swell. Rei was alright, and he was running, the *khaaja* still embedded in the stone from its failed assault.

An idea started to grow.

'I'll try to trap it,' Amika said at last. The once-silent earth howled at the disturbance, sending a pulse thrumming up her legs and through her veins. She'd commanded it before, back in Honnah with the wannari. There'd been more life in the soil then. But still, she had to try.

Amika stretched her *khe'torla* towards the *khaaja*, running her awareness around the lip of the crater, through the cracks in the stony ground. She clenched her fist and the earth obeyed. The fissure constricted, crushing bone and rock alike. The *khaaja* shrieked, long and high like a kettle whistling on the stove. Amika squeezed until the muscles of her hands started to strain, the tendons of her wrist taut.

But there was resistance. Something pushing back. Her grip loosened, failed, and the *khaaja* burst free in an explosion of chipped stone.

Amika hit the ground, head covered. Kio remained on his feet, firearm loaded and ready to fire. He dropped the hammer and the bullet flew. It bounced off a gnarled horn protruding from the crown of the beast's head. Snarling, it curled its serpentine form towards them.

'Do something, Amika,' Kio growled through clenched teeth, reloading. His cheek was bruised from wrestling with the recoil, but he held the firearm steady and levelled his aim. The next bullet ripped through the *khaaja*'s left eye. It burst like a summer fruit, congealed golden slop spraying into the air.

Enraged, it gained speed, a snake preparing to strike. Kio shot it again to little effect.

'Amika!' he shouted. But she couldn't move, stunned by her broken trap. The beast was close to them now, so close she could smell the acrid rot of its flesh, feel the heat of the roaring breath billowing from its great open maw. She raised her hands, feeble and hopeless, and reached for the first thing her *khe'torla* could find.

It. She found *it*. Her *khe'torla* twisted around the *khaaja*'s length and it flowed from her, permeating scales, muscles and bone. She felt every painful inch of its decaying body, as though it were an extension of her own being, a nerve she could twitch, a finger she could curl.

A boot she could stomp.

Amika brought her hands together, slowly, as if closing a big, heavy book. The *khaaja* thrashed and howled and foamed, black froth bubbling from his mouth as its body crumpled head to tail. She crushed it like a fold of parchment in her fist. Bones splintered. Entrails burst. Its last good eye popped in its skull.

Searing pain burned through Amika. Blood trickled from her nose, her ears. The pressure inside her head was immense. But she couldn't stop, couldn't sever the connection between her *khe'torla* and the *khaaja*. Not until it was dead.

The beast imploded, crushed by the weight of Amika's will. A torrential black shower of fluid and flesh swirled around them. The ground sizzled and smoked from the acidic downpour as the *khaaja*'s shrivelled remnants plummeted to earth, as dry and brittle as an old leaf.

Amika hit the ground hard. Kio lay atop her, a shield against the fallout. The earth rumbled beneath her and something, somewhere distant, cracked like broken glass. But Amika was no longer conscious to see it.

23

REI-HAI

There was shrapnel in his leg. A sliver of rock, thick as his thumb, driven deep into the meat of his calf. Rei limped through the gore and ruin of the *khaaja*. Its corpse lay in a foot-deep crater, bones and viscera now outside its flesh. Throat dry from running, his hoarse voice called desperately for Kio. Panic swelled within. All he could see were smoking piles of black, acidic slop.

When the *khaaja* fell, the whole world had swayed like a boat at sea and a great crack of rolling thunder echoed in the distance. Now, it was silent as gravestones.

'Kio!' he called with a cough, lungs heavy with inhaled sediment. 'Kio! Answer me, please. Kio! *Fuck.*'

Rei lost his footing and stumbled, wounded leg screaming. Pain kept him down a while. Frozen, right there on the ground, hands and knees in the *khaaja's* black blood. How many Siephymn died when this beast fell? How many lives, just like his? Did they implode in a shower of blood and bone, bodies twisted inside out, just like their sire who lay behind him on the Waste? Or did their hearts just simply ... stop?

'Kio!' he screamed himself raw. Finally—a groan, a cough, a curse. Rei pushed himself back to his feet, hopping as he rushed in the direction of the sound.

'Over here!' a dusty voice croaked, and warmth spread through Rei's body like a flood.

Kio huddled on the ground, half covered by a rocky outcropping, blood and dirt smeared across his beautiful face. Rei dropped before him, hands clamped along his jaw, kissing his lips.

'I'm alright, I'm alright,' Kio insisted, breaking away. Their foreheads pressed together and Rei breathed the moment down deep, savouring the relief that was sure to be short-lived. Kio's left hand curled about Rei's neck, but the other grasped something in his lap.

'She won't wake up,' the prince said, voice breaking. 'She won't open her eyes.'

Amika lay on her back, head turned away from them, a trail of dried blood snaking down her neck from her ear. The same red stains seeped from the corners of her eyes, and her lips were paler than the moon. Rei pressed his fingers to her throat.

'She's alive,' he confirmed. The pulse was faint, but it was there. 'She probably used too much *khe'torla* to slay the *khaaja*. She'll be fine with rest.'

He tried to recall the Meah-Hyren's lessons back in the Li'Nea Wood, something about balance and resonances and things he didn't quite understand. Demonspawn were different, Grey had said; no internal *khe'torla* to draw on. Amika must have used her own to bring it down. But how much ...

Kio looked at him as though Rei had spoken another tongue, but now was not the time to explain Amika and her gifts. 'Are you hurt? Can you stand?' Rei asked instead. 'I took a wound to the leg. I'm fine, but I can't carry her.'

'Show me,' Kio demanded. He reached towards Rei's leg, fussing like a nursemaid, until Rei batted his hands away.

'I said I'm fine. Just … give me a minute. Help Amika.'

Reluctantly Kio withdrew, got to his feet and stretched out his muscles with a stiff groan. He looked unharmed—filthy, but unharmed, save for a cut on his forehead that looked worse than it was. He slung Emanais's rifle across his back and bent down to scoop Amika into his arms, her body limp. Once she was balanced precariously over his shoulder, he stretched a hand towards Rei.

'Shall I carry you too?' he said, half-hearted smile on his lips.

Rei placed his hand in Kio's, squeezing tight. 'I'd hate for you to overburden yourself, my prince,' he said, grimacing as he was hauled upright. He melted against the taller man's side, silently grateful for the weight Kio was able to support with an arm curled protectively about his back.

Together, they took their first tentative steps towards camp.

Their arrival was hardly the hero's welcome they deserved. Recovery was underway, with the abled frantically tending to the injured and assessing the damage. Additional tents were being erected, those crushed in the battle salvaged and repurposed. Demonspawn were piled and put to the torch; Rei no longer felt any nearby.

'We need to find a healer for Amika,' Kio said as they hobbled through the collapsed gates. His breath came in heavy pants, sweat thick on his forehead. All around them, the maimed and dying moaned—or worse, lay grave-still and forgotten.

Rei peeled himself away from Kio's side, away from his support. His leg buckled and he reached for the prince's arm to prevent the inevitable fall.

'And for you, too,' Kio added.

Rei hissed in pain. The stone shard shifted, sending fresh hot blood streaming down his leg and into his boot. The shrapnel needed to come out, but not until it could be properly cleaned and sutured.

'I'm fine,' he insisted again and eased weight back through his leg, with slow, gradual caution. It was hardly the worst injury he'd endured, but being a lower limb, it was as cumbersome as it was painful. He pulled away from Kio, steady on his feet now, and scanned the camp for any signs of command or order among the chaos.

Emanais stood outside the entrance to the tunnels, perched on a crate to increase her already imposing height. The child clung to her thigh, bandage wrapped about his arm where Rei had cut him, black and splotchy against his pale skin. Their eyes met across the camp and she disentangled herself from the child, hopped down off the box to race towards them.

'You did it,' she said, though the words were more question than statement. 'Brave Hirathi, *how?*'

'It was Amika,' Kio said, breathless. 'I don't know how, but she did it, and now she won't wake up.'

'Give her to me.' Emanais held her arms out like a mother awaiting a babe. Kio passed his sister to her, Amika's form lolling against the Qhoraakese woman's chest. 'Come. I'll take her to Forykke, our chief chirurgeon. He will see to her.' She started leading Kio away.

'I guess I'll go find a lesser chirurgeon, then,' Rei said, pointing towards a row of tents obviously used for triage. 'Should be good enough for me.'

Kio paused and made to return to his side, but Rei shook his head. Amika *was* more important; he just didn't like the hold Emanais had on Kio.

She saved him, Amika had said. The words had explained his lover's attachment to the Qhoraakese woman. It did not, however, justify Emanais's obsession with *him*.

Rei limped through the heavy canvas flap to a wall of hot air thick with wine, blood and fragrant herbs. Twelve cots had been cramped into the long but narrow tent, some housing two or three injured. Healers flitted between patients, administering strong mandrake tea to the worst of them and plying the rest with buckets of wine. Everywhere Rei looked he saw blood and bonesaws, scalpels and gauze. He hadn't seen a lot of hospitals, wartime or otherwise, and being confronted with such filth, agony and inevitable death sent an uncomfortable shiver across his skin.

'Full, full!' a healer said, looking up from his comatose patient. Blood-stained linen covered the man's abdomen, shredded by a demonspawn to the point that his shit-filled bowels spilt out; the stench was horrendous. Even Rei could see he was beyond saving.

'Sorry?' Rei asked stupidly, unsure if he'd heard the man correctly through his thick Qhoraakese accent.

The healer pulled the length of fabric wrapped around his nose and mouth down to make his words more audible. 'This tent full,' he said clearly. 'Go next one.'

In the next tent, Rei was greeted by a young girl so panicked by the ruins of battle that she stared at him, frozen and wide-eyed.

'My, uh, leg ...' He gestured flippantly at his bleeding calf, but the girl continued to stare. He noticed now that this tent was empty—silent. Had he stumbled into the wrong place? She was definitely a healer; her white apron, face mask and blood-stained hands told him that much. She'd likely come here seeking a moment's respite, but Rei didn't have the energy to hobble off in search of *another* triage tent.

'I'll just ... take a seat ...' he panted, limping to a cot. He collapsed with far less grace than he would have liked, but he was exhausted and in pain, and frankly didn't care much for dignity. The stiff fabric groaned under his weight, slight though it was, as he lay back and brought both legs off the ground.

Rei closed his eyes, groaning as the adrenaline drained from his body and left behind a cavernous void ready to be filled with ache. Hands touched his leg and he startled, pulse spiking; the timid girl recoiled from her attempt to inspect his wound. She mumbled something in Qhoraakese and the onslaught of incomprehensible speech dropped a heavy stone of dread on Rei's chest. Her breathless words and frantic pace brought back memories of the farm, of his designated workmate's desperate pleas. His skin prickled, muscles tense.

'Pain,' she said, having located words in the common Meytaran tongue. She reached for his leg once more.

'Yes, pain.' Rei jerked away on instinct and sent more agony ripping through his muscles. 'Much fucking pain.'

The girl nodded, shuffled away, then returned with a wineskin, full and bloated like a drunkard's belly. Rei's stomach churned. He had no thirst for alcohol; a sip here and there was all he could swallow. The residual trauma from the drunken batterings of his childhood was enough to quench his thirst for a lifetime. But the thought of surgery sans anaesthetic …

Rei reached for the skin, pulled the cork free with his teeth. He was dehydrated from running, and although wine wouldn't help, he chugged it down with desperate need for oblivion.

He felt the effects almost instantly. It wasn't just wine he'd been given—it was some awful cocktail of whatever liquor they had at their disposal, mixed to be potent and unforgiving. It burned the whole way down his throat before setting his insides ablaze from the pit of his stomach. His body grew hot, heavy, and finally, detached.

The Qhoraakese healer's speech was distant. Soothing in a way he hadn't felt before. He still didn't know what she was saying, but he supposed it didn't matter. His whole world spun. Through the blur of his vision, a moment of clarity: the flash of a scalpel. The kiss of a blade. The searing pain of torn flesh.

Blackness.

There was a foul taste in his mouth, the lingering tang of alcohol and bile. Had he vomited? If he had, he'd been cleaned, along with the tent around him. Rei eased himself up on his elbows, stomach roiling and head pounding. He'd expected to feel worse, actually. Perhaps what made him susceptible to liquor's effects also hastened his recovery.

The healer was long gone, the tent around him eerily empty for a hospital in a battle zone. But as he looked around, he saw this place was more storage than triage, with crates of supplies stacked haphazardly like they'd been brought here in a rush.

Rei swung his legs over the side of the cot and sat up. He grimaced from the pain in his calf, tightly bandaged in bone-white linen, the leg of his pants cut away from the knee. He was about to try to stand when a rustling outside the tent drew his attention. Habit saw his hand search for a blade; his fingers found a scalpel beside the cot.

Kio stumbled through the flap, batting it aside like he was tangled in a spider web. His skin was flushed, eyes glassy, gait unsteady. Gods, he was drunk—drunk like Rei had never seen before. He set the scalpel aside as the prince staggered towards him and fell to his knees in the dirt.

'Praise Miatha, you're alright,' he slurred, nuzzling into Rei's chest. 'I thought you were going to die. I was so *sure* you would die. Everybody dies.'

'Kio ...' Rei parted his thighs to pull Kio closer, arms wrapping about his broad body. But instead of savouring the intimate warmth of their entangled limbs, he bristled. His fingers brushed across something rough, something crusted, hard and wet. Rei pushed the prince away, tried to turn his much larger frame to get a look at his back.

'Deities dead,' he breathed. 'Fuck, Kio. Didn't you get a healer to look at *you?*'

The prince was peppered with charred craters burned into his flesh like a beetle boring through wood. They were black and weeping, a mix of his own blood and whatever acidic slop had splashed on his body from the decaying *khaaja*.

'Shit. *Fuck.*'

'Pick a curse, Rei-Hai,' Kio muttered. 'No need to be so fucking foul.'

Rei ignored him and slipped out from beneath his slumped form to manoeuvre him face first onto the cot. He touched the wounds gingerly, unsure if Kio even *felt* them. It certainly didn't seem like he did, but the wine would have numbed his senses. Rei hissed as he pulled back the ruin of Kio's shirt; the singed fabric had melted into some of the larger, fleshy caverns.

'Sit up,' he instructed. 'We need to get this off.'

Kio mumbled something unintelligible but managed to oblige. Rei swung a leg so he straddled the narrow cot and scooted forward until he was almost flush with Kio's back. He curled his arms around the prince's body to help him undress. Deft fingers blindly unlatched the clasps of his surcoat and loosened the laces that held his undershirt closed, just as they had many times before. But not like this.

Never like this.

Rei slid the well-worn clothes carefully off Kio's shoulders, fighting the instinct to press his lips to the warm skin he'd exposed. There were some marks he didn't remember; souvenirs picked up from Kio's time in the Cirahk dungeons and a string of bubbled silvery scars down his left flank. Numbers—a brand.

His fingers traced the outline of the old burn before he even realised what he was doing.

57892.

A number denoting proof of purchase.

A receipt in a ledger.

Nausea bubbled in Rei's gut once more. But this time it was anger, and not the lingering effects of the alcohol he'd ingested. To see the man he loved more than this world reduced to a string of *numbers* ...

'What is she?' Kio mumbled groggily. His voice was so small Rei hadn't been sure if he'd even spoken. 'My sister,' he said. 'Amika. What is she?'

Rei took a deep breath, fingers pulling away from the brand. 'Powerful,' he said. Plain. Simple. Because there was no other explanation for Amika, even if Kio *was* in a state to hear it. 'She's powerful.'

Kio nodded, his head dipping low against his chest, shoulders slumped and spine curved. The shape of a man defeated.

Just like you, my prince, he wanted to add. *If only you'd remember.*

While he was still and quiet, Rei set about tending Kio's wounds. He knew the basics, had stitched his fair share of holes during his time at the Tower. Kio's burns didn't need to be sutured, but the quicker they were cleaned and dressed, the less likely infection would set in.

He reached for the array of implements spread out beside the cot, remnants from his own treatment. Anything stained by his inky blood had probably been destroyed, leaving only pre-cut wads of sterile gauze, various tweezers and probes, needles, and twine on the tray. Rei lifted a polished tin with its lid half unscrewed and brought it to his nose. The salve was shiny with beeswax, fragrant with calendula, comfrey and plantain. He inspected the assortment of glass phials and discovered more tinctures; there was even a little jar wriggling with maggots.

'I'm going to clean these,' Rei said, moistening a strip of gauze with a clear liquid, sharp with the scent of alcohol. He pressed it to the first of many scabbed pits and braced himself for recoil.

Kio did not flinch.

Rei worked meticulously, as swift and precise as he could with Kio swaying drunkenly atop the cot. The discarded gauze piled up on the ground by his foot, dark with dried blood and dead, charred skin. Kio lurched forward suddenly and a snore escaped to rouse him from his stupor. His head whipped around in panic.

'Kio,' Rei soothed, fingertips stroking his neck. 'You're alright. I'm here. We're back at camp.'

The prince flopped backwards, head colliding with Rei's shoulder. He stared up at the sloped ceiling, at the spot where the central pole pierced the highest peak, sapphire eyes unfocussed. The coarse stubble on his cheek brushed against Rei's neck, but Rei just nuzzled closer, savouring the sandpaper roughness of the intimate proximity. Kio's skin was *very* warm.

Rei's pulse thundered through his veins. He turned his face into the crook of Kio's neck, inhaling the thick scent of him, all the wine and sweat and blood. Kio moaned, raised his hand to curl through Rei's hair. Soft and hesitant, Rei pressed his lips to the prince's throat, his jaw. Up to his ear, where he sucked the lobe, once adorned with jewelled piercings, between his teeth.

Kio gasped, and time blurred. There was no distance or years or trauma between them now—just a familiar dance of tongues and touch, lips and hands. Hot kisses and breathy moans. Rei found himself in Kio's lap, the pain in his leg a forgotten memory as their bodies ground ever closer. His hands gripped the prince's face as if he needed their kiss to survive—needed *him* like the oxygen he needed to breathe. And in a way he supposed he did. Kio was why he held on, why he still fought to live. It wasn't for a prophecy, or fear of death, or even the pain of becoming demonspawn. It was Kio. It was always Kio. It had always *been* Kio.

A nip at his collarbone drew a gasp of his own; Rei's fingers pulled at Kio's hair in delight as he finally came alive beneath his touch. His cock strained painfully against his pants, against Kio's taut belly, as Kio squeezed him so hard he couldn't breathe. The cot protested beneath their writhing weight as Kio upended Rei onto his back. He descended upon him with an obvious intent to devour, an animalistic hunger that made Rei purr with desire. Fuck, he was so hard, and Kio was too. But Kio was also drunk—so *fucking* drunk. Did he even know where he was? What was happening? Who he was with?

Rei whimpered Kio's name, teeth around his nipple, and bucked his hips to ease his arousal against the prince's own. There was a hand inside his breeches now, fingers teasing, stroking, probing. Rei groaned again, his grip squeezing the wounds on Kio's back. The other man tensed and Rei's heart stopped.

'Kio—'

'Don't,' he slurred, eyes hooded, lips barely moving. 'I don't want to think. I don't want to *fucking* think. I don't—'

'Then don't,' Rei said quickly. He stroked Kio's face, his cheek. Brushed his hair back out of his eyes. 'Don't think. Just close your eyes and kiss me.' Rei craned his neck to take Kio's lips, once, twice. Gentle, calm, coaxing kisses. 'See? That's all you need to do. Hold me. Kiss me.' *Love me.* 'I'm right here.'

Rei wrapped his arms tenderly around Kio's back, guiding him slowly atop his own body. He kissed him, deeper this time, a gradual attempt to rekindle the moment. Kio's mouth was inviting, and soon he reclaimed control, forceful and strong. Rei moaned into the kiss, lips caught between teeth, tongues entwined. Kio's lips wandered south, down his neck, down his chest, abdomen, where they stopped just above the waistband of his open breeches. But instead of taking him in his mouth, Kio clutched Rei's hips and flipped him. Rei gasped as the awkward twist set the wound in his calf aflame, pain spreading up his leg. But it was soon forgotten.

Rei's pants were wrenched from his hips, skin prickling as his bare arse was exposed to the world. Kio's hands caressed up his back, his sides, over his shoulders. He kissed Rei's spine. A loud groan burst free as Kio entered him, hard and strong, lifting his pelvis up off the cot to meet his own. Rei pawed fistfuls of the pathetic excuse for a pillow. Kio was rough like he'd never known—erratic, deep and sharp, one hand gripping Rei's hip, the other clamped on his shoulder, slamming him back with every thrust. It was not the reunion he'd envisioned, face pressed into the sheets like he was back at the Tower. But still he moaned, wanting more—needing more. It was perfect because it was Kio. Perfect, because nothing, nothing, *nothing* in this whole fucking world smelt, felt or tasted like the man he'd always loved.

'Rei-Hai ...' Kio moaned breathlessly, curling his hand around Rei's length. Rei shuddered, pleasure burning through his body. He reached back to grip Kio's thigh, his arse, driving his cock even further inside. They were both groaning now, climax close. It was too quick, too soon, but Kio was drunk and it had been so long—*too* long—there was no way they could last much longer.

Rei's arms gave out as he came, falling face first into the pillow with Kio slumped over his back. They were both spent, their bodies slick with sweat and seed and heavy with exhaustion. Rei didn't want to move. Kio's weight atop him was a comfort, his softening length a welcome intrusion. The prince was nuzzled into the curve of his back, his face pressed in the gap between his shoulder blades, drawing long, deep breaths.

'I love you,' Kio mumbled, lips moist against Rei's skin. 'I love you so much, Rei-Hai Shaw. Sickness take the both of us if you ever leave me again.'

'I won't,' Rei said. He found Kio's hand and laced their fingers, giving it a squeeze. 'I promise, I won't. I'm yours.'

There was so much more he wanted to say, things he desperately wanted Kio to know. But before he could voice them, the prince had already slipped off to sleep.

Rei eventually freed himself from beneath Kio's unconscious form. He tidied and dressed himself, covering the prince's nakedness with his discarded clothes. Rei sat on the end of the cot, the other man's knee pressed against his thigh. Kio had lost so much weight, Rei realised now, wasted away from his imprisonment in Cirahk and whatever horrors he'd endured on his voyage here. He rested his hand on the small of Kio's back, thumb stroking the smooth skin. It was the only part that wasn't marked with burns, though the wounds didn't look quite as horrific now they were cleaned and shadowed by the darkness falling outside the tent.

Rei turned his attention to his own wound, to the spots of blood seeping through the dressing. Must have split a stitch. Not that he cared; it didn't hurt that much, compared to other scars.

Footsteps shuffled outside the tent. Rei straightened but otherwise made no effort to move. There was no hiding what had happened here, and he felt no shame, despite the chaos of the camp around them. It was only dumb luck no one stumbled in on them fucking.

Emanais entered. She glanced silently at Rei, then at Kio, and a wide feline grin stretched across her face. 'And who says drunks are useless?'

'Clearly not you,' Rei said venomously, 'seeing as how you like to keep him wasted. Tell me, Emanais: what use do you have for him?'

The Qhoraakese general folded her arms and cocked her head to the side in curious bemusement. She'd left the tent flap curled open behind her and Rei could see the comings and goings of the camp outside, the movements of soldiers marked by flickering torches. More tents had been erected throughout the complex, a new row hemming the triage tents.

'I assure you, my *uses* for your lover in no way interfere with your own,' she said, grin fading. 'So put a muzzle on that jealousy.'

Rei snorted. It wasn't jealousy that made his blood run hot—it was suspicion. The Qhoraakese were responsible for the Siephymn farms, and whether or not Emanais sought to destroy them, he would not trust her. Not when she enabled Kio to drink himself to oblivion.

'Why do you do it?' he asked. 'He's hurting, and you ply him with wine instead of comfort.' He already knew of Kio's ... habits. The self-destructive remedy for grief was one he shared with Rei's childhood guardian, Geraad Shaw. His skin prickled at the thought.

'Kio thinks you saved him,' Rei pressed. 'But you haven't. You've just trapped him with booze instead of irons. So I'll ask you again: why?'

Emanais scratched at her scalp between her braids, seemingly more irritated by Rei and his questions than any itch. Her hazel eyes washed over Kio's prostrate form and lingered on the possessive hand Rei kept on the tilt of his pelvis.

'Because he is me,' she said softly, words tinged with a melancholy Rei did not expect.

'Tortured in a Bararanite prison, were you?'

'No,' she said, still distant. 'But I lost my crown, my family, and was exiled as a traitor to my people. I manage my grief with rum, and I am filled with hate because someone I love is sentenced to die young and there is nothing I can do to stop it. All I want is to feel powerful again.

And if drinking my fill of booze is what it takes to achieve that, then so be it.' Her tone had sharpened to a razor's edge, eyes cold and hard. 'Still think I don't know how to help him?'

Rei shrank, humbled. His finger traced a soothing pattern on the small of Kio's back and he hoped the gentle touch brought him strength he didn't need to find at the bottom of a bottle. The prince stirred, but didn't wake.

'He needs to sleep it off,' Rei mumbled, avoiding Emanais's gaze.

'He can do it later,' she said. 'His sister is awake.'

24

KRIAH

Nell was grey-skinned and face down in a pool of blood. Panic pierced Kriah's chest until he saw Nell shudder with a violent cough. Crimson mist sprayed from his mouth. Kriah rushed to his side and pressed a hand to his back for comfort. Nell's body burned with fever, the heat of it seeping through his sweat-sodden clothes.

'Come on, Nell, sit up,' Kriah said, turning him onto his back. The young man groaned. He was barely lucid, lips flapping wordlessly.

'He's already dead,' Yae'ilston observed, tone flat.

'No, he's not. He's—'

'He's *dead*, Kriah. Look at him. That is not living.'

The blank, unseeing stare of Captain Yless returned unbidden to Kriah's thoughts—as did the mercy Nell granted him. Could Kriah offer the same gift to his friend?

Despair sat heavily on his chest. He took Nell's hand, gave it a squeeze and, to his surprise, found that it squeezed back.

'... find ... her ...?' he croaked.

Kriah leant closer. 'What?'

'Ste ... laya. Did yer ... find ...?'

His throat tightened. If he'd seen her, he'd not noticed; the people of Trendon had been so horrifically burnt, their bodies were reduced to charred logs. Kriah swallowed as he searched for words. None came.

Another hacking cough rattled Nell's body and he inhaled with audible stridor, blood dribbling from the corner of his mouth, from his ears. Kriah cradled his head, trying to elevate it, but it did little to alleviate the horrible wet choking gasps coming from his throat.

'He's your friend and yet you let him suffer?' Yae'ilston scoffed. He stood over them, arms folded.

Hot tears stung Kriah's eyes as he stroked Nell's hair back from his face and fixed Yae'ilston with a withering glare. He knew what he had to do, but that didn't make it easy.

'Stelaya ...' He swallowed, turning his attention back to Nell. 'Stelaya was at the inn. She was sitting at the bar, nice hot bowl of stew before her and a pint of ale in her hand.'

Nell tried to chuckle at the imagery, but a cough came out instead.

'I sat down beside her, and I said, "Nell loves you, dear Stelaya. But he"'—Kriah sniffed— '"he has to go back to sea. To be with his family".'

'D-d-d-d-did she ... say...?' His words were weak, barely audible.

'She put her hand on mine.' Kriah took Nell's hand as he spoke. 'And placed a single kiss on my cheek. Then she said, "Take him home".'

Kriah's voice broke as he uttered those final words, his free hand reaching for the dagger in his belt. Tears spilt down his face now; he hadn't the strength to hold them back. His eyes washed over the stony visage of Yae'ilston before settling again on Nell. He leant close, pressed a kiss to his friend's cheek as though sharing Stelaya's parting gift ... and pushed the tip of the dagger through his skull.

Kriah sat beside Nell's body until nightfall. Despite Yae'ilston's attempts to get him moving, he stayed rooted to the spot beside his friend's corpse. The wound had bled immensely. It leaked from the hole at Nell's temple like wine from a splintered barrel, spreading outward across the floor, where it soaked into the seat of Kriah's trousers.

He didn't care.

He didn't care about anything. Not now. Not in this moment. Perhaps never again.

Yae'ilston had returned to biting his nails—anxious or impatient, Kriah couldn't tell. He didn't imagine the dead Meah-Hyren could smell the thick scent of blood in the air, but he seemed uncomfortable all the same.

'What are the Bararnite customs for honouring the dead?' Kriah rasped, voice raw with emotion. He was sure he'd read about it somewhere but he couldn't find the memory among the grief.

'I don't suppose it much matters,' Yae'ilston mumbled around his thumbnail. 'Second Born die all the time. Surely no one ca—'

'*I* care!' Kriah shouted, so loud he expected Nell to twitch in shock. He didn't, of course, which dragged Kriah with another wave of anguish. 'Because this is our fault. Not yours. Not mine—*ours.*'

'I was following orders,' Yae'ilston hissed.

'You *chose* to obey! And now I choose to fight back. I will release the Goddess and send Azet'haal and his army back to the very fringes of this world. You have no choice but to help me. I die, you die, right?'

The young Meah-Hyren simmered with a surly scowl on his fine-featured face. His arms were folded tightly across his chest in a protective shield. It made him look smaller than his slight frame already was.

'Then we should burn his body.'

It had been days since he'd slept. As a halfblood, he required mortal sleep far less than the average Second Born, but this was the first time he'd counted ten sunrises without closing his eyes. Now the world had gone fuzzy around the edges, like the cuffs on a well-worn coat, and he couldn't quite tell where one thing ended and another began.

'What's wrong with you?' Yae'ilston asked as Kriah tripped over a small branch, hidden beneath the long grass. He didn't manage to break his fall, instead landing heavily on his chin. Blood trickled hotly down his neck before Kriah realised what had happened.

'I, uh ...'

Why was it so hard to answer? He stared blankly at Yae'ilston's visage, slack-jawed and confused. He took a moment to take in his surroundings, to get his bearings and shake lucidity back into his brain. The Holanian capital lay to the southeast of Trendon, and he'd headed more or less in the right direction, if not a little too far south. The setting sun shimmered off a river on the horizon.

Kriah rubbed the heels of his palms into his eyes. They stung furiously, heavy as lead, but the act brought fleeting clarity to his blurred vision. 'Just tired,' he told Yae'ilston, staggering back to his feet. 'I've not slept since Cirahk.'

The Meah-Hyren clicked his tongue. 'Yet another weakness of your tainted blood.'

Kriah steeled himself for another tirade over the absurdity that someone like *him* had stolen Yae'ilston's life. Massaging his temple, he waited for the venom.

But it didn't come. Not this time. He turned back to the space where the Meah-Hyren's spirit had coalesced only to find him standing there, arms folded, resting his chin on the back of his hand.

'Is sleeping ... difficult?' he asked with caution, as though any genuine curiosity in the Second Born's ways would earn him rebuke. 'If it's necessary, why not do it?'

Kriah scratched his head. 'It's not difficult, it's just ...' *Azet'haal.* Sleep would beckon him back inside Kriah's mind. Draw his attention towards Holania and beyond. No, Kriah had to stay awake. Let Azet'haal think he died in the chaos that befell Cirahk.

Don't let him know what I plan to do.

'What happens if I dreamscape?' Kriah asked Yae'ilston. 'Would you join me there too?' *Would Azet'haal?*

'I imagine so,' Yae'ilston nodded. 'This blending of consciousness is designed to drive you mad—a punishment for stealing the life and *khe'torla* of your kin. I would think that means you'd be denied the peace and solitude of your own dreamscape.'

Kriah wanted to curse under his breath, but managed to keep his frustrations hidden. This was not Yae'ilston's doing; he had not asked to be killed.

Despite his exhaustion, he kept walking, arriving at a riverbank right on sundown. The Faethou River—it had to be. The border separating Holania from Bararn. It was still and wide, shining like liquid bronze in the evening light. Kriah scanned the banks, but found no bridge. Unsurprising, really, considering how far he'd strayed from the main roads. He had no way of telling how deep it was, if he could ford it without drowning. He never had learnt to swim, so isolated and landlocked in the Li'Nea Wood.

'Well?' Yae'ilston prompted impatiently.

'Well, what? I'm thinking,' Kriah snapped. 'There's no bridge.'

'So move it.'

Kriah turned to him, incredulous.

Yae'ilston shrugged. 'You're Meah-Hyren,' he said, as though it were something Kriah could forget. 'You don't need a bridge. If there is an obstacle in your way, *move* it.'

He spoke as if it were the natural solution to the problem, as if Kriah himself should have already considered it. Azet'haal had parted the seas to make his way to the mainland; surely Kriah could displace a river. But it wasn't a lack of confidence that paralysed him—it was fear. Fear Azet'haal would feel the ripples. Fear he'd fall too deeply into the alluring depths of his new *khe'torla*.

Determined to find another way, he noticed something hidden in the reeds. Flat and wooden, it was barely discernible among the earthy hues of the riverbank. Kriah pawed the waist-high grasses aside for a better look. An incredulous laugh escaped his chest in a single puff of air.

A flat-bottomed barge had been abandoned here, upturned and balanced over a boulder to keep it out of the water. The pole for traversing the river was speared in the mud beside it. It had seen better days; patches of mossy green algae splattered across its underside like a quilt. Whoever had used this to cross the river had clearly not done so in some time.

'You'd truly rather push yourself across than simply move it out of your way?' Yae'ilston observed with curiosity.

'There's nothing simple about moving a river,' Kriah grunted as he strained to manoeuvre the awkward boat onto the bank. He kicked it into the water, relieved to see it float. 'Besides,' he continued as he stepped onto the barge, 'I'd rather not risk rousing Azet'haal's attention.'

The old wooden planks creaked beneath his feet but were not so rotten that his boot went straight through. He let himself breathe again.

'I already told you, no one can sense beyond the chaos you left in Cirahk,' the Meah-Hyren muttered, irritation evident in his clipped words.

Kriah didn't wait to listen to his complaints. He thrust the long pole into the silty earth and pushed away from the bank. His legs wobbled as the barge cut through the weedy shallows, but he soon regained his balance once he was out into the smooth waters of the river. Kriah flashed a triumphant grin when he turned to see Yae'ilston's grumpy silhouette shrinking in the distance. He could do this without *khe'torla*. He could—

An earth-shattering quake ripped through him, knocking him to his knees as the boat threatened to tip. His bones rattled. Kriah clutched his head against the sudden sharp pain and looked to the sky, expecting to see it crack open like an egg.

But it was not a seal that had broken.

'A reverberance.' Yae'ilston confirmed Kriah's grim suspicion in his dry, matter-of-fact way. 'You need not worry about drawing Azet'haal's attention to *you*. That reverberance lit a beacon we would have seen in Kherunis.'

Kriah's heart thundered in his chest. Amika—it had to have been Amika. He closed his eyes in search of any remaining echoes of *khe'torla*, trying to pinpoint the source of the disruption. He could still feel it roil through the earth, somewhere deep below the ground and very, *very* far away.

In Qhoraak.

'She's ... not here,' he breathed aloud, panic rising up his throat. The immediate joy he'd felt upon realising she was alive was swiftly replaced by a sweeping despair that he was not moving in the right direction.

Kriah took up the barge pole and pushed on. It didn't matter that she wasn't here. She was alive—in Qhoraak, where Sha'arn said Hirathi's Chosen would be. Heat spread through his body. After all that had happened, she'd remained true to the Prophecy. She would find the seal there and break it. And soon, they would rendezvous in Kheshtarl. He could feel it.

But the road to Adria was not as smooth as Kriah hoped.

Once across the river and on Holanian banks, he soon saw the devastation of the war that had drawn Amika home. Within a day's travel, he arrived at the skeletal remains of a village, naught but charcoal and scorched stone. Unlike Trendon, which set itself to the torch, this destruction was long past; bodies no longer lined the streets to be coated in the silvery film of moisture left by the misty rain that had been falling since morning. The village was solemn in a way Trendon hadn't been; peaceful despite the wreckage.

Kriah trudged through the damp ashes, searching for anything that would serve as shelter for the night. Nothing stood.

'The whole town's been razed,' he said softly. 'Not even the buildings were spared. This is ...'

This is war.

Historians had a funny way of documenting war. Heroes on one side were key aggressors on the other; massacres could be presented as decisive victories depending on who authored the text. Even barbarism was confused for enthusiasm. They recorded casualties and major battles, but no one bothered remembering *these* losses—the townships and livelihoods snuffed out simply for living on the wrong side of the battle lines. This was the future that awaited Whyt'hallen. The realisation chilled Kriah's blood.

'This was not our doing, either,' Yae'ilston asserted cautiously. 'Our goal was to fully enthral Bararn before pushing any further west.'

'I know,' Kriah murmured, unearthing a broken pot with his boot. 'These are old wounds. That's why she came back.'

If Yae'ilston pressed for details of *her*, Kriah didn't hear it. His senses drowned in the wreckage of the Holanian village and remained muted long after they'd left. The rain had stopped and, unable to sleep anyway, Kriah continued through the night, guided by the crimson glow of the Tear. It was never truly dark now, even when the moon sat aloft in the sky. Would the divide between night and day lessen with every seal they broke?

At dusk on the second day, they approached another village, the destruction far more recent than the last. There were skeletons beneath the ashes here, buried under soot and fallen beams instead of respectfully within the earth. No one had attempted to recover them. Kriah's belly clenched in fear.

She escaped the capital, he had to remind himself when worry for Amika's safety swelled afresh. *She's gone west and she's alive.*

Kriah repeated those words like a mantra as he finally sat to rest. He'd been walking for days now and could no longer rely on his immortal stamina to keep going. He was bone-tired, with blisters on his feet so deep the skin peeled away in white, bloodless layers. Kriah hissed as he pulled back the wrinkled dead skin to reveal the red, glistening wound beneath. The raw flesh stung as it met the cool night air.

Yae'ilston's lip curled in distaste. 'Must you do that?'

'It has to dry out,' Kriah said. He positioned his calf up on a rock to allow air to circulate around his heel, though he had no idea how to dress it when it came time to walk again. Exasperated, he lay back in the dirt and stared up at the festering sky. All he wanted to do was sleep.

'Why aren't you using *khe'torla*?'

Kriah's eyes snapped open—when had he closed them? He propped himself up on his elbows and glared at the spectre perched on a broken wagon.

'Why are you still here?' he snapped childishly. 'Always talking, talking, *talking!* Can I not rest without an interrogation?'

Fatigue had given his tongue a sharp edge, one he could not sheathe. But instead of recoiling at the lashing, Yae'ilston smiled a cruel grin.

'Not yet a full turn of the moon and you're already maddening at my presence,' he laughed. 'Your sanity will fall long before the next seal does. You brought this upon yourself, you know. When you cut off my fucking head.'

Kriah ran his hands down his face, fingertips massaging his tired eyes. Temper extinguished by Yae'ilston's mocking observations, he now felt foolish as well as exhausted. The question over his hesitancy to use *khe'torla* pinched a nerve he hadn't realised was exposed. Kriah tried to regain his composure; he didn't need his fear becoming another weapon in Yae'ilston's arsenal.

'I know, I know,' he groaned instead. 'This is my punishment.' He opened his eyes and waited for his blurred vision to clear before setting his gaze on the Meah-Hyren. 'Will you linger like this forever? Or will you lose yourself eventually, too?'

Yae'ilston brought his thumb to his mouth and started chewing on the nail. He didn't speak for a while, and the silence was somehow louder than anything he'd ever uttered before. He spat a nail fragment off into the darkness before muttering, 'I think perhaps you really should try to sleep.'

Adria would have cut a beautiful morning skyline if it weren't for the collapsed spire of the grand central castle. Grey against the rising sun, Holania's capital seemed a dry corpse compared to the golden pastoral city Kriah had read about.

But it wasn't just the leached colour or the grave-stillness of the city that made Kriah think of death—it was the bodies lining the streets like waystones.

'I suppose you weren't involved in this either,' he said dryly. But instead of professing innocence, Yae'ilston was eerily quiet. Kriah glanced over his shoulder to check his phantom was still with him and found the Meah-Hyren stony-faced and white.

'You know we weren't,' he muttered once the shock had lessened. 'Our purpose was to enslave, not ... slaughter.'

He had floundered looking for a suitable word, but Kriah failed to recognise an alternative. Slaughter was exactly what they faced here. Men speared anus to throat, propped up like scarecrows to warn people off the city. Maggots writhed in the wounds, and the dry, cracked parchment of their lips had turned black with decay. The reek was worse than a latrine pit left to bake in the sun—a putrid concoction of shit and rotting meat.

Kriah swallowed his rising bile and edged closer, disrupting a swarm of flies that sucked at a corpse's sunken eyes. The man had been dressed in a fine surcoat of crimson brocade, stitched with gold thread now as dank and tarnished as old jewellery.

'These were noblemen,' Kriah observed, covering his nose and mouth against the stench. He looked down the row of scarecrow men and found similarities in their grime-covered dress. Gold and crimson—Bararnite colours.

The creak of a bowstring echoed around the desolate castle town.

Kriah raised his hands. 'I'm a peaceful traveller, I mean no harm!' he announced, careful to keep any measure of threat from his voice. It took all his strength not to turn his head in search of the assailants. His heart hammered in his ears; the Skrevaar Blade stirred in his veins.

'City's closed to travellers!' a male voice responded. There—on the wall. A young man in a popped up from a crumbling crenelation, long-bow drawn taut by his cheek. Two other soldiers flanked him, though they looked younger and less sure than the man who spoke.

'I have important information regarding the safety of your people. Please—let me speak with your commander. I am unarmed.' Kriah spread his hands a little wider in emphasis.

This declaration made the younger soldiers waver, the bowstrings slackening as they relaxed their arms. Their helmeted comrade remained vigilant.

'Fools,' he growled. 'Doesn't matter if he's armed or not. No one goes in. You heard what's happened in—'

'I have news of that!' Kriah shouted, watching their ears prick up at the announcement. 'News of what's happened in Bararn—and the west. I also believe that your princess is still alive, so if you would just—'

An arrow careened into the earth by Kriah's boot, sending up a spray of ashes and splintered rock. He remained steadfast, feet anchored to the spot, though his *khe'torla* subconsciously went in search of a pulse, ready to defend him from a second volley. It found little more than death.

The soldiers jostled atop the wall. Half-helm elbowed the loose-fingered subordinate in the ribs. 'Deities dead,' he rumbled through clenched teeth. 'I didn't say *shoot* him, boy!'

'But he said Amikharlia's still alive,' the young soldier protested. 'If that's the case, then we ... all of this ... was for nothing.'

Half-helm grunted and lowered his weapon. He returned the arrow to its quiver and leant the bow against the brick crenelation, hard stare never faltering. 'Keep those hands where we can see them,' he barked, stabbing his finger towards Kriah. 'We'll take you to see the Lord Regent.'

25

AMIKHARLIA

Something felt wrong, but she couldn't quite put her finger on it. Amika's head throbbed with immense pressure, like her brain was trying to escape through her ears, nose and eye sockets. Dehydration, the healer had said; she should feel better soon. There was a tube stuck in her arm connected to some sort of animal bladder filled with liquid. Clear, not crimson, like they fed Rei. She inspected the thin needle speared in her flesh, noting the way it did not hurt like she expected. Qhoraakese medicine was a magic of its own.

Amika expected to find herself in the underground hold, but when lucidity returned to her in full, she discovered she was stretched out on a low cot in a tent much like the one she'd previously occupied. It was smaller; designed to be private, perhaps cosy, with a few personal items stacked in the corner. She'd seen them before, she realised. Fur throws and wooden blocks carved into animals.

As if summoned by thought, Emanais appeared, ragged and dishevelled. Blood and grime stained her ruffled white shirt as though she'd been tending the wounded herself. There was an unsteadiness to her gait that suggested intoxication, but she otherwise seemed alert, if not exhausted.

'Here she is,' Emanais said, gesturing for others to follow her inside with a wide sweep of her arm. Kio entered, supporting a limping Rei over his arm. Amika's heart warmed at the sight of them, alive and well despite their injuries. If nothing else, she'd succeeded in keeping them safe.

'I left Sylar with Zhayar,' Emanais said. 'I'll sleep there tonight. We'll talk more once we've all rested.'

Kio nodded at the departing woman, then helped Rei sit at the end of Amika's cot. Her brother came to kneel beside her and wrapped her in a long, tight embrace. 'I'm glad you're alright,' he said into the mess of her hair. 'Deities dead, I thought I'd lost you again.'

'I'm fine,' Amika said, smiling as he withdrew. 'I'm fine.'

But she wasn't. Something was broken and she didn't know what. She kept feeling for a pulse and coming up dead. Her mind was fuzzy, distant. Even the edges of her brother's face were blurred. She shook her head, trying to clear her vision, but he caught the uncertainty of her expression and frowned.

'You're not fine,' he said, cupping a hand against her cheek. He looked back at Rei. 'No one is fucking fine. Why won't you tell me anything?'

Anger rose in his voice, ignited by the alcohol on his breath. He was drunk—or had been very recently. Unsurprising, considering everything that had happened. But it was why Amika held back telling him all she had done—all that she *was*. Kio's world had changed enough lately; he wasn't ready for more upheaval.

She took a deep breath and searched for lies to placate her brother, but she caught Rei's eyes and they urged her to speak the truth. Hesitation stole her voice a moment, but when it returned she told him. She told him everything. The scope of her powers. The Prophecy. Rei's betrayal of the Tower. Reminas's death. The Tear in the sky—all of it.

And Kio stared at her like she was a stranger—a *monster*.

He retreated to the corner of the tent, arms folded, and paced like he thought moving would help it make sense. The tremor returned to his hands and he rubbed at his face, at his eyes, as if pushing back tears.

'Kio ...' Rei said softly, and stretched a hand towards him, beckoning him back. He did not take it.

'You did *that*,' Kio repeated, pointing to the wall of the tent, where the sky bled red beyond. 'To bring back the Goddess? *Fuck*, Amika!'

'It was a mistake,' she said quickly. 'The Meah-Hyren tricked me. But now that it's started, we can't turn back. We have to release the Goddess so she can fix it. Make it right. That's why we're here. To find the next Chosen and break the Hirathi seal.'

She regretted the words as soon as she spoke them. Kio's face hardened, eyes narrowing.

'And I thought you were here for *me*,' he growled. Shaking his head, he stomped from the tent, glancing at neither of them as he left.

Rei released a forceful sigh before catching his forehead in his hands. Amika braced herself for his rebuke, but instead he just patted her leg through the thin sheet. The comfort was fleeting, but it was enough.

'He's such a fucking mess,' Rei muttered, seemingly to himself.

'He thinks I'm a monster,' Amika spat, voice thick with emotion.

'I *am* a monster,' Rei insisted, 'and yet he loves me still. He'll forgive you, Amika. Just give him time.'

She nodded and sniffed back the tears she would not let fall. Gods, she had made a mess of things. That's all she did. Calamity Amika, raising chaos wherever she went. She'd come to find Kio to set things right, but instead of mending the wedge between them, all she'd done was drive them further apart.

The tent began to spin and the ground rose up to meet her. She would have landed with a mouthful of dirt had Rei not thrown himself at her.

'Ah, fuck. *Shit*—' There was pain in his voice as he eased her back into the cot. Amika couldn't open her eyes, the vertigo too intense, but she heard the way he muttered under his breath. He was injured because of her, wasn't he? It all felt so far, far away.

She melted into the bedding, adrift on a black ocean, darker than the night. It was quiet here, too quiet. It was never quiet inside her mind. There was always something—always ants.

Ants ...

The pieces came together, slow and lethargic like fingers through honey. She saw it now. The thing that was broken. The thing that was wrong.

The thing that was gone.

Amika spent days drifting in and out of consciousness. She had vague awareness of people coming and going, dark silhouettes passing the fringes of her perception. Healers, perhaps; Rei most likely.

'... aside from mild dehydration, we can find nothing wrong...' A voice she didn't recognise.

My khe'torla*!* she wanted to scream. *My* khe'torla *is gone!*

'Figure it out.' Kio. That was definitely Kio.

Still, she could not wake.

When she finally did find her way back to reality, there was movement in the camp outside. Amika glanced at her arm, found she was no longer connected to any strange contraptions, and made to get out of the cot. Her legs were unsteady, weak, but she caught her balance on the central support post, making the canvas walls ripple like water.

Breathe, she thought, turning her focus inward. She reached desperately for the marching in her veins, the familiar sensation that should have been easy to access with even the weakest of concentration. But there was nothing. She was silent. *Hollow.* For a moment she couldn't even breath from the shock of it. A part of her was gone. Severed like a useless, rotten limb.

Her breath came in shuddering sobs. Amika stuffed her fist in her mouth, bit down on the knuckles to the bone. Sinking to her knees, she wailed—wailed for a loss that ripped through her core.

She could have wallowed for hours were it not for increased activity outside. Pawing the tears from her eyes, she got back to her feet, steadier this time. Whatever was happening to her could wait—would *have to* wait. There were still people here who needed help.

The glare of the bright crimson sky stung her eyes as she stumbled out into the camp. Signs of the carnage still remained: rubble from the crumbled gate and watchtower had been cleared and stacked out of the way; the wounded had been taken care of, the corpses burned or buried—she wasn't sure of the custom here. But the camp was cluttered. When she'd arrived, Emanais and her army had lived mostly below ground, save a handful who chose to sleep beneath the stars. Now it seemed they all preferred that arrangement.

The commotion that had drawn her out stemmed from an arrival in camp—one of Emanais's scouts returning from recon on the back of a very sad and overburdened mule. His face was familiar, but Amika hadn't seen him since before the demonspawn attack. By the way a crowd seemed to pool around him, his return was well-anticipated.

Amika trailed from a subtle distance. He was heading for the tunnels when one of the gathered soldiers intercepted him and pointed him back the other way—towards her. Instinctively, Amika slipped into a tent to avoid being caught. She wasn't doing anything suspicious as such, but with so few people milling about ...

Why is no one underground?

The tent she entered was a hospital, one apparently dedicated to those stable and on their way to recovery. Amika turned to see half the cots empty, and those still occupied were filled by men and women sitting upright while they chatted, covered in neat stitches and freshly dressed wounds. At the back of the tent, a flash of crimson hair caught her eye, vibrant against the white of the canvas walls and linen bandages.

Rei stood with his back to her, talking with Kio, who had a masked medic inspecting his naked back. Their fingers danced tenderly together, eyes fixed on each other, Rei distracting Kio from whatever treatment he received. The healer injected a clear fluid into his back through a glass syringe; Kio grimaced slightly with each prick.

When he glanced up and saw Amika, fear and guilt clenched her gut. She hadn't even known he was wounded, and the memory of him storming drunkenly from her tent rose in her mind. She froze.

'Amika!' Rei came hobbling towards her, a pronounced limp in his left leg. He opened his arms and smiled. 'You're awake!'

She returned his embrace earnestly but looked past his shoulder at Kio. 'Is he alright?'

Rei's cheer melted faster than wax beneath flame. 'Infection, maybe. He was burned by the *khaaja*'s sludge. Emanais said they've not seen anything like it. It wasn't that bad a few days ago. They're doing their best, but …' He shook his head. 'Can't you … Can't you do something?'

Amika's heart tore. She'd never healed anyone before. She'd tried once—the boy, Vyktor, outside Ollyn after the Bararnite attack on Adria. It hadn't worked, but she'd been close and she was stronger—

Was. Was stronger. Her *khe'torla* was now as dry as the desert outside. How could the Goddess be so cruel?

Kio groaned and thumped the bed with his fist, drawing their attention back to him. 'Surely you have something for the pain!' he demanded with a shout.

'All gone,' the masked healer mumbled.

'Wine, then.'

Amika rushed to his side. 'Squeeze my hand,' she said and knelt before him, offering up both hands. Kio held her gaze silently, face hard, before taking them in his own. His grip tightened almost immediately.

'Rei-Hai,' he said. 'Find me something to drink.'

'Absolutely fucking not.'

'*Rei-Hai.*'

The couple exchanged a look and Rei's eyes narrowed before he stormed out of the tent as irately as he could manage with a limp.

Kio hissed as the chirurgeon continued his work. The syringe had been swapped for a blade to debride the dead flesh from the wounds. Amika's lip curled away from her teeth as she imagined the pain. No wonder he wanted a fucking drink.

'Do you remember,' she said suddenly, 'when I broke my leg?'

Her brother nodded. 'What were you—eight?'

'Something like that. Fell off the wall in Lower Adria. Rei-Hai's fault, I'm sure.'

'He wanted to see who could climb the fastest, knowing very well he'd win.'

'Master Antor said I was too young for mandrake tea,' Amika recalled, goosepimples rising on her skin. 'Said we'd have to set the bone without it. So Mother sat beside the bed, took my hands like this and told me to squeeze as hard as I needed.'

'You broke three of her fingers.'

'And she never complained.'

Amika didn't realise she was crying until a sob hitched in her throat. She hadn't spoken of her mother since she'd learnt the queen was dead—killed during the Bararnite invasion of Holania. Had Kio watched her die?

'I'm sorry, Kio,' she blubbered through tears. 'I'm sorry for everything. It's all my fault. None of this would have happened to you, if only I—'

She pulled a hand from her brother's grip to wipe her cheeks, turning away in shame. Not of the tears that fell now but of every foolish decision that led to this moment. There were so many of them and the weight crushed her.

'You may have placed a sword in Reminas's hand,' Kio said evenly, turning her face back towards him. 'But he was the one who swung it. Adria, our mother, me ... That's all on him. The Tear?' He gave a wry half-smile. 'Well, can't be too hard to fix, right?'

Amika cried in earnest now.

'Hey, hey, hey. Look at me.' It was his turn to squeeze her hands. 'You're my sister, Amikharlia. I love you. And I forgive you.'

Kio pressed a kiss to her forehead and she leant against his shoulder, letting the tears fall. He curled an arm around her back as best he could, patting her as though she were a small child seeking solace. Amika had meant to bring *him* comfort, and yet—

A horn sounded outside. Three short blasts. Pause. Three more. Adrenaline flooded Amika's veins as she broke away from her brother's embrace. Was it another attack? No—the chirurgeon was not at all alarmed.

Rei-Hai ducked under the tent flap, wineskin in hand. 'Emanais calls a war council,' he said snippily.

'What's happened?' Amika asked, dusting off her knees.

Kio gestured for the drink and allowed Rei to help him into his shirt. He took a long swig and then turned to Amika and said, 'Guess we go find out.'

Twelve confidantes had been summoned to Emanais's war council, packed into a tent filled with supply crates that now served as a table around which they all congregated. The man Amika had seen arrive earlier stood beside Emanais at the head of the group, the woman Zhayar at the other. The rest were faces she did not recognise, but they were all part of Emanais's inner circle and thus privy to whatever news she was about to share.

'A mine shaft has collapsed, northwest of Xant,' Emanais declared, arms folded and face hard. 'The same tremor that claimed our newest tunnels.'

A shiver jittered over Amika's skin.

I did this, she thought—she *knew.* The unstable cast she had unleashed on the *khaaja* ... The power had been immense; of course the reverberance had been too. Amika may have saved Emanais's troops—saved herself, Rei and Kio—but how many other lives had she ended in that mine?

'The Allchief is distracted with the recovery effort,' Emanais continued. 'Now's the time to storm the Citadel. Time to liberate my sister and whoever else he has imprisoned there.'

'Would Waqar really compromise Xant's security because of a mine?' interrupted a soldier unknown to Amika, a man with locs bleached golden by the sun.

The returning scout answered. 'He would for firesand. By all accounts the mine at Uhloch has been flattened. It's the richest vein in Qhoraak. Waqar will want it operational.'

A murmur rippled around the room. Amika's eyes settled on her brother, who stood at the edge of the group, arms folded, Rei seated on a crate beside him. It was well known Qhoraakese mines were manned by slave labour from the convict trade, even if the practice was officially abolished. Her skin prickled with a cold sweat. Kio could have been among the wreckage, had things played out differently.

Emanais placed a boot on the edge of their makeshift table and leant down to inspect what Amika now saw were etchings on the wood. With a long charcoal stick, she scribbled amendments on what appeared to be a crude sort of map.

'Yeni was accosted running recon on the farm in Polterk.' She slashed a long cross through the diagram, drew an arrow pointing away from it. 'But the farm's been emptied. Pulled west to the capital. So that's where we'll go.'

The tent fell silent. There was no disapproval—or perhaps they were too scared to voice it. Those standing to the right with Zhayar slowly nodded, muttering quietly among themselves.

'When do you plan to set out?' asked a tall, slender man with snowy flecks through his natural curls, arms folded and rigid. He had a distinct hooked scar down the right side of his face, cutting through his eye, which was milky with blindness. Amika had seen him somewhere before—in the healing tents, perhaps?

'Before the Hirathi Moon hits its peak,' Emanais said.

'That's within two days. Much of the army will not be ready to mobilise. We are still healing.'

'So leave them behind,' another offered. He spoke Meytaran with a natural inflection. Bararnite, by the look of him.

'And approach Xant with a depleted force? Suicide!'

'Better depleted than weak and slow,' Kio mumbled. Her brother was right; if he hadn't spoken, Amika would have.

Venomous words were shared in Qhoraakese. Emanais kicked the table and the group shuddered.

'The Little Prince speaks true,' she said into the hush that followed. Her gaze swept the crowd, levelling a challenge at any would-be combatant. 'It will take an army fourteen days to reach Xant. We must arrive while Waqar has his forces busy with the mine. That earthquake was indeed fortuitous, in spite of the damage it caused us. We could never take the capital otherwise.' Emanais turned to the scarred man. 'How many remain in the infirmary?'

'Twelve abed. Twenty-some are still receiving treatment, but otherwise mobile.' His one-eyed gaze washed over Kio and Rei. 'And a further five are in hospice. They will not survive their injuries. I have kept them comfortable.'

Emanais nodded gravely. 'Thank you, Forykke. Ease their passing—we don't have the resources to waste. Stay behind and treat those still recovering. I don't want to see this post abandoned while we're away. We've worked too hard to seize this camp. It can be rebuilt.'

Forykke dipped his head, accepting the order.

'Dhenka, Zhayar and the Little Prince will leave for the shadow base to retrieve our surplus stores and the pack mules,' Emanais continued. 'Everyone else: pack up the camp. We're to be on the road by sundown tomorrow. Go. Now,' she barked when everyone lingered a moment.

The sharpness of her tone snapped them into action, and they filed out of the tent in a less-than-orderly scrabble. Kio stayed behind, giving Rei's shoulder a squeeze. His eyes met Amika's across the tent. He opened his mouth to speak, but was silenced by Dhenka and Zhayar directing him to follow.

'It's a day's ride to the shadow base,' Emanais said in explanation as they hurried him off without a word. 'The quicker they leave, the quicker they return.' She paused before Amika, touching her arm fondly. 'Glad to see you up and about, Chosen. Your gifts will be more than welcome in the battle for Xant.'

Amika moved towards Rei, who glowered sourly at the space Emanais had occupied.

'I don't like this, Amika,' he growled. 'We came here for Kio. We have him. Let's go home.'

Home, she thought. Where was home now? She'd left Adria in ashes, her death alongside Reminas all but confirmed. Kio too was assumed dead. Had Bararn retaliated? Who sat atop her father's throne? Too many questions she'd pushed aside when they fled; if she let them in now, she would drown.

Amika offered her arm to Rei, helping him stand. She knew why he hated it here, why he was so desperate to leave. But they couldn't. Not yet. Not with a seal so close.

'Emanais is Chosen,' she said, wrapping an arm around Rei's back as they hobbled from the tent. 'The one of royal blood—I'm sure of it. She's the daughter of the last Allchief, before Waqar slaughtered her family and took the throne.'

'She told me,' Rei confirmed with a nod. He squinted in the brightness of the red sky outside, but otherwise no longer seemed affected by the Tear and its poison. Wounded leg aside, he *was* stronger now—would that change if more seals fell?

'That's why she cares for Kio,' he continued, grumbling now. 'She shares his pain. It's half the reason she keeps him drunk beyond oblivion. Because it helps *her*.'

He pointed out a tent in a row of several identical dwellings, some of which were already in the process of being packed away in accordance to Emanais's directive.

'Kio drank too much long before he met Emanais,' Amika reminded Rei gently. 'Even before I left Adria, he was far too fond of his cups. I don't think any one thing caused it.'

Rei didn't respond to that, instead hobbling over to the pile of bedding he and Kio must share; an upended bottle rested in the dirt to one side. Rei kicked it further away with the toe of his boot.

'So you mean to go along with it, then?' he asked, and it took a moment for Amika to realise what he was saying. She dragged her hands down her face, exhausted. Supporting Rei on the trek across camp had depleted her more than she expected.

'I don't know,' she said, exasperated. 'Is it even a choice now?'

Rei shrugged. 'You seem pretty good at finding options when there supposedly are none.'

Amika eased herself down onto the bed beside him. She let the silence grow between them. There was so much she wanted to say, but she couldn't find the courage to give life to the words. Secrets, doubts, regrets—everything she kept locked away because talking seemed too disastrous. Her strength was bound to her *khe'torla*—her *purpose*. Without it, what was she?

Rei released a long, heavy sigh. 'We'll have to face the Tower,' he said, fingers worrying the frayed edge of the bed linen. 'To get the Nirhana Blade. If they don't find us first—Goddess only knows what Elles reported back to them.'

Amika placed her hand on her friend's knee and gave it a firm squeeze. 'We've survived them this far,' she said. 'We'll survive them again.'

But first, they had to survive Qhoraak.

26

KIOKHAREN

Emanais ordered the army depart at sunrise, following Kio's late-night return. The shadow camp had been little more than a hole in a crag, well hidden by even more rocks and debris. There was a small pen housing six mules, and a bedroll where someone obviously stayed to oversee their care. After loading the animals with as much as they could carry—sacks of grain, lentils, rice and salt—they headed back to base, arriving well after the lanterns had been extinguished for the night.

Dhenka tried to coax Kio to join Zhayar and himself in Emanais's tent, but Kio declined, his head spinning from hours bobbing in the saddle with a belly full of booze. The Qhoraakese man had been bruised but didn't push it, and instead stood back and laughed as Kio stumbled into his own tent. Amika and Rei were asleep in a tangle of blankets, various limbs exposed to the cool night air. Kio pulled the linens over his sister's shoulders; she did not stir, but Rei's eyes flicked open at the slight disturbance.

'Sleep,' Kio insisted, kicking off his boots. 'Emanais wants to leave at dawn.' He slid into bed beside Rei and his sister, settling on his side to avoid the searing pain in his back, which throbbed hotly now the alcohol was leaving his system.

'How generous of her to grant us a whole night's rest,' Rei grunted, shuffling closer. Kio curled an arm around his lover and breathed him in, absorbing the warmth from his small body. Gods, he would have taken him right there, if Amika wasn't asleep beside them. His mind could not interfere with his body, drunk like he was. He'd managed to keep the terror at bay before, even if he could barely remember it afterwards.

But moments after hitting the pillow, Kio drifted off into sleep that was fitful and broken by dehydration—and a thirst he could only slake with wine, whiskey or rum. He supposed he was hungry too, though it didn't bother him quite like the need to wet his tongue.

In the morning he went searching for a drink, but found the bottles and casks already packed neatly away into one of three wagons used to haul the larger, heavier supplies. Much was to be carried in personal packs—bedrolls, weapons, additional rations—with only the communal stock and shelter to be carted by the mules.

'I'm sure Emanais would prefer I stay back with the other injured liabilities,' Rei-Hai grumbled as Kio helped him into the saddle of one of the pack animals.

'*I'd* prefer that, in a way,' he said, placing the reins in Rei's hands. Kio stroked the mule's long neck as if doing so would comfort him, too. 'But I need you close. It's the only way I can make sure you're safe. Amika said the Tower's hunting you.'

'I can take care of myself.'

'I know that, my love. I can just do it better.'

He smiled, and Rei's prickly facade softened to a grin of his own. Warmth spread through Kio's body. He so badly wanted to kiss him, and not just a passing, casual peck. He wanted to *kiss* him. Deeply, intimately.

Wanted to feel him—and remember it. Rei deserved more than a drunken fuck. What if that was the only way they could be together now?

The army marched at a steady pace, taking breaks only when necessary. The sun was unrelenting and the barren red stretch of wasteland seemed endless, devoid of any trees or grasses. The heat only bothered the newest inductees of Emanais's rebel army, those not yet acclimatised to Qhoraak's acrid heat. Sweat poured off Kio's body and made the wounds on his back sting anew. By the time they stopped to make camp, peeling off his shirt felt like removing a sock from a fresh, sticky blister.

'Maybe you're the one who should have stayed with the sick and dying,' Rei said coolly as he redressed the wounds, applying the thick salve with careful fingers.

'I promised Emanais,' Kio mumbled before curling his lips around the spout of his wineskin. His flesh prickled at the texture of the leather, at the way it puckered at the seams like a wrinkled old face. But it had been a long day without drink, and his tongue craved liquor like his mind craved silence. He'd forget his discomfort soon enough.

Across the camp at a low-burning fire, which was more for cooking flatbreads than warmth, Kio found Amika engaged in serious conversation with Emanais. Ema nodded as Amika spoke, her hands threading Sylar's hair as the boy played with wooden figures at her feet. They were too far away for Kio to read lips—or perhaps he was already drunk—but the deep furrow of Ema's brow hinted at the weight of their words.

Kio glanced up at the sky, at the Tear that pulsed like an infected wound in bruised flesh. Had Amika really done that? Did she really intend to make it *worse?*

'You haven't forgiven her,' Rei observed, smoothing his hands down Kio's shoulders. He leant close, breath hot on Kio's cheek. 'Not really.'

'I should,' he conceded, melting back into Rei's touch. 'I want to. It's just ...'

She fucking terrifies me.

Kio stood with a sigh, turned and offered a hand to Rei. 'Bed?'

'Why yes, my prince, I fear I am far too tired to even walk,' Rei said dramatically, pressing the back of his hand to his forehead like a damsel.

'You sat in a saddle all day.'

'Yes, and unfortunately for you, my arse is exhausted.' Rei took the proffered hand and hauled himself up, forcing out a groan. He stretched to place a quick peck on Kio's cheek, but Kio swept him up into his arms.

'I'm kidding,' Rei laughed lightly, pushing against his chest. 'I can walk. Put me down.'

Kio obliged; his back burned from the exertion. His head started to spin but Rei steadied him before he lost his balance.

'Perhaps you should sleep as well,' he said, voice hardening.

'I'm fine, I'm fine,' Kio insisted, blinking slowly to clear his vision. 'I want to talk with Amika.'

'Goodnight then, my prince,' Rei said, brushing his arm before pointing at the tent they'd erected for the night. Kio watched him hobble away, his limp improved but not perfect, until he disappeared inside.

Taking another swig from the wineskin, Kio made his way across camp to where Amika sat with the others.

'... in the audience chamber of the Great Hall,' Emanais was saying. 'Hirathi's seal, patterned into the mosaic on the floor. His spear, the symbol of his power, hangs above the Allchief's chair.'

'Sounds like everything we need is all in the one place, then,' Kio said awkwardly, as a way to join the conversation. He took a seat beside Sylar, ruffling the boy's raggedy red hair.

'Your sister believes me Chosen,' Emanais beamed. She offered Kio the bottle of rum she was drinking, but he shook his head, showing her the wineskin.

'How fortuitous our paths should cross, then,' he muttered.

'And some don't believe in destiny.' Emanais raised a toast to the sky, slipping drunkenly into Qhoraakese for a moment. 'Idiots, I say! What are we if not puppets for the gods? I was born to sit upon the Seat of Hirathi. Being named his Chosen reinforces that fate.'

'I still struggle to accept that our paths are mapped for us,' Amika confessed softly.

Kio felt her eyes on him as he played with Sylar, bouncing one of the wooden animals through the dirt as though it were running. The boy squealed in delight, one of the few sounds he ever uttered.

'But I guess some of us can't always be trusted to make the right decisions,' Amika muttered, mostly to herself. The words speared straight towards Kio's gut. He had forgiven her for leaving Adria, absolved her of any blame for what he'd endured in the aftermath. But this business with the Tear, with its magic and prophecies, was a lot harder to accept.

Kio was about to open his mouth to explain when Emanais started shouting gleefully in Qhoraakese at a passing soldier; she scurried off into the dark after him, tripping over a supply sack as she left.

'The two of you really do make quite the pair,' Amika observed with mild amusement.

'I never thought anyone could replace Moyna,' Kio admitted to his wineskin. 'I never saw my life without her. Now, I can't imagine it without Ema. She's ... an anchor. And I'm a drifting boat. She keeps me steady.'

Amika burst into laughter. 'Sorry. Sorry, that's just very … *deep.*' She struggled to speak through her giggles. 'It's not like you at all!'

Kio bristled. 'Oh, fuck you. I happen to think very deeply about things! All the time. Not just when I'm'—he took a long drink—'drunk.'

Amika's mirth subsided as Kio's mood took a sombre turn. 'So if Ema's the anchor,' she asked, 'and you're the ship … what does that make Rei-Hai?'

Kio deliberated considerably longer than he would have if he'd been sober—but if he'd been sober, they wouldn't be having this ridiculous conversation in the first place. 'Rei-Hai is … Rei's the entire ocean.'

He braced himself for laughter. When it didn't come, he turned towards his sister and found her looking at him with a warm smile on her lips. She reached across and gave his forearm a squeeze. 'That's beautiful, Kio.'

He shrugged her off. 'Shut up.'

They both chuckled and Amika beckoned for a share of the wineskin. She took a long drink then passed it back, silence now consuming their merriment.

'I hope she comes with us,' Amika said, entranced by the fire. 'Whether she's Chosen or not. I hope she sees it through to the end. Helps us get *our* throne back.'

Kio hadn't given much thought to what would happen when he left Qhoraak. A part of him supposed he would die here, or at the very least, never see Holania or his loved ones again. Could they really just go home after this? After they shatter the world to defeat an enemy who has never attacked?

Kio drained what was left of the wine and found the amount unsatisfyingly sparse. His tongue burned for more, but at least his hands were still, his mind fuzzy and blissfully unfocused. He stared at the fire and tried to imagine a life they might return to. A life that included Rei, Amika *and* Emanais.

As the silence stretched on he lost himself in the warmth of the glowing coals, and eventually drifted off to sleep.

By the fifth day, Kio was sick of seeing red. Red sand. Red rock. Red sky. It all blurred together in such an oppressive veil of crimson that he almost recoiled when he woke to find Rei's hair splayed across the pillow.

They were heading northwest, towards the coast, and now even the great spine of the mountains that bisected the Waste shrank flat into the horizon. Kio couldn't remember what trees looked like, couldn't recall the soft feel of grass or the smell of rain. It was a different world here—vast, barren and empty. Anyone attempting to traverse the desert alone was sure to go insane from the all-consuming nothingness.

'Your footwork is sloppy,' Rei chastised from the sidelines as Amika and Kio sparred with wooden sticks while the others made camp on the sixth night. 'And your riposte is shit.'

'Forgive me, Master Shaw,' Kio grunted, parrying Amika's vicious swipe. 'It's been a while.'

'You're certainly not forgiven. Poor skills get you killed.'

'So many ... opinions ... from somebody ... who doesn't ... even ... fight ... with ... a sword—*yes!*' Amika squealed triumphantly as Kio's weapon went careening from his hands into the dust. She wiped sweat and dirt from her forehead, beaming wildly. 'Perhaps I should be in charge of training the troops, brother.'

'You seem to forget I'm carrying an injury.' Kio massaged the back of his neck, not game enough to touch the crusted wounds themselves. Even from here he could feel the heat burning up his flesh. The pain was not so bad, but ... it didn't seem to be getting better either.

'I need a drink,' he said, and Rei went rummaging through the supply pack he was sitting atop for a wineskin. He tossed it to Kio, who caught it, and pulled the cork free with his teeth. His mouth salivated as he drank long and deep—

It was water. Kio swallowed it down all the same, parched from the sparring match. He glared his disappointment in Rei's direction, but the redhead just smiled sweetly.

'It's my turn to help cook tonight,' Amika said, glancing off towards the main cohort, who were a shroud of dark silhouettes against the setting sun.

'May the Goddess protect and watch over us,' Rei said sardonically.

A laugh burst from Kio's lips. 'That bad?' he asked, grinning at the pair of them.

'That bad,' Rei confirmed.

Amika rolled her eyes and tossed the sparring stick aside. 'You'—she speared an angry finger towards Rei's chest—'can starve, then.'

Huffing, she made her way back towards the central campfire, weaving her way between the rising rows of tents before disappearing into the crowd.

'Should get our own tent sorted,' Kio said, eyes on the darkening sky as he swallowed another mouthful of water.

'Oh, fuck it. Let's just sleep under the stars,' Rei grumbled. 'Not like it's going to rain.'

Despite his complaints, the moment their tent was up, Rei immediately set about unfurling his bedroll. He sat with his legs out straight, gingerly flexing and rotating his left foot to stretch the healing muscles of his calf. He could walk much better now, for a few hours anyway, before pain and fatigue set him limping again.

'Are you … alright?' Kio asked uneasily from the entrance flap, where he lingered, having noticed Rei was not following him out to dinner. 'All you do is hide away. Is it … the curse?' He swallowed dryly, not wanting to remember the state Rei had been in when he and Amika stumbled into camp. She'd said he'd been weakened when the Tear reopened, but Rei seemed relatively fine since receiving treatment from the Qhoraakese healers.

He stopped unlacing his boots and glanced up at Kio, his breath loud and deliberate. He chewed on his lower lip in an uncharacteristic display of vulnerability, and Kio noted the way this conversation made him shrink.

'I hate it here,' he said quietly. 'I thought it'd be better away from that damn farm, but it's not. Everything about this place makes my skin crawl.'

Kio nodded solemnly. He understood, better than Rei likely knew. He would never set foot in Cirahk without feeling the same; he couldn't even drink from a wineskin without feeling sick to his core. Memories were more stubborn than scars, fading but never vanishing entirely.

'I'll bring you some food. Surely even Amika can't ruin salt pork and lentils.'

Rei laughed acerbically. 'Just grab a serving before she puts any fire peppers in.'

Kio left the tent for the campfire, feeling light in a way he hadn't for years. So much of their childhood friendship had been defined by playful chiding, the savagery of their jibes increasing with affection. Although he'd grown close to Emanais, this banter was missing from their relationship. Kio never felt comfortable teasing the woman who saved his life—it was just not part of their dynamic. But now that Amika and Rei were with him again and he'd regained a part of himself he'd long thought lost, this ragtag crew of rebels had become more of a home than Adria had been in years.

'I don't know how I burned them,' Amika muttered to herself as she slopped a spoonful of stewed lentils into the bowl Kio held. A dry crust, black with pan scrapings, dusted the serving she dealt him. She garnished it with three slivers of salt pork, hiding her face in shame. 'Here's Rei's,' she said, passing Kio a bowl that had been set off to the side.

Kio raised an eyebrow. 'How come *his* isn't burnt?'

'I took it out early because he doesn't like spice. May not be burnt, but it won't have any flavour.'

'I'm sure it'll be fine. I starved for weeks in a dungeon, remember?'

Kio's words were lighthearted, but Amika retreated behind a cloud of angst, turning a fake smile to the next in line to be served.

Ruminating on his failed attempt at humour, Kio wove back through the rows of tents. He dipped his head in friendly acknowledgement as he passed familiar faces, until one caught his attention with an alluring grin and arms that opened wide as he approached.

'Little Prince,' Dhenka said in greeting and pressed a kiss to Kio's cheek before pulling back from the embrace. 'I've barely seen you. Ema and I miss you in our tent. We are almost in Xant. Perhaps you should join us and make the most of this peace before wartime is upon us.' He ran his hand down the length of Kio's arm, across his fingers, which still gripped Rei's dinner.

'Another time, perhaps.' Kio stepped around him; Dhenka reached out and caught his waist.

'I never have understood what's so special about Siephymn,' he said, voice low, gaze flicking between Kio's ear and his mouth. 'Maybe you could bring yours along.'

Kio shoved him back with the flat of his forearm, eyes narrowed and nose crinkled in distaste. Hair stood up on the back of his neck at the memory of Dhenka's touch.

The other man laughed. 'I jest, of course. Can't blame a man for trying,' he said, tracing a finger along Kio's jaw. 'And this man has been trying, *very* hard.'

'Another time, Dhenka,' Kio insisted forcefully and walked away, shaking his head.

When he arrived back at the tent, Rei on his back, idly twirling a long needle around his fingers as he stared at the canvas canopy. He stopped as Kio entered, spiriting the curious weapon away to sit up on his elbows.

'She burned it, didn't she?'

Kio laughed and took a seat opposite his lover. They conversed while they ate, partly to distract themselves from the questionable taste and weird texture, but also because doing so was such a rarity. When had they last sat and talked over dinner? It must have been *years*. Before Moyna? Before the Tower? Kio truly couldn't remember. They'd been apart so much of their adult life.

But no longer.

'How's your leg?' Kio asked, setting his empty bowl aside. Rei'd rolled his trousers to the knee and removed the dressing, allowing the healing wound to breathe.

Rei shrugged and shifted so his feet landed in Kio's lap. The prince walked his fingers tenderly around the wound, inspecting the neat stitching holding the torn flesh together. It looked viciously red against the porcelain white of Rei's skin, but didn't seem infected or inflamed in any way—unlike the searing heat radiating from Kio's back.

'Does it still hurt?' he asked.

Rei shook his head, face hidden in shadows cast by the dim light of the waning lantern. 'Not so much,' he said, rubbing at it as though itchy. 'I could probably run the final stretch to Xant now.'

'Please don't,' Kio said softly. His hand skimmed up Rei's leg. Over his knee. Up his thigh. 'I hope we never arrive. I like it here.'

'I like it when I'm with you,' Rei breathed, tongue flicking out to wet his lips as his beautiful golden gaze danced between Kio's mouth and his eyes.

Kio curled a hand behind Rei's neck, pulling him in. Lips clashed, tongues tangled, and the smaller man clambered atop Kio's thighs. Kio held him so tight their bones touched, their hard angles fitting together in perfect complement.

Rei's hands found their way into Kio's dark hair where they desperately sought purchase, careful and conscious of the wounds on the prince's back. But Kio didn't care. He just wanted to touch Rei, taste him, *feel* him, no matter the cost—no matter the pain. He inhaled deeply, sucking down the sweet salty scent of him, teeth nipping at his soft neck.

'Kio,' Rei breathed, sliding a hand down between them, down his chest, down his groin. Panic grew with his arousal, breath hitching as Rei reached for his belt.

No, no, no!

With a howl of frustration, Kio shoved Rei from his lap. He kicked the discarded dinner bowls, sending utensils flying. When he turned back to his lover he expected to see offence. Disgust. *Pity*.

But Rei-Hai Shaw just watched him, expression soft and lips silent. He stretched a hand towards Kio and the prince took it. Squeezed it tight. Rei shuffled closer and brought their entwined hands to his lips, kissing Kio's knuckles.

'I'm sorry. I—'

Rei shook his head. 'You're not drunk,' he muttered, more to himself than to Kio. He sighed heavily. 'Do you want—'

'No, I don't!' Kio snapped. 'I want you. And I want to have you as I am, not as a drunken shell who can't even tell what he's fucking. I just—*urgh!*' He screamed and banged on his forehead with the heel of his palm. 'I know I bedded you,' he said, pushing the frustration and disgust out through his teeth. 'The night after the *khaaja* attack. But I can't remember a damn thing. It had been so long and I ... We'll never get that moment back, Rei-Hai. I'm worried I'll never feel anything again.'

Rei leant against him and pressed his mouth to Kio's in a slow, tender kiss. 'Then I'll just have to remember for the both of us.'

He nestled into his chest and Kio folded his arms around him. Tears stinging his eyes, he set his cheek atop Rei's head and tried not to think about how much he wanted to die.

27

KRIAH

There was nothing grand about Castle Adria—not anymore. A heavy coat of gloom hung off every surface, rendering the royal halls as dark and desolate as the ruined markets below. Sword slashes and scorch marks covered the stone where portraits and tapestries should have hung. Curtains were little more than shredded ribbons, singed at the edges; blood spilt as carelessly as milk.

Battle had raged in these halls. Swift and bloody and brutal. The torment of it still lingered in the air, in the shoulders of the soldiers who escorted Kriah through the bleak passageways. He'd expected the Lord Regent to receive him in a grand audience chamber, with a throne and dais and two dozen shining knights throughout. Instead he awaited in a long, narrow room that was barely large enough for the ten-seat table in its centre. A candelabra sat atop it, half its candles melted down to stubs, casting more shadows than light. A figure stood before the high window, back to Kriah and the door.

'Lord Regent,' Half-helm addressed him.

The man turned, regarding his guests with sullen, distant eyes. He was older than Kriah expected—or aged by war, perhaps—but still held a few youthful familiarities. A relative of Amika's, surely, with chestnut hair, the same button nose and a playful curl about the lips. He held himself like a boy playing at manhood; even Half-helm's respect seemed uncertain.

'Captain Crawlton,' the Lord Regent said wearily. 'I thought no one was to enter the city until we knew more about Cirahk?'

'This man says he has news concerning that, Lord Regent,' Crawlton muttered, doubt and distrust still heavy on his tongue. 'Also claims Princess Amikharlia is still alive.'

The Lord Regent's face suddenly whitened and he turned to acknowledge Kriah. 'Truly? We'll take any information you have. While there's not much to offer in the way of coin, I can provide a dry bed and warm meal. Tell me: what is your name? I'll hear all you have to say.'

'Uh, Kriah, Your M—Lord Regent.' The man spoke so rapidly, so full of hope, that Kriah needed a moment to catch up. 'I travelled with Amika out of Ciraselo. We parted ways four Nirhana Moons ago, back in early autumn, but I know she's alive—and where she's headed.'

The Lord Regent nodded as though accepting Kriah's words for now. Addressing the captain, he said, 'Crawlton, have a chamber prepared for our guest and see that the kitchens bring wine and something to eat. No one else is to enter this room but the serving girl, do you hear me? I want that made very clear. '

'Yes, Lord Regent.' Crawlton said flatly. He retreated without haste and bolted the heavy door behind him with a metallic clunk.

Kriah stood, awkward and unsure, until the Lord Regent gestured he sit at the table that consumed the space between them. 'How do you know my cousin is alive?' he asked as he took a seat directly opposite Kriah, leaning close as if they were two friends sharing a secret.

Kriah swallowed. There was no easy way to explain this. Not to a Second Born. He risked a great deal sharing the truth now; spoken aloud it sounded so far-fetched, so *unnatural*. Nell had understood, thanks to the transference of memories. It had not been without consequence, but …

Kriah stretched a hand towards the Lord Regent.

'Stop,' Yae'ilston insisted.

He froze, then turned over his shoulder to where Yae'ilston lingered in the corner.

'You'll draw Azet'haal and his army straight here,' the Meah-Hyren cautioned. 'Is that what you want? Find another way.'

Kriah withdrew his hand, returning it to rest on the table in front of him. The Lord Regent regarded him with curious concern, but said nothing.

'Amika is …' Kriah hesitated. 'Amika is special. We share a … connection. I can feel her. Sometimes, anyway. She's not here. And wasn't when your castle burned.'

He braced for a roar of laughter. An order to have him beheaded. But the Lord Regent just slumped in his chair, head resting on its high back, as he stared up at the shadowed ceiling above. 'Thank the Goddess,' he breathed. 'I'm reluctant to believe in miracles but … we've been so long starved of hope. I need to find something to hold onto.'

'… You believe me?' Kriah pressed incredulously. 'Just like that?'

'I never wanted to proclaim her dead,' the Lord Regent insisted. 'We never recovered a body. Not for Amika—or Reminas, actually. Chirurgeons said the blaze burned so hot it cremated their remains. They found fragments here or there, but there was no way to say if they belonged to one person or to two. I never thought she was dead, but we …'

He rubbed his hands down his face, and Kriah saw him for the young man he truly was. Tired. So tired. Tired in a way Kriah understood now, having not slept or dreamscaped in weeks. Whatever happened here went beyond grief.

'The bodies on the pikes ...' Kriah prompted gingerly. 'You ... did that?' His stomach turned in memory of the corpses, at the stench of rot and shit and blood. He'd never seen barbarism on such a scale. For the briefest of moments, he understood why his grandfather believed the Second Born *dangerous*.

The Lord Regent shook his head vehemently. 'I didn't *do* anything! The people, they ... When word broke that Reminas and Amikharlia were dead, they rebelled. Pushed back against the Bararnite occupation. Many Holanians fled the city when the walls were breached, but those who remained endured through *so much*. They saw the queen beheaded on the balcony. The king's body hung from the cathedral tower like a flag after the wedding. Amikharlia's return was the only salvation they held. For it to be snatched away ...'

Kriah could do nothing but nod. As he absorbed the moment, a meek blonde girl tapped on the door, bearing a tray of offerings from the kitchen. She entered at the Lord Regent's behest and set the meal down on the table between them: hard cheese, crusty bread and a stew thick with beans and root vegetables, along with a glass carafe. Silently, the girl righted two upturned goblets, filled them with a rich red wine and bowed out of the room as though she were never there.

'Please, eat,' the Lord Regent insisted, reaching for a dry roll. 'It is by no means the feast we would usually take pride in offering, but our stores were depleted well before any of this happened. Kiokharen was the only one who saw Reminas for what he was, for what Bararn was doing ...' He drank deeply from his wine, draining the goblet in one gulp. He repeated the process until the carafe was empty.

Kriah slid his own goblet across the table. 'If it please you, Lord Regent ...'

'Tarken,' the young man corrected, reaching for the proffered wine. 'Tarken, please. That title just reminds me of what I've lost.'

Tarken looked like a man resigned to never feeling anything again. He was stone, inside and out. Kriah saw it in the set of his jaw, in the rigidity of his shoulders. What sort of suffering did one have to live through to abandon joy so completely? But Kriah had seen the aftermath of the Holanian uprising; it was not hard to envision the blood and chaos that preceded it.

Is this what I will become?

Kriah's attention turned to Yae'ilston, who wandered around the narrow chamber like a bored child seeking stimulation. He poked at an ornate vase on the shelf that ran the length of the far wall, despite his presence having no impact on the physical world. The moving visage did little to erase the memory of his severed head tumbling through a fountain of blood—a memory so vivid that when Kriah closed his eyes he could still see it, still *taste* the metallic tang on his lips.

Perhaps it was a good thing he didn't sleep anymore.

'... did she go?' Tarken was saying. Kriah blinked rapidly, dragging his attention from Yae'ilston and back to the living, breathing person before him.

'Amika?' he guessed; he'd missed half the conversation. 'Qhoraak, I think. But she'll be heading to Kheshtarl next, and we have to warn—'

He stopped abruptly. They hadn't yet gotten to *that*. Tarken accepted Amika's survival out of desperate hope—would he be open enough to believe Kriah about Meah-Hyren enslavement as well?

Kriah rubbed his eyes, heavy with exhaustion now he'd been sitting, and reached for some food to distract himself. He dipped his bread into the stew and watched it soak up the thin brown liquid like a sponge. It wasn't overly flavourful—water had been added time and time again to make it stretch—but it was a warm meal, and Kriah hadn't eaten in days.

Not since Nell—

He cleared his throat, banishing the emotion that threatened to choke him, and looked at Tarken with grave sincerity. 'There are more concerns brewing in Bararn.'

It was Tarken's turn to swallow dryly. 'We've always feared retaliation. It's been too quiet for too long. What are they planning?'

'It's not anything they've planned, as such. It's ...' Kriah stared blearily at his plate as he struggled to find words that would not incriminate him, either. Having been in contact with plague, he was ... he was ...

'... you scampered off to?'

That wasn't Tarken.

Kriah lifted his head. The Lord Regent was looking at him, tight-lipped and intent. But he hadn't spoken. Kriah blinked again and saw Azet'haal amble through the room, casually surveying his surroundings as if admiring a masterful display of art.

Kriah tumbled off his chair. He landed heavily on his back. Wind burst from his lungs in a suffocating gasp. He opened his eyes but Azet'haal was still there. Still talking. Still walking towards him.

'Ah, so you've crossed the border?' The Meah-Hyren surmised. 'It's been hard to keep track of you, Halfblood. It must be so *tiring* keeping me out.'

'How ... are you ... here?' Kriah choked.

'He's not here, you fool—you're asleep,' Yae'ilston shouted from across the room. He sounded muffled and distant, like he was underwater or somehow fading away. 'Wake up, Kriah. WAKE. UP.'

Kriah drew a gasping breath as he woke. The Lord Regent hovered over him in concern as Kriah lay immobile, sprawled on his back but still in the chair. He struggled to sit up, but dizziness and Tarken's steady hands pinned him down.

'Easy, easy,' he hushed, but ultimately relented and allowed Kriah to right himself.

'What happened?' Kriah asked, rubbing his eyes. The edges of his vision were frayed like the hem of an old cloak. As it cleared, he saw no sign of Azet'haal.

'You fainted,' Tarken said simply. 'Was like you just fell asleep.'

Asleep!

Panic ripped through him. If he'd slept, that meant Azet'haal had not been a hallucination; he had been here, inside Kriah's mind—had seen where he had gone.

We're not safe here.

'We need to go,' Kriah said, pushing past Tarken and up to his feet. 'We need to get out of Holania. We're not safe. He'll come. He'll come and he'll bring it here.'

Pacing the length of the room, down the narrow space between the table and the wall, Kriah pounded the heels of his palms against his temples. How could he fall asleep? He hadn't meant to, hadn't even known it was happening. Stupid. Stupid. *Stupid.*

'Kriah, you need to calm down,' Yae'ilston coached. But Kriah was too caught up in his mind to locate the Meah-Hyren phantom.

Stupid. Stupid. Stupid.

'You're losing control—'

The candles on the table blazed. Great pillars of flame shot up to the ceiling. A gale burst through the open window.

Tarken cowered, back against the door.

Stupid. Stupid. Stupid.

'Kriah!'

Wailing, Kriah dropped to his knees. He pressed his face on the floor and covered his head with his hands as though he expected the whole world to collapse. A part of him wished it would. Wished the ground would open up beneath him and swallow him whole. Anything was better than this. Anything—

Hands hauled him upright, onto his backside. He was trembling, disorientated, surrounded by more faces than he remembered being in the room. Scooting back on his heels, he collided with the wall. Cold terror ripped through him.

'You're alright. You're safe.'

A gentle voice. A familiar voice—Tarken? The Lord Regent came into focus before him. He placed a comforting hand on Kriah's knee.

'You've been through a lot. You're exhausted.' Tarken turned his gaze to meet an approaching figure, and reached for something on a proffered tray.

A teacup. A small, simple teacup. White porcelain. Fluted lip. Cloudy tan liquid swirling within. It was pressed to his lips.

'This will help you sleep,' Tarken said, and Kriah started to struggle.

'N-no!' he moaned, turning his head aside. 'No!'

'Hold him down.'

Hands everywhere. On his shoulders. His jaw. Fingers prying open his teeth. He bit. He thrashed. But someone pinched his nose and he had to open his mouth to breathe.

The bitter brew burned his tongue. Hot like fire. Numb like ice.

And then like nothing at all.

Sickness came to Adria on the fifth day of his confinement.

Kriah heard the bells toll and watched the white-haired rider enter the city from the window of the guest chamber that had become his prison. Two days later, the first whispers of fever swept the castle.

If Azet'haal had joined him in sleep, Kriah didn't know; the mandrake tea the Lord Regent had forced upon him had induced an unconscious state so deep that not even Yae'ilston recalled the days that were lost. Either way, the Meah-Hyren were here, and Azet'haal's plague had begun its march through the Holanian capital.

'Do you suppose they'll kill you?' Yae'ilston asked, more curious than cruel, as Kriah continued his watch by the window. The little room was well-furnished with a wide bed, thick blankets and a side table stacked with several books. Kriah flicked through the offerings once or twice, but couldn't sit still, let alone quiet his thoughts long enough to read.

'Probably,' he muttered bitterly, watching the drizzly grey day outside. Rain fell as sleet and left slushy puddles of mud and ice across the ruins of the castle town. The markets, which had been razed to ashes long before Kriah's arrival, contributed to the monochromatic haze hovering about the city. Adria was supposed to be beautiful, he recalled, lush with foliage and golden from glorious sunsets reflected off the river. Now it was just dead.

'And you're just going to let that happen?' Yae'ilston was incredulous. He sat cross-legged on the bed Kriah had not touched since he recovered from the mandrake stupor, arms folded across his chest.

Kriah turned back from the window. 'What else am I supposed to do?' he snapped. 'Fight my way out? Level the city entirely? No. I won't do it.'

Amika needs somewhere to come home to.

He scratched the back of his head, ruffling his curls even more out of place. It was hopeless. Azet'haal was closing in, spreading his disease, while Kriah had been locked inside a room by the very people he sought to help. Soon, the Meah-Hyren would find him and—

A knock at the door sent his heart jumping from his chest. As he sucked down breaths to calm his pulse, he waited in silence for the visitor to identify themself.

'Kriah?' It was Tarken.

The Lord Regent's presence gave Kriah no comfort. He'd not heard from Holania's current ruler since his imprisonment. Tendrils of fear and anger slowly uncoiled within him and Kriah prepared to defend himself from whatever onslaught awaited beyond the door.

But the bolt did not clatter free, nor did the knob even shudder. Instead he heard the shuffle of feet and a slight thud as something solid leant against the wood.

'Do you really think my cousin is alive?' Tarken asked, voice tired and meek. It was low, as well. Not in pitch but direction, as though he were sitting.

Kriah matched the Lord Regent's discretion and took a seat by the door. 'I know she is. I told you—I can feel her. Or I could, anyway. Recently.'

There was a pause, and Kriah imagined Tarken nodding through the silence. 'The council thinks you should be executed.' The words were thin, distant. 'A rider came, warning of a plague spreading through Bararn. Said they were chasing an infected man who escaped their quarantine. Now, some of the guards are stricken with fever and bloody flux—'

'*I* came to warn you of that,' Kriah pleaded and stretched towards the wood that separated them as if it would make a difference. 'The rider came to spread it, not me!'

Yae'ilston snorted. 'You really have made a mess of things—'

'Shut up, Ilston!'

Kriah's scream echoed around the small chamber. He'd never spoken to the Meah-Hyren's phantom like that, not aloud nor in the presence of another. Reclining on his feet, Kriah closed his eyes and breathed deliberately in and out through his nose, shame and resignation shrouding him like a cloak.

'I believe you,' Tarken whispered.

Kriah straightened, eyes snapping open.

'I was in that room with you for hours and I am not sick, and those who *are* didn't have any contact with you at all.'

'Then why keep me locked in here?'

The Lord Regent sighed in frustration. 'Because it is the will of the council. I am just a figurehead, Kriah. A symbolic custodian of the throne. Queen Clareesa was my aunt, but there is not a drop of Holani blood in my veins. No one follows my decisions, not really. I was just a captain in the royal guard before this happened. And when Bararn invaded I ...' A *thunk* against the door—his head. 'I submitted to their rule. And now ... Kiokharen is gone. Amika. My aunt, my uncle. My fa—' Sobs choked his words and a small cry escaped with his breath.

Kriah let the young regent sit with his grief. He didn't know how to comfort someone grappling with the pain of mortality, even after all the death he'd seen. Foolishly, he glanced at Yae'ilston for some sort of suggestion and he found the spectre reclined on the bed, staring at the ceiling in boredom.

After a long silence, Tarken said, 'I don't want to be responsible for any more blood spilt in these halls. But ...'

'Then let me *go*,' Kriah urged; Yae'ilston laughed at his desperation. 'I'll find Amika. Bring her back. And then we'll—'

'I can't do that, Kriah.' Tarken's voice was louder, but he just sounded more tired. 'Not yet.'

It was Kriah's turn to hit his head on the door. Once, twice, three times. The vibrating thump eased his frustrations for just a second. On the other side, Tarken shifted to his feet.

'I'm sorry,' the Lord Regent said weakly. 'I'll do what I can to change their minds.'

Footsteps trailed away from the chamber until Kriah could hear nothing but the sound of rain splashing on the windowsill. Despondent, he flopped back on the stone floor, turning his head so he could look out at the grey sky. He caught Yae'ilston staring.

'What?' Kriah grunted.

'You called me Ilston,' he said, the faintest of lines creasing his brow. 'Why?'

Kriah sighed heavily. He didn't have the energy for Yae'ilston's cruel jibes right now. But as he studied the Meah-Hyren's posture, the shine of curiosity in his eyes, he could find no trace of mischief or malice.

'It's, uh ...' Kriah sat up on his elbows. 'Something I picked up from the Second Born. They shorten names.'

Yae'ilston's frown deepened. 'Is it really such a hassle to pronounce one's full name?'

Laughter burst from Kriah's lips. 'I said the same thing!'

Yae'ilston failed to respond to his mirth, and Kriah's chuckles soon died.

'It's not about difficulty,' he added. 'It's about frie—' Friendship was not the right word to describe Yae'ilston, and mentioning it to him would open up more ridicule. 'Familiarity,' Kriah said instead. 'It's about familiarity. They shorten the names of people they speak with most. I'll never be rid of you, so ...' He shrugged, lamenting that an emotional slip of the tongue had led to such an awkward conversation.

'So I'm supposed to call you *Kri*, then?' Yae'ilston quipped. 'Or maybe just, *Ah*. That sounds more like you, seeing as how you're always confused by everything.'

Heat inflamed his skin. 'Shut up, Ilston!'

Kriah turned towards the wall to hide the smile spreading across his lips.

The next time a knock arrived at the door, Kriah knew something was different; no greeting followed. After a second tap, he barked, 'What is it?'

The lock clicked and fell free. Kriah's pulse spiked. Tarken must have failed to placate the council. Fists curling, he prepared himself for an attack. If a Meah-Hyren walked through that door, he'd have no reason to hold back his *khe'torla*.

A cowled girl entered the room, bearing a bowl of grey-looking porridge on a tray. Kriah did not drop his defences; the serving girls always announced their presence and brought meals under the supervision of a guard. This maid was alone.

Kriah watched like a hawk as she shuffled over to the side table and set the meal down with trembling hands. Was she injured—or just afraid? Instead of bowing out of the room, her task now complete, she closed the door and turned back to Kriah.

'You're the halfblood,' she said, shaking off her hood. A golden braid swung down her back, matted and dull and flecked with dried blood. Her face was dotted with a multitude of thin cuts, still red and healing.

'You're not ... Meah-Hyren,' Kriah observed carefully. His posture relaxed, albeit slightly.

'No, I'm not.' The girl pulled up her sleeve, exposing four black bands tattooed around her forearm. 'If you want to get to Kheshtarl, you have to trust me,' she added quickly, before Kriah could react to her revelation.

'Why would the brethren help me?' he levelled at her suspiciously. 'You attacked Amika in Ciraselo.'

'That was my master,' she said, shaking her head. 'And she attacked the traitor, Rei-Hai Shaw, not your precious princess.' The girl grimaced, fingering her shoulder as she gingerly relaxed her arm by her side. 'You were right when you said she was still alive. I encountered her in the Meytaran hinterland, en route to the sea cliffs on the Qhoraakese border. But that was weeks ago, now. I suppose she could be dead.'

'Amika did that to you?' Kriah asked, dipping his head towards the girl's wounded shoulder, to the hundreds of little incisions across her flesh.

She laughed bitterly. 'No, not that. That fucking little shit Rei-Hai put a knife in my back as I made my retreat. In haste, I portalled here instead of the Tower. I must have dropped my home stone somewhere and have been holed up here ever since. Need to recover properly if I'm to make it back on foot. Tell me, Halfblood: you know how to put that magic of yours to good use?'

'My name is Kriah,' he snapped. 'And if I did, I wouldn't heal you anyway. Not with the Meah-Hyren so close.'

The girl staggered over to the bed and took a seat where Yae'ilston had been reclining. Perturbed but otherwise undamaged, the phantom shifted further up the mattress, where he muttered his indignation to himself in the Meah-Hyren tongue.

'Ah, yes, the flaw in Meah-Hyren magic. I certainly see why the Yaians poured their *khe'torla* into stones instead.' She slipped a hand into her robe and produced a fistful of luminescent blue gems. 'Crush a few of these and no one is any wiser.'

Kriah's eyes widened at the Skrevaari magic stones—shards of glacier ice the Yaian exiles imbued with their *khe'torla* so they could continue to cast without betraying their survival to Kherunis. It was a strange thing, seeing *khe'torla* before him but being unable to sense its pull or hear its melody.

'If you have these, why are you still here?' Kriah asked, brow furrowed.

'I told you: I lost my home stone,' the girl muttered, returning the gems to their hidden satchel. 'Portal stones are anchored to a specific place—I can't just go anywhere I please. I have to have been there before. And have a stone that remembers.' One shining shard remained in her hand and she rolled it over between her fingers. 'All I have left is one for Kheshtarl.'

'And you want to portal me there?' Kriah shifted on his feet to ensure he was between her and the door. This was too easy, too convenient. He kept waiting for the trap, but he couldn't see it.

'I know you're trying to find Amika,' she said confidently. 'I know you think she'll head to Kheshtarl. And I also know wherever that powerful little witch is, Rei-Hai Shaw will be skulking at her heels. They know my face now; they'll kill me as soon as I get close. But if I'm with you ...'

'You want to use me to get to Rei.'

'Of course. What's he to you, Kriah? Nobody.'

He's Chosen, Kriah reminded himself. *And his seal's in Kheshtarl.* 'He's my friend.'

The girl laughed cruelly. 'Rei-Hai Shaw doesn't have friends. He has *masters*. And he's betrayed them.' Apparently tired of Kriah's deliberation, she stood, magic stone clenched tight in her fist. 'You can stay here and die with your sentimentality if you like,' she said, crushing the gem. The shards liquified in her palm and seeped out between her fingers. Instead of falling to the floor, the droplets rained upward, forming a puddle in the space between them.

'Or you can come with me.'

She took a step forward, into the shimmering pool, and Kriah exchanged a fleeting glance with Yae'ilston before diving into the water after her.

28

AMIKHARLIA

They smelt the corpse long before it came into sight. The sharp, rancid stench, thick with sulphur and rot, began its assault on the senses when the decaying body was little more than a blip on the flat horizon.

'Deities dead, what *is* that?' Kio groaned, burying his face in his elbow.

'Nothing that was recently alive,' Amika said as she wrapped the tails of her long scarf around her nose and mouth. Many of the others did the same, repurposing the shawls they used to protect against sun and sand as masks to mitigate the awful stink. It had little effect; Amika still felt the heavy, putrid reek clawing at the back of her throat.

Emanais brought the procession to a halt. 'I don't believe it,' she was muttering to herself when Amika pushed her way through the ranks to investigate the reason for the hold-up.

The great corpse of *khaaja* lay in the Waste some five hundred feet before them, black with bloat and disfigured beyond recognition of the creature it once was. But it *was* a *khaaja*—there was no mistaking that. It was larger than the one that drove the attack on the base, or maybe Amika's memories were just clouded by the shrivelled and crumpled state she'd reduced it to. It hadn't looked so imposing once it had imploded on itself. A shiver raced across her flesh, but her veins were still, silent. She pushed the painful swell of grief down low.

'It's been dead a while,' Amika said. 'A full cycle of the moon at least, by the look of it.'

The *khaaja*'s hide had turned papery thin. If it once had fur, it had since sluiced away, leaving only a husk stretched over bones and dust. Its gut had burst open, spilling putrefied entrails, alive with wriggling maggots, onto the red earth. But that was not the wound that had killed it.

'Do you recognise it?' Amika asked Emanais.

The commander shook her head, braids dancing. 'No,' she said slowly, carefully, her eyes barely connecting with the corpse. 'No, I don't think so. It's not Yeni's sire.'

Amika placed a hand upon Emanais's shoulder and squeezed. She knew her pain all too well. It was a specific kind of need—a core-deep ache that drove you to save someone who was an extension of your very soul. The longer you were separated, the more agonising it became.

Distant and distracted, Emanais stroked Sylar's hair as he clung to her leg, face turned into her thigh so he could not see the gore. Wordlessly, Emanais led him away, prompting the army to keep marching.

As they moved upwind of the corpse, the *khaaja*'s death continued to play on Amika's mind. They were within a day's walk of the capital and the creature had been left undisturbed in the Waste. When the *khaaja* she slayed hit the earth, it left a crater; the one they'd passed hadn't even left tracks. Given its size, it seemed implausible for it to have been dumped, but ... something just didn't sit right.

'Amika,' Kio called from where he marched with the first of several supply wagons. She turned over her shoulder to see her brother flick his head, beckoning her close. Amika peeled away from the vanguard and made her way to him.

'What's wrong?' she asked, frowning. Rei had a finger to his temple.

'There are demonspawn coming,' the redhead said, massaging the obvious pain in his head.

Amika's heart leapt to her throat, adrenaline pumping. 'A horde? Like back at the camp?'

He shook his head. 'No, there's not that many. And they … feel different, somehow.'

The wasteland around them was flat and bare; they could see assailants coming for miles, even with the heat haze blurring the edges of the horizon. Demonspawn had to be close for Rei to feel them, and yet …

'Go tell Emanais,' Amika said to Kio. 'There's an ambush waiting for us somewhere.'

Her brother nodded and pushed grumbling soldiers aside as he made his way to the front of the procession. Amika's nerves were alight, hand twitching by the hilt of her sword.

'Can't you do anything?' Rei asked, shaking off the last twinges of his headache. 'Reach out with your *khe'torla* and find them, or whatever?'

A hard lump plugged her throat; she swallowed it away. 'I, uh—no. No, it doesn't work that way.'

Amika scrambled for more explanations, more excuses, when a thunderous crack erupted overhead. They cowered, arms curled reflexively over heads as though the sky itself were crumbling.

But it was the ground.

Darkness erupted over a hidden ridge like ants fleeing the nest. Firearms cracked warning shots into the air as the mass spilling out of the ground took the shape of an army—an army with demonspawn among its ranks.

The beasts lined up beside their Qhoraakese counterparts, rikkara and ukarat and creatures Amika did not recognise, each more foul and savage than the last. Instead of launching into an attack, they held still in perfect formation. Emanais's troops were enclosed in a ring of spears, loaded pistols and snarling demonspawn.

'Why aren't the demonspawn attacking?' Amika whispered, hoping Rei was close enough to hear.

'Because they're tethered,' he whispered back. 'That's why they felt strange. They're being controlled. Those witch-fuckers have Siephymn for soldiers.'

Commands were issued in Qhoraakese, but the dialect was so rough Amika could make no sense of it. The army encroached and the ring tightened like a fist around her throat. Her hand curled about her sword, but she didn't dare draw it—not with so many weapons pointed at her chest.

Behind her, Rei sank into her shadow. Never before had she known him to look so small, so unassuming. He was ... scared.

'I don't believe it,' an accented voice drawled in Meytaran.

Stepping out of formation, one of the enemy soldiers sauntered towards them, shaking braided locs free of his hood. His piercing hazel eyes regarded her with curious familiarity as a cavalier grin split his face in a porcelain crescent.

'The most beautiful huntress in Meytar! Here, in Qhoraak. I truly do not believe it.'

Amika glared at the man with fierce contempt. He knew her, somehow, but she couldn't place him. There was something familiar about his voice, his smile. It lingered on the edge of her memory, irritatingly out of reach.

'Tell me, girl, how is my dear sister? Still working that tavern of hers?'

Amika gasped as the pieces fell together. '*Lamber?*'

Lamber Deen—Lominah's estranged younger brother. The man who had taught her to hunt.

'The one and only.' He gave a dramatic bow. 'To think I get to introduce you to the Allchief after all these years. He has such a need for someone with your ... talents.'

Lamber stretched his hand towards Amika; she slapped it away. He bristled but chuckled, eyes growing dark as he looked to the space beyond her shoulder. His smile grew again.

'I see that's not the only gift you offer.' Lamber shoved her aside, his strength deceptive, and Amika stumbled, leaving Rei exposed. Lamber seized him by the wrist. 'Another little Siephymn for the Allchief's collection.'

He tried to drag Rei away, but the redhead dug his heels into the earth. Snarling, he bashed at Lamber's grip, foot kicking at his knee. But Lamber was larger, stronger, and Rei was so terrified he trembled even as he fought.

With one fierce tug, Lamber pulled Rei close like a lover, clamping a hand about his face with brutal force. Rei went as still as death. The cold muzzle of a firearm pressed into the soft underside of his jaw.

Somewhere, Kio shouted, 'Get your fucking hands off him!'

The Qhoraakese army silenced her brother before Amika had the chance, knocking him face-first into the sand. A heavy boot crunched on his back and he screamed in bone-deep agony. Amika flinched. Anger roared through the rebel forces, but Emanais soothed them before any blood could be spilt.

'You certainly look familiar,' Lamber said, turning Rei's head from side to side as if inspecting a piece of meat. 'Where did *you* come from?' He released Rei's face only to grab a fistful of his hair, wrenching his head sideways to steal a glimpse of his neck.

'Lamber, stop! He's my friend.' Amika started towards them—and halted when the pistol turned on her.

'*He* is a prized stallion who ran away from the stud,' Lamber snapped, waving the firearm in her face. Rei hissed as he was dragged about by his hair. 'And didn't the Allchief want my balls for that! First an escapee, then a rebellion, and I had to go crawling back to Xant to tell Waqar fucking Koll that an entire farm was lost! I'm lucky to still have my head. So when I heard Emanais Ulande and her terrorist army were on their way to the capital, it seemed like the perfect opportunity to redeem myself.'

Lamber scanned the rebel ranks in search of their commander, his savage grin broadening when he found her. Amika couldn't bring herself to turn her back to him, to turn her back on Rei. Emanais yelled something venomous in Qhoraakese; Lamber only laughed.

'I'll take this one back to Yeni and the other little fillies,' he said and shoved Rei to start walking. 'Bound to be a touching reunion for them.'

'You'll have to fucking kill me!'

Rei broke free of Lamber's grasp, swept beneath the groping hands of another soldier and made a run for the opposite side of the ring. It was suicide; they all knew it. Kio screamed helplessly, mouth full of sand, as ranks began to mobilise, raising firearms and readying spears. The demonspawn snarled and thrashed, eager to pounce.

Rei dodged one spear and then a second, rolling back to his feet right into an arching swipe from his blind spot. Amika flinched, closed her eyes, expecting to see a head roll when they opened. But Rei lay crumpled in the sand, a smattering of black blood seeping from his forehead—unconscious.

Unconscious, but alive.

Amika's lungs resumed their function and she gulped down hungry gasps of air, hunched over. Sick. She felt *sick*. Behind her, Kio screamed and thrashed ferally. He was still pinned; his violent outburst had done little more than worsen his pain. Blood seeped through the layers of his shirt, a large dark stain blooming across his back.

Lamber sauntered over to Rei and nudged him casually with a boot. He whistled, snapped his fingers, and two soldiers stepped forward to collect Rei like a stray dog from the gutter. Lamber passed Amika, regarding her silently for just a moment, before striding on to Emanais.

As the commander, the Qhoraakese woman had been stoic, quietly calculating her next move even while other pieces acted out of turn. But beneath that stony facade Amika felt the rage shredding through her, red-hot like wildfire. She would have stayed locked in that silent battle with Lamber for hours ... had she not made the unconscious mistake of touching Sylar's head.

Laughter burst from Lamber's lips as he threw his head back in delight. 'Don't tell me,' he chuckled at the discovery. 'You've got a Siephymn child. Is he one of ours?'

'You will not fucking touch him,' Emanais growled. She bared her teeth like a cornered dog, ushering the child behind her.

'Lamber, don't do this,' Amika implored as he menacingly closed on the child. Sylar whimpered and buried his face in his aunt's body.

Emanais whipped a dagger from her belt—and a dozen rifles were soon levelled at her chest.

'Waqar wanted you alive, but I'm sure it won't matter if I bring one of our lost little lambs back instead.' Lamber lashed forward and grabbed Emanais's wrist to wrench the blade free. In the struggle, a soldier snatched Sylar from her leg. The boy screamed, high-pitched and desperate, as he was dragged away in a storm of flailing limbs.

'Do something!' Emanais screeched as the boy disappeared behind the wall of assailants. 'Someone fucking do something!'

Tears choked her voice. Amika's own eyes stung.

'Do something! Do something!' she continued to shout.

Amika clenched her fists, blood pumping hot but silent through her veins.

There was nothing she could do.

They were loaded onto a barge at dusk, hands bound in chains. It was dark, the air greasy. Xant rose in the distance, a city of smoke and steel on an island across the strait, visible only between narrow gaps in the cargo. Never before had Qhoraak seemed so foreign, so far removed from everything Amika knew.

It was not a place she wanted to die.

'Why, Amika?' Emanais rasped. There was a bruise around her left eye, purple and angry; she caught a fist to the face during the struggle. She sat opposite Amika on one of the many low benches, while her rebels were packed shoulder-to-shoulder. 'Why didn't you use your gift?'

Shame rushed to Amika's face in a blanching stain. Kio glared at her too, just as betrayed. She squeezed her fists against the guilt, a torn nail drawing blood from her palm with its jagged edge.

'Because I can't,' she whispered, almost inaudibly. 'I can't use it. It's gone.'

Emanais pressed her elbows to her knees and leant forward, closing the space between them. 'What do you mean, gone? It's part of you, isn't it?'

Her tone had been comforting, but it provided Amika no relief. Deities dead, she felt so weak—so *helpless*. She couldn't even raise her arms in these stupid chains, rusted though they were. Some *Chosen* she was.

'I'm sorry,' she whimpered. 'I don't know what to do. I don't know how to get them back.'

The barge gave a metallic belch as it pushed away from the dock, the last of its passengers finally loaded. The shift left a sickening lurch in the pit of Amika's stomach. She'd never been on a ship before—not at sea, anyway. The river boats on the Faethou were small and open-aired, designed to carry no more than two or three people. But this steel serpent was made for carting freight—living or otherwise. She didn't need chains to feel a prisoner here.

'You knew that man,' Kio said out of the silent darkness that engulfed them. 'Lamber.'

Amika nodded as more sickening shame swelled within her. 'I met him years ago in Ciraselo. He was hunting demonspawn. Got me started in the trade. He said he was working for the Allchief, but I didn't …' She swallowed. 'I didn't know what that meant then.'

'How did he know we were marching for the capital?' Emanais added. There was an accusatory edge to her voice Amika did not like; her skin prickled at the implication.

'Emanais, you can't think—'

'Of course we don't,' Kio interjected. He'd stopped fidgeting with his hands for the first time since they'd been captured, the skin now red and raw. He suddenly straightened. 'Where's Dhenka?'

Emanais glanced around the rows of subdued faces, searching for the man known to be her lover. Her gaze met that of Zhayar, the ranger who'd brought Amika to camp, and she barked a desperate question in Qhoraakese. Zhayar shrugged, shook her head, and Emanais let slip a curse that needed no translation. Some naive, optimistic part of Amika wanted to voice the possibility that Dhenka had slipped capture and was instead planning their rescue. But she knew that wasn't likely.

He had betrayed them.

The realisation hit them hard, sinking their spirits faster than lead. If Kio was outraged, he didn't show it. But Emanais ... Emanais trembled with a palpable fury so hot it brought sweat to shine on her forehead. Her muscles were as hard as the steel all around them, tense and taut but restrained.

'I'll kill them,' Emanais rumbled to herself. 'I will fucking kill them all.'

And there was no doubt in Amika's mind that she would.

Xant was a mechanical city, filled with steel and gears and oil the likes of which Amika had rarely seen. Steam rose from vents along paved streets, lined with orange lanterns perched on tall metal posts. The glow they emitted was ethereal, bright, unlike the meagre flicker of candles back home. Steel was used for more than weaponry here, built into the structure of the multilevel brick buildings.

'Lomi always said Xant was nothing like Ciraselo,' Amika mused idly as they marched alongside the channel leading from the bay towards the centre of the city. 'I finally understand what she meant.'

'Meytaran folk assume we're primitive because we're isolated,' Emanais muttered. 'But isolation has made us strong. Rich—industrious. Why else do you think your indentured never return home once their debts are clear? Xant may be the only city in Qhoraak, but it is the greatest settlement Whyt'hallen has ever seen. And Waqar stole it from me.'

The sun was rising as they approached the Allchief's castle. The Citadel, Emanais called it, or so was the closest translation. It was a great sprawling manor of red brick and black steel, tall and illustrious but also dark and imposing. A bonfire burned in the centre of the paved courtyard, crimson flames licking the skyline. Hirathi, the Deity of fire, was alive and well in Qhoraak.

'How long's it been since you last set eyes on the Eternal Flame, Ulande?' Lamber said coolly, stopping where Amika, Kio, Emanais and Zhayar were huddled. His hand rested casually on the hilt of the stiletto blade he wore at his hip, but Amika was more threatened by the pistol nestled inside the holster beneath his jacket. 'Must be almost fifteen years now,' he continued, his gaze fixed on the flickering fire. 'How old would you have been? Fourteen? Fifteen, maybe? Half your life spent in exile only to return to be executed. Death just follows you everywhere, doesn't it?'

'How many of our people died to put that *bastard* on my throne?' Emanais spat venomously. The chains rattled as she strained against them, itching to fight.

'And how many more died in your crusade against the farms?' Lamber turned to face her, eyes flashing. 'Siephymn are not our equals, Ulande. Your family's ideals were outdated. That is why you lost the throne. That is why your followers turned against you. Waqar has the vision to make us strong—strong enough that even those white-haired witches won't dare challenge us again.'

'The Meah-Hyren are coming for us regardless of your army,' Amika burst. 'They will do to us what you do to the Siephymn. If that's your justification for all this, then surely you can see it's flawed!'

Lamber scoffed and turned to one of his men, calling him over with the flap of his hand. They conversed sharply in Qhoraakese, just loud enough for Amika to hear.

'Take the would-be rebels to the old foundry,' he said. 'These three can come with me.

29

REI-HAI

Rei's forehead was sticky with dried blood. He awoke face down on a damp stone floor, smelling like piss or old water—maybe a combination thereof. He sat up and vigorously wiped his face with his sleeve, listening to the wheezing breaths and rattling coughs echo in the darkness. There was little he could see aside from shadows, but the chill in the air made one thing certain: he was underground.

Rei pawed about blindly, chest seizing as his hands hit something fleshy. He hissed in a breath—no. Someone else did.

'It's alright,' he said quickly, sensing fear fill the space. 'I won't hurt you, I'm ...'

In the dim light, Rei could see the soft outlines of a boyish face, the golden sheen to his eyes. He swallowed. It was the child—Sylar.

His child.

'Oh, fuck,' he breathed, then inwardly chastising himself for his choice of words. Even he knew not to speak like that around a child. Could the boy understand him?

Rei had kept his distance from the child ever since he'd pieced together his parentage. At least he didn't look like her, not really. Not that it made it any easier. The boy—*Sylar*—stared at him intently, like he expected

"

Rei held all the answers and knew how to save them. It made his skin prickle, his stomach flip.

'I, uh,' he began awkwardly. 'Do you know what I'm saying?'

Sylar nodded.

'Okay, that's good. I guess. Don't like talking?'

A head shake.

'No ... I didn't like talking much when I was small either. My father thought I was broken. Maybe that's why he beat me.'

Rei stopped himself from saying anything more. He took a deep breath and surveyed the room now that his eyes had fully adjusted. They were definitely underground—an ornate ironwork grate loomed far overhead, filtering light down in a murky haze. There was no hope of climbing. The walls were wide, smooth and rounded like a dome—a cavern with no rooms or passages leading beyond. Just row after row of cages filled with bodies bundled tight against the bars. Most did not move.

A tiny hand caught his wrist as Rei made to stand. Sylar's grip was tight, his golden eyes wide with fear. Rei's irritation flared but he repressed the instinct to wrench himself free; he too had been a small child locked away somewhere strange.

'I'm just going to check the locks,' he said and gestured at the bars. 'See if I can get us out of here.'

'You wouldn't be the first to try,' a dusty male voice coughed from across the chamber.

Rei reached for the dagger in his boot; it was gone. He had other weapons—needles, sewn into the seams of his leather bracer—but he couldn't ease them free with the boy clinging to his wrist.

'And would you try to stop me?' Rei challenged. The voice spoke with a heavy Qhoraakese accent, all vowels and clipped consonants, but it was not menacing.

The man chuckled. 'No. In fact, I implore you.'

Another prisoner, then.

'Where are you?'

'To your left. I'd wave, but ...'

Rei turned towards the voice and briefly caught the flare of two luminescent eyes cutting through the darkness like a golden beacon. He'd never seen Siephymn do that before. Not at will, anyway.

Easing his hand out of Sylar's grip, he took a needle from the hidden pocket in his sleeve. Despite Qhoraak's advanced medical technology, the lock before him was embarrassingly simple; Rei picked it with little effort and the iron gate groaned open.

'Come on,' he whispered, pulling Sylar into his shadow as he stepped beyond the threshold of their prison. His heartbeat drummed in his ears, so loud he barely heard the boy shuffle after him. An empty cage separated them from the Siephymn who'd spoken. A pile of filthy straw filled the space—bedding for a since-departed occupant. Rei refused to think about where that *guest* had ended up.

The cage at the back of the domed room did not house a crimson-haired Siephymn but a Qhoraakese man. Mature but not old, with silver streaks twisting through the black coils of his locs, he'd been strapped to a high-backed chair, iron manacles chewing at his ankles, wrists and neck. He was naked from the waist up, all muscled and scarred. A network of many needles pierced his umber skin and connected to long, thin tubes that climbed the brick wall behind him like vines up a lattice. His eyes, which had been luminescent from across the room, were now as cold and dark as onyx as they watched Rei's approach. He smiled wickedly, sharp teeth bright.

An icy chill swept across Rei's flesh. 'You're not Siephymn,' he said, forcing saliva down his suddenly dry throat. 'You're a *khaaja*.'

The man's grin widened, eyes flashing gold once more. He looked past Rei to where Sylar cowered behind his body. 'There is no need to fear, child. You're of my blood.'

Rei glanced down at Sylar, then back to the *khaaja*, shock and terror ripping through his limbs.

'Not *you*,' he sneered. 'I don't know *you*. Don't even recognise your scent. Your sire is not from these parts.'

'Kheshtarl,' Rei confirmed.

The *khaaja*'s lip curled as if he'd caught a rancid stink. 'You befouled a daughter of mine.'

'Not by choice.'

The *khaaja* flinched, fists curling against his restraints. The tubes on the wall danced as something raced through them into the *khaaja*'s veins. It pained and then placated him—made him docile. When his muscles relaxed, his head lolled drowsily to the side.

'My name is Pak-Ruhn-Qar and I demand you release me,' he drawled.

'How did they capture you?' Rei found himself asking. 'How did they even know what you were?'

Pak-Ruhn-Qar's head rolled across his shoulders, his dark gaze searching for Rei with an unfixed stare. 'They used my blood against me. Your kind were never meant to breed. Just devolve and join the herds. Instead you mix bloodlines, develop ways in which even our powers can be subdued. Potency with which we cannot contend.'

Rei surveyed the room, looking for other cages that may contain children. There must be another child here, someone like Sylar—someone born to the farms.

'Ironic you condemn the result of our *breeding*,' Rei hissed. 'How many women have you killed by spreading your seed? How many lives have you destroyed?'

'I was worshipped as a god!' Pak-Ruhn-Qar wailed. A shudder rippled through his body as another dose of sedative came pulsing through the tubes. He was in immense pain; tears glistened down his cheeks. 'Women prayed for my attention. It was a blessing, not a sacrifice. Siephymn were celebrated!'

Rei cackled, near-manic. There was nothing about his life to be *celebrated*. His whole existence had been one shitstorm after another. He'd been beaten and raped, exploited and hated—traumatised inside and out. But his kin were supposedly *celebrated?*

Pak-Ruhn-Qar had fallen silent—dead or unconscious, Rei didn't care. He would have spat on his corpse had the child not been there, attached to his thigh. He bristled. If this *khaaja* was Yeni's sire, would Sylar die along with him?

Rei's hand fell atop the boy's head in a gesture that was strange and unwelcome. He pulled back after the brief pat and turned his attention to the prison around them. If there were other farm-bred children here, he would find them—save them from whatever fate those Qhoraakese bastards had in mind. He just needed to know where to start looking.

As he moved away from Pak-Ruhn-Qar's cell, he caught sight of a deep depression in the opposing wall—a tunnel. Rei detached himself from Sylar and headed towards the opening on cautious feet. An oppressive smell wafted from the corridor's mouth, so heavy in the air Rei could almost see its cloud.

He stopped suddenly and turned back over his shoulder to Sylar. 'Wait here,' he said, tongue sharp. 'I mean it. Wait. Here.'

The boy nodded, his obedience taking Rei by surprise. Was this truly his son? But with those sad eyes and hawkish edge to his otherwise fine features, there was no mistaking his parentage. He saw *her* in him too.

Rei steeled himself to enter the tunnels, the stench churning his stomach as much as his nerves. Whatever had been stored down here had been left to rot in the damp and the dark like—

Corpses. Piles and piles of corpses. Stacked along the wall of narrow tunnels, almost as tall as Rei himself. And if they weren't already dead, they were close to it, their emaciated bodies shrivelled like husks bearing little resemblance to the people they had been.

But they're not people, Rei realised, edging away from a fleshy heap. *Not any more.*

They were demonspawn—devolved Siephymn. Discarded and forgotten now their purpose had been fulfilled—or their time expired. Rei clamped a hand over his mouth to stop the bile. He'd witnessed death time and time again in all its stages but never like this and never on this scale. He tried to swallow the rising acid by drawing long, steady breaths to anchor himself. He'd always tried to detach himself from his fate by thinking of Siephymn—of *himself*—as something less than human. But it was hard to draw that distinction now. Some of the corpses were in various stages of devolution: human limbs protruding from beastly bodies; claws and horns and leathery wings attached to human torsos; cat eyes and serpent tongues.

Rei retreated from the sight. Hit the wall. Wetness spread across his shoulder blades. Sticky and dark—blood.

He looked up. The meagre light caught the greasy sheen of blood down the walls, made it sparkle like oil on a pond. He could smell it now, too. All around him. On him.

In him.

Panic devoured him like a wave. It broke over his head and held him under. This was what awaited him if he stayed here. This was what awaited him if he left.

Somewhere, someone was crying. Rei brought his hands to his face, checking for tears. Not him. The distraction was grounding. He straightened, paused, listened intently. The sobs interspersed with groans of *Help me*, echoing from deep within the tunnel.

Rei glanced back to check on Sylar and found the boy sitting outside Pak-Ruhn-Qar's cell, knees drawn up to his chest. He was small and immobile, a dark silhouette in an already dark room. At least he couldn't see what lay but a few feet beyond him—what Rei would forever try to purge from his thoughts.

At the end of the tunnel, the corridor curved sharply to the right before diverging into another network of paths. A shiver broke across Rei's skin, the narrow, labyrinthine halls so reminiscent of the underground farms. He swallowed down his fear and walked towards the left-most tunnel, which boasted a weak, flickering flame within.

'... help me ...' he heard again. A dusty, hollow cough. A cry of pain. Another desperate plea. '*Help me!*'

Rei quickened his footsteps. He rounded the corner into a dim chamber—and immediately stopped dead.

A woman hunched on all fours, panting and groaning. Sweat glistened on her Siephymn-pale skin. His first assumption was that she laboured, deep in the throes of giving birth.

But she wasn't.

Her spine rippled under her skin. Ribs cracked. Shoulders buckled and dislocated. Body twisting grotesquely, she screamed.

Rei started towards her. She'd collapsed face first in the filthy straw, her bones all back in their rightful places. She looked up at him, blood-black tears streaming from the inner corners of her golden eyes.

'Help ... me ...'

That face. Not that fucking *face.*

'N-no ...' Rei gasped, retreating. '*No.*'

Yeni spat a string of hysterical Qhoraakese in his direction before succumbing to another wailing scream. The sound triggered a deeper fall into panic. He was back in that room, back on the bed. Drugs in his veins and weight on his chest. He could feel Yeni's nails on his skin, sharp and cold like a razor across ice. Her fingers were clawed, now. They gouged the stone floor as she crawled towards him, her deformed legs dragging behind her.

Rei wanted to run, but he couldn't; he'd backed himself into a wall. Yeni inched closer. Blood spilt from her mouth, her eyes, her ears. Her moaning face distended from her skull as it grew into a beastly muzzle.

Rei reached for his dagger—still gone. Shit. He couldn't breathe, couldn't *move*. Muscles so taut they were sure to snap off the bone. Yeni swiped at him with a clawed hand and he staggered to the left. His injured leg. It buckled under the sudden weight and he fell, knee hitting the stone hard. Rei howled in pain. And then in fear.

Yeni gripped his ankle. He shrieked, tried to kick her off. She was wailing still, her voice jarringly human, though her face was now deformed beyond recognition. She was impossibly strong. Legs useless, she dragged him towards her, a fisherman reeling in his catch. Rei pounded her hands to no avail. She wouldn't let go, and he had no weapon—nothing that would pierce the leathery thickness spreading across her skin.

'Get the fuck away from me!' Rei screamed as her snapping maw made a play for the soft flesh of his belly. He grabbed her head, clamping his hands either side of her skull like a vice. Yeni thrashed under his grip, bloody spittle flicking from her jowls. Rei kicked at her gut, trying to knock her back, but she just kept coming, snapping and clawing and growling. With a cry, Rei *squeezed*.

A *crack* and then there was a dead weight against his chest.

Rei's breath left his lungs in a gush as Yeni collapsed atop him, neck bent at a grotesque angle. She was dead. Stuck somewhere between woman and beast.

Rei could feel the tears on his cheeks, but he hadn't the strength to wipe them. He lay there, numb and spent beneath Yeni's body, fighting to keep the memories of their encounters at the farm at the edge of his awareness.

But then he heard a child scream.

30

AMIKHARLIA

Footsteps echoed on the polished obsidian floor as Amika and the others marched through the Citadel towards the Allchief. Flames flickered in sconces along the wall, in great braziers posted around the room, and in a large central cauldron identical to the one they'd passed in the square. Reverence for Hirathi was as oppressive as the heat in the room; the fire brought it to near-sweltering levels, causing Amika to sweat and chafe beneath her clothes. Kio too muttered his complaints, but Emanais's face was as stoic as a mask.

Amika surveyed the room, absorbing her new surroundings. The large, high-ceilinged chamber was ringed by several arches cut through the red brick on either side, but without a breath of wind, the open-air design did little to alleviate the stifling heat. It did, however, provide many routes of escape—or entry points for reinforcements. The ground around the crackling cauldron was a disc of ornately wrought iron, a grate over whatever catacombs lay below. And beyond the fire, perched high atop a dais that allowed him to be seen above the flames, sat the Allchief.

'*Zim hel ghar, Waqar Koll! Qhoraak er daz kelletmar!*' a herald announced, tapping the butt of his spear against the stone. The procession of soldiers came to an abrupt halt, the room deathly silent without the stamping of their feet. With a synchronised step, they pulled back into a new formation, leaving Amika, Kio and Emanais exposed and alone before the Allchief's throne.

Waqar Koll looked down from his perch, his copper gaze fixing immediately on Emanais. He wasn't a large man—certainly not what Amika was expecting for someone hailed as *Allchief*—and his balding head glistened with a thin coat of sweat. Despite his modest stature, there was a cold, conniving curl about the edges of his mouth that set Amika's nerves alight.

'My all-powerful Allchief,' Lamber announced as he sauntered forward, arms opening in a grandiose arc. 'I bring to you the most priceless of gifts: Emanais Ulande, the exile terrorist; a convict, sold to you by the King of Bararn; and a woman whose power rivals that of the gods themselves.' He grabbed Amika by the elbow and slung her forward. 'Strong enough to slay a *khaaja*.'

'You think these are *gifts*, Lamber?' Waqar drawled tiredly. There was a cadence to his vowels Amika couldn't quite place, but the persistent paleness of his skin suggested somewhere north—the Ice Coast of Bararn, perhaps. 'Ulande is an exile, brought before me under law, not reverence. And I have no interest in an offering sent by a little upstart king from the east,' he added with flippant disinterest. 'Word is, Reminas is already dead.'

'He is dead,' Amika confirmed. 'I killed him.'

'Did you, now? And a *khaaja* as well? My, is there anything you *haven't* killed?'

'You.'

Waqar laughed at her venom and Amika's rage swelled. If her magic hadn't abandoned her, she would have welcomed its indignant march through her veins; instead the silence cooled her temper and made her feel small.

'That honour will be mine,' Emanais growled. Hate radiated from her body, spreading through the room like a fog. Her fists were clenched so tight her arms shook.

Waqar turned to her. Just his eyes. As if she wasn't even worth the effort it took to move his head. 'Ulande. The only death in these halls will be yours. You broke exile. Another word from you and I'll have you cut down where you stand.'

Emanais raised her chin in defiance. 'Then all your disciples will see you for the coward you are. I invoke *Echtaz Maal*!'

Silence swept through the chamber. Amika's pulse thumped in her ears.

But then Waqar erupted into a delayed but violent guffaw, as if Emanais had told a joke that took some time to unravel.

'Girl, your father couldn't best me at *Echtaz Maal*. Nor could your brother, your uncle or your aunt. Don't tell me you're so eager to join them in defeat?'

'Are you denying my challenge, Waqar?'

A sneer grew on the Allchief's lips, crooked and lopsided thanks to a scar running down his left cheek. He pushed himself up from his throne, shrugging off the robe clasped about his shoulders. He was taller than Amika first thought, no longer slouched down in his throne, his chest as round and solid as a tree trunk. Despite lacking the ridges and ravines of taut muscles, he was obviously powerful.

But can he topple her hate?

If Emanais was intimidated, she did not show it. She stood tall as Waqar stepped away from the throne; statuesque, even as Amika and Kio were dragged aside to clear a ring for battle.

'Let go,' Amika growled, snatching her wrist away from the man who grabbed her. If *Echtaz Maal* was a duel, then she understood the rules: any interference would mean Emanais's death.

'What shall it be, Ulande?' Waqar asked, an arrogant grin on his lips. With a meaty fist, he tugged the thick golden cord hanging behind his throne and revealed an arsenal mounted on the wall. Spears, halberds, swords, scimitars—the weapons were as varied as the people in this room. Had he conquered all foreign upstarts and kept their blades as trophies?

Amika watched Emanais deliberate her options. The offerings were wide and varied; the only thing missing was Qhoraakese firearms. Nerves started to dance in Amika's belly. She'd never seen Emanais wield anything else.

'I want the Hirathi Blade,' Emanais demanded.

Waqar laughed and reached for a polearm set in the middle of the wall. 'This is the symbol of the Allchief, girl.' He pulled the weapon from its holster, the vicious blade catching a glint of flickering firelight as he gave it a preparatory thrust. 'You want it back? Come pry it from my dead fingers.'

Emanais sneered and stomped towards the dais. She plucked a short, stocky cutlass from the wall and immediately went on the offense. Waqar raised the glaive to parry, Emanais's blade sliding down the shaft with a metallic whine. She retreated quickly, barely avoiding the counter-lunge thrust at her bowels.

Beside Amika, Kio tensed. 'She chose the wrong weapon,' he growled, voice low, fists clenched. 'She can't best a spear with a short sword.'

'Not easily, anyway,' Amika agreed grimly.

Emanais was on the defensive now, edging backward down the stairs from the dais. With Waqar holding the higher ground, she could do nothing against the greater reach of the glaive but deflect each thrust and retreat further. She was trying to lure him onto even ground, and he willingly took her bait.

But Waqar was every bit in control, and he knew it. Arrogance shone in the way he walked, closing like a predator, the tip of the blade scraping along the stone in a shower of sparks.

'What's the matter, Ulande?' He released a powerful upward swing, one that Emanais just managed to deflect. 'Regretting your choice?'

'Never!'

She swept the speartip aside and tried to step inside Waqar's guard. But the Allchief was quick. He recovered from the shifting balance by ramming the blunt iron-tipped butt of the spear into Emanais's breastbone and sent her careening across the ground with a screeching gasp. She skidded to a halt on her back, sucking down air with a sickening stridor. Coughing, she winced through the pain.

Kio started to her aid; Amika caught his elbow. 'You can't,' she hissed, eyes turning cautiously to the guards surrounding them. Two soldiers armed with pistols saw her brother's impatient movements from across the makeshift duelling ring and their fingers curled against the triggers. With their hard-set jaws and suspicious, narrowed eyes, Amika knew from just one glare they'd not hesitate to open fire if either of them intervened.

Beside her, Kio radiated fear. Amika slipped her hand down his arm and pressed a squeezing grip around his fingers, feeling the tremble rattle through the bones. If she didn't calm him soon, he would do something rash, something impulsively foolish. Her brother may have changed in many ways, but that was certainly not one of them.

'She's alright,' Amika soothed, dipping her head towards Emanais. 'She's getting up.'

With a groan that was almost a growl, Emanais rolled onto her side and sat up, stretching for her sword that lay just out of reach. She scooted closer and light engulfed her in a blinding flash.

Gasps burst from the onlookers, many raising forearms against the light. An updraft blew from the illuminated pattern beneath Emanais, locs dancing in the gale.

'What did you do?' Kio demanded of Amika, though he did not pull his gaze from the maelstrom of light and wind before them.

'Nothing,' Amika breathed. 'That's the seal. I was right. Emanais is Hirathi's Chosen.'

She'd witnessed the awakening of a seal already—back in Ciraselo, when she'd stood among the ruins of the imperial palace and ruptured the sky. But seeing another Chosen fulfil their role in the Prophecy left her stricken with awe—and guilt. Emanais was now shackled to the same yoke of destiny; from this moment forward, her life was not her own. She would be pulled in whatever direction the Prophecy dictated, just as Amika was.

As the wind died, Emanais's manic laugh filled the room. 'You see, Waqar!' she cackled. 'Hirathi not only recognises my claim to his throne, he endorses it! See how he bathes me in his blessing!'

Despite the pain she no doubt carried in her chest, Emanais stood tall, sword raised and ready. Emboldened, she went on the attack, forcing Waqar to adjust quickly to her upward swings, aimed at sweeping his thrusts off-target. He howled as her sword nicked his forearm; a shallow wound, but enough to see Emanais shriek with victory at having drawn first blood.

'You can't dance around me forever, Ulande!' Waqar roared, swinging the glaive towards her in a wide horizontal arc. With its eight feet of reach, Emanais would not be able to pirouette or backstep out of the attack. The viciously long blade on the polearm would gut her like a fisherman's fresh catch.

Kio exhaled sharply through his nose; Amika squeezed his hand. But instead of retreating, Emanais lunged forward, extending her full reach to pierce Waqar's shoulder. The brash counterattack saw her take the haft to her thigh; had her lunge not broken his momentum, her femur could have shattered.

As it was, she lost her balance, dropped to her knee, fortunate that Waqar also stumbled back to assess his wound. Blood leaked between the fingers of his meaty hand and he growled at the sight, more frustrated than maimed. Emanais had been at the edge of her range; the puncture would be skin-deep at best.

'I don't like this, Amika,' Kio whispered, voice hoarse. 'She's losing. I thought you said she was Chosen?'

'She is,' Amika insisted, eyes flicking back to where the curling flame sigil of Hirathi lay emblazoned in the stone. 'She just has to get the key.'

Emanais got shakily back to her feet, clutching her thigh. The bleeding within the muscles would be immense, the pressure painful, making it difficult to bear weight. She endured it well.

'You want to hear how your family died?' Waqar taunted. He took up the glaive once more, blood from his hands slick on the haft. He advanced towards her, blade angled low as if trying to spear fish on a riverbank. 'Your aunt I got in the back. Sliced her top to tail down her spine like I was carving a roast bird.'

He sent a mocking thrust towards her chest; Emanais deflected, but was once again being driven back—back across the ring, back towards the seal.

'Your brother fell next. I believe I got him—'

Waqar gave a quick push-thrust towards Emanais's exposed throat. She swept the blade aside, steel ringing around the chamber.

'And where were you, Ulande?' he mocked venomously. 'Where were you when I snatched the Hirathi Blade from your father's dead hands? Hiding in the tunnels somewhere with your whore sis—'

Emanais screamed. She feinted right, drawing Waqar's thrust. With the blade sent wide, she snatched the haft, tucking it tight against her body. The Allchief snarled and jolted as he tried to wrench it free. Anchored to the entangled weapon, he couldn't defend. Couldn't attack. Couldn't move. He was vulnerable to a death blow, and Emanais saw it, raising her sword to hack at his head.

He let go.

Waqar relinquished his hold on the Hirathi Blade, freeing himself from an attack that would have split his skull. The sudden shift in force sent Emanais tumbling backward, her sword clattering aside as she hit the stone.

'She fucking did it,' Kio whispered, his tone more shocked than relieved. But Amika was less inclined to cheer. Waqar was still breathing, and *Echtaz Maal* was a battle to the death.

'Not yet,' she cautioned, heart in her throat as Emanais chambered back to her feet even slower than before.

'Yield!' Emanais roared, Hirathi Blade stretched out to Waqar in command. 'Admit defeat and I'll grant you a clean death. Make me wait, and I'll make *you* wait. Make you watch as I dismantle your fucking farms piece by piece, as I dismantle *you* piece by—'

The ground began to shake. Fissures snaked outward from beneath Emanais's feet. Hirathi's sigil pulsed like a heartbeat.

'What—' Emanais gasped as she looked down. The weapon in her hand was glowing brighter and brighter and—

It shattered.

The Hirathi Blade burst in a crystalline shower. Emanais screamed, hands groping at empty space as the shards dissipated into nothingness. She patted around on her hands and knees as if searching for dropped coins in long grass—unarmed and vulnerable.

'It's inside you, Ema!' Amika shouted, recalling Kriah's recount of melding with the Skrevaar Blade. 'Concentrate and bring it back!'

'What the fuck are you talking about?' she screeched. 'It's gone. It's fucking gone! Where is Hirathi?'

Another tremor shook the room; Emanais cowered, covered her head with her arms as dust and debris rained down from above. The unstable ceiling drew Amika's eyes away from the duel and towards the great brick arches, through which she could see the sky. There was a rumbling, celestial groan as the Tear widened with the newly broken seal. Fragments of the sky fell away like pieces of a cracked porcelain vase. The Allchief's guard readied their firearms, aiming the barrels skyward in preparation for a new threat.

But Waqar was not distracted.

He stormed across the stone arena, thunder cracking at his back. Among the chaos, he picked up Emanais's sword and raised it to strike.

Her back was still turned, paralysed by the fear and panic of finding herself unarmed.

'No!' Kio screamed, breaking away from the line. He threw himself at Emanais, just as the blade began to fall.

'Kio!' It was Amika's turn to scream. She gave chase, heart pounding—

But she was too late.

The blade landed in her brother's belly, slitting him open hip to hip. He hit the ground, crimson blood spreading beneath him.

Pain ripped through Amika's chest. Had she been shot? She collapsed, the rough stone floor grating skin off her palms with the momentum of her fall. There was screaming—so much *screaming*—but it wasn't coming from her. It was raw and unrestrained, a rageful wave spilling over a dam. The room shook even more.

Amika found enough strength to clamber to her hands and knees. She saw Emanais hunched over Kio's crumpled form, tears streaming down her cheeks, fists clenched so hard her whole arms trembled.

'Fuck you,' she spat at the advancing Waqar. He flicked blood off his sword as if swatting a fly as he continued to stalk towards her. 'Fuck you, Waqar. I swear on Hirathi's fucking grave—on this very seal. I will *fucking* kill you!'

Emanais sprang forward, vaulting over Kio as if she intended to hit Waqar bare-handed. She drew back her arm, ready to strike. But instead of her fist connecting with the Allchief's jaw, scarlet light shot from her palm.

The Hirathi Blade pierced Waqar through the face, its curved steel tip erupting through the back of his skull in a burst of blood and grey matter.

The Allchief's body went limp, but Emanais still screamed. She thrust the spear further, pushing three, four feet of the haft through his head. Then, with deadly fury, she split his skull even further, removing half his face with the pull-back.

Waqar's body fell bonelessly to the floor beside Kio. But instead of roaring in triumph, Emanais fell to her knees in anguish.

'No, no, no!' she wailed, tossing the Hirathi Blade aside as she made to cradle Kio's head in her lap. The blade shattered into glass and raced back towards her body like a scattering army of ants. 'Amika!' she cried. 'Do something! Quick!'

Amika scuttled to her feet, but her legs were so weak she could barely stand. She could feel her tears now, dripping off her chin. Despair had sapped the adrenaline from her veins, rendering her slow and sluggish.

It can't end like this, she thought, expecting the soldiers to swarm her and Emanais in the chaos. But they were just as stupefied as she, watching on with shocked, blank expressions, some focused on the duel—but most on the crumbling sky overhead.

Another tremor shook the earth, knocking Amika off her already unstable legs. She braced for falling debris, but it wasn't the ceiling that shattered.

The ground erupted before her, an underground explosion sending brick and iron and smoke up into the air.

And darkness spilt forth in its wake.

31

REI-HAI

'**D**on't look,' Rei implored, taking the boy's face between his hands. His voice caught in his throat. 'Don't fucking look.'

Sylar fought against his grip, thrashing about as he wailed in hysterics, desperate to be at his mother's side. Rei hadn't wanted the boy to see that. Hadn't wanted to tarnish his memories with the sight of *that* creature.

Hadn't wanted him to see her die.

'Look at me,' Rei said. He lowered himself to his knees with a grimace, the wound in his leg throbbing from the earlier struggle. 'Look at me, Sylar. That's it. I know you're scared. I'm scared too. But it doesn't have to end like that for us, okay? I'm going to take care of you. We're going to get out of here. But we'll come back for her, okay? I promise.'

Sylar sucked in his lower lip and nodded, his sobs abating. Rei stretched out his hand and the boy took it, squeezing it tight; he was stronger than he looked.

In more ways than one

The darkness of the tunnels seemed more oppressive than before. The air was thick and hot and made Rei's skin crawl. He felt ... odd. Numb, yet overstimulated—a swarm of bees in a glass jar. He still sensed Yeni's hands around his ankles, claws cutting into his flesh. The thought set his nerves aflame, gut churning.

Taking a breath, he concentrated on the warmth of Sylar's hand to anchor his mind. The tremor in the small boy's body was so intense it sent vibrations up Rei's arm. He was in so much shock Rei was amazed he still walked—or was he just dragging him along?

As they moved through the tunnels, the strange sensation simmering through his body strengthened the closer they got to the chamber where Pak-Ruhn-Qar was imprisoned. It was a dull ache, similar to the acidic pang that burned through his body on the cusp of a transformation, but muted—or restrained.

Sylar suddenly gripped his head and started making the awful keening sound from when the *khaaja* attacked the underground base. He collapsed to his knees and thrashed about, trying to shake off unseen assailants.

Was he going to devolve? No—he was just a child. Rei had only started to lose control around his twentieth birthmoon. But if that was what was happening, Sylar must have been in so much pain. Rei wrapped himself around the boy and held him tight.

'Fight it, Sylar,' he said, jaw clenched against the surprising strength in the child's limbs. '*Fight* it. You can do it.'

Thunder boomed overhead. Wails and moans rumbled from the cages in the central cavern, bouncing off the walls of the dome in a sorrowful cacophony of pain. Rei understood now—he'd felt this before. But this time he was shielded by whatever Emanais and her crew had pumped through his veins.

A seal had fallen.

Cracks raced through the walls, displacing a shower of dust and crumbled brick. He could hear shouts from above—firearms, maybe—and distant, panicked screams. Were more demonspawn coming through the weakened Tear? Had they been able to leverage it wider, spreading more poison—spreading more fear?

Whatever was happening affected the Siephymn so acutely they threw themselves at the bars of their cages in an attempt to alleviate their torment. Some were devolving, banging themselves bloody against the iron and stone. Others did not move at all, already dead. But Sylar ... He lurched forward like a tumbled bag of grain, seizing as his body hit the ground.

'Shit—*shit!*' Rei hissed, panic squeezing his chest as the boy shook violently. Carefully, he rolled Sylar onto his side and withdrew until the fit passed. Vomit trickled from the corner of the boy's mouth as his jaw and other muscles started to slacken.

After the boy had stilled, Rei checked Sylar's pulse. It was steady. He could breathe again.

When did I start holding my breath?

Rei brushed the crimson hair back from the boy's eyes and let his hand linger for a moment. When he eased himself back to his feet—gods, his leg was throbbing now—he hobbled deeper into the cavern, more determined than ever to find an escape.

The Siephymn, driven mad by the breaking world above, had smashed their own skulls into black bloody pulp. Now, they were little more than mounds of broken bone and brain matter, twitching with residual energy. Bile sped up Rei's throat.

This could have been me. This could have been—

Movement in the *khaaja*'s cage snatched his attention. Pak-Ruhn-Qar writhed in his fetters, an eldritch screech escaping his gaping mouth. His movements were obscenely fast: fragmented and flickering, blurred in their speed. The Qhoraakese face the *khaaja* had worn slid off his skull like melting candle wax. Splitting open at the crown of his head, it peeled away in sloppy layers, sluicing off his shoulders, his arms.

'Help ... me ...' Pak-Ruhn-Qar seemed to wail, before he burst—an overfilled waterskin cleaved with a knife.

Rei shielded his eyes from the explosion, but was not showered in blood and viscera as he'd expected. From the ruins of the *khaaja*'s human form unfurled an immense skeletal beast with a fan of elongated, multi-jointed limbs spreading from its back like spidery wings. It howled and Rei shuddered, catching a glimpse at the cavernous void that was its face. Free of its chains and network of tubes, it burst through the ceiling, spilling like an oil slick into the world above.

Tangles of iron and brick fell in a cascade of deadly chunks. Rei cowered from the debris, glancing behind, relieved to see Sylar safe from the fall zone. The boy stirred but didn't wake, even with the clamour.

When the detritus ceased falling, Rei stole a glance skyward.

The Tear drifted further apart. It crackled like lightning. Pulsed like an infected wound pumping blood across the sky. Everywhere he looked was hot and scarlet—more vibrant and more sinister than before. He felt the way it tugged on his body, probing for *khe'torla* to syphon into the void. No wonder it drove the other Siephymn mad, those who weren't protected by whatever tonic had been flushed through Rei's body back at the farm.

'... anybody there?' a distant voice echoed.

Rei's head snapped; everyone down here had been dead or dying. His gaze caught the wall behind Pak-Ruhn-Qar's cell, where the network of tubes connected to his body had been ripped away as he tore free of his constraints. Light flicked between gaps in the brick where the iron frames had been wrenched from the wall, leaving fist-sized holes in their wake. A shadow moved past one of the openings.

'Hello?' Rei clambered over the rubble towards the fissure. The red glow from above provided enough light that his eyes needed some time to adjust. As he approached the gap, he caught glimpses of a face be-yond—no, several. They were a mix of Qhoraakese and immigrants, wearing no discernible uniform or weaponry.

Prisoners.

'Is anyone hurt?' Rei asked, standing on his toes to press his face against the hole. 'The ceiling caved in over here.'

'No, we fine,' a Qhoraakese woman said in broken Meytaran. She looked vaguely familiar with a tangle of locs piled atop her half-shaved head. The startled look in her hazel eyes suggested she recognised *him* too. 'Little Prince's Siephymn,' she said.

'Rei-Hai,' he corrected. He knew her face from Emanais's camp—Zharla, Zharka, or something.

She pressed a hand to her chest. 'Zhayar.'

Close enough. 'Is anyone hurt?' He wouldn't be able to dig through the wall on his own, not with his size and injuries.

Zhayar shook her head. 'No.'

'All right. Good. There's no exit on this side. Not that I could find, anyway.' He wasn't about to go creeping through the tunnels again, considering what awaited him last time. 'What about over there?'

Voices conversed in Qhoraakese, pulling Zhayar's attention towards the other captives for a moment. Rei tried to crane his head further into the hole, but with its height and angle, his vision was limited.

There was movement, and another figure came forward: large, imposing and distinctly Bararnite. His swollen face was mottled black, purple and yellow from a thorough beating, though it looked older than anything the guards could have dealt him.

'I'm not from Kheshtarl, yer dumb witch-fuckers,' he grunted upon seeing Rei.

'Good thing I'm not either,' Rei said coolly. 'Are you one of Emanais's men?' He didn't look familiar, but his broken face could have been distorted beyond recognition.

'Aye. Ylan.'

'Rei-Hai.'

Ylan guffawed. 'You're the southern fucker that Dally was dippin' his prick in? Moaned about you an awful lot. None of us ever could get any damn sleep.'

Heat raced up Rei-Hai's neck, a burning combination of embarrassment and rage. He had to piece the information together, but once he placed the name, he recognised the insult.

Reminas's runty mutt.

'Well, I'm sure Kio didn't sleep much either,' Rei muttered through his teeth.

'Kio, aye? That'll take some gettin' used to.' Ylan fingered his misshapen nose, then scratched at his patchy beard. 'Yer gonna get us out of here, are yer?'

Rei flinched as more debris crumbled down from above. 'Are there any exits to the surface over there?'

'Must be,' Ylan conceded. 'Guards brought us food earlier, if you could call it that.'

'Then help me widen this gap.' He glanced back at Sylar, assessing the boy's size. 'Just a little. I'm not sure how stable it is.'

The Bararnite gestured back to his fellow captives and another male came to assess the breach. Wordlessly, Ylan managed to convey what they were planning to do and together they started wiggling at bricks to see which could be removed. Rei felt around the rubble for anything he could use to leverage the stone free. It was dangerously unstable, but if he could just get Sylar to the other side, perhaps he could find a way to climb out.

He glanced at the opening above. The ornate grate had been destroyed, its gilded tendrils stretching up like menacing iron fingers towards a blood-red sky. Something was happening up there, but he couldn't see, couldn't hear anything discernible above the screams and clangs of steel. Had Pak-Ruhn-Qar attacked the city? Was Amika there to contain him? Where was Kio?

'Careful!' Ylan shouted, pulling Rei back to the present. The wall groaned as a Qhoraakese man made to wrench a large piece free. 'That's gonna bring it down. Pull from the bottom. And you—start pushing. We can get this section free.'

Rei leveraged a tangle of iron as a crutch to lean on while he kicked at the wall with his good leg. His injured calf screamed with the responsibility of even partially holding his weight, and he wasn't sure how much help he offered. But the brick started to crack away from its mortar, dust and dirt flying out with every kick.

'Look out!' Ylan called as the chunk fell free, Rei's foot going through the wall with that final push. The sides of the opening began to shake, and Rei pulled himself back before they gave way, filling the space in an avalanche of brick.

Rei groaned as he rolled down the pile of debris in his hasty escape. 'F-fuck ...' He'd landed on something sharp, a hot pain spreading through his flank. He lay immobile for a moment, hand pressed to his side, expecting blood. The skin had not ruptured.

While recovering from the initial shock of pain, feet shuffled to his side, and he felt a hand on his back. It rolled him onto his back and he saw Zhayar hovering over him, brow furrowed with concern.

'I'm alright.' Rei waved her off, grimacing as he sat up. He watched her face pale as she glanced around the cavern.

'*Kaeya magh,*' she breathed, cupping a hand over her gaping mouth.

It was hard for Rei to reconcile Zhayar's grief for the slaughtered Siephymn with his own experience in Qhoraak, despite knowing Emanais and her army fought to destroy the farms.

'Sylar!' She abandoned Rei as she spotted the boy, leaving Ylan to help Rei to his feet instead. Rei gripped the big Bararnite's arm as he got his balance, watching as Zhayar summoned others to her side.

'Where're Kio and the others?' Rei demanded of Ylan while Zhayar busied herself with Sylar. 'Tell me they're alright.'

Ylan sneered and gave a one-shouldered shrug. 'How would I fuckin' know? They separated us after we arrived. Dally, the Boatkeep and that witch. We got sent down 'ere, they got taken elsewhere.'

Rei bit the inside of his cheek as he thought. The Hirathi seal had been broken, that much he knew, which meant Amika was likely involved in whatever chaos was unfolding over their heads, Kio by her side. The warm embrace of hope spread through his body; he would get out of here and back to their side where he belonged.

'Yeni?' Zhayar called, eyes probing the darkness. When no response came from the cages around the chamber, her gaze settled on Rei-Hai. 'Yeni?'

Guilt swelled in Rei anew. The whole reason Emanais had marched on Xant was to find her sister—to free her from the Allchief's dungeons.

And he had killed her.

'I, uh ...' he started, lost for words, which was very unlike him. He could drown the truth in excuses, but would it be understood? Zhayar's Meytaran was rudimentary at best, so his being subtle would just come out sounding obtuse.

Rei swallowed his reservations and said, 'She's dead. She changed. I killed her.'

Zhayar's face hardened, but not in a way that made Rei feel threatened. She assumed a practised mask and asked, 'Where?'

'End of that corridor.' Rei pointed to the narrow passage where he had encountered Yeni in her state of devolution. He would not go down there again.

Rei turned his back as Zhayar sent two of her companions down into the tunnels to retrieve the body. Would Emanais truly want to see it? His skin crawled at the thought of Kio finding him that way, at that hideous, deformed face being the only thing his lover remembered.

They returned quicker than Rei expected. Silent and solemn, the only indication of their arrival was the sharp intake of air through Ylan's teeth. 'Deities fucking dead, boy,' he said. 'That's a Siephymn? That's what we're trying to save here?'

'No, we're trying to save *that*.' Rei gestured indignantly to Sylar. 'Children. Children who didn't ask to be born and certainly don't deserve to die. Or be bred like animals in a stud.'

'Who'd want to fuck that?' Ylan sneered with disgust. 'Dally know what you are? And he put his cock in you anyway? What depraved—'

Rei's hand lashed out. He took the much larger man by the throat, fingers finding the edges of his windpipe and *squeezing*. Ylan gave a pained choke, his own hands coming to bat Rei away, but Rei's savage grip was too strong.

'His name is fucking *Kio*,' Rei growled, words punctuated with a final, vice-like squeeze. He pushed the Bararnite back so hard the big man stumbled.

Rei prepared for retaliation, his muscles tense and ready for a fight. He'd been on edge since the seal broke, his nerves frazzled and alight beneath his skin. If Ylan came for him, he'd take him down—even if he had been useful in breaching the wall.

'Sylar,' Zhayar said gently, followed by a string of murmured Qho-raakese. Rei turned away from Ylan to see the boy stirring, rolling towards where Yeni's corpse had been set beside him.

'No, don't—' Rei started, rushing to steal the boy's attention. Zhayar raised a commanding hand and brought him to a halt.

'His mother,' she said sharply. 'Must say goodbye.'

'And see her like *that?*' Rei gestured incredulously towards the mutated figure that no longer resembled the woman she had been.

'He is Siephymn,' Zhayar said. 'He must know.'

A hand clamped down on Rei's shoulder to stop him interfering. It belonged to a man he didn't know, and the grip was more supportive than threatening; Rei shrugged him off, but remained still, heart hammering as Sylar edged towards his dead mother. Tears spilt down his cheeks, but he sobbed in relative calm, unlike the hysteria that had consumed him when he saw her die—saw Rei kill her.

He wrapped his arms around his mother's head, nuzzled his face into what would have been her neck and stayed like that a moment. A cloud of shared grief descended upon the cavern as Zhayar led the rebel captives in some form of Qhoraakese prayer. When complete, Sylar withdrew and sat back on his heels, tears dry. His eyes seemed more golden now—more luminescent—and his pupils had taken on a narrower shape.

Rei's heart fell. The widening Tear had stimulated the progression of his curse, something that hadn't manifested in Rei himself until puberty. The *khaaja* had said the boy's blood was potent—did that mean his curse was too? Would he devolve even quicker than Rei?

Rei clenched his fists, pushing the thoughts down deep. Sylar looked at him and Rei stretched out a hand. The boy shuffled closer, taking it wordlessly. Rei gave it a squeeze.

'Come on,' he said. 'Let's go find your aunt.'

32

AMIKHARLIA

There was so much fucking blood.

On her hands, her clothes—even her face. She pulled Kio into her lap, pressed all over his body in a feeble attempt to stop the bleeding, to stop his guts spilling across the floor. But it was pointless. There was too much of it, all hot, thick and sticky. The more she tried to hold it back, the more it seemed to flow.

'F-fuck!' Amika choked, her eyes so heavy with tears she could barely see. But she didn't need clear vision to know that everything was red, red, *red*, and that Kio's colour was melting faster than snow in spring. Blood spilt from his lips as he coughed, his sapphire eyes dull and unfocused.

'Do something, Amika!' Emanais screamed, falling to her knees beside them. She took a hesitant peek at the wound beneath Amika's hands and swore viciously in Qhoraakese. 'He's going to die. Why aren't you doing anything?'

'I c-can't!' Her veins were still silent, still empty. Even with Emanais's hands joining her attempt to stem the bleeding, it was hopeless. The wound was too wide, too deep.

Don't let him die. Don't let him die.

'You stupid fucking fool!' Emanais screeched, gripping Kio's face between her bloodied hands. 'Why!'

Kio's lips fluttered as he tried to speak. 'Sick ... of watching ... people ... die ...'

'So now we have to watch *you* die? You selfish prick!'

He coughed violently, blood bubbling up his throat. 'Tell R-Rei ... Hai ...'

'N-No!' Amika squeezed him closer. *Don't let him die. Don't let him die.* She roared so viciously her ears popped from the pressure, blood vessels bursting in her eyes. Lost in her rage, her grief, her frustration, she vaguely heard Emanais's voice barking at the crowd closing in around them.

'I fucking won!' she screamed. 'Back down. I *FUCKING WON!*'

Waqar's soldiers would kill them all. Even though the Allchief was dead, the terms of the duel had been broken first.

Don't let him die. Don't let him die.

'Miatha!' Amika shrieked at the sky. 'Help me, Miatha! Or I swear on your fucking chains I will leave you trapped in the Tear! I will never set you free!'

It was a hopeless, empty prayer. A desperate dying wish. Amika didn't know if Miatha could hear her—if she was really even there. But her gifts could only have come from the Goddess herself; Miatha must have the power to restore them.

'Miatha, *please!*' she implored. 'You cannot let my brother die! Give me your strength, damn you!'

Thunder rolled through the bruised sky, pulsing like a vein. Warmth spread across the nape of Amika's neck as though a breath tickled her skin. It raced through her shoulders, down her arms, all the way to the tips of her fingers. Her nerves came alive, crackling like lightning down an iron rod.

Ants, she realised. Millions upon millions of ants, racing through her body in unprecedented numbers. They spewed from her hands in a burst of light, bright and brilliant and all-consuming.

Amika closed her eyes against the blinding glow, blocked her ears against the chorus of screams. Despite the rising cacophony, the voices were distant, muted, Emanais's commanding wails little more than a whisper in a storm.

The power flooding through Amika was hot and raw. She syphoned *khe'torla* from the earth—from the *air*—and funnelled it through her brother's body. With her eyes squeezed shut, she couldn't see if it was working, if his wound was stitching closed like she intended.

Don't let him die. Don't let him die.

With a scream of her own, she gave one last push. One last desperate surge of *khe'torla* from wherever she could steal it.

A screech and a flash, and the flow severed, repelling Amika back like a magnet. She hit the ground hard, white light bursting across her vision. The world around her fell silent.

When she regained her senses, the stark silence prevailed. She eased herself up onto her elbows.

Kio's head still rested across her lap where she had held him. He was white as marble, a still, stony form in a mess of blood. She felt for a pulse.

It thrummed steadily beneath her fingers.

An audible sob bubbled from Amika's lips. She'd done it. Somehow, she'd done it. The familiar march of *khe'torla* danced through her veins, and she was so lost to euphoria she could do nothing but laugh *and* cry. She threw back her head and cackled—wept. Through tear-heavy eyes, she stared up at the sky, at the great jagged cleft that was wider than before. As she gazed into the infected, celestial wound, lightning blinked within, calling to Amika like a beacon.

Raise ... me ...

Amika turned away from a voice she couldn't have heard and found Emanais picking herself up from the stone. A gaping hole lay behind her where the ground had opened up and unleashed *something* into the world above.

'Oh, *fuck* ...' Emanais exhaled shakily. 'Amika, what did you do?'

The tone of her voice sent a spike of fear through Amika's chest. Swallowing, she followed the other woman's gaze.

Bodies. Toppled like tokens on a game board. The Qhoraakese soldiers lay crumpled about the room, still and silent. They bore no wounds. No injuries of any kind. But they were grey. Dry, shrivelled and dusty. Husks sucked empty of all moisture—of all life.

Amika looked down at her bloodied hands, pulse thunderous in her ears. Syphoned. She had *syphoned khe'torla* from somewhere. But it had come from Miatha ... Hadn't it?

She looked up at the sky again, and the swirling lightning within the Tear pulsed once more in recognition.

Raise ... me ...

'Did I ...' Amika began, voice cracking. 'Did I do this?'

Emanais shuffled closer. Blood trickled from a wound on her forehead. Her eyes were wide with panic—with fear—as she looked from Kio to Amika and back to Kio. His face crumpled in a grimace as he coughed, head turning slightly as he started to wake.

'*Kaeya magh*, how—'

Emanais's words were eclipsed by a piercing shriek from across the room. 'No, no—!'

Amika looked up to see Rei-Hai Shaw racing towards them, screaming as he pushed a child from his arms and ran. He closed the distance with inhuman speed and threw himself at Kio, eliciting a pained groan from the prince. His hands swept over Kio's body, searching for wounds among the blood and shreds of shirt, confusion fighting with distress across his features.

'What—'

'It's alright, I'm alright,' Kio rasped, reaching for Rei's hands. 'I'm alright.' He eased himself up off Amika's lap with a groan of pain that made his words far less convincing. She smoothed a hand across her brother's back to steady him and noted it was no longer peppered with burnt craters. She'd healed him—*all* of him— not just the wound that threatened his life.

But at what cost …?

The paper-thin corpses drew Amika's attention once again, their hollow dark eyes staring at her in accusation. Emanais's rebels, who had arrived with Rei-Hai from whatever dungeon they had escaped, inspected the fallen soldiers with wary prods of their boots. Emanais herself stood over Waqar's crumbled form. He too was a dried-up husk.

'Guess he wasn't dead enough,' she spat, and summoned the Hirathi Blade to hand. She thrust the tip of the spear through Waqar's already ruined face. It squelched thickly with dead, congealed blood. 'That's some devastating power you got there, Chosen.'

Amika looked down at her hands. They trembled beneath lashings of Kio's blood. She felt no more powerful than before, her *khe'torla* pulse no more pronounced. Miatha hadn't gifted her more power—she'd stolen it. Sucked the very life force from those around her and pumped it into her brother.

And Miatha had allowed her to do it.

'I didn't …' she stammered, still reeling from the horrific aftermath of the miracle. 'I didn't mean to—'

'You must have had some control,' Emanais insisted. She plucked the Hirathi Blade from Waqar's face and it shattered into light, dissipating up her arm. 'I'm still here.'

'You're Hirathi's Chosen,' Amika said, sounding far more confident than she felt. 'Surely that protected you.'

Emanais rumbled low in her throat as she mused, gaze turned towards the pulsating rift. 'That's all that happened,' she said sadly. 'A greater Tear in the sky. I didn't see Him walk free …'

'I'm sorry, Ema,' Amika said, the apology little more than an empty solace.

She turned away from the emaciated corpses and took in the rest of the wreckage that lay around them. The ceiling had been wrenched open, shattered by whatever fiend escaped the bowels of the Citadel when the seal fell. The shadowy mass moved so quickly it had been hard to see in any detail among the chaos of the duel—but given its sheer size, there was only one thing it could have been.

'I think Waqar had demonspawn imprisoned beneath the city,' Amika concluded gravely.

'A *khaaja*,' Rei confirmed. He'd helped Kio back to his feet and, despite being dwarfed by the much larger man, supported him to stand with a hand laid protectively on his chest. 'Pak-Ruhn-Qar. He lost his human skin. All the Siephymn below devolved and went mad.'

'What? Are you alright?' Kio demanded suddenly, stepping away from Rei's hold to inspect him instead.

'I'm fine. Whatever I was given back at the farm seems to have protected me. And Sylar's age protected him. He had some sort of fit, but—'

'Did you find Yeni?' Emanais pushed her way towards Rei, took him by the shoulders with panic and desperation. 'Was she down there?'

Rei stiffened, his face turning to stone. He looked past her—not at Amika or Kio, but at nothing. 'She's dead.'

'Liar!' Emanais shrieked and shook him as if trying for a better answer. 'Liar—'

'Ema, stop.' Kio pulled her off and held her back, an embrace rather than restraint. 'It's not his fault.'

'It is,' Rei said flatly. 'I killed her.'

'*NO!*' Emanais beat against Kio's chest as she screamed in Qhoraakese, violent and venomous. 'How could you! No, no, no ...' She was exhausted, hysterical, and although her fists flailed every which way, her blows lacked any real fight.

Amika edged towards Rei. Despite his callous tone, she had seen the tears glistening in his eyes, his jaw clenched. She slipped an arm around his shoulders and found he was trembling.

'I did it. I killed her,' he repeated. 'I killed her. I killed her. I *killed*—'

'Rei, stop. It's not your fault.' Amika pulled him against her body, trying to break whatever loop he had found himself caught in.

Emanais was no longer fighting against Kio. She dropped to her knees and now sobbed against his legs, boneless and distraught. Kio himself had turned back towards Rei, brow furrowed in concern.

'I killed her. I killed her. I killed her ...' Rei's chanting confession trailed off as he too gave way to tears. Amika squeezed her friend tight, but he was stiff and unresponsive. She needed to snap him out of it, but couldn't bring herself to tap into her *khe'torla*—not so soon after it had caused a massacre.

Kio untangled himself from Emanais and folded his arms around Rei and Amika both. She savoured her brother's warmth, his strength—the life coursing through him once more—before stepping aside so he could comfort Rei in a way she could not. He pressed a kiss to the smaller man's forehead and enveloped him in an embrace.

Cheek resting atop Rei's head, he turned to Amika and said, 'What happened here?'

Amika opened her mouth to explain, but a woman's voice cut in first, screaming for Emanais. The Qhoraakese leader looked up from her misery as Zhayar and the other rebel forces came towards them, Sylar in tow. The scout held something in her arms—a bloody tangle of fur and bone and shredded clothes.

'Deities dead, is that—' Kio gasped, shifting so Rei could not see them approach.

'Yeni!' Emanais screeched, scrambling towards Zhayar and the others on all fours. The disfigured corpse was lowered before her and she threw herself across it and wailed.

Amika kept her distance and watched the tragic reunion unfold from the sidelines with Rei and her brother. Zhayar had a hand on Emanais's back, talking softly in Qhoraakese, presumably explaining what had happened. The boy, Sylar, nestled into Emanais's side.

The emotion was contagious; hot tears prickled Amika's eyes as Emanais mourned her sister, her army sullen by her side. Some knelt over the shrivelled soldiers and wept—friends and family members they'd come to the capital to liberate before Amika slaughtered them. Guilt and disgust swelled in her anew.

'I don't need to remember what happened to know something isn't right,' Kio said, his voice low and for Amika's ears only. Rei's face was buried so deeply in her brother's chest he didn't seem able to breathe let alone hear, but Kio squeezed his arms tight around Rei's head before adding, 'Did you kill these people to save me?'

'I—I ...' Amika's lips quivered. There must have been fifty men and women lying in a broken circle around them, all having fallen where they stood. Lamber as well, she realised, was crumpled near the Allchief's throne, little more than a withered husk in a long leather coat.

'... Could you do it again? For a Sieph—' Kio whispered, but Amika cut him off before he could finish.

'What? Kio! F-fuck—*no!*' she spat incredulously, stepping back in stone-cold shock. Even if she had the means at her disposal, she wouldn't bring back someone so far gone. Someone like Ye—

Not Yeni.

Rei. He was talking about Rei.

Amika didn't know how clearly her brother had seen Yeni's corpse before Emanais set upon it in grief. Amika herself only caught a glimpse, but it was enough to see that she was a twisted horror of a thing, more beast than woman now. If Rei died in such a way, would he be stuck inside that broken shell when he returned? He wouldn't want that. No matter how much Kio begged.

Rei pushed away from Kio's chest, gaze distant and face hard. If he'd been crying, or if he'd heard Kio's request, he didn't show it. 'The damage is isolated to this chamber,' he said, voice small and hoarse. 'We came above ground just outside the Citadel and saw others lingering in the halls, staring at the sky from their windows.'

'Then we need to take control of the city,' Kio said, looking from Rei to Amika. 'Put Emanais back on her throne where she belongs.'

'There's no one alive to verify her victory,' Amika muttered, her icy words slicing up her own back like a blade. 'And if there are reinforcements coming, it wouldn't be much of a fight. None of us are armed. All of us are exhausted.'

'The ruling of *Echtaz Maal* is absolute,' Emanais rasped, approaching them with a limp as Sylar hung off her thigh. 'There will be no resistance. Waqar is dead. I hold the Hirathi Blade. No one will dare take my fucking crown from me again.'

Amika was surprised to see Emanais so full of fire so soon after her sister's death. But the woman's fierce eyes were red with tears, her muscles trembling with emotion that had nowhere else to go. Amika knew that feeling. That need to keep moving to avoid having time to feel. She'd done that when she first left Adria. When her mother died. Reminas. The Tear. Now, with a hundred hollow eyes burning into her flesh like acid.

'Tell us what you need,' Amika said, stilling her own tremors.

Emanais met Amika's gaze and nodded. 'We need to build some pyres.'

Yeni's body was shrouded in linen and laid on a pallet before the Great Flame in the Citadel's courtyard. Pyres had been built for the Allchief's soldiers, with ten, fifteen corpses placed atop, each as dry as the kindling below, ready to be lit.

It had been a sobering affair, building the pyres. One that Amika felt in every aching joint and muscle as she stacked the wood and loaded the bodies *she'd* created. Many of the surviving residents of the Citadel had been vicious in their grief, unleashing vitriolic tirades of incomprehensible Qhoraakese at Amika and the other foreigners. She lapped it up. Soaked it into her bones, even as the hysterical survivors were dragged away by Emanais's troops. From what she'd gathered, Emanais's rule as Allchief had been widely accepted, as was the way here; but there was lingering distrust towards the outsiders due to the widespread destruction that had followed Waqar's death and the fall of the Hirathi seal.

'There's no room for regret here, Princess,' Rei said softly, appearing by her side as they took a break from rummaging through the rubble and debris. 'You did nothing I wouldn't have considered myself.'

They both watched Kio across the courtyard as he worked tirelessly alongside Emanais and Zhayar to lift corpses atop the most recently constructed pyre. His torn shirt had been discarded against the heat of the city, confirming Amika's earlier suspicions that his infected burns had also been erased. There were no scars—from the burns or the fatal slash across his belly. It was as if the wounds had never been there at all.

When night fell, it was time to light the pyres. Emanais summoned everyone she could find to join in farewelling the dead. Waqar's body had been laid by the Great Flame as well, on the opposite side of the cauldron to where Yeni was placed. He too was wrapped in linen, his silhouette distorted beneath the cloth due to his sunken skull and fractured face. Emanais stood over him, ceremonial dagger in hand.

'Fuck you,' she hissed, dragging the blade across her palm. Blood dripped on the crisp white linen of his shroud. 'You don't deserve the Rites. You denied them to my father. I should deny them to *you*.' She squeezed her hand into a fist, the blood falling like thick, heavy raindrops. 'But then we'd be no different. *Zim hel ghar,* Waqar Koll,' she spat in cold mockery. '*Qhoraak er daz kelletmar-nak!*' Raising her head to the crowd, she shouted in the Meytaran tongue, 'All hail Waqar Koll—the *former* Allchief of Qhoraak!'

A single echo of '*ghar*' burst from the congregation along with a raising of fists. Emanais stepped back from Waqar to allow Zhayar and a man Amika did not recognise to lift him into the fire. The Great Flame roared as it accepted the offering, swallowing it with a tangle of fiery tongues. *Khe'torla* stirred beneath Amika's skin. The fire pulsed with an intensity she hadn't felt when they first walked into the city. It rumbled like a war drum, low and slow but palpably strong. Goosepimples rose across her flesh, cold and prickly.

Has Hirathi risen after all?

Kio was summoned to help Emanais lower Yeni into the flames. Amika closed the gap he had left beside Rei and took the redhead's hand in her own. He didn't look at her, but nor did he turn away as the mother of his son was interred in fire.

'I killed her,' he repeated, voice distant. Amika squeezed his hand and he pressed back, harder. 'It was too late. She'd already turned.'

'I haven't forgotten,' Amika said softly. She had made a promise and she would keep it, no matter how much it hurt.

'Thank you,' Rei said, and they turned silently to watch the pyres light up like lanterns in the night.

33

KRIAH

The inertia upon exiting the portal left Kriah's head spinning and insides churning violently. He collapsed on his hands and knees and hawked up the meagre contents of his stomach. Behind him, the woman from the Tower laughed.

'One of the most powerful beings in Whyt'hallen and you can't even keep your guts in check?' she jeered, exiting the strange floating puddle without so much as a break in her stride.

'This is hardly a normal way to travel,' Kriah groaned, wiping his mouth with the back of his hand as he straightened. For a moment he'd wondered if they'd truly gone anywhere, having stepped out into yet another small room. But unlike the stone chamber that had been his cell in Adria, his new surroundings were timber and tightly woven straw, soft and springy beneath his feet. It was also stiflingly hot; an oppressive, damp heat, unlike anything he had felt across the Middle Kingdoms.

There was a shuttered window to his left and Kriah scrambled to open it. The air was in desperate need of circulation, especially now the sharp tang of stomach acid mingled with musty confinement. Outside was an assault of greenery in every shade and texture. Trees with long, scaled trunks shot up thirty, forty feet into the sky, feathered fronds spanning out like parasols overhead. Ferns filled the undergrowth much like they did in Kherunis, but there were no silvery trunks breaking the verdant landscape. Moss grew on rocks, on bark, on soil, and everything was uncomfortably damp.

'Is this ... Kheshtarl?' he asked, turning back from the window to where the Tower brethren stood. Yae'ilston's visage coalesced beside her but he too was drawn to the forest outside, mouth agape like a bewildered child.

'I'd bloody hope so,' the woman grunted. 'That was my last home stone.' She pushed past Kriah to stick her head out the window; Yae'ilston muttered a complaint as she passed through him. After a brief survey of the world outside, she swore savagely in a dialect Kriah didn't recognise. 'Not exactly *where* I thought we'd land, but Kheshtarl nonetheless.' She stretched her tattooed arm towards the east. 'Kessar is that way.'

Kriah glanced around the room, which was barely three paces wide in any direction. There was a sliding door behind him, partly open, though it was too dark to see much beyond. The room itself contained not much of anything: a couple of storage crates; a bedroll and blanket stacked in the corner; a dish of candle stubs.

'What is this place, then?' he asked.

'An abandoned hunting shack,' she said with a shrug. 'Not much use to anyone.'

'So why bring us here?'

'We all need somewhere to lie low at times.' Gingerly, she prodded at the back of her shoulder, at the wound she'd sustained from her encounter with Amika and Rei. It was likely infected, given the way she grimaced and held herself, but it was hard to tell if her pale colouring was natural or from illness.

'What's your name?' Kriah asked, realising she had never shared it.

'I'm of the Tower, Halfblood,' she snarled. 'We do not give our names.'

'And you find *me* prickly,' Yae'ilston quipped dryly; Kriah ignored him.

The woman dropped her hand from her shoulder and eased herself into a seated position, leaning forward across her raised knees instead of back against the wall. 'You already know more than you need to,' she said with a grimace.

'I know that wound isn't healing,' Kriah surmised boldly. 'You said it's been weeks, yet it troubles you like a fresh cut. I could help you.'

She looked at him, grey eyes narrowing behind a tangled fringe of pale blonde. Her hard jaw softened. 'Elles,' she said, as though relieving herself of a great burden. 'My name is Elles.'

'Let me see your wound, Elles.'

Kriah knelt down beside her and waited for the young woman to wriggle out of her clothes. Despite accepting assistance, Elles remained guarded and pulled off her cloak without daring to break eye contact. A dull sheen of dried blood crusted the coarse fabric of her tunic, rendering it stiff. With a groan, she stripped down to her breastband, grey with sweat and grime.

Kriah hissed in a sharp breath. The stench hit him first, pungent as rotting meat. The heat of infection radiated from her back. The wound itself was yellow and glistening with thick, milky discharge. It was hard and black around the puncture, but so full of pus and fluid Kriah couldn't see how deep it went.

'*Ch'lor amasnay!*' Yae'ilston swore with a gasp, nose wrinkling in disgust. Kriah shot a warning glance in the spectre's direction before turning his full attention back to the wound. Fear tingled down his spine. He had no idea what he was doing. He'd watched his mother treat a few patients in Ciraselo, but nothing like this. He didn't even know where to start. Only that aimlessly flooding *khe'torla* into her body like he'd tried with Nell wouldn't work.

'That bad, huh?' Elles said gravely.

'I, uh ...' Kriah stumbled. His roving gaze caught on the supply crates, and he shuffled towards them in search of *something* to use as a catalyst. Ka'ella's healing had been founded on enhancing the innate properties of herbs and tonics. Perhaps there was something here he could use ...

The first crate was filled with dusty old parchment, twine, sealing wax and a dried pot of ink. Kriah shoved it aside and dug into the next. Linen, oiled pouches filled with ground spices and dried herbs. He was about to dismiss them as cooking supplies when he found a glass canister filled with thick golden paste.

Honey.

Kriah rechecked the bags—dried calendula petals and ground turmeric root.

'These ... might work,' he said, trying to rein in his surprise. He was sure his mother had mixed a poultice of similar ingredients for drawing out infection. It would not be exact, but it might be *enough*.

Kriah pulled the stopper from the glass pot of honey and upended the calendula and turmeric inside. Yae'ilston wandered closer to inspect but for once had nothing to say.

'Can't believe that's all still here,' Elles said, watching as Kriah whisked the concoction into a thick, tacky paste with an old quill from the writing box. 'No idea when someone last used this place.'

'That's the good thing about honey,' Kriah said, making his way towards her. 'It never goes bad.'

He scooped the sticky salve up with his fingers and spread it across Elles's back with as much care as possible. She flinched reflexively before recovering her composure, teeth audibly crunching in her jaw against the pain. Heat spread from her skin, hot and shiny with infection, and up through Kriah's fingers. He pushed *khe'torla* through the gritty salve, felt it tangle and tug against the toxins filling her flesh. Pushed so much he felt lightheaded, even with Yae'ilston's surplus *khe'torla* flooding his veins. With a gasp for air, he withdrew.

'Try to keep it covered,' he said. 'We'll scrape it off and try again in a day or two.'

Elles pulled her tunic back over her shoulder. 'I know this will kill me,' she said softly. 'I'm not a fool. But I need to complete this mission before it does.'

Kriah wiped his hand clean on one of the old blankets. 'Why?'

'I've lived my life in the shadow of Rei-Hai fucking Shaw. An insolent little prick, yet the masters doted on him, his mistakes pardoned while ours cruelly punished. He was the first of our batch to receive a band and all because he chose to spend his nights on his fucking knees instead of training.'

It was a very different picture than the one Rei had painted of his time at the Tower. But the way Elles spoke with such vicious hate suggested it was real—for her, at least. Kriah's chest tightened with empathy. He knew what it was like to feel unworthy and overlooked, even when all you ever did was try to prove yourself. Kriah had done everything his grandfather had asked. Believed his mad prophecy with blind, stupid faith. And still he'd been treated as nothing. As a replaceable piece in a larger game he was never truly taught how to play.

'You think turning Rei over to the Tower will earn the recognition you deserve,' Kriah surmised, speaking each word with care.

She laughed bitterly. 'No. I just want to see the little fucker punished. I'd have to do something truly impossible to heighten my esteem with the masters. Something like returning from Kheshtarl with the Myrahn Blade.'

Kriah's ears pricked up. The Skrevaar Blade stirred within him at the mention of its kin. What did the Tower know of the Myrahn Blade? And more importantly—why did they want it?

'What's so important about an old sword?' he said instead.

Elles turned to him, grey eyes sharp. 'Oh, don't feign ignorance, Half-blood. The masters know all about your little Prophecy. They're trying to beat you to the keys.'

'Why? If they know what we're doing, why interfere? The Yaians hate the Meah-Hyren—I'm trying to stop them.'

The woman attempted a shrug. 'Don't know, don't care. But they want the Blades and they want Amika—even more than they want Rei-Hai Shaw.'

Kriah's pulse began to quicken. Allowing Rei to return to the Tower was one thing; bargaining with Amika another. 'I will not—'

'Oh please,' Elles injected with a snort. 'The Tower will catch up with her eventually. They always do. But should I return to the masters with the traitor Rei-Hai *and* the Myrahn Blade, well—I may just earn enough gratitude to make sure Amika walks away unharmed.'

She gave Kriah a conspiratory smile and stretched out her hand. 'Do we have a deal?'

The thundering heartbeat in his ears drowned clear thought. Kriah swallowed, mouth dry. 'I thought you said it was impossible,' he rasped, desperate to find the flaw in the otherwise convenient solution.

'It is,' she said. 'For me. Not for a Meah-Hyren.'

Somewhere, Yae'ilston clicked his tongue but Kriah pushed his protests aside. A better solution would not present itself. He needed the key and he needed Amika safe. What was a Siephymn's life against hers—against the thousands who would die or be enslaved at Azet'haal's hands if Miatha wasn't restored to her throne? Rei was going to die soon. He would understand ... Wouldn't he?

Would Amika?

Closing his eyes, Kriah took a long, slow breath, dragging clarity into his lungs and mind. Elles's hand was still waiting. And Kriah took it in his own.

The Myrahn Blade was held within Kessar Castle, beyond the reach of the Tower. The king was a deeply scrupulous man, especially when it came to the security of his palace. No one came in and out except for his personal attendants. Even guests were entertained outside of the castle, at a public hall in the city, to which he travelled via palanquin and entourage.

'His personal guards are selected through bloodline,' Elles explained before Kriah left the Tower's safe house for the Kheshtarli capital. 'Born and bred within the castle itself. We haven't even been able to get a Watcher on the inside to observe. But with your ... *warlockery* ... there must be something you can do to slip by.'

She wanted Kriah to glamour himself, to assume the guise of a personal guard in a far more convincing manner than any of the Tower's powders or dyes could achieve. It could be done, Kriah knew, having watched his grandfather distort the perception of the Second Born to him as a decrepit old man instead of the ageless Meah-Hyren he was. But it was not something Kriah had ever learnt.

'I thought you didn't want to mess with the Second Born's minds,' Yae'ilston observed, trailing behind Kriah as he cut an angry path through the dense, wet forest. Kriah had slipped on more moss-covered rocks and logs than he cared to admit, and the exertion of hacking away vines and ferns left his clothes as damp as if he'd crawled out of a river. He was in absolutely no mood to deal with Yae'ilston's mockery.

'I don't,' he grunted.

'What exactly do you think *glamour* is?'

'Look.' Kriah stopped, releasing a branch he'd brushed aside so it cut through Yae'ilston's incorporeal face. 'I don't have a choice. And it's better than drowning them in distorted memories or creating mindless zealots. But if you have another suggestion, then please, I'd love to hear it.'

Yae'ilston brought his thumb to his lips, started chewing on the nail. 'No. This is the most effective way.'

Kriah groaned inwardly, picked up his knife and continued hacking at the wayward frond cutting across their path. Sweat trickled down his neck, between his shoulder blades, setting his nerves alight with irritation and sticky heat.

'Why are you eager to do as you're told?' the Meah-Hyren pressed. 'Now that someone's giving you orders again, you jump without question. Are all Second Born that fickle with their loyalty, or is it just—'

'I said shut *up*, Ilston!' Kriah roared, whirling around in rage. It built up in his chest like steam in a kettle, uncontrolled and unjustified as he screamed his frustrations at the man who wasn't there. 'Shut up, shut up, *shut up!* You want to tell me I'm useless? I already know that. I have fucked up at every turn and I am so lost I don't even know where the sun sets anymore. I am faced with impossible choices every—'

'Kriah ...'

'—fucking day, and I am doing it alone. So yes, when someone made a decision for me, I accepted it. Because I'm tired, Ilston. I am so fucking tired and I cannot sleep. I cannot dreamscape. I can't even have a moment to my fucking self because—'

'*Kriah!*'

Yae'ilston's desperation broke through his hysteria and Kriah smelt the smoke almost immediately. Tongues of flame licked from beneath his boots, hot and vicious despite the damp undergrowth. Panic took hold of Kriah; the fire burned as though doused with fuel.

'Kriah, look at me,' Yae'ilston was saying, voice calm and even, despite the danger. 'Look at me. That's it. Look at me and breathe. In ... and out. Nice and slow.'

Kriah did as he was told, even mimicked the exaggerated way Yae'ilston pretended to suck air through rounded lips. Smoke continued to rise, thick and white, obscuring the Meah-Hyren's visage.

'That's it, Kri, keep looking at me. Very good. Now relax your *khe'tor-la*. That's it, nice and slow.'

The tightly wound coils of *khe'torla* began to loosen, retreating into the crevices of his subconscious like scattering snakes. It had spread from his body without intention, moving with his rage like a sentient beast. Greist'hal's *khe'torla* had done the same thing—flaring in uncontrollable waves when his thoughts became unstable, his emotions heightened. Now he understood why his grandfather had been so dazed, so distant, after one of those episodes. Losing control was truly terrifying.

'You're back,' Yae'ilston said, smiling faintly between the dissipating smoke. His hand was pressed to Kriah's chest, a comforting gesture that Kriah, of course, could not feel. His flesh tingled all the same.

'Was that ... Am I ...' Kriah gasped, panic rising like bile again. The ferns beneath his boots were a tangle of smouldering ash and charcoal.

Yae'ilston shook his head. 'No, you're fine. You just need to learn how to control the stolen *khe'torla*. Soon, it won't overwhelm you.'

'How did you know how to do that? To talk me down from the panic?' It had taken decades for Kriah to learn the skills necessary for diffusing one of Grey's outbursts. Yae'ilston had done it on instinct.

'Azet'haal and your grandfather aren't the only Meah-Hyren to have taken lives, you know.'

Yae'ilston withdrew his hand. Abruptly, as if only just realising it was still there. He continued on their previous bearing, passing through the foliage unencumbered. Kriah followed, unnerved by Yae'ilston's taciturn behaviour. Moments earlier he had been wishing for silence, but now he had it, it was eerie and unsettling.

The rest of the day passed slowly as a result. Kriah cut his way through the overgrown forest until he came upon a road, where Yae'ilston was waiting for him, staring off at the tall buildings of Kessar now visible above the treeline on the northern horizon.

'Does it feel like Kherunis?' he asked, referring to the forest around them. Kherunis had been so alive with *khe'torla* it was intoxicating; the mainland was sparse by comparison. Like inhaling deeply but unable to fill your lungs. Kriah had grown up with such a small reservoir of *khe'torla* in the natural world around him, one that grew thinner the longer the Tear remained open in the sky. This was normal for him. But for Yae'ilston …

'No, it doesn't,' Kriah admitted, somehow glad the Meah-Hyren spirit could no longer perceive the lack of life force he had once enjoyed in abundance.

'Pity,' he said wistfully. 'It's really pretty here.'

Now that they followed a road, and Kriah was not preoccupied with having to hack his way through the forest, he could appreciate the beauty to be found here. The canopy reached even higher than the deepest misty hollows of the Li'Nea Wood and all manner of beast and bird flitted about overhead. Occasionally he caught the golden twinkle of an elkaven's eye, but the majority of animals seemed native—*natural.*

Distracted by the creatures above, Kriah collided with the shoulder of another traveller who had stopped on the road towards Kessar.

'E-excuse me,' Kriah wheezed, air knocked from his lungs. The Kheshtarli man barked what he assumed were obscenities before shooing Kriah away as if he were a stray dog begging for food scraps.

'You don't make the best impressions on people, do you?' Yae'ilston observed dryly, ducking out of the path of another sneering traveller.

'Let's just get to the city. We'll deal with that then.'

The Kheshtarli capital was everything Kriah expected a castle town to be: wide, paved streets lined with shopfronts; strings of colourful lanterns stretched overhead; music spilling from taverns; laughter and smiles and children weaving through crowds. It was clean and bright—even the dark tiles of the curved rooftops had been scrubbed free of bird shit.

After the chaos of Ciraselo and the ruins of Adria and Cirahk, Kriah had given up hope of ever seeing a peaceful, functioning city. He could have happily lost himself in the winding streets that teemed with tea houses and food stalls and carts selling bowls of broth and salt-grilled fish and meat seared on skewers. Saliva welled in his mouth at the rich, savoury scents filling the streets—a welcome change from rot and ash and smoke.

'That's a distinct uniform, wouldn't you say?' Yae'ilston pointed through the crowd towards a figure robed in a pristine ivory cloak trimmed with emerald.

Castle guard.

Elles had spared no details when it came to describing the royal attendants Kriah would need to impersonate to gain entry to the castle. White was the colour of the king in Kheshtarl, and only members of his household and guard were permitted to wear it.

'It's not enough to just don their garb,' the Tower brethren had warned, 'or even mimic their mannerisms. They know each other inside and out. Even our most skilled Watchers have been caught.'

I have to become them, Kriah reminded himself.

The guard was genderless, as far as Kriah could tell, with sleek black hair cut into a sharp bob at the jawline. Their eyebrows were plucked until only short, thin wisps remained in the inner corners. They had stopped to purchase fruit from a market vendor, though Kriah saw no coin or token exchanged for the goods.

He tailed the royal guard as they slipped away from the merchant, bowing pleasantries in their retreat. They walked with purpose, but without hurry, and it was hard to follow such a distinct target without drawing suspicion.

'I don't suppose I can use glamour to make myself invisible?' Kriah muttered to Yae'ilston as he awkwardly sidestepped around a roving peddler pushing a cart through the streets.

'No, of course not,' the Meah-Hyren scoffed. 'You can distort what they see, but you cannot make them see nothing.'

The guard put distance between them, and Kriah swore, losing sight of them altogether for a moment. He was about to fall into panic, stumble under the threat of another failure, when he caught a white flash turning a corner. He quickened his pace.

When he entered the alley, it was empty. Kriah's pulse hammered. Not even a Tower brethren could disappear so suddenly, so completely—he must have turned into the wrong street. He pivoted on his heel and made to retrace his steps.

His path was blocked.

The castle guard held a small, squat blade to Kriah's neck, no larger than an arrowhead.

'*Nyol tae kka?*' they hissed, stepping closer. The height difference was profound—could that perception be overcome? Kriah had already set his *khe'torla* to work, washing over the guard's body and face, charting a map of their features. To project this appearance to others, he had to understand, had to know every plane and dimple.

The knife at Kriah's throat relaxed and the guard's dark eyes widened in shock. Their lips quivered. It had worked.

He was wearing their face.

'*Nyol tae kka!*' they screamed. They still held the knife aloft, but the fight was slowly fading as they edged away.

'You'd better hope they don't run,' Yae'ilston added.

Unhelpful though the observation was, he *was* right. Kriah grabbed the retreating guard's wrist. The struggle revealed a strength not visible beneath their heavy robes. They slashed out at Kriah, the short blade surprisingly deft and deadly in their hands. It nicked Kriah's forearm, and the pain was immediate and immense.

An acidic burn raced up his arm. Poison? No—poison shouldn't work on him. He was immune. But he could *see* it spreading, black rivulets threading up the network of his veins.

'Kriah!' a familiar voice was calling. Who was that? They sounded so far away.

'*Kriah!*'

His legs buckled. Darkness crept into the edges of his vision.

'Kri—'

And consumed him.

34

KIOKHAREN

K io's lips traced soft kisses along Rei's collarbone, up his neck. The crimson light of dusk through the large windows stained Rei's skin a pale pink. He was warm and soft and deeply asleep, unusually slow to rouse.

But the bed *was* sinfully comfortable, and Kio himself found it hard to wake—or leave its luxurious embrace for anything other than getting wine or relieving himself. The mattress was filled with some sort of metal spring, making it firm but supportive, unlike the uneven sag of a featherbed that lost shape with more ... vigorous activities.

Emanais had allowed them full rein of the Citadel to recover after everything they'd endured since their arrival. It was a precious and welcome respite, one Kio was not about to waste. Ahead of a tireless string of war councils and ceremonies, the new Allchief had ordered seven days of rest—the traditional mourning period for her people.

Kio had spent six of those days in bed already.

Rei moaned softly, starting to stir. He turned his head away from Kio and exposed the full length of his neck. Kio nipped at it playfully while his hand slipped beneath the covers to fiddle with Rei's cock. It came to life between his fingers.

'You're up early, my prince,' Rei mumbled sleepily.

'I could say the same to you.' Kio's kisses trailed up Rei's throat, along the ridge of his jaw before ghosting breathily atop his lips. 'Though you seem particularly lazy today.'

'I feel like I haven't left this bed,' Rei said, voice thick and husky. He turned towards Kio now, golden eyes flickering open. A slight smile tugged his lips as their gazes met, and heat blazed across Kio's chest. 'But somehow I feel that's intentional.'

'I finally have you where I've always wanted you.' Kio reluctantly pulled his hand from Rei's cock to brush hair from his face instead. 'I've spent more time with you these last few weeks than I have in ten years. I don't want to ever let you go.'

'Then don't,' Rei breathed, the words sounding a challenge. His jaw jutted towards Kio at a provocative angle, demanding his mouth be seized.

Kio curled a hand around Rei's neck and brushed a thumb over his soft lips. They parted, tongue flicking out to wet the digit with alluring torment. Kio's body came alive, blood rushing everywhere all at once. Rei took the thumb inside his hot mouth, eager and hungry as though it were a cock, and Kio felt his neglected appendage twitch with jealousy. He lurched forward, seizing Rei in a ravishing kiss. Deep and frenzied, it stoked his arousal—and then the familiar cold swell of terror consumed him.

Kio pulled back from the kiss, heart clenching as Rei's lips made to follow him in retreat. He opened his eyes, but Kio couldn't bear to see the hurt and confusion reflected in them once more. He reached past Rei for the carafe of wine he'd left on the dresser the night before. It was mostly full, and Kio downed it like air, the lukewarm temperature of the liquid enhancing the fruity bouquet. It was so good, and he wanted more—wanted to taste it alongside the saltiness of Rei's skin.

He tossed the empty carafe onto the bed and reached for Rei almost immediately, dragging him atop his body. Rei's arousal pressed against his belly, hot and hard, as he ground down against Kio's length. The prince growled, took a fistful of Rei's hair and tugged him back, sucking on his throat like a babe at the teat. Rei hissed and then gasped as Kio's fingers started probing at his arse.

'Do you want me to fuck you rough?' Kio said, teeth around an earlobe as he tried to burn the icy terror away. *I am in control. I am in control.*

'Fuck me how you like, my prince,' Rei breathed. 'So long as you remember this time.'

The barb was intended to hurt, and indeed it *stung*. For all the times they'd fucked since their reunion—and Kio ensured there had been *plenty*—his memories of each encounter were broken and blurred. To keep the terror at bay, he drank until he couldn't feel, couldn't *think*. But that salve came with an unbearable sacrifice. His body remembered the friction of Rei's skin, the taste of his seed in his mouth; but he couldn't recall the sound of his pleasure or the way his face contorted as he spilt. But he wanted to. He wanted to so badly his soul ached. If he remained in control, remained *powerful*, then maybe, just maybe, he could—

Kio pushed Rei back on the bed so hard he heard the air leave the younger man's lungs. He tore open Rei's thighs and descended between them, a starved animal on the prowl. As he sucked Rei into his mouth, he felt his lover tremble, breath falling free like a shiver.

'A-ah, Kio—*fuck!*' Rei squirmed against the pleasure, hips bucking. He tried to grab Kio's head, to guide him, control the rhythm, but Kio snatched his hands away.

I am in control. I am in control.

He crept up Rei's body, where he pinned his wandering hands above his head. The bones of his wrists felt small, fragile, and Kio knew it would bruise were it not for the black leathery skin of the devolving limb. He was so beautiful, lying there like that. Kio took a deep breath, traced a finger down the ridges of Rei's chest, committing every inch to memory. He'd not had much wine, and in this moment of pause, he felt terror's fist curl around his heart and start to squeeze.

Kio hoisted Rei's knees over his shoulders and pushed into him, bending forward to take his lips in a kiss. Rei cried out at the intrusion, his freed hands reaching for Kio immediately. He gripped his neck, his biceps, his thighs, trying to pull Kio deeper, and Kio was happy to oblige.

'K-Kio ...' Rei whimpered, head thrashing side to side. 'Ah, Deities dead, *fuck.*'

'That's it, darling boy,' Kio groaned, turning to bite the soft inner flesh of Rei's calf as they squeezed against the sides of his head in the building pleasure. 'Scream for me.'

Kio dropped a hand between them to grip Rei's cock. It took less than two strokes to have him spilling onto Kio's stomach, to have him panting and trembling with Kio's name on his lips. And Kio made himself watch. Made himself remember the touch and the sight and the scent and the taste and the sound as he came, holding onto Rei so tightly he could feel the imprints in his muscles, on his bones.

He collapsed with a groan, his face in the crook of Rei's neck. He stayed inside him a little longer, twirling the long ends of Rei's crimson hair around his fingers. His body grew heavy, along with his breathing, and he felt himself drawn towards the elusive tug of sleep.

Kio let himself fall and hoped, wished, *prayed*, he would still remember when he woke.

The bed was empty. The sheets were cold, abandoned hours earlier. Kio sat up, fear in his heart.

But Rei stood by the window, naked from the waist up, watching the dying pyres crackle below. They'd been kept alight all through the week, more kindling added when the flames grew weak; but now the mourning period was over they were finally left to rest.

Rei's back was to Kio, arms wrapped around himself as if against a chill Kio couldn't feel. He slipped out of bed and went to his lover.

'Couldn't sleep?' Kio asked dreamily as he ran his hands down Rei's shoulders. There were bruises on his biceps, the size and shape of Kio's fingers from where he had grabbed him the night before.

'Not anymore,' Rei replied without turning. 'I feel like I've slept half my life away already. How's your head?'

Kio winced, expecting to be brutally reminded of a hangover. But there was no pounding at his temples. No stale, bitter taste in his mouth. His stomach felt still and at ease, if not a little hungry, and his memory was as crisp as the dawn outside.

'Good. Great, actually,' he added with a grin. Lowering his lips to Rei's ear, he whispered, 'How kind of you to ask, *darling boy*.'

He felt the shiver ripple through Rei's body. The smaller man tilted his head back against Kio's chest to meet his gaze, a warm smile parting his lips. 'You remember.'

'And you were perfect.'

Kio stretched down to take Rei's lips in a kiss, arms folding around his body as Rei squirmed so they stood chest-to-chest. Kio wanted to take him again right then and there. They were so used to their meetings being brief that spending every second naked and in bed felt as normal as breathing.

'... are your clothes still outside? We were supposed to meet Emanais in the council room an hou—*shit!* Oh, Deities fucking dead, Kio!' Amika screeched, hiding behind the door she had so rudely opened.

Kio scrambled to cover himself with the blankets. Rei's skin flushed so red it almost matched his hair but he was otherwise close to bursting with laughter.

'Five years living in a tavern and you never learnt to knock?' he asked, choking back a chuckle.

'I knocked yesterday when I left these and got no answer,' Amika shot back, eyes still squeezed shut as she shook a fistful of clothing in their general direction.

'Well, we were *busy*, Amika!' Kio hissed.

'Sickness take me now ...' she groaned through her teeth. 'Are you decent yet?'

'Yes,' he said, fastening the last few buttons on his trousers. 'Why are you here so early?'

Amika stomped into the room and tossed a pile of clothes on the bed. She herself was dressed and powdered, her short hair braided awkwardly like a crown across her head. Her tunic and breeches were of Qhoraakese fashion, leathers and linens in earthen hues of tan and ochre, shot through with accents of cobalt and gold. Kohl was smeared thickly around her eyes.

'Ema wants to see us before the *lopaghnar*,' she said.

'The what?'

'*Lopaghnar*. Her coronation, I think. Something similar, at least.'

Kio examined the garments. There were two sets—one for him, one for Rei—of the same style as Amika's. The linen was softer than he expected, though after months of shirts held together by patches and twine, a merchant's hessian sack would have been a welcome change. He turned back to Rei, who was already shrugging into the tunic, the sharp lines of the garment's cut adding breadth to his shoulders while cinching his already narrow waist. Kio felt his blood stir, thirst tingling on his tongue.

'When does she want to see us?' he asked.

'An hour ago. She sent me to come find you when you didn't show.'

'An hour! Amika, it's barely dawn!'

'And she wants to see us before the ceremony. I suggest you hurry up.'

She slammed the gilded iron door closed, but the lack of echoing footsteps suggested she waited just outside. Not wanting to become the target of his sister's ire—or Ema's, for that matter—Kio dressed without delay and met Amika in the corridor. She led them through the wide, brick-lined halls, which were more like breezeways between the castle wings than internal passages. With Qhoraak's stifling dry heat, it was little wonder the Citadel had so much open-air architecture to promote circulation and decrease the temperature inside the buildings.

'Why does Emanais need me at her war council?' Rei grumbled, fiddling with the cuffs of his tunic. He walked two paces behind as he always did, a foolish but ingrained practice from their childhood in Adria.

'You know why,' Kio said.

Rei's steps faltered. 'If you say something fucked up like *blood connection* or *family*, I will stab you with some—'

'Because *I* want you there.' He grabbed Rei's wrist and dragged him into step beside him. 'I told you: you're never leaving me again.'

'Somehow I don't think that's entirely up to you, my prince,' Rei muttered bitterly under his breath, but kept walking in stride despite Kio's longer gait.

When they arrived at Emanais's audience chamber, the heavy iron doors were open in anticipation. There wasn't an awful lot of wood used in Xant's construction, Kio noted absently to himself as Zhayar scowled and ushered them inside with a flurry of impatient arms.

'I truly regret never getting you into bed, Little Prince, seeing how reluctant you are to leave it,' Emanais said with a smirk from where she was seated at the head of a large table that almost filled the entire room.

'Well, good company and good wine certainly helps.' Kio reached for a carafe among the goblets and bottles strewn across the detailed map of Qhoraak that was painted onto the wood.

'That it does!' Emanais straightened and gestured for him to pour a drink. 'We have both in abundance. Now it's time to get to work.'

Filling a goblet, Kio offered the carafe to Amika and then Rei; both declined, and a swell of shame washed over him. He took a sip and it was gone, already forgotten.

'Zhayar and I have discussed our next move.' Emanais's hazel eyes flicked to the other woman and then back to the sprawling map. 'There are four other farms that we know of.' She pointed to some vague locations in northern Qhoraak. 'I will send envoys to oversee their closure and the release of the captives held within. Should we be met with resistance—'

'With all due respect, Ema,' Amika interjected, 'we agreed to help win back your throne. We've done that. It's time we moved on—to Kheshtarl. To the next seal.'

'Your brother pledged himself to my cause,' she said, her gaze settling on Kio. 'And there is still much work to be done.'

'Then do it without him,' Rei growled from the back of the room, arms folded and head turned towards a window.

'Emanais, please,' Amika urged, not exactly polite. 'He is the rightful ruler of Holania, not an indentured soldier. He's paid his debt.'

'And he's standing right here and can *fucking* speak for himself!' Kio shouted, slamming the goblet on the ground. The pewter chalice bounced off the stone, splashing the remaining wine over his shoes.

The room fell silent—and then Emanais threw back her head and laughed, a single cackle that was as devilish as it was amused.

'Amika's right,' he said through clenched teeth, reining in his bubbling temper. 'I am a prince of Holania. I will decide my own course of action, damn you all.' Kio turned to his sister, who stood tall and rigid like a hired blade ready for a back-alley scrap. 'I gave Ema my word; I will see this through. Once that is done, we will head to Kheshtarl.'

He allowed silence to fill the room as his directives sank in. It was a clear, decisive plan—one that met everyone's needs. But Amika closed her eyes and sighed. Kio's chest pounded with uncertainty.

'We don't have *time* for that, Kio,' she said with stretched patience. 'Now the Hirathi seal has fallen, we must get to Kheshtarl and break the next. Rei and I have to go.'

Kio turned back to his lover, who raised his leathery, clawed hand in explanation. 'Borrowed time, and all.'

'Siephymn are weakened by the Tear,' Amika explained, before Kio had to shamefully admit his confusion. 'The wider it opens, the worse they suffer.'

'I watched a dozen Siephymn bludgeon themselves to death as they devolved,' Rei said flatly. 'Even if you march on the remaining farms, all you'll be liberating are corpses and caged monsters. The longer the Tear stays open, the less time we all have.'

Kio felt dizzy. He reached for a chair to steady himself, wishing he hadn't tossed the last of his wine away. Everyone spoke with an urgency he didn't understand—agendas they'd neglected to share. He was so angry. Angry at Amika and her secrets; at Rei for seeming fine when he clearly wasn't; at himself for being so *fucking* stupid.

Emanais slammed her hands down on the table. 'Then why did you have me break the fucking seal?'

'Because the cogs were already in motion. We can't wind them back,' Amika said. 'Miatha is the only one who can fix this, and she's stuck inside the Tear. We have to set her free to set things right.'

'You're chaos, girl. Pure and simple,' Emanais said, though much of her spark had cooled. She gestured for Zhayar to pour her a drink, and this time Amika took one too. Kio retrieved his goblet and refilled his cup, wine splashing over the lip as he trembled.

'So it seems we must divide our forces,' Emanais mused after a long silence. She twirled a knife absently around her fingers as she thought.

'Or you could come with us,' Kio offered. 'You're part of this now.' *Whatever* this *is.*

'Would that I could, Little Prince,' she said. 'But the Siephymn are not my only worry. I must also deal with Dhenka. His body was not among those sucked dry in the Citadel. I must hunt him down and kill him for his betrayal.'

Kio shared that sentiment viscerally. Dhenka had been seductive, and the last time Kio had seen him, he'd invited Kio to share his tent. Had he been that burnt by Kio's rejection? And why betray Emanais? Had they not been lovers?

'What will you do about the *khaaja*?' Rei asked, still lingering at the edge of the room. 'Pak-Ruhn-Qar is out there somewhere, wearing his own horrific skin.'

Emanais stabbed the knife into the table, right where Xant was depicted as a towering city that consumed the entire island it was been built upon. 'Yet another mystery I must solve. I suppose that's related to the Tear as well?'

Amika shrugged. 'If it causes Siephymn to lose control of their human forms, then it seems likely. Though I couldn't say for sure.'

'If the *khaaja* die, so too do their offspring,' Emanais said, lips drawing a thin line as she thought. 'There has to be a way to bring them back.'

'Pak-Ruhn-Qar told me why Waqar created the farms. Why he was so interested in breeding Siephymn,' Rei muttered, almost to himself. Louder, he said, 'Down in the cells, before he turned ... he said Sylar's blood was potent—a weapon to be used against his kind. Waqar used it like a sedative, kept him chained up below. The *khaaja* back at the farm wasn't drawn to Sylar's blood—it was threatened by it. Wanted to kill him.'

Kio turned to where the boy was playing silently in the corner behind Emanais, immersed in a game of wooden toys and oblivious to their conversation. He was painfully like Rei, so obvious now Kio knew the truth. His heart ached as he watched Sylar play—a boy so similar in age to the son he'd lost, fathered by the man he loved. Kio took a long, deep drink of his wine, draining the cup again.

'Sylar should come with us to Kheshtarl,' he declared.

'*No,*' Rei and Emanais said, instantly and in time.

'If those beasts are trying to kill him, why not take him across the sea where they cannot get him?'

'Because there are *khaaja* in Kheshtarl, too, Kio,' Rei said wearily. 'He's no safer there. At least here he's with family.'

Arguing with Rei about this could damage their relationship in ways Kio might not be able to repair. He took another drink to help swallow the words he shouldn't say.

'Will you join us in Kheshtarl, Ema?' Amika asked. 'When things are stable here? You're Chosen, after all. We may yet need you.'

Emanais stood, straightened the long coat that had crumpled from her slouched recline in the chair. 'Maybe,' she said, dismissive. 'But I'd best go get my damn crown first.'

Emanais's coronation—her *lopaghnar*—lacked the grandeur Kio expected of a crowning ceremony. The Adrian streets would have been filled with flower garlands and silk bunting, bright in the cerulean blue of the Holani, lutes, horns and harps singing out from every corner.

In Qhoraak, a single drum pounded like a battle march and a silent crowd gathered to watch Emanais ascend the dais towards the Hirathi Seat. Kio, Amika and Rei joined the witnesses at the front of the assembly, where Zhayar led Emanais through the wreckage of the Citadel's audience chamber. Much of the rubble had been cleared, the fissure in the floor boarded and reinforced, but the pyres still smouldered like snuffed candles behind them, a grim backdrop to what should have been a joyous celebration.

Emanais paused before the Great Flame, the same cauldron to which she had offered her sister's body just days before. She had been stripped to a simple linen shift, her locs restrained in a single thick braid. After dipping her head in reverence to the flame, Emanais lowered herself to her knees to press her forehead to the stone. One by one the crowd followed suit, Kio and Amika too.

'*Rei!*' Amika hissed under her breath, reaching out to pull the obstinate redhead down with the others.

Prayers to the Deity complete, Emanais made her way towards the dais, where Zhayar and Sylar waited beside the throne. The drums increased in tempo as a heavy cloak encrusted with all manner of gemstones and gold was swung around Emanais's shoulders. She turned back towards the crowd, threw her fist in the air. The Hirathi Blade shot out like a bolt. The assembly gasped and recoiled, the drums pound, pound, pounding towards a frantic crescendo.

'*Zim hel ghar,* Emanais Ulande!' Zhayar shouted above the noise. '*Qhoraak er daz kelletmar!*'

The drums ceased, and a heartbeat later, the gathering erupted in a frenzy of cheers and whistles. Kio clapped, chest swelling with admiration for the woman standing atop the dais, power and pride hanging off every inch of her being. She embodied everything he thought a ruler should be—everything Moyna *had* been and so much more.

'I hope I live long enough to see you ascend the throne, my prince,' Rei whispered, his words almost inaudible over the drums and crowd.

'I'll make sure of it,' Kio said, tangling their fingers together as he grinned. 'You'll be right by my side.'

And that woman will make the perfect queen.

EPILOGUE

The darkness was silent. And cold. He hadn't been *cold* since he'd arrived in Kheshtarl. Was he back there now? Whisked across the continent by someone with the Yaians' magic stones?

Water dripped from a broken pipe. Slow and irritating and the only sound he could hear. Underground, then.

Kriah sat up. His limbs ached, but he was intact. Weak, but well, considering the poison that had been pumped through his body.

What was *that?*

He'd never heard of a toxin that could affect his Meah-Hyren blood before. Panic seized him in an icy grip. Had Azet'haal's reach already spread to Kheshtarl? Had he bolstered the potency of his plague to strike Kriah from afar?

'Yae'ilston,' he rasped, voice cracked from disuse. He coughed to clear his throat. 'Ilston?'

The chamber was dark, but Kriah should have been able to see him. He was always aware of Yae'ilston. Like an extra limb. An extension of the *khe'torla* flowing through his—

No. It wasn't possible.

The march in his veins was silent.

'Ilston!' Kriah screamed again, desperate and terrified. He tried to light a spark in his hands, to illuminate the space around him. Echoes bounced off the walls, revealing the breadth of the cavernous chamber. But that was all. His *khe'torla* told him nothing. Told him nothing because it *was* nothing.

His *khe'torla* was gone.

Kriah wrapped himself into a ball to stop the shakes. He was alone. He was actually alone. Back adrift at sea and waiting to die. What had he achieved since being dragged ashore?

Death. Only death. Nell's death. Yae'ilston's—would it finally end now with his own?

He spent hours huddled in the dark. Hours, or it could have been days. His hollow stomach clenched and churned, but not with hunger. He didn't want to eat—didn't deserve it. He just wanted it to be over.

A metallic clunk resounded somewhere behind him, but Kriah didn't turn towards the noise. Footsteps accompanied a dim light, growing brighter and brighter as someone approached with a lantern. They stopped before what must have been the bars of Kriah's cage.

'I almost didn't believe them,' a male voice said. Heavily accented with the southern inflection, but proficient in the Meytaran tongue. 'When they saw your face change shape. Impossible, I said. So few creatures are capable of such a feat.'

Kriah raised his head, turned to look over his shoulder. A tall Kheshtarli man stood in the shadows of his flickering lantern, his long black hair loosely bound at his nape. He looked small under the many layers of his white robes, but held himself with a warrior's rigidity. A delicate gold circlet sat atop his head.

'You do not look Meah-Hyren,' the King of Kheshtarl mused, head cocking to the side. 'So why did Ni-Dahn's blade affect you as it did? Could it be that you're a halfblood?'

Kriah gritted his teeth and forced himself to remain quiet.

The king scoffed and flicked his wrist. A small knife, like the one Ni-Dahn had carried through the markets, appeared in his hand.

'I suppose it does not matter,' he said, words frosted. 'Your kind is not welcome here. I suggest you start talking.'

He set the lantern down by his feet. And as the light danced across his face, Kriah could have sworn the man's dark eyes flashed gold.

End of Book II

The story continues in Book III.

Coming soon...

Enjoy this book?

If you enjoyed reading **The Blood Curse** and other installments of the *Gardens of War & Wasteland* series , please considering leaving a review.

As an indie author, reviews are essential to getting the story into the hands of more likeminded readers.

Every little bit helps.

ACKNOWLEDGEMENTS

This book nearly killed me.

So many authors warned me of the dreaded Second Book Syndrome and my god, were they *right*!

The Blood Curse blew through so many deadlines, I was almost certain it wouldn't make a 2024 release let alone launch before the end of March—just days shy of the *The Ruptured Sky*'s first anniversary.

But I did it. It's here. And I could not be happier.

Trying to juggle two part-time jobs, two kids, a burgeoning writer's career and write a follow up book in 12 months could not have been possible without the veritable army of support at my back. So first and foremost, to my family—my parents, sister and husband: the strength you give me emotionally, physically and finanically have been instrumental in me being able to achieve my dreams. I would quite literally not be here without you.

To my editing crew—Sean, Mardie, Jo-Anne and Claire: thank you for your dedication (and patience) in helping this rushed, messy draft turn into something I'm proud to publish. Your feedback, encouragement and critical eyes mean the world to me.

To the writing family I've built along the way: I dived into authorhood with very little community at my back; but the way everyone has welcomed me and my little book with opened arms—especially during the gauntlet of SPFBO9—means more than I could put into words. Krystle, Connor, Beth and JC, thank you for enduring the rants, catching the falls, and most importantly, celebrating the victories. The community is the greatest part of being an indie author and I am so *so* blessed to have connected with each and every one of you.

And last but not least—to you, dear reader: thank you for taking a chance on my little book and even coming back for more! Whether you're a vlogger, reviewer or silent lover of stories, you are the reason I do this. The support you provide is immeasurable.

Here's to many more adventures together!

xx

jam

NEWSLETTER JAM

Can't get enough of Whyt'hallen?

Sign up for **Jessica A. McMinn**'s mailing list to receive exclusive insights and updates from her #writerslife, including two FREE **Gardens of War & Wasteland** novellas: **The Collector's Lost Things** and **Call of the Huntress**.

About Author

Jessica A. McMinn is a speculative fiction author based in regional NSW, Australia, with a passion for dark fantasy, coffee and cats.

Since graduating from the University of Wollongong with Distinction in BCA (Creative Writing) and BA (Japanese), Jessica spent five years in Japan teaching English and refining her craft. She now works as a freelance writer.

When she is not writing, Jessica enjoys playing video games, drawing, crafting and raising her two beautiful children while constantly pleading for the cat not to piss on the carpet.

https://jessicaamcminn.com/